TALES FROM THE STRANGER TIMES

VOLUME 1

C.K MCDONNELL

To Yvonne
X
Caime

Copyright © 2025 by McFori Ink

All rights reserved.

No part of this book may be reproduced in any form or by any electronic or mechanical means including information storage and retrieval systems, without permission in writing from the author. The only exception is by a reviewer, who may quote short excerpts in a review.

This book is a work of fiction. Names, characters, places, and incidents either are products of the author's imagination or are used fictitiously. Any resemblance to actual persons, living or dead, events, or locales is entirely coincidental.

Caimh McDonnell

Visit my website at www.WhiteHairedirishman.com

First edition: August 2025

Paperback ISBN: 9781912897636

Hardback ISBN: 9781912897667

CONTENTS

Introduction	v
The Raven	1
Do the Research	41
Love and Death in the time of Planned Engineering Works	53
The Other Side	78
The Owl and the Pussycat	99
A Dog's Life	125
Paint by Numbers	144
Fire in the Skies	164
Dance with the Devil	177
Before Your Very Eyes	211
The Lady Rises	235
A Good Book	252
Yes, Prime Minister	267
The Blitz Spirits	284
'Twas the Night Before Christmas	301
Ring The Bells	317
Free Goodies	319
Also by Caimh McDonnell	321

INTRODUCTION

My mother is a wonderful woman in many ways; smart, loving, generous, practical, with a 'solution-orientated approach' to life. That is the best way I have to describe the fact that I discovered remarkably recently that she has always held the firm belief that she can sign my name to any legal form she so wishes. Not just mine in fact, but any of her children's or indeed her husband's. She's never specified but I'd guess family pets are also covered. This can be termed 'mammy privilege' and apparently it extends to not just her, but all Irish mothers. Legally, it's categorically one hundred per cent fraud, but there isn't a police force in the world who wants to go up against them. People say the SAS or Navy Seals are the world's most elite fighting force, but those people have never had someone respond with "Well, sure, I'll be dead soon" to a request to move a family gathering back a week. If they'd been in charge of finding Osama Bin Laden he'd have handed himself in after a week tops.

INTRODUCTION

All this is by way of introducing you to one of Mammy McD's favourite phrases. She rolls it out when I explain I'm doing a book tour, or writing an article, or doing pretty much anything. That phrase is 'and you get paid for that?' I should point out, it's not delivered disbelievingly but rather in an effort to confirm that nobody is taking advantage of her youngest child's naïve and trusting nature. He, being one of the few family members without even one qualification in the field of accountancy. I can't specifically remember it happening, but I'd bet the big bag of magic beans I just traded my cow for that she said it when I'd explained to her what a podcast was. I'd have done so in 2020 on one of our daily phone calls. Yes – that 2020. You remember the one. I'd have mentioned this new project to my mother as despite knowing it'd be met with only confusion and suspicion, it's hard to come up with new topics of conversation when one of you has been told she can't leave the house even to go to mass, and the other spent most of his time hanging out in his shed/office with the dog even before they announced we were having a pandemic. I would then have explained that no I wasn't getting paid, but it served other purposes, and she'd have made grumpy noises before immediately ringing my sister and asking her to quadruple-check I definitely have a pension.

If you're interested, the reason I started doing *The Stranger Times* podcast back in 2020 was, well, it was 2020. What the hell else was I going to do? Once I'd got up at the crack of dawn to walk the dog while the missus battled online for the glittering prize that was a supermarket delivery slot, I found myself with quite a lot of unasked-for free time. Sure, I could have written a novel, but a large part of a novelist's job is finding ways of avoiding doing that. Besides, as a former stand-up comic myself, I was fully aware that the entire comedy circuit was sitting at home on their sofa trying to find a reason to put on trousers, so I'd have a literal embarrassment of riches when it came to finding narrators. Comedians, in normal times, spend more time on the road than long distance lorry drivers and hence you will not find a community more obsessed with audiobooks. Turns out, lots of them have been chomping at the bit to record one. And so it was, I wrote some stories, and some truly excellent people recorded them.

That's how it started. How it kept going, even after we all got told we could finally leave the house again to go to mass and stop pretending banana bread was worth the effort, was that I discovered I loved writing these stories. Yes, I'd found a way of doing my job that, much to my mother's horror, actually cost me money as opposed to making it, but it was also one of the most creatively rewarding things I've ever done. The wonderful thing about short stories is that they're short. The clue is very much in the name. You know how you go to see a sci-fi film because it's got a cool concept only for it to collapse in on itself after thirty minutes because the idea runs out of juice? Well, that doesn't happen with a short story. You get to squeeze all the juice out of it and then it's done. Bam! Onto the next one. You don't need to keep going and introduce a love interest that someone can point some form of gun at in order to generate an ending.

While the odd character hopped the wall from the novels to the short stories or vice versa, that wasn't their primary

INTRODUCTION

role. Their role was to knock down walls entirely. With each of them, the world of *The Stranger Times* got bigger and richer, so that every time I came back to write the next novel, there was so much more there. People love asking writers if they worry about running out of ideas. I can't speak for anyone else, but I worry about the exact opposite. I have so many ideas, I worry I won't get a chance to use them all. Short stories should be a way of knocking some of those off the list but unfortunately, they seem to just generate more. Thanks to the ever expanding universe that Banecroft and his unlikely found family of misfits and vagabonds find themselves living in, I've got so many ideas for the next *Stranger Times* novel, and the forty-nine after that, I'm actively considering joining a gym so I can conceivably write as many of them as possible, before I get taken up to attend that great big mass in the sky. (Not to be picky but if you're reading this God – first off, big fan, secondly if there is a heaven and I happen to sneak in, please God don't let it be like mass.)

So, in summary, the reasons for this short story collection, volume one of a planned twenty-nine, are numerous. Firstly, it's to share with anyone whose interest in podcasts matches my mother's, a selection of the stories I've been cranking out over the last half-decade or so. Secondly, it's to remind me what's in them as, to be honest, re-reading them for this collection has given me yet more ideas to add to the never-ending pile. But above all that, the most important thing is this; seeing as you've (presumably) been kind enough to actually buy this collection, when Mammy McD next asks if I get paid for this, I can answer yes! And not in artistic fulfilment, because she bloody hates that answer, but cash, which she likes. So, thank you, you've made an old woman

INTRODUCTION

very happy. Well, all right, not happy. Happy is a strong word for it. Irish mothers don't do happy, but you've made her less disappointed, or at the very least, she can now focus that disappointment on the concept that somehow, she wanted grandchildren and got dogs.

THE RAVEN

Eddie Poe stared at the blank page in front of him, pen poised. He scribbled down the words 'There once was a girl from Nantucket', and looked at them for far too long before tearing out the sheet and tossing it in the bin beside his desk. It had plenty of company in there. Things were not going well.

He scratched his forehead irritably as he regarded the latest blank expanse of paper in his Moleskine notebook. It lay open before him, taunting him for his total lack of inspiration. He thought for a moment, pen hovering, before he wrote the words 'Inspiration is ...' and then promptly ran out of ideas. That page quickly followed the first into the bin.

All around the room candles flickered in the draught, the source of which he'd never been able to find. He had access to electricity and all other twenty-first-century conveniences, but he preferred to work by candlelight, for Eddie Poe fancied himself a poet and was thus predisposed to pretension.

He looked out the window of his house dejectedly. It was

a dark, drizzly night, as opposed to one of those bright nights you hear so much about. Manchester's weather was deeply uninspiring. Maybe he should move some place where the climate had more of a flair for the dramatic? Scandinavia always looked relentlessly bleak on TV. Perhaps somewhere over there? Come to think of it, they actually had bright nights. The sun didn't set for months at a time during the summer, and then stayed set for even longer. God, how could you not be a poet in such a desolate place? *Dark Days in Heaven, Bright Nights in Hell* – that could be the title of his collection. It virtually wrote itself. He'd just need to stick his verse in a gothic font, pop it up on Instagram, and he'd be a literary sensation by Christmas. He might get himself a photogenic dog, too. One with a limp or, ideally, a more interesting disability. Wheels for back legs would be perfect. He'd need to go out every morning and de-ice the poor little bastard so it could go to the bathroom. That, right there, would be the opening paragraph of his profile in the *New York Review of Books*. Give it six months and he wouldn't be able to move for buxom young ladies with a penchant for lace, leather bodices and dramatic make-up choices, vying for his affections.

Eddie's attention was pulled away from his dreams of living in an igloo with nothing but an epileptic, two-legged husky for company by a tapping on his chamber door.

He froze. It might be Mrs Parnecki looking for the rent. As it happened, Eddie had recently come into some money and cleared all his back rent. However, his landlady was eighty-three and not tech savvy – this had initially meant that he could buy himself time by claiming payment had already been sent, but now he'd finally come up with the money he had no way of convincing her of that until her nephew in

Belfast rang to confirm receipt. He didn't have the stomach to go through another long and drawn-out explanation about that right now. He was writing. Why did people keep impinging on his precious writing time? Was it any wonder that he'd been so unproductive recently?

There it was again. That tap-tap-tapping on his chamber door.

It didn't sound very Parneckian. She may have been a little old lady but she was surprisingly strong, and being deaf apparently meant she had also lost her sense of touch that informed her she was pounding on someone's door. If it wasn't her, who else could it be?

Eddie was a reclusive artist who, at that time, made most of his money by selling poorly rated, distressed-wood sculptures on Etsy. He was very careful to keep his home address private, having received his one and only return via the medium of it being hurled at his window at 3 a.m., wrapped in a piece of paper bearing a two-star review. Heaven knows what they'd have done with it had it only merited one star. The glass, thankfully, hadn't broken, given that the softness of the wood was one of the regular complaints he received.

Besides, with the exception of Mrs Parnecki, anyone else would have just rung the doorbell. All things considered, it stood to reason that nobody was in fact tap-tap-tapping on his chamber door. He was about to dismiss the sound as a figment of his feverishly creative imagination when it happened yet again. It even seemed more insistent this time.

Eddie rose to his feet, a sense of dread engulfing him. Now he'd dismissed the obvious answer to the question of the identity of this mysterious tapper, more sinister possibilities were presenting themselves. Kids. It could well be kids. He found solace in the thought, even though it meant this was the prelude to some form of inevitable attack. Eddie's determination to keep the cape alive as a sartorial choice for the discerning gentleman had drawn the ire of the heathen progeny of Stockport.

He quietly disengaged the latch on the front door. His best option was to open it suddenly, in the hope of catching the miscreants in the act and scaring them off. Whatever happened, this time he would not attempt to deal personally with any burning brown paper bags or Amazon boxes on the welcome mat. This was a rental property – he'd call the fire brigade and hope they arrived in time to control the blaze before it burned the house to the ground. It was a preferable alternative to ruining another set of silk slippers battling a flaming bag of excrement, the content of which was so large he could only hope it had come from a very big dog who needed more fibre in his diet.

Eddie hurled the door open to find nothing but the aforementioned dank and drizzly night awaiting his attention. The only activity he could see was a lost and lonely Uber Eats bike riding forlornly into the night. Shit, that rhymed! He slammed the door shut and raced back towards his desk. In his haste, his slippered foot caught the corner of the desk and he howled in pain. He was hopping in place, clutching his abused tootsie, when once more he heard that tap-tap-tapping on his chamber door.

No, not the door. Now he was standing upright, he realised the sound was, in fact, coming from the window. A tree branch? But there was no tree in the garden. Not any more. He'd recently taken it down as part of an extensive remodelling project. Mrs Parnecki had been to see him about that, too – some nonsense about not being allowed to make substantive changes to the garden of a rental property without permission. Typical capitalist bullshit. For better or worse, this was his home now. Dreams of Scandinavian bleakness leading to international adoration were just that. Dreams. He had to stay here, and that meant whoever or whatever was tap-tap-tapping on the window was his problem.

He approached it slowly, the drawn curtain swaying slightly in the damnable draught. Eddie steadied himself. This was his mind, his brilliantly creative, fervent mind playing tricks on him. That was all. There was nothing in his garden apart from a tastefully designed, if criminally underappreciated, rockery that spoke of nature's eternal battle with man, featuring as it did rocks interspersed with chunks of concrete he had found in a nearby skip. One day Mrs Parnecki would be selling it for thousands of pounds, and then she'd feel pretty damn stupid for saying it was fly-tipping. He would only allow the property to be sold if there was a cast-iron guarantee the rockery would be left in place and preserved to be enjoyed by future generations. A Poe original.

He drew a deep breath and yanked the curtain open. His mind hadn't managed to form a particular expectation, but he was nevertheless taken aback by the sight of a large, black bird on his windowsill, glaring at him. It was too big to be a crow. A raven? Whatever it was, it could bugger off.

'Shoo!' shouted Eddie. 'Be gone, you foul bird.'

In response, the bird fixed him with a beady eye then pointedly tap-tap-tapped on the window again.

'Oh, it's like that, is it? I'm not afraid of you.'

Eddie banged on the glass to make his point.

The raven tap-tap-tapped to make his.

'Right.' Eddie stepped forward and opened the window. As he did so, the raven scooted across to avoid getting hit. He'd fully expected the bird to fly off at that point, but it stood its ground.

'Go on, get lost!' hollered Eddie, waving his hands about.

In response, the raven raised its beak and cawed. 'Nevermore!'

Eddie felt a chill travel down his spine, which had little to do with the breeze coming through the open window. He staggered backwards. 'What? What? What did …'

'Nevermore!' repeated the bird.

'It's …' Eddie stood there, clutching his hand to his chest. 'Shut up. You're just a stupid bird. You're not actually talking; it just sounds like you are.'

'Rude.'

The shock of this interjection caused Eddie to lurch backwards so fast that he lost his footing. He landed arse-first on the carpet, narrowly avoiding hitting the back of his head on the TV he regularly claimed not to have, both at literary gatherings and to the TV licensing people.

'What in the—'

In answer to his question, the raven hopped in through the open window, and another smaller bird followed.

''Bout bloody time,' said the second bird – a starling. ''Bout bloody time. Freezing out there. Rude leaving somebody out there. Rude.'

'You can … you can talk,' said Eddie, gawping at the bird in disbelief.

In response, the starling looked at the raven and shook its head. 'Yes, I can talk. Talk I can, indeed. It's not that impressive. I mean, you can do it.'

'Nevermore!' squawked the raven.

'See?' said the starling. 'Even he can do it and he's a raven.'

'Nevermore!'

'No offence,' said the starling. 'Although, be honest, Frank – you aside, your brethren ain't the smartest birds on the wire, are they?'

'Nevermore!'

'I said, you aside. And it was you who asked me to get involved. Let's not forget who is doing who a favour here.'

Now that Eddie had heard him talk a bit more, he realised the starling spoke with a lilting Welsh accent. The raven didn't have an accent, other than sounding a lot like a raven.

Eddie felt things were rather getting away from him and he decided to try to regain the initiative. 'Be gone, foul beasts!'

At this, both birds stopped their conversation and turned to stare at him again.

'Oh, here we go,' said the starling. 'Back to hurling insults around, are we? Honestly, how the hell dolphins let you lot become the dominant species I will never know. Never know, I will. Give a monkey opposable thumbs and all of a sudden it thinks it can go around hollering "foul beast" at whoever it likes. What's the world coming to, I ask you?'

'Nevermore!'

'All right, Frank – I'm building up to it. Give me a chance. Not even finished the introductions. I have to tell him my name is Gordon, he will inevitably make some kind of remark about that being a weird name for a bird and then I—'

'Nevermore,' interjected Frank the raven.

'But we're still in the hurling-insults phase,' protested Gordon the starling. 'I've not even hit my stride yet. This bellend is wearing a kimono, and you'd better believe I've a few minutes of killer material locked and loaded on that.'

'Nevermore!'

'Wh-why does he keep saying that?' stammered Eddie.

'What?' asked Gordon.

'Nevermore.'

'Nevermore!' squawked the raven, as if in confirmation.

'He's not saying "nevermore",' said Gordon. 'He's saying "Neville Moore".'

'It sounds like "nevermore".'

'Oh, right,' said Gordon, before turning back to his companion. 'The stones on this kimono-wearing dandy – in less than a minute he's gone from birds can't talk to criticising your diction. Unbelievable.'

'Nevermore!'

'I'm not Neville Moore,' said Eddie. 'You've got the wrong man.'

'Oh, we know that,' said the starling. 'That we know. We know you aren't Neville Moore because Neville Moore is …'

Gordon left the sentence hanging and looked pointedly at Frank, who stared back at him. Eventually, the starling shook his head in despair. 'Nevermore! He is nevermore. Honestly, Frank. It was right there. There's a rhythm to these things. You've got to get on the same page as me if this double act is going to work.'

'I don't know a Neville Moore,' interjected Eddie, as not only could the starling talk but he also gave the impression that he'd keep doing so unless someone interrupted him.

'Know him? You don't know him, and know him you won't because he's dead. Dead. Dead. DEAD!' hollered Gordon.

'Nevermore!'

'Better, Frank, better. Get in the flow.'

'I'm sorry to hear that,' said Eddie.

'Really? Because you killed him.'

Eddie clutched at his kimono. 'I haven't killed anyone.'

'Oh, is that so? That is so, is it? I have two words for you – fat balls!'

There followed a long pause, which Eddie eventually felt compelled to fill. 'Is that supposed to mean something to me?'

'Unbelievable!'

'Nevermore. Nevermore. Nevermore!' squawked the raven, flapping his wings irritably.

'All right, Frank,' said Gordon. 'Keep the cool, son. Keep the cool. We gotta play this by the book. You can't just peck his eyes out like in the good old days.'

'Nevermore.'

'He wants to peck my eyes out?' asked Eddie, horrified.

'Nobody said that.'

'You just did.'

'No, I didn't.'

'Nevermore.'

Gordon looked at Frank. 'Really? You're siding with him?'

'Nevermore.'

'Well,' said the starling, turning back to address Eddie, 'good luck making that stand up in court. The legal system is even less inclined to believe a bird can talk than ordinary saps like you are. I've been trying to lodge an objection to that new housing estate for months and they keep saying I've got to put it in writing. Like it wasn't hard enough getting hold of a phone to make the call in the first place. It takes a team of three of us to dial the number, and believe me, that is a massive pain in my feathery backside. Doug and Rachel try their best, but there's a reason starlings don't build nuclear reactors. Let me put it that way. And now the council wants me to fill out a form and email it! I'm a bloody bird, mate. That's basic discrimination, is that.'

'Am I ...' began Eddie, rubbing his hand across his face. 'I've had a stroke, haven't I? This is some kind of dream. I've been working too hard and my brain has overheated or whatever.'

'Hark at Kimono Boy. Trying to establish the insanity defence, are we? Not gonna work, sunshine. You've already been found guilty. This is about sentencing.'

'I haven't murdered anyone.'

'Is that right?' said Gordon. 'And what would you call putting out fat balls laced with bleach?'

'I—'

'Don't deny it!' said Gordon. 'Seriously, don't,' he repeated in a softer voice. 'Frank will go old school if provoked, and I do not have the stomach to watch that.'

'There ... I ...' Eddie cleared his throat 'I may accidentally—'

'Nevermore!'

'Inadvertently—'

'Nevermore!'

'While distracted—'

The raven flew across the room straight at him, wings spread, a vision of terror. 'Nevermore. Nevermore. Nevermore!'

Eddie dropped to the ground and curled up in a ball, his arms wrapped around his head. 'I'm sorry. I'm sorry. I'm sorry. It was all the bloody chirping. It was driving me mad. Mad. MAD! I'm trying to write and I need peace to work. I just want peace.'

He lay there on the carpet, expecting something to happen.

Nothing did.

'Hello?'

There came no response.

Eddie slipped his right hand over both eyes and waved the left in front of his face, fully expecting to find a raven standing there. Nothing. He risked a quick peek for confirmation.

'Relax,' said Gordon. 'Your eyes are fine.'

'Really?'

'Really. We've got rules about these things.' Gordon's tone implied he wasn't so much a fan of the rules as a begrudging abider. 'So, now that you've confessed to the poisoning of poor Neville Moore, a robin redbreast in good standing in this here community, we can move on to the sentencing. Would you like to offer any mitigation?'

'I ...'

'Sit up. Frank isn't going to do anything to you. You have my word.'

Hesitantly, Eddie did as he was told. He glanced around to see that Frank was now perched on top of the TV behind him and Gordon, the starling, was standing on the coffee table. Gordon looked at the small candelabra beside him. 'Not to get off track, but what's with all the candles? You not paid your electricity bill?'

'Nevermore,' cawed Frank irritably.

'Never mind,' said Gordon quickly. 'Back to the subject of the dearly departed Neville ...'

'I ... I didn't realise—'

'If the rest of that sentence is that you didn't realise poison was poisonous, I really wouldn't.'

'OK,' said Eddie. 'Look, I wasn't in my right mind. I'd … I'd just broken up with Lenore, my girlfriend, and—'

'Ah,' said Gordon, 'that explains it.'

'It does?'

'Not what you did,' clarified the starling. 'We talked to the local birds, y'know, gathered testimony. They said someone used to have a birdfeeder in the garden and leave out fat balls and all that, before this. That was her, then, was it?'

'Yes – I mean, we both did.'

'Right, but mostly her. Her mostly.'

'We had a joint bank account and that paid for the shopping. Fat balls aren't cheap, y'know. I … I had to make some cutbacks, and the birds kept coming around, looking for food …'

'So, you thought murder?'

'I didn't. I mean, it was just a …'

'Bird?' finished Gordon in a quiet voice that was a lot more alarming than any of his shouting had been. 'Well, now, that brings us to the crux of the matter. I think we can move on to sentencing now, don't you?'

'Nevermore!'

'Agreed, Frank, agreed.'

'Look, I'm sorry,' said Eddie. 'I'm truly sorry.'

'I have no doubt you are now,' said Gordon, 'no doubt. How much money do you make a year?'

'How is that relevant?'

'Relevant? Neville was a family man. Eight months old, prime of his life. Wife and five chicks to support. Reparations. I presume you'd be more amenable to that than the …'

'Nevermore!'

'Let's call it the eye-for-an-eye approach.'

'But I am a humble artist.'

'*Riiiiight*.' Gordon drew out the word in that way people were in the habit of doing that so irritated Eddie. Like the woman at the job centre. Like the man at the bank. Like the voice in his head regularly did. 'Does that pay well?'

'Indeed it does, for nothing is worth more than the work of those who are brave enough to hold the mirror up to the whole of human existence and say, here, look upon this and see who we truly are in all our tarnished glory.'

'Yeah,' said Gordon, 'I was really looking for pounds and pence. Ballpark figure. To be honest, not a big fan of mirrors. My friend Miguel got into a fight with one, broke his own beak.'

'Nevermore!' interjected the raven.

'Well, excuse me for injecting a little colour into the conversation, I'm sure.' Gordon turned back to Eddie. 'Frank would like us to nail down this whole compensation thing.'

'I'm not a rich man,' protested Eddie.

'Ahhhh,' said Gordon, 'was the kimono a charity-shop buy, then? Doesn't excuse it entirely, mind. Excuse it entirely, it does not.'

'I want to make this right,' said Eddie. 'Sincerely, I do. In fact, I think I might have a solution.'

'OK,' said Gordon. 'Well, now we're talking. What kind of solution?'

'Just give me one moment,' he said, making his way to his feet slowly. 'I need to get something.'

The starling and the raven shared a look before Gordon said, 'All right, but don't try anything funny.'

'No, no, no,' said Eddie. 'I know precisely how to resolve this.'

He opened the hall cupboard and put his right hand into the inside pocket of his long leather coat, which was hanging on one of the pegs. 'I'm just trying to find my wallet and ...'

As soon as his left hand found the handle of the oversized tennis racket that he'd remembered was also in the cupboard, a thrill passed through Eddie's body. No thugs, avian or otherwise, were going to come into his home and push him around.

He spun about, almost catching the starling with a vicious backhand before it darted away.

'WHOA!' hollered the bird.

'Begone, you feathered demons!'

Eddie turned and volleyed the raven away as it flew towards him. The bird was sent crashing into the array of framed photos beside the record player. Feathers flew. One of the candles toppled over and landed on the carpet.

'Nevermore!'

The raven, dazed, regained its footing and staggered about before it set its gaze back on Eddie, vengeance burning in its beady little eyes.

'Leave it, Frank,' called Gordon from across the room. 'He's not worth it.'

'You dare to come into my home and threaten me!' roared Eddie. 'You have no idea who you're dealing with. I am a man of exceptional determination. You shall not cow me.'

'What?' came the response from Gordon, who was now perched on the window sill. 'Who mentioned cows? This ain't got nothing to do with cows. Cows, it has nothing to do with.'

Eddie pointed the tennis racket threateningly in the direction of the raven. 'This is your final warning. Be gone or suffer the same fate as your chirpy little friend.'

'Nevermore!'

'Yes,' said Eddie with a twisted little smile, 'Neville Moore. May he rest in peace.'

He and the raven locked eyes for a long moment before the bird flew straight for the open window and out into the night. Gordon, the starling, hopped on to the window frame between inside and out, and looked back at Eddie.

'This was a big mistake.'

'Yes,' said Eddie defiantly, 'messing with me was indeed a big mistake. Now, bugger off!'

Having closed the window, Eddie rushed to stamp out the smouldering carpet where the candle had fallen. He extinguished the rest of the candles, turned on the lights and examined the room to confirm he was now alone. Then he checked every window and door in the house to satisfy himself that they were all secure. Only when that was done did Eddie take out the bottle of whisky he'd been saving. With shaking hands, he poured himself a healthy measure and knocked it back in one. He had fought off the barbarians at the gate. Destiny had come calling, and he had not been found wanting. He poured himself another.

He'd never felt more alive!

Eddie felt like death.

Or, to be more precise, if offered the opportunity of death, he'd leap at it – not that leaping was something he felt capable of. Or movement of any kind, for that matter. His head was pounding, his stomach was broiling, but, more than that, every fibre of his being hurt. Even his fingernails ached. How could your fingernails ache? His mouth felt as if someone had used it to mix cement in.

Something was pressing against his cheek. In an act of

magnificent bravery that deserved to have songs written about it, he opened one eye to look at whatever the thing was. An empty bottle of whisky. That explained quite a lot.

He winced as a deafeningly loud noise ripped through the air. After a few seconds of agony, he realised it was Rachmaninoff's Piano Concerto No. 2, aka his mobile ringtone. He closed his eyes again and lay there, waiting for it to be over. Finally, blissfully, it ended, only to restart again a second later.

Forced to concede that life was going to continue whether he liked it or not, Eddie managed to pull himself upright. As he did so, his foot found a wine bottle lying on the floor. That explained a whole lot more. He'd had the weirdest of weird dreams. Talking birds. Was there no limit to his imagination? Perhaps he should branch out into novels, screenplays, writing for the stage? He would consider all of this just as soon as he'd done some hearty throwing up.

He noticed that he'd removed from the wall the framed picture of him and Lenore at the Grand Canyon – about time, too – and in its place now hung her old tennis racket. He stared at the object in confusion. His phone stopped ringing then immediately started again. Who the hell could want to speak to him this badly?

Somewhere inside his throbbing skull, two brain cells met and a flashpoint of inspiration occurred. The bursary. He had applied to be the poet in residence at one of the Johns Hopkins libraries – a position that came with a not insignificant stipend – and only yesterday he'd been wondering why he hadn't heard anything back. Maybe this was them, finally, ringing to give him the good news?

Finding himself suddenly in possession of the motivation not only to continue living but also to find his phone, he started scrabbling around. It appeared that while in his cups last night, he had rearranged a few things, removing photographs, trinkets, anything that had belonged to her. The one who had betrayed him. It was all gathered in a pile in the fireplace. Thankfully, he hadn't set fire to it, the fireplace having been bricked up years ago.

There were empty beer cans strewn around the floor, too. Beer? They'd only had it in the house because Lenore had insisted on inviting Ruth from work and her even more bourgeois buffoon of a husband, Tim, over for dinner. He'd seemed intent on discussing with Eddie not only the exact route he'd taken there but also routes he had driven to other locations. Over dinner, Eddie had made clear that *Strictly Come Dancing* was pap fed to the ignorant masses to keep them distracted and happy while they were metaphorically boiled alive in their own juices by the patriarchy, and Tim and Ruth had left without having dessert, or drinking any of the beer. Lenore had pecked away at him about that, too.

Finally, Eddie found his phone under his notebook. He picked it up but didn't answer, his attention drawn instead to the pages of paper. He'd written something. He didn't even remember doing so, but there it was, in his distinctive scrawl. Several sides of it.

He flicked it over and started to read.

Once upon a midnight dreary, while I pondered, weak and weary

Good opening.

The phone in his hand sprang into irritating life yet again

and, if for no other reason than to stop its infernal bleating, he answered it. 'Hello, Edgar Poe Senior speaking.'

He'd never referred to himself as 'Senior' before, but he instantly liked it. True, there was no Edgar Poe Junior from which to differentiate himself, but the title nevertheless had a certain gravitas to it.

The voice on the other end of the line was like a glass of cold water being thrown in his face.

'Good morning, Eddie,' it said.

'Who is this?'

'Who is this?' it repeated. 'I'll tell you who this is, this is who. This is Gordon – we met last night.'

'I ...' Eddie looked up at the tennis racket hanging on the wall. 'I don't know what you're—'

'And you can knock that crap off, Eddie Boy. You know damn well who I am and what you did.'

From somewhere, Eddie summoned some anger. 'And I'd do it again,' he hissed. 'You do not come into my home and threaten me.'

'Nobody threatened you. Then. I'm doing it now, though. Consider yourself being threatened.'

'I'm not afraid of you. You're a bird. Just a bird. What can *you* do to *me*?'

At this, the voice laughed. Something about it chilled Eddie to the bone. Then it said, 'I want you to remember, Eddie, that we gave you a chance – a chance to do the right thing. Remember that, and brace yourself. It's about to get ironical, sarcastical and more than a little scatological.' The voice started laughing again.

Slightly lessening the effect, Eddie then heard it say, 'Right, press the thing now. No, not that thing, Doug – the other one. We've been through this. Rachel, stop hitting that.

You're stopping him doing the ... C'mon, people – work together here!'

Eddie jabbed his finger at the screen to end the call. He sat there, staring at the device for a few seconds, before he pulled himself up and staggered to the bathroom, his hand clamped over his mouth.

He almost made it.

Try as he might, Eddie could not convince himself that all of this was just a dream now. Once he'd finished parting ways with what appeared to be every morsel of food he'd ever consumed, he crawled into his bed, stopping only to confirm the bedroom window was firmly closed and locked before he drew the curtains.

Several hours later he awoke and, after a moment, with a terrible sense of dread, he recognised the sound that had roused him.

A tap-tap-tapping on his window.

He shouted an extensive and heartfelt barrage of abuse at whatever was on the other side of the curtains, but it achieved nothing.

Dragging his duvet and pillow with him, he moved into the spare room, quietly shifting some boxes off the bed to make room. As soon as he'd crawled under the covers, there it was again. That tap-tap-tapping on the window.

He relocated to the sofa but sure enough, yet again, the tap-tap-tapping followed him.

It was only at that point that he allowed himself to cry hot, wet, salty tears at the sheer injustice of it all.

For the rest of the day he sat there on the sofa, wrapped in his duvet and watching TV at the highest volume possible.

He swore that even then, behind the noise from the screen, he could feel as much as hear that tap-tap-tapping. At some point he must have fallen asleep from sheer exhaustion because the next morning he woke to bright winter sun pouring through a crack between the curtains that he'd never been able to close fully.

Grief may have its five stages, but persecution has a less clear-cut trajectory, clearly. He'd passed through self-pity and had come out the other side angry. He clung to that – let it give him energy. Even when the tap-tap-tapping started again, Eddie sat there and resolutely ignored it while he drank his morning coffee.

He made it to Lenore's car, which she'd been nice enough to leave behind when she ran off to Portugal, without incident. Some googling over breakfast had provided him with a plethora of ideas and it was time to go shopping.

It took him the best part of the day, but Eddie found most of what he was looking for. As soon as he got home, he busied himself rushing around the perimeter of the house, installing the countermeasures he'd acquired, all the while keeping his head on a swivel and watching for any winged menaces. It was only as the sun set that he sat back at his desk and allowed himself the reward of reading through the verse he had written the night before.

And the Raven, never flitting, still is sitting, still is sitting
   On the pallid bust of Pallas just above my chamber door;

. . .

It was good. Really good. What made it all the odder was that he didn't remember writing it. If he was entirely honest, he wasn't one hundred per cent certain what some parts of it meant, but nevertheless it was undeniably good. The thing with poetry was the reader didn't always have to know exactly what it meant, just that it definitely meant something. In fact, clarity was generally a disastrous idea, as then there'd be no point in people analysing it ad nauseum, which was how a piece of work became truly eternal.

The poetry world was loath to admit it, but one of the most successful poets of all time was Nostradamus. The man had been a genius because he realised that if you were vague enough, your awful poetry could become immortal by reverse engineering it into a chilling prediction of everything from 9/11 to the rise of K-pop. Eddie had considered getting into the prophesying game himself, but in order for it to really bear fruit, you had to be dead. While he wanted his work to live on, he wanted the same for himself. Besides, predictions for the future tended to attract odd men who wore anoraks, had sweaty handshakes and smelled of rotten soup, and Eddie still hadn't given up on the dream of buxom young ladies with a penchant for lace, leather bodices and dramatic make-up choices.

Another notable thing about *The Raven* – that's what he was calling his masterpiece – outside of its obvious brilliance, was that it bore little resemblance to what his actual meeting with the bird had been like. He was glad there was no reference whatsoever in it to Gordon the starling – the motor-mouthed vermin did not deserve the honour of being mentioned in such a magnificent piece of work. Let him die in obscurity. Let him die. Please, god, let him die. In the space of twenty-four hours, Eddie had written his masterwork and found his nemesis, all before leaving the house.

In the background, he could hear the merry tinkle of the wind chimes he'd bought, swaying in the winter breeze – one was hung in the back garden and the other by the front door. Their sound would disturb birds, as would the motion of the trio of spinners he'd dotted around the place. He was quite proud of his novel solution to needing to find shiny silvery objects that would also deter birds. He'd acquired a dozen CDs of James Blunt's seminal album *Back to Bedlam* from a charity shop for a pittance, and they were now dangling outside every window and door of the house. Let's see the little bastard and his cawing friend get by all of that.

That night, just as Eddie was lying in bed, dropping off to sleep, there came a tap-tap-tapping on his window.

The following morning, when Eddie didn't awake so much as finally give up on the concept of sleep, he dressed and, with grim determination, prepared to head out for some more serious defences. As he opened the front door, he stepped back in shock. There, on his doorstep, were the three spinners, both wind chimes and a pile of James Blunt CDs, with a framed picture of the man himself sitting atop it all, signed 'To my good friend, Gordon'. Stuck to the frame was a scrawled Post-it note that read 'Do not disrespect the Blunt'. It seemed Eddie had underestimated his opponent; he would not make that mistake again.

By the time evening rolled around, the new defences were in place. On this occasion, he'd gone with rubber snakes located all around the property. Supposedly, according to a website he'd found written by a corn farmer, they frightened all birds on a primeval level. He'd also got hold of a large scarecrow with glowing eyes set in its plastic pumpkin head.

It was so scary that Mr Nabar from next door had come around to ask Eddie to take it down, which he'd refused to do. He'd also installed chicken-wire screens on all the windows.

That night, as Eddie lay in bed, the tap-tap-tapping on his window came again despite all the above precautions. He'd also bought a set of noise-cancelling headphones, which he put on to block out the sound, but to no avail. It was as if the infernal tapping could bypass his hearing and chip away at his very soul.

The following morning, the chicken wire had been removed, as had the snakes. The scarecrow was still there but had been turned around and was now mooning the house. As Eddie dragged it down angrily and disposed of it, he could feel Mr Nabar's eyes on him.

Fine.

So be it.

It was time to take a drastically different approach. In an effort to let bygones be bygones, Eddie put out a new birdfeeder full of seeds and several fat balls.

That night, he slept on the floor in the hallway, wearing his noise-cancelling headphones again, but still he fancied he could hear that tap-tap-tapping.

As soon as he awoke the next morning, his neck sore from the awkward position in which he'd finally grabbed a couple of hours' sleep, he opened the curtains tentatively. The bird table was completely bare and the feeder was empty. He couldn't help but smile.

The seeds had been fine, mostly, bar a few select ones in the middle that had been coated in odourless rat poison.

Similarly, only one of the fat balls contained something that gave it an extra kick. True, it was a stunt like this that had sparked Eddie's feud with the feathery bastards in the first place, but he couldn't see how striking back against their unfair oppression could put him in any worse a position. If your enemy is dead set on war, then showing them the cost of it is the only way to stop them. Eddie liked that and found himself wondering if it was a quote he'd picked up from somewhere. If not, he should make it one and take ownership of it. He'd stick it on an appropriate background and throw it up on social media after he finished breakfast. You could never tell what might take off. As he poured himself a bowl of Sugar Puffs, there came an unexpected thud. Eddie looked down to see a fat ball staring up at him from the middle of the bowl.

After he'd dressed, Eddie packed a bag and headed out the door. He was greeted by the sight of Lenore's car, his car, surrounded by Mr Nabar and a couple of the other neighbours. They were all standing there, staring at it wordlessly.

'Ehm,' said Mr Nabar eventually, 'I ... I believe it is supposed to be lucky.'

'I think they say that,' said Mr Barker, the retired quantity surveyor from across the road, 'if one bird shits on your car, or your shoulder, or something like that. This' – he waved a hand at the car – 'looks like every bird within a hundred-mile radius has crapped on the lad's car. It's ...'

'Is this one of your art things?' asked Mrs McMillan, the part-time GP receptionist from number thirty-four. 'Like, an installation?'

Eddie finally found his voice. 'No, it is not.'

'Just as well,' said Mr Barker. 'Because if it was, I was

gonna say it's shit!' He looked around expectantly. 'Shit? Get it? It's shit!' He rolled his eyes at the lack of response. 'Fine – please yourselves.'

'This is unbelievable,' said Mr Nabar. 'You should contact the papers, or that Donal MacIntyre man from the TV.'

'Are you mad?' said Mr Barker. 'That bloke goes after gangsters and nonces. Why is he going to care about a load of birds crapping on this poor fella's car? You want to contact GB News. This is probably something the government is responsible for. Or get in touch with that fella who left and now has his own YouTube channel. He's not afraid to speak truth to power. He tried to light a cigarette live on air and they fired him.'

'Why was he trying to smoke while on air?' asked Mr Nabar.

'I dunno. Something about free speech.'

'Was it like the Sex Pistols taking a poo on the desk of the head of their record label?' asked Mr Nabar.

'No,' said Mr Barker, looking thoroughly appalled. 'That's disgusting.'

'True,' conceded Mrs McMillan, 'but it is arguably less damaging to the health of those around you than passive smoking.' She turned back to Eddie. 'I think you should contact the *Guardian* or—'

'Thank you all for your assistance,' barked Eddie, so aggressively that they all took a step back, 'but I will deal with this matter privately. Good day.'

The neighbours all walked away and, as Eddie spent the next couple of hours cleaning off enough of the mess so that he could drive to the car wash safely, he couldn't help but feel several sets of eyes watching him through various blinds. No doubt the Neighbourhood Watch WhatsApp group, which

Eddie had left in protest following criticism of how he'd chosen to dispose of his Christmas tree, would be abuzz with discussions of his behaviour. He cared not. He had other, literal, actual shit to deal with. After three trips through the car wash, the car was as clean as it was ever going to be, although the paintwork would never be the same again.

That evening, Eddie checked himself into a Premier Inn.

He was not in the least bit surprised to hear, as he lay on his bed that evening, a tap-tap-tapping on the window.

The woman standing behind the counter at the cat shelter smiled nervously at Eddie. Earnestness was coming off her in waves – that and cat hair.

'Oh, yes,' she said brightly, 'we have a great number of cats available. In fact, truth be told, we're full to capacity. There's currently a crisis in rescues in this country.'

'That is terrible,' said Eddie, as he felt it was expected. 'I'm looking for something quite specific.'

'Hypoallergenic?' guessed the woman.

'No.'

'A kitten?'

'No.'

She slapped the desk excitedly. 'A snuggle buddy? An older cat. One who just wants to spend the twilight of their life snuggling up on the sofa with you, watching a box set.'

'Good god, no,' said Eddie.

The woman recoiled slightly, her enthusiasm replaced with suspicion.

Eddie smiled to reassure her. 'What I mean is … What I'm looking for … What would be most of value to me …' He stopped as he noticed the large plaster on the back of the lady's hand. 'That!' He pointed at it. 'What happened to your hand?'

She covered it protectively. 'Oh, that's just a little scratch from one of our more challenging residents.'

'Excellent,' said Eddie. 'I love a challenge.'

Eddie was very aware of the whispered conversations going on behind his back, but he studiously ignored them. Instead, he focused all of his attention on the creature sitting in the cage, staring back at him. The cat had only one eye, but it packed more homicidal intensity than most creatures could possibly manage from two. Its fur was a weird mixture of brown, grey, ginger and white. It was quite possible it'd taken some of it off another cat. Eddie kept his eyes firmly locked on it. Now was a crucial moment to attempt to establish dominance.

One of the shelter volunteers, clearly the senior member of the cat-lovers coven, eventually stepped forward. 'Ehm, I really don't think this is the cat for you, sir.'

'Nonsense,' said Eddie. 'He seems lovely.'

'Really?' She coughed. 'I mean, he's a very challenging cat.'

'Yes, so I hear.'

'To be fair, he's not bad with people.'

Her comment drew an odd groaning noise from one of the other women.

'By which I mean,' clarified the first woman, 'he has more of an issue with other animals.'

'I see.'

'We'd hoped neutering him would calm him down. It usually does the trick. Seems to have had the opposite effect on him, though. He came around suddenly and violently after the op, when the vet was checking his stitches – some of us think he was faking.'

'Devious.'

'That's one word for it. Nathaniel won't come back any more. In fact, I hear he's thinking of leaving the veterinary profession altogether. Seriously, we have a lot of other cats.'

'And you say he doesn't get on with other animals?' asked Eddie, ignoring her suggestion.

'Oh, yeah. After his procedure, he got into a fight with another cat and, well, sort of, well, performed his own version of the operation on the poor bugger. Seriously, don't adopt him.'

'He sounds like he just needs a little TLC.'

'I ...' He could sense the woman looking back at her colleagues and them doing that irritating thing people do where they silently mouth things back and forth. The cat, meanwhile, was licking one paw casually – like a feline Hannibal Lecter. 'If,' said the woman, 'you were to adopt him, you'd have to sign a waiver indemnifying the shelter against any issues.'

'Of course. I'd be happy to do so. What's his name, by the way?'

There followed an unexpected few seconds of silence before the woman eventually said, 'We've not really given him a proper name.'

'All the other cats have names,' said Eddie. 'Surely you must call him something?'

'Well, ehm ...' He could hear the woman failing to make up a lie and, in a state of panic, reverting to the truth. 'Bastard. We've been calling him Bastard.'

'I see.'

'You know,' she added weakly, 'as a joke.'

'Of course. One final question: how does he get on with birds?'

Once Eddie had signed the waiver, the shelter couldn't get him and Bastard the cat out the door quick enough. He was pretty sure that their absolutely-no-returns-allowed policy had been invented entirely for his benefit. He didn't care. He had a good feeling about Bastard. They'd even thrown in his cage for free, mainly because nobody wanted to open it to get him out of it. The pair headed home, stopping on the way so that Eddie could pick up supplies.

An hour later, he was standing in front of Bastard's cage, holding a plate of tuna in his hand. He set it down a couple of feet away. Then, as the cat watched him curiously, he used the tennis racquet to open the cage door from a safe distance. Bastard sat there looking at Eddie, who had now stationed himself on the far side of the room. After a few minutes, the cat casually sauntered out and started sniffing the tuna. Seemingly satisfied it was legit, Bastard scoffed the lot.

That was the easy part done. Now for the considerably harder next step. Eddie cleared his throat. 'OK, now, Bastard, did you like that?'

The cat sat down and tilted his head.

'Good,' said Eddie. 'There is a lot more where that came from. In fact, every day for the rest of your life, and catnip and anything else your little heart desires.' Feeling foolish, he held up the picture he'd printed out from the internet. It was of a starling. 'All you need to do is get one of these. Or, come to that, as many of them as possible. Any bird, in fact, that comes tap-tap-tapping on our window. Deal?'

Some part of Eddie's mind appreciated that he had quite possibly slipped into madness, but then if birds could not only talk but also orchestrate a sophisticated campaign of intimidation, why couldn't he make a deal with a psychotic feline?

In response, Bastard stood up and sauntered off towards the back door. Eddie, dodging his new 'pet' carefully, opened the door to let him leave. Bastard paused on the threshold and peered up at Eddie with his one good eye.

'Anything you want,' reiterated Eddie.

As soon as Bastard left, Eddie poured himself a stiff drink and made his way to the sofa.

That night, Eddie got into bed but left the headphones and all the other accoutrements he'd been using in a futile effort to block out noise to one side. Instead, he lay there, listening carefully. Sure enough, after a few minutes, it came – that infernal tap-tap-tapping. Eddie closed his eyes, waiting, wishing, hoping.

Eyes wide open, he shot upright at the ferocious feline yowl that came from outside the window, followed by the sound of a struggle, followed by ... nothing. Silence. Blissful, wonderful, magnificent silence.

Eddie settled back down and, for the first time in a long while, enjoyed a glorious night of blissfully undisturbed sleep.

He awoke feeling refreshed and invigorated. He wasn't naive enough to believe the war had been won, but perhaps he had finally landed a blow against his enemy. Those birds needed to realise that he was a man of greater resolve than they could imagine. He had to be – he was a purveyor of verse in a world of tweets. It took a special kind of person to get booed off stage at an open mic night that was eventually won by a guy doing impressions of household objects, and to still go back the following week and try again. They were just animals. He was a goddamned poet!

With a sense of trepidation and a bowl of cat food in hand, Eddie opened the back door. Bastard the cat was sitting at the other end of the garden, basking in the winter sun while licking his paws. Hearing the door open, Bastard sauntered towards it casually, only stopping to pick something up in his mouth. As he drew closer, Eddie realised with a shock of excitement that the thing was a bird. He was bringing him a dead bird. And not just any bird – a starling. Like a returning Roman general paying tribute to his emperor, Bastard laid down his trophy on the mat in front of Eddie. It was definitely a starling. He couldn't be sure it was the dastardly Gordon, but something inside him told him it must be. He punched the air in delight.

'Who's a clever boy?' said Eddie joyously. 'You are such a clever boy.'

He screamed as the starling twisted its head and looked up at him. 'Thanks very much,' said Gordon.

'But ... But ... How did ...'

Gordon righted himself and took a bow. 'Surprise.'

Eddie looked at Bastard. 'You. You ... traitor!'

'Oh, dear,' chirped Gordon, 'I wouldn't have said that.'

Eddie barely had time to react before the cat hurtled, claws first, into his face.

And so it went. After Eddie eventually fought him off, Bastard ate the food Eddie had lovingly prepared, took a pee on the rug in the front room, and then left, never to be seen again.

When he was getting his wounds tended to in A & E, he'd made the mistake of explaining events to the nurse. A couple of minutes into his subsequent 'chat' with the nice doctor, he realised she was a psychiatrist and that he was being assessed. He quickly explained he was an artist and that he'd been speaking in metaphors. Halfway through his recitation from memory of one of his poems, the doctor abruptly and rather rudely left the room, and he was discharged shortly thereafter.

The scratch marks on Eddie's face eventually healed, except for the one down his left cheek. In truth, he felt it lent him a more mysterious, rugged edge, so that was some slight consolation.

Every night the tap-tap-tapping sounded at his window and no matter what Eddie tried, where he went, nothing stopped it. Without ever giving him any explanation, the two pest control companies he contracted both abandoned their posts and stopped returning his calls. The bird netting, spikes, all of it – every measure he installed proved useless. Eddie had held out some hope that the falconer he'd hired with his two highly trained birds might have some effect, but the man had dared to blame Eddie when both birds went against a lifetime of training and buggered off, never to be seen again. Eddie had even bought himself an air rifle and built himself a hunting blind in the back garden. The police had come round and explained that while it wasn't illegal for him to have the weapon, they were taking it off him as a 'public safety concern'. Eddie had seen Mr Nabar's lace curtains twitching.

Through all this, he'd slept only a couple of hours on any

given night and found himself living in a state of perpetual exhaustion. So much so that when the fateful phone call had come, he'd thought it was a dream at first.

While the majority of Eddie's time had been taken up attempting to battle back against the unassailable forces of his avian oppressors, during a brief respite he had submitted *The Raven* to a few competitions. He'd promptly forgotten all about them until the phone rang that morning. Initially, his tone had been frosty, given that Gordon had taken to ringing up regularly for a 'chat' – but it wasn't him. Instead, it was a lady called Ms Marcioni from the Allan Institute in Baltimore. They'd been trying to get hold of him for several days. She was delighted to inform him that *The Raven* had been selected unanimously as the winner of the prestigious Wallace Award for excellence in the field of poetry and he was to be honoured at a ceremony in Baltimore the following week. As well as being feted by the great and the good, he would also receive his prize of one hundred thousand dollars. The poetry world's richest such award.

He'd struggled to take it all in as Ms Marcioni had mixed gushing over his work with firing details at him, including how him not having a publishing deal had caused quite a stir in the industry. After he'd put down the phone, part of Eddie's mind had jumped instantly to thinking the whole thing was a ruse. But then the emails from Ms Marcioni and others started flooding in. He looked at the Allan Institute's website and there it was – an announcement confirming the whole thing. All he needed to do was turn up, accept his prize and he would be set to be the darling of the literary world, courted by publishers, fawned over by the press and undoubtedly inundated by all manner of invitations from buxom young ladies with a penchant for lace, leather bodices and dramatic make-up choices.

His ecstatic reverie was interrupted by a noise. That noise. A tap-tap-tapping on his chamber door.

Eddie had spent most of the week making plans while batting away the increasingly insistent solicitations from agents and publishers. That made sense. Nothing stirred up a frenzy more than those in it being told no. It wasn't why he was doing it, though – it was more of a happy byproduct of his preoccupation. Everything he'd ever wanted – no, deserved – was now finally within his reach, and the only thing standing between him and it were some feathery little monsters. He'd spent most of his remaining money making it happen, paying well over the odds to make sure everyone involved would be exactly where they needed to be when they needed to be there. He told anyone who asked that he was taking these measures to escape the attentions of religious extremists who were targeting him for his work. It wasn't even that far from the truth.

And so it was on the big day that he'd driven to the supermarket, just like he did every other Tuesday morning. Luckily, it was raining, so Eddie, wearing his deerstalker hat, hadn't even looked out of place. He'd been worried about that. From there, he'd swapped outfits in the gents' toilets with an out-of-work actor who'd then proceeded to do a shop before taking Eddie's car and returning to Eddie's house where he would stay inside and out of sight for the next two days.

Eddie, meanwhile, had nipped into a taxi in the supermarket's loading bay. It drove him to the Trafford

Centre, where he met four Elvis impersonators who were all dressed in identical clothes to him. He'd ended up using Elvises as it turned out it was quite hard to find a bunch of people of a similar build who were all looking for work on a Tuesday morning and were happy not to ask many questions. They all entered the changing rooms in Marks & Spencer simultaneously, before each heading to a different exit where a dedicated taxi was waiting.

Eddie remained in the changing rooms, having rather brilliantly swapped outfits yet again with yet another Elvis who had been waiting in there. This Elvis had been in drag, and so it was that Eddie, in a tasteful blue dress, long blonde wig and sunglasses, had hopped into the private hire car that had been waiting exactly where it had been instructed to wait. The driver had coughed and commented on the amount of perfume Eddie was wearing, but even this was intentional. Eddie didn't know if birds could track scents, but he wasn't about to risk finding out. From there, he'd been driven to Liverpool John Lennon Airport, to catch a connecting flight to Dublin and then on to Washington. He'd remembered to change clothes yet again in Dublin, as US Customs would probably have questions if someone turned up in drag.

Only when he was settled in his seat in business class (of course) and the plane had taken off did Eddie allow himself to enjoy the complimentary glass of champagne. He'd done it. Everything he wanted would be waiting for him when this plane landed. From the airport, he would be whisked by limo to Baltimore where, the following evening, in front of an audience of thousands, he would be celebrated as the voice of his generation.

. . .

Eddie had read and heard people talking about the downside of fame. How a demanding public could wear on you. He'd only experienced it for a day, but he'd already hazard a guess that none of those people had ever come last in an open mic night where, never mind the household objects impressionist, a mime and a bloke who could pat his head and rub his tummy while doing a bad rendition of 'Baby Got Back' by Sir Mix-a-Lot had made up the podium finishers. They hadn't even announced any other placings except that he'd come last. From that to this – this, he could get used to. Shaking hands, trying to look humble as people lavished praise upon him, publishers dangling bigger and bigger numbers in front of his face as he played it cool – every inch the principled artiste. This was it. The dream. And he hadn't even needed to move to Sweden or de-ice a dog to achieve it.

Eddie had tried to look magnanimous as the ceremony had rather dragged on. He sensed that the several thousand people in the auditorium were all really going through the motions, waiting for him. He'd been practising his reading both on the flight over and all morning. He wanted to absolutely nail it. As the head of the institute delivered her speech eulogising his worthiness as a winner, he stood in the wings, preparing himself. The stage was immense. The massive glass windows displaying the Baltimore skyline provided a wondrous backdrop that made the lectern in the middle of the stage look positively tiny. He'd have to be big. Own the space.

As he walked out, the lights were blinding and the ovation deafening. Once his eyes had adjusted, he could see the crowd spread out before him. Every man, woman and, he assumed, the occasional child were on their feet, applauding him. He shook the chairperson's hand and, when the tumult eventually died down, he turned his attention to the speech he had prepared. He was humble, gracious, funny – his joke received a massive response. And then it was time to deliver his reading.

A hush fell.

He left it for a few moments, drinking it in but also allowing tension to build. It was just as he took a last sip of water that he heard it.

He smiled. Tried with every inch of his being to resist the urge to turn around and look.

There it was again.

A tap-tap-tapping on the glass behind him.

Eddie cleared his throat.

Tap-tap-tap.

Unable to resist any longer, he glanced over his shoulder. He couldn't see anything but the lights of the skyscrapers in the distance.

The chairperson thew him a concerned smile.

He nodded back, giving her a tight smile in return.

It was just his imagination. Just—

Tap. Tap. Tap.

A manic giggle escaped his lips. He placed his hand over his mouth, trying to control himself.

It happened again.

He noticed a few anxious faces in the crowd now.

He cleared his throat and took a large, long sip of water. It wasn't real. All in his mind. He just needed to—

Tap. Tap. Tap.

'Shut up!'

He'd meant for the words to stay only in his head, but his mouth had delivered them loudly into the microphone.

The room truly was tense now.

Relax. He was a poet. People would think it was just part of the performance. He just needed to—

Tap.

He spun about and pushed the chairperson away as she tried to calm him. The last thing he remembered was running towards the immense glass window, and then ...

Darkness.

Three Months Later

Eddie sat down on the bench. It was sunny. He enjoyed the feeling of the sun on his face. Manchester in the sun was a glorious thing. They only got an hour of outside time a day, and that could be taken away if they misbehaved. Eddie didn't misbehave. Everyone said so. To be fair, he was on such strong drugs, he didn't have the energy. Even if he'd wanted to, the restraints made it rather difficult. Still, he was happy, in a way.

The two burly guards were standing at a distance, resting on the wall of the yard, and Eddie heard the flick of a lighter as one of them lit a cigarette.

'Who is this bloke, then, Mick?'

'Are you kidding, Stevie? Do you not read the papers?'

'Papers? Who reads a newspaper in this day and age?'

'Whatever. He's been all over the news. The poet.'

'A poet got on the news?' Some small part of Eddie's brain registered the shock in Stevie's voice and he almost managed to feel indignant.

'He does if he loses his shit at some big award ceremony and starts attacking people.'

'Jesus.'

'That's not even the best bit. They fly him back here, say he's had a breakdown or something. Then, someone starts asking questions about where his girlfriend Lenore has gone, and they find her. She's only buried under the rockery in the back garden.'

'Christ.'

'Yeah. Initially, people thought he was faking it to try to lodge an insanity plea, but nobody is this good an actor. I mean ...'

It was at that point that Eddie tuned out of the conversation, his attention drawn elsewhere. A bird had landed on the backrest of the bench beside him.

'Hello, Eddie.'

'Hello, Gordon.'

'You don't look well.'

Eddie laughed. 'Oh, I'm not. Ask anyone. I'm crazy.'

The starling tilted his head slightly. 'Can't help thinking you've only yourself to blame. Blame yourself. Self to blame.'

'Do I?'

'I mean, you could've made a deal.'

'I'm not a rich man.' They'd taken the prize money back before he'd even actually received it.

'Yeah, but you can get a big old tub of worms for a tenner a month.'

'What?'

'For poor old Neville Moore's family.'

'That – that's all you wanted?'

'They're robins. What did you think they wanted – a house in the country and an annual holiday in Ibiza?'

Eddie started laughing, and then, as was often the case, even as tears streamed down his cheeks he found he couldn't stop. Stevie and Mick dragged him away and back to his room.

It was a nice room – or cell, to be more accurate. Still, it had a window that was some form of plexiglass as opposed to bars. Once they'd secured him in the jacket for his own safety, the nice nurse gave him one of the big pink pills and Eddie felt himself relaxing again.

The last thing he heard before he drifted off into a fitful sleep was the tap-tap-tapping on his window. Somewhere, maybe only in his mind, a harsh voice cawed the word 'nevermore', or something very similar.

DO THE RESEARCH

Razor looked at his screen and shook his head. Balander69 was such a newb. The idiot probably believed that man really had been to the moon. Mind you, some of the young guns you meet on these boards, nothing would surprise him. Razor had been in a chat last week that had descended into a flame war, an increasingly common occurrence since the schism. He'd dismissed the other guy as a tourist who didn't even know who JFK was. The guy had hit back that he'd been into him since his early demos. Kids.

He was about to get into it when the doorbell rang. Lucky escape for Balander69. Razor would rip him a new one about how international banking really worked some other time. Right now, dinner was here, and he was starving. He'd spent the entire day researching whether the supposed foot-and-mouth animal 'cull' was actually an operation to stockpile meat stocks for the chosen few after the Great Reset. It was all coming together. Everything was there if you dug deep enough.

He pulled the cord to draw the curtain he'd installed to

cover his charts. Security was paramount. He couldn't have civilians stumbling upon what he was working on. The deep state had eyes and ears everywhere. Razor needed to stay off the grid. It was the only way. As far as anyone else was concerned, he was just an ordinary dude living in a terraced house in Salford, and that was how he wanted it to stay. Be the unseen enemy.

The doorbell rang again.

'All right. I'm coming,' said Razor, as he tightened the belt on his dressing gown.

'Do it faster,' replied a female voice on the other side of the front door. 'I haven't got all night and your pizza's getting cold.'

That was odd. The normal guy was, well, a guy. Razor squinted through the spyhole in the door. A girl was standing there, with long blonde hair but totally shaved on one side. A ring through one eyebrow and a streak of red through her mane added to her distinctly punk look. She was chewing gum with ferocious intensity while glaring at the door. As if on cue, she held up a pizza box and pointed at it with a sarcastic smile. How the hell did she know he was looking? There was no way she could see that.

'Thanks,' said Razor. 'Just leave it on the step.'

'I can't do that.'

'The normal guy does.'

'The normal guy did a lot of things – that's why he got fired. Although some of those things, to be honest, were not that normal. I'm not allowed say, but you might want to check you're not pregnant.'

'What?'

'Nothing. I'm joking. I have a very dry sense of humour.

Not everybody gets me. I also have a pizza. Nobody gets that unless they open the door.'

'I don't normally open the door.'

'Cool,' said the girl. 'On behalf of myself and the other drones trying to make a living in the zero-hour contract, minimum-wage service industry, may I thank you for your big tipping ways. Still, in the twenty-five-minute-long unpaid training session I had before starting this gig tonight, they made it really clear we can't just dump the pizza. You've got five seconds to take it from me like a human being or I'm going to eat it while you watch.'

'You've got a real attitude problem.'

'And yet my finishing school voted me most likely to succeed. Five ...'

'Hang on.'

'I have been. Four ...'

Part of Razor's brain was tempted to tell the girl exactly where she could go. However, a much larger part of his brain really wanted pizza. He began unlocking the four locks he'd installed. He decided he'd give her a piece of his mind right after he took the food.

'Two ...' said the girl.

'What happened to three?'

'It got bored and left. Can't say I blame it.'

Razor finished unlocking the door and went to open it. 'OK, give me the—'

He was interrupted by his own front door smacking him straight in the face, propelled by a well-placed Doc Marten boot. He staggered backwards, stumbled and fell over the coffee table. When he looked up, the girl was in his house, closing the front door behind her.

'What the hell?' shouted Razor.

'Yeah,' said the girl, sounding infuriatingly calm. 'You shouldn't have opened the door. That was a good instinct you ignored there.'

Razor held his hand up to his face. 'You broke my nose.'

'No, I didn't, you big baby. It's just bleeding a little.'

'I'm going to ring up and complain about you.'

'Seriously?' she asked with a smirk. 'You're part of an outlaw group, fighting to open the eyes of the sheeple to the true nature of the global elite. Somebody kicks in your door and you still think they're from the local pizza place?'

Before she could stop him, Razor turned and threw himself under his desk. He reached out a hand in each direction, simultaneously hitting the two large red buttons under either end of the workstation.

He looked up at the girl and smiled. 'I've just wiped clean every last one of my hard drives.'

She shrugged. 'Cool.' She turned her head to take in the rest of the front room and peered into the open-plan kitchen to the rear. Her face formed into a mask of disgust. 'Fingers crossed this is the start of the full-on cleaning blitz this whole place needs.' She nodded pointedly at a pile of pizza boxes in the corner of the room. 'You're going to other pizza places too? Wait until the guys at home base hear about this – they'll be so upset.'

'I'm calling the police,' said Razor.

'Interesting,' replied the girl. 'I thought you'd be all "the cops are the pawns of the global fascist elite, working for Bill Gates, blah, blah, blah, blah".'

'Who the hell are you?'

'See, now you're actually asking semi-sensible questions. That smack in the face did you the world of good. Besides, I imagine that raggedy beard you've got going there took most of the damage. You look like Tom Hanks in that *Castaway* film only, y'know, sadder. Anyway, I'm Tina. What should I call you?'

'People call me Razor.'

She barked a laugh. 'Well, I'm not going to be able to do that with a straight face. Let's go with Brian, seeing as it's the name your mum gave you. She says hello by the way.'

Brian/Razor narrowed his eyes. 'My mother is dead.'

'Well,' said Tina, 'that would certainly explain the smell.'

'I think you should leave,' said Brian as he started to stand.

'I feel you. I didn't even want to come here in the first place but, well, I got myself into some trouble and let's just say this is like my community service.' She flipped open the pizza box to reveal it was empty except for some crusts. 'Thanks for the pizza, by the way. Although, seriously – cheese-stuffed crust on a quattro formaggi? C'mon, dude – that's less of an order and more of a cry for help.'

'I don't want to hurt you,' said Brian, pointing at the door, 'but I will if I have to.'

Tina nodded. 'Thank you for the information, Brian. I'll be honest, I don't think it's going to become an issue, but nevertheless, good to know. Take a seat.'

'I don't want to ...'

It was hard to say what confused him more. The fact that even as he was objecting to the very idea of sitting down he was already doing it, or that the chair from his workstation was suddenly behind him. It hadn't been there before. Then again, he'd just received a blow to the head so perhaps he wasn't thinking straight. Yes, that must be it.

'So, as I was saying, your mother – may she rest in peace –

is not, in fact, resting in peace. Her spirit is highly agitated because she's worried about you.'

'Oh, please, you haven't seriously come here to peddle some ghost mumbo jumbo, have you?'

Tina sighed. 'First off, you fuzzy-faced incel, I'm not here peddling anything. I'm here because I did the teeny-tiniest bit of messing about with a traffic warden who was being rude and it was "do this thing for John Mór or else you're on probation again". And second ...' She moved across and pulled the cord to reveal the wall full of charts. 'You believe that there's a link between the Clintons, a mining company in Peru, UFOs, and is that Phillip Schofield from off the telly?'

'I wouldn't expect someone like you to understand.'

'Good,' said Tina, 'because I don't and have no interest at all in trying. Although, with ...' She pointed at the board again. 'Is that the comedian Harry Hill?'

'That is need-to-know information.'

She leaned in. 'It's written below the picture so now I know. So yeah, with Harry Hill as my witness, if at any point you speak the words "do the research", I will not be responsible for my actions.'

Brian said nothing. Instead, he stared back at her in a way he hoped could be described as defiant.

'I'm here because your mother's spirit is bugging Mrs Shanyaski from three doors down, night and day, and she's had enough of it. Her downstairs is giving her terrible trouble and she doesn't need any more stress right now. I appreciate you didn't want or need to know about Mrs S's downstairs issues but neither did I. I just came from there. Honestly, I'm not sure if she meant downstairs in an architectural or a biological sense, but some questions you just don't ask. I'm here, we're going to sort this out, and then we can both get on with our lives.' She looked around again. 'Or at least whatever you're doing in lieu of having one.'

'Right,' said Brian. 'Well, let's just say for one second I believe you, which I don't – how come Mum is bothering Mrs Shanyaski and not me?'

Tina kept her eyes on the board, seemingly transfixed by the lines of thread connecting the various pictures. 'Not to go all Bruce Willis on you, but Mrs S has a strong sixth sense. It's like any other sense – sight, smell … Some people are a lot more sensitive than others.' She turned to Brian. 'Speaking of which, can you really not smell that?'

'What?'

She waved a finger around. 'All of this. This place reeks of old socks, stale food, body odour and despair. You're really not getting that?'

'No.'

'Do your eyes work?' she continued, scanning the room. 'I mean, seriously. If I photoshopped a picture of a seal living in this squalor, you'd have Madonna protesting on your doorstep by morning.' She pointed to the desk. 'Has that jar got wee in it?'

'Of course not. It's Snapple.'

'Drink it.'

'I'm not thirsty right now.'

'Look,' said Tina, softening her tone considerably, 'how long has it been since your mother passed away?'

'Two years.'

'And it was always just you and her?'

Brian nodded.

Tina looked around for somewhere to sit, then thought better of it. 'Do you think that maybe you're not dealing with it great?'

'I'm doing fine.'

'Brian, quick reality check – if I were to set fire to your house, I'd be done for burning rubbish in a suburban area. When was the last time you went outside?'

'I've been very busy.'

She shook her head. 'Oh, come on, Brian. You're a young man. You have your whole life ahead of you. You're only what – thirty-seven? Thirty-eight?'

'I'm twenty-four!'

'Wow. You really need to get some sunlight.'

Brian jabbed an angry finger at the pinboard. 'Look, this is important stuff. I don't expect you to understand.'

'Is it, though? What are you – QAnon?'

'No,' Brian scoffed. 'How dare you. Nothing like that. QAnon was just a false flag disinformation operation carried out by the deep state to hide what's really going on. It's all there if you …'

Brian stopped himself.

'Say it,' said Tina, her eyes narrowing. 'I dare you.'

'… look into it,' finished Brian.

Tina puffed out her cheeks. 'Look, dude. I get it. We all go through some stuff and it's easy to get sidetracked, but you need to get yourself back in the game. Do it for your mother if not for yourself.'

'Right,' snapped Brian. 'Can we just skip to the bit where you give me the pamphlet about joining your church or whatever this is.'

'You are one stubborn so-and-so, do you know that?'

Brian jabbed a finger at the pinboard again. 'This is vital. All right? You have no idea how the world really works. What kind of stuff is secretly going on behind the …'

Brian trailed off. A jar of your own urine floating across

the room in front of you will make you do that. He sat open-mouthed as it stopped and hovered in the air a couple of feet away.

'Oh, I'm sorry. Did I break your concentration? You were explaining how the world works?'

'But ...'

'And, by the by, it's not my area of expertise, but that's looking a little cloudy. You might want to get that checked out.'

'How are you doing that?' asked Brian in a near whisper.

'What? Oh, that? The floating jar of cloudy pee-pee? That's nothing. This, on the other hand ...'

Brian watched dumbfounded as the pile of pizza boxes in the corner rose into the air and proceeded to dance around each other, like low-rent UFOs. He was forced to duck as the jar of pee returned to its place on his desk.

'This is the kind of stuff you learn when you have way too much time on your hands.'

'It's incredible,' said Brian, unable to keep the awe from his voice.

'Here's the reality of how the world works, Brian,' Tina said, as the pizza boxes continued their display. 'Most politicians are just power-hungry narcissists who weren't hugged enough as children. Rich people just want to get richer because it's how they keep score. The vast majority of the bad crap that happens is not part of some big evil plan but just people not thinking about anything other than making a ton of easy dirty cash. Life is terrifyingly random, and if you're wondering how the planet is still here, well, you're not the only one.' The eight pizza boxes had now arranged themselves into a big smiley face that hung in the air in front of him. 'Any questions?'

'How?' asked Brian.

'Oh,' said Tina, then clicked her fingers theatrically. The pizza boxes piled themselves back up in the corner again. 'All of this? Well, Bri, there really is magic in the world. Wonders more than you can possibly imagine, and there actually is a battle going on between good and evil' – she pointed at the pinboard behind her – 'but none of it involves the Clintons, Beyoncé, 5G, the Rothschilds, Harry Hill or Phillip Schofield. What's more, I guarantee you'll find none of it on your websites, chat forums, or wherever else you're "doing the research".' She nodded towards the front door. 'The only place you'll find out about it is out there.'

'Are you a …'

'What?'

'A witch?'

'We don't use that word. It has a lot of negative connotations. "Wizard", on the other hand – see the difference? There's your basic sexism. So no, we prefer "practitioner". Also, people don't tend to burn practitioners at the stake.'

'And there's lots of these practitioners? What can you do exactly? Are ghosts really real, then? What does that make UFOs? Which—'

Tina raised her hand. 'You've obviously got a lot of questions and I'll answer all the ones I can …'

'Cool.'

'… in exactly two months' time. When I'll meet you in the Kanky's Rest pub at eight p.m.'

'What?'

'By which time, you'll have restarted your university course in …' She eyeballed him pointedly.

'Electronic engineering.'

'Yep, that. You'll be dressing in clean clothes every day, leaving the house, having showered. You'll have dropped a good ten pounds. This place will look fit for human habitation and, in the name of all that is good and holy, if you pee in another jar in your life, I will stop you from doing that permanently in a way you definitely won't like. Are we clear?'

'I have to do all that before you'll tell me anything?'

'No, you have to do all that to allow your poor mother to move on, safe in the knowledge that she didn't raise the next Unabomber. Then, I'll tell you a little of what I know.'

Brian ran his fingers through his hair. 'What am I supposed to do in the meantime?'

'Do you mean other than cleaning?'

'Yes.'

Tina looked around again. 'I mean, I think that will take up most of your time.'

'Please?'

Tina puffed out her cheeks and tapped her foot. 'Hmmmm.' She clapped her hands together. 'I got it.' She pulled a rolled-up newspaper from her jacket pocket and handed it to Brian. 'Here you go.'

He unfurled it. '*The Stranger Times*? This is that weird paper full of all the lunatic stories.'

'People who live in bad *X Files* re-runs shouldn't throw stones, but yes, that's the one.'

He held it up and pointed at the headline. '"A Dragon Ate My Pasty". You're telling me this is real?'

'Oh, no, most of it's nonsense. Most of it. Still, if you know what to look for ...'

'And how will I ...'

'You'll figure it out. You're a smart boy when you're not being an idiot. Besides, it has a cartoon strip that I always enjoy.' Tina rubbed her hands together. 'Right, my work here is done.' She turned towards the door.

'Wait!'

'Nope. I'm making a dramatic exit.'

'Please?'

The note of pleading in Brian's voice made Tina stop with her hand on the door handle.

'My mum,' said Brian. 'Can you give her a message? Tell her I love her and I'm sorry.'

Tina looked at Brian for a long moment. 'She knows. And for what it's worth, the reason she can't move on is because she clearly loves you, too.'

Brian looked at the carpet and nodded, tears pushing at his eyes.

Tina opened the door and waved. 'Later, gator. Two months, to be exact. Next time I see you, you'd better be wearing trousers.'

And with that, she slammed the door shut.

Alone again, Brian looked around the room. He coughed to clear his throat. 'OK, Mum, I guess I should get cleaning.' He scratched at his beard. 'Where do we keep the sponges?'

LOVE AND DEATH IN THE TIME OF PLANNED ENGINEERING WORKS

Karen put her hands on her knees and took a few deep breaths. That was the thing with grand romantic gestures – nobody told you how bloody inconvenient they could be. Sure, Holmes Chapel Viaduct looked lovely from a distance, but the damn thing was surprisingly difficult to get onto. Admittedly, it was designed for trains and not people, but still.

She'd had to get a taxi because she couldn't figure out the buses, and the trains weren't running for some stupid reason. Then, she'd ripped her jeans climbing over a fence. She'd ripped herself too. It was only a small cut, but the material kept rubbing against it in an irritating way. She could feel the trickle of sticky blood on her leg. And these jeans were new. True, it didn't matter in the grand scheme of things, but still. She hadn't thought to bring a torch either, and was forced to rely on the one on her phone, which wasn't great to begin with and was running down the battery fast.

She was considering giving up on the whole thing, which was ironic. The only thing keeping her going was the thought that once she got there, she wouldn't have to come back again.

She needed to focus and just keep following the train tracks. If nothing else, it would take her mind off the noises.

Karen was a city girl – one who knew almost nothing about the countryside. As far as she was concerned it just existed. Bits of it looked quite nice, a lot of it seemed to smell bad, and for some inexplicable reason, a lot of the people who lived there voted for Brexit. This gap in her knowledge was one of the things – one of the many things, apparently – that had annoyed Becca. She was always banging on about how Karen needed to be more at one with nature, as if she were David Attenborough just because her parents had a holiday home up in the Lake District.

Karen hugged her denim jacket around herself more tightly. She hadn't really dressed for the weather. Technically, it was the Sunday of the August bank holiday weekend. 'Technically', because the words 'August bank holiday weekend' conjure up an image of summer and warmth, but this was supposedly the coldest one on record. It felt more like a November day, and not a good one at that.

She wasn't a total idiot. Karen knew what the country looked and smelled like, but the noises did come as a particularly unpleasant surprise. There seemed to be constant rustling noises at either side of the tracks. Things kept moving about around her. Scurrying. Scrabbling. Hooting. Cooing. There was far too much of all of it. Frankly, nature needed to cut that shit out. It was past 11 p.m. Shouldn't everything have gone to sleep by now?

In the meantime, she tried studiously to ignore it. It'd just be squirrels or rats or badgers or something, probably – nothing that could hurt her. She was out here alone in the dark, but it was Cheshire, for God's sake – the only thing likely to kill you was a speeding footballer in a ridiculous sports car. Pretty much the worst thing that could happen was what she was here to do.

Karen yelped at a particularly loud rustling noise to her right that was way too big to be a badger – not unless six of the buggers had teamed up to put the shits up her. If they had, congratulations – it had totally worked.

Her body started running before her brain had a chance to lodge a vote. What's more, once she started, she found she couldn't stop. Panic surged through every fibre of her being. It was like a feedback loop. She ran because she was afraid, and then the fact she was running merely confirmed that there was definitely something to be afraid of.

She didn't dare to look around. She was too busy looking down at the ground illuminated by the wan light from her phone; too busy concentrating on trying not to trip over the tracks. She might know bugger all about the countryside, but she'd seen more than enough horror films, thank you very much. It was the foolish girl on her own who tripped and fell that got eaten – or worse – by whatever was chasing her. She was not going to be that girl.

Stuff like that in horror movies drove her up the wall. How women existed primarily as victims or, occasionally – in a sneaky bit of expectation subverting counterprogramming – plucky heroines. Only last week she had strongly made the point to Becca on WhatsApp that there were nowhere near enough female monsters in horror movies. Like women couldn't be villains. Becca, the bitch, had rather proved Karen's point on that front. Karen could think of many words to describe her, and 'villain' was at the tamer end of the scale.

Karen had been so focused on not tripping that she

hadn't noticed the trees falling away from either side of the track – not until she felt the wind against her face. She was properly on the bridge now. Clouds were skittering across the sky in sporadic clusters, but at that moment, the moon had an unencumbered view of the Cheshire countryside. It did look very pretty. Karen slowed to a half-hearted jog, then turned around abruptly to confront the nothing that was chasing her.

Her whole body sagged as she allowed herself to relax. Her heart was beating like an untalented but enthusiastic child with a new drum kit. She stood there, heaving in erratic breaths while pulling at her T-shirt under her denim jacket, where the sweat was causing it to cling to her. Once she'd determined that she wasn't going to die from the most ironic heart attack imaginable, Karen turned back around and screamed.

A figure was standing down the track from her. She couldn't make out much in the way of details, because as soon as she'd turned around, Karen had been caught in the beam of a powerful torch. The only details she could make out were the creature's distinctive horns.

Karen screamed again.

The figure screamed back. It also sounded female.

Karen started to back away. 'Stay away from me.'

'I'm not coming anywhere near you!' The voice was definitely female.

'What are you doing up here at this time of night?'

'I could ask you the same thing.'

'That's none of your business.'

'Likewise.'

'You scared the living shit out of me!'

'Right back at you, sister.'

'Will you stop shining that bloody torch in my face?'

'Oh, right,' said the voice, lowering the beam to the ground. 'Sorry.'

Now that she wasn't being blinded, Karen could get a better look at her non-attacker. She was probably in her early twenties, same as her. She was a little shorter, and was wearing a warm-looking fleece under a waterproof jacket. It appeared she had done a considerably better job in the planning-ahead stakes than Karen.

Karen relaxed a bit. Serial killers seemed unlikely to wear sensible fleeces. She had no data to back up that reasoning, but still, it felt like it made sense.

'What are you wearing on your head?'

'What?' said the woman.

'On your head,' said Karen, pointing. 'Why've you got a horned helmet on your head?'

She couldn't see the girl's face clearly, but she sounded embarrassed. 'It's a family heirloom. Like, a traditional thing.'

Karen's nickname in school had been 'Questions'. She didn't know why, but she always had to ask further questions. She was very aware it annoyed people – it'd annoyed her parents, her teachers, her classmates, and she was pretty sure it had annoyed Becca. She couldn't stop herself, though. Some people just wanted to understand the world, whether the world liked it or not.

Karen took a step forward to get a better look at the headgear. She also got a better look at the girl. Ginger hair poked out from what was really more of a hat now she could see it a bit closer. It sat over a roundish face that featured wide inquisitive eyes and dimpled rosy cheeks. The girl looked more nervous than Karen did.

'Are you, like, Vikings or something?'

'No,' said the voice. 'And Vikings didn't actually have horns on their helmets. That was an affectation invented by Hollywood.'

Damn it, Karen had known that. She hated when she gave people the opportunity to point out stuff to her that she already knew. 'So, what are you, if you're not a Viking?'

'Is this a test?' asked the girl.

'What? Why would it be a test?'

'Did Dad send you? Or Barry? That'd be just like Barry. Such a prick!'

'What are you talking about? I was just walking here, minding my own business, when you popped out of nowhere and frightened me half to death.'

'I didn't pop out of anywhere. I was sitting just there.' The girl pointed the torch at a deckchair at the side of the track, with a blanket, a flask and a rucksack beside it. 'And you came running up the track like a maniac, flailing your arms.'

'I was not flailing my arms.'

'There was definitely flailing going on.'

'There couldn't have been that much – I was holding my phone out to see the ... Ah crap!' Karen started to slap her various pockets. 'Yep – I must've dropped my bloody phone when you leaped out at me.'

'Again, there was no leaping out. I just calmly stood up and waited for you to notice me.'

'All right. Whatever. Just help me look. Please.'

With a tut, the girl trained her torch along the ground where Karen was standing. They searched in silence for almost five minutes before they found the phone, despite it being only a couple of feet from Karen's original position. That was because it had landed right beside the iron track, which was also why the screen was smashed into a spiderweb.

'That's great. Just great,' said Karen. 'Look at that. Ruined.'

'Our Darren can fix that. He runs a repair shop in town. I'm always dropping mine.'

'Right,' said Karen, shoving it into her jacket pocket. 'Thanks. Doesn't matter.' She indicated up the track. 'Well, it was really weird to meet you, but if you don't mind, I'll be on my way.'

The girl shook her head. 'No can do.'

'Excuse me?'

'This is my bridge and you can't cross it without my say so.'

'Are you taking the piss?'

'No,' said the girl, drawing herself up to her full height and puffing herself out. 'I most certainly am not.' She pointed at her helmet-type hat affair with the horns. 'I'm a troll.'

Karen nodded. 'Right. So you are taking the piss, then?'

'No,' said the girl, sounding really annoyed now. 'I am not.'

'You're a troll. Do you, like, say horrible things about people on the internet?'

'See. That is a prime example of the kind of bullshit we have to put up with. We trolls were a thing long before the internet was a twinkle in Sir Timothy John Berners-Lee's eye, but our name gets co-opted. Have you any idea what it's like to constantly get associated with shitty behaviour that is nothing to do with you?'

'Actually, I do. It's 2020 and my name is Karen. Apparently, everyone with that name is now a stupid racist.'

The girl paused. She seemed slightly mollified by this. 'OK. Fair point. Well, then you know.'

'I do.'

'For the record, I always thought that particular meme was unhelpful bullshit.'

'Exactly. When did we start attributing stuff to names? Names are random.'

'You're not wrong,' agreed the girl. 'That kind of thinking makes astrology look like a science.'

'Yeah. I mean, I've been going on anti-racism demos for years. I protested against those EDL cockwombles marching – even when it happened in the middle of my exams.'

'Well done, Karen,' said the girl, with apparent absolute sincerity. 'My name is Maisy by the way.'

'Hi.'

'Hi.'

This exchange was followed by a long pause, during which both girls looked around awkwardly before Karen's need to ask questions trumped the silence.

'Sorry, can I … You're a troll?'

Maisy looked embarrassed, and fidgeted self-consciously with one of the horns on her hat. 'Yeah. Yeah, I am.'

'Is this, like, a "bet" thing?'

'No. If you must know, I come from a very long line of trolls.'

Karen opened her mouth to ask a follow-up question, but nothing came.

'Trolls,' continued Maisy, 'are actually indigenous to this island. We were here long before mankind was.'

'You're not human?'

'Well, don't say it like that. What you know as so-called "humans" are actually a lot of similar but different species that can pass for human, but aren't. Or at least, aren't fully.

We get referred to by the catch-all term 'the Folk'. My mum is full human but Dad is seventy-five per cent troll.'

'Right,' said Karen, sounding sceptical.

'If you did your DNA – like, the real DNA and not the made-up one – there's a good chance you'd have some Folk blood in you too.'

'My granny is from Wales,' said Karen, as if that was meant to mean something.

She licked her lips. She was aware that sensitivity wasn't her greatest strength. At least, not conversationally. It wasn't that she wasn't sensitive or didn't care, it was just that she wasn't great at phrasing things in a gentle manner.

She cleared her throat. 'Are you ... Have you, maybe, recently left – or escaped – from somewhere?' Karen winced. Not even close to sensitive.

'Oh yeah. Bloody typical. Faced with another culture you don't understand, you naturally assume the other person is a nutter. How unsurprising!'

'No. God, no. It is just that ... I mean, I'm sure you believe what you're saying, but ...'

Maisy nodded her head so furiously that the hat almost fell off. 'Here we go. Here we go. Fine. You want proof?'

Karen said nothing, already deeply regretting challenging the poor delusional girl.

'Brace yourself. Shit is about to get weird.'

Maisy angled her torch so it illuminated her face and then shut her eyes tight, as if concentrating.

Karen stared at the girl's pained expression. Nothing was happening.

'Give it a minute,' said Maisy. 'Sometimes it takes a minute.'

Karen looked behind her. Maybe this was a good moment

to head back the way she had come. Maisy didn't seem dangerous, but Karen had seen a documentary about Ted Bundy, and he'd got away with killing a load of people by not looking like a guy who'd kill a load of people. If history proved anything, it was that you shouldn't judge people by their appearance. As false indicators went, it was right up there with what they say or what they put on their dating profile.

Karen was about to turn to go when …

It must be a trick of the light.

She gasped.

Maisy's bottom teeth appeared to be growing.

'What the hell!'

Maisy opened her eyes and spoke. 'Tusks,' she said, unnecessarily pointing at her newly acquired facial feature. 'See? Troll tusks. We can make 'em come out and disappear at will. Mostly, we keep 'em hidden – for obvious reasons.'

'But …'

'Yeah,' replied Maisy triumphantly. 'That blew your tiny little m— Ouch!' Her expression turned decidedly more sheepish, or at least, whatever a sheep would look like if it had massive tusks on its face. 'Nipped myshelf. These things are a bit awkward to talksh around. Hang on.'

Maisy closed her eyes again and Karen watched, dumbstruck, as the tusks shrank and then disappeared.

'Does it hurt?'

'Like a bastard. Still, proved my point.'

Karen nodded. She really had. 'OK. So, this is your bridge?'

'Well, Metaphorically speaking.'

'How can you metaphorically own a bridge?'

'As it happens,' said Maisy, 'my uncle John is an engineer

with the rail company. He's a few miles up the track right now, leading the team doing the upgrade work that's shut down the line for the weekend. He's technically in charge of it, and he gave me the bridge for the night.'

'Your uncle can't give you a bridge.'

'He can,' insisted Maisy. 'Metaphorically. I'm not claiming to own the actual viaduct, but I'm standing my post on it for the night, as is tradition.'

'What kind of a tradition is that?'

'A bloody stupid one. Male trolls prove they've become men by standing a post overnight at one of the family's bridges.'

'But you're not a male?'

Maisy made no effort to keep the sarcasm from her voice. 'Gee, thanks for noticing. Being the youngest and only girl with four older brothers, I was unaware of that fact.'

'Sorry.'

'Yeah, well,' said Maisy, appeased. 'Anyhow, I said it was sexist bullshit and I demanded to stand my post – same as all the boys had done. Keith had to do his twice, seeing as he got caught drinking cider the first time. Idiot.'

'So, you demanded to be put out here all night?'

'I'm proving a point!' said Maisy, crossing her arms.

'Fair play. Smashing the patriarchy.'

'Yes. It might not be throwing yourself in front of a racehorse or refusing to sit at the back of the bus, but the only way to destroy prejudice is by confronting it head on.'

'Right,' said Karen, still not entirely sure what to make of all this. 'Can I ask – aren't trolls supposed to live under bridges?'

'See, there you go again. More lazy stereotyping and misinformation.'

'Sorry.'

'It isn't your fault. I blame fairy tales. They were the tabloids of their day. Some Scandinavian git has a falling out with the local troll, and suddenly we're attempting to eat talking goats, and smashing babies into pâté.'

'So, do you live under bridges?'

'No, and we never did. I mean, logically, if you're in charge of a bridge and it's raining, where are you going to stand?'

Karen nodded, understanding the expected answer. 'Under the bridge.'

'Under the bridge,' agreed Maisy. 'I mean, all right, there might be the occasional young troll, out on his own, on his first bridge, who maybe is camping out ...' She slapped her hand to her forehead, nearly toppling the horny hat. 'Sorry, I left out the most important bit – the bit all of the fairy tales leave out too. The reason trolls are associated with bridges? We built the bloody things!'

'Oh.'

'Yeah, see? We were making a living while providing vital infrastructure investment at a time before government existed. So, you paid the troll a toll – which is where the word comes from, yes – but it was just a simple fee for using the fruits of their hard work. If you didn't want to, you could just cross the river, or whatever, in the same way you used to. Trolls are engineers. Always have been, always will be. Isambard Kingdom Brunel – he was a troll. Probably. Well, I'm not one hundred per cent certain on that, but I've heard lots of people say so.'

'OK. Well, thank you. I feel like I've learned a lot.'

'Well, good,' said Maisy. 'Glad to hear it.'

'Now, if you'll excuse me, I'll be on my way.'

Karen took a step forward and Maisy took a sideways step into her path, one hand held out in the classic bouncer pose.

'Whoa, whoa, whoa – what have we just been talking about? For the night, this bridge is mine.'

'So, I have to ask permission?'

'No. You've got to pay the toll.'

'Fine, how much is it?'

'Five pounds.'

'Five pounds?' repeated Karen, incredulous. 'For a bridge that isn't really yours?'

'Still, it's a cracking bridge. This viaduct is the longest on the line at 1,794 feet, with a whopping twenty-three arches each of sixty-three-feet span – a considerable feat of engineering for something constructed 180 years ago. This bridge is an absolute belter. All right, before you say it – yes, Stockport Viaduct is higher, but it's also shorter.' Maisy leaned in conspiratorially. 'I could've stood my post on that one, but the view here is way nicer.'

'Whatever' said Karen, taking out her wallet. 'I'll ...' She looked inside it. 'I don't have any notes. Do you take card?'

'I'm afraid we don't. Strictly a cash-only business. Troll Code. The terms are stated on the sign that is clearly displayed over there.' Maisy pointed up the line into the darkness.

'Where?'

'There's a sign up there. You ran right by it when you were screaming and waving your arms about.'

'How was I supposed to see it in the dark?'

'The Troll Code predates electricity. Even in olden times, people brought torches. In fact, they occasionally used to gather in mobs and wield them. They'd come after trolls who were just trying to make a living from their own entrepreneurial spirit and engineering endeavour.'

'I'm beginning to see their point.'

'What was that?' said Maisy accusatorially.

'A joke.'

'Not a good one.'

'You can't charge me to use a bridge you don't own,' said Karen, stomping her foot.

'I can. Weren't you listening? Uncle John works for the company that owns it and he's put me in charge of it. Under the Troll Code, that means it's mine. If you get by without paying, I fail my test. I'll be tuskless.'

'Big deal. Who cares?'

Maisy gasped, truly scandalized. 'I care. A lot. I would bring shame upon my tribe.'

'All right. Sorry.'

'If it makes you feel any better, any money raised will go to the Dogs 4 Rescue shelter.'

'I've heard of them. Aren't they the place that offers kennel-free living?'

'Yes.'

'I love them! I follow them on Facebook. They take in the dogs nobody else wants and then you see them in the videos, running about happily with all the other dogs.'

'Have you seen the videos with the dog with only two legs?'

'Stop it. I love him. I cry every time.'

'They do great work. I did a 10K for them last year.'

'Nice one,' said Karen. She patted her pockets. 'Unfortunately, I've still not got any money.' A thought struck her. She took her phone out of her pocket. 'I could transfer a fiver to them directly, though?'

Maisy considered this for a moment, then her face lit up. 'That works!'

'Great.' Karen tried to open her phone. The fingerprint recognition didn't work.

'Try the code,' suggested Maisy.

'OK, I ...' Karen touched the screen a few times and then shook the device in frustration. 'Damn it. This thing is completely shot.'

Maisy tutted. 'That is unfortunate.'

'Well,' said Karen hopefully, 'the intention was there.'

Maisy shook her head. 'Sorry. That butters no bread.'

'All right. How about you lend me a fiver?'

'No can do. Know why?'

'Let me guess. Troll Code?'

Maisy nodded. 'Afraid so. No credit. It's right there on the sign.'

'This is ridiculous. Actually, I don't need to pay the toll.'

'Yes, you do.'

'No, I don't,' said Karen, stomping her foot again, 'because I'm not crossing the bridge. I'm going to jump off it.'

Even in Karen's extensive experience of being able to kill conversations stone dead, that was a doozy.

Maisy looked at her for a long moment and then spoke in a soft voice. 'Don't joke about that.'

'I'm not,' said Karen, trying to sound defiant. 'It's my choice and none of your damn business.'

'Fair enough,' said Maisy quietly.

'Right. Good. Well, if you'll excuse me, then.'

She brushed past Maisy and started to walk up the track. After a few seconds, the beam of Maisy's torch followed behind her as Maisy ran to catch up, having gone back to grab her rucksack. She eventually stopped in front of Karen, her arms extended.

'Whoa there, missus. Hang on a minute. That – that thing you're going to do. It still counts as using the bridge. Five pounds!'

'Bullshit.'

'Rules are rules,' said Maisy as she fumbled with the rucksack before pulling out an alarmingly large stick. 'I don't want to use the cudgel, but I will.'

Karen couldn't believe what she was hearing. 'Have I got this right? I've got to give you five pounds I don't have to cross a bridge you don't really own, or else you're going to assault me?'

Maisy thought about it and then nodded. 'Pretty much, yeah. Well, either that, or we go old school.'

'Old school?'

'All right,' said Maisy, lowering the cudgel. 'Before this bridge is crossed by thee, you must answer for me these questions three.'

'You're kidding?'

'Look, do you want to cross or not?'

'Fine. Get on with it.'

'OK. Right then, question one – are you willing and able to pay the toll as clearly indicated on the sign over yonder?' Maisy nodded pointedly. 'Yeah, there's something they left out of the fairy tales. In reality, the first question was, would you just like to pay up like a responsible citizen. Yet more anti-troll—'

Karen waved her hand. 'Let's not go through all that again. No, I can't pay the stupid toll.'

'Right. Question two ...' Maisy stood there, biting her lip.

'Well?'

She looked embarrassed. 'I, erm, I'm supposed to have a riddle ready.'

'And don't you?'

'All right, smart-arse. It's a rail bridge on a closed line. How many customers do you think I was expecting tonight?'

'That's as maybe, but it's not my fault you're underprepared, now, is it?'

Maisy took off her helmet and started to pace, twirling it in her hands. 'Just give me a minute, OK?'

'I'm kind of in a hurry here.'

'Really? Do you want to explain how exactly? It's not like they turn the gravity off at midnight.'

Karen huffed. 'All right, fine. But I'm not waiting all night.'

'OK. Here we go. What has four legs in the morning—'

'A man!'

'Shit. No. I mean, no, it wasn't.'

'It was. The answer is a man. Question three.'

'No way,' said Maisy. 'I hadn't finished. Doesn't count.'

'Rubbish.'

'According to the Troll Code, I have to finish the question before you answer.'

'OK. Prove it.'

'All right, I will.' Maisy picked up her rucksack and rummaged inside it again. 'As it so happens, I have a copy of the Troll Code with me for just such an eventuality.' After some extensive digging around, she produced a small book, which she held up triumphantly. 'Got it.'

Karen held out her hand and Maisy gave the Code to her. 'Light?'

'No problem.' Maisy moved across and shone the light at her, being careful to keep far enough away to abide by social distancing guidelines.

Karen opened the book and squinted at it for a moment before looking up. 'What the hell is this? It's all gobbledeegook.'

'How dare you! That is Trollish. It's not my fault you can't read it.'

'Oh for …' For one moment, Karen considered tossing the book off the bridge and into the darkness, but she resisted the urge. Even she realized that it was unlikely to deescalate the situation. Instead, she handed it back.

'OK, then. Finish question two.'

'Thank you,' said Maisy, before puffing out her cheeks and closing her eyes.

'Will this take long?'

'All right, I've got one.' She lowered her voice. 'Erm … Why do you want to kill yourself?'

Karen looked away. 'That's not really any of your business.'

'Well. Normally I'd agree with you but, y'know, it kind of is. I mean, I own this bridge for the night. If you jump off it, questions will be asked.'

'Just tell them I paid the fiver and whatever happens happens.'

Maisy held up the book.

'Really? That's against the Code?'

'It violates it in several different ways, actually. There's the rule about lying. The rule about assuring bridge safety. Not to mention the rule about once you start the three questions, you can't stop.'

'It's personal.'

'I appreciate that. If it helps, you're the first non-family member who knows I'm a troll. Nobody but my closest family has seen my tusks except you.'

'Fine,' said Karen, turning back defiantly. 'If you must know, it is our bridge.'

Maisy looked confused. 'We've been through that. Technically—'

'I don't mean it like that. Me and my girlfriend, Becca. It's our bridge. Our first date – like, a proper date – was a picnic over there.' She jabbed a finger into the darkness. 'Actually, it might have been over there. The point is, we fell in love looking at this bridge.'

'Right.'

'Yes. I mean, I say we fell in love. I did. Her? God knows. I sure as shit don't. Not any more. I mean, we were about to move in together. Her idea. But then Covid-bloody-19 happened and Becca had to stay at home with her mum, who's vulnerable. So, y'know, we couldn't see each other. Restrictions being what they were, and then her mum with her heart problems, she said it was too risky to go out, even when the restrictions were eased. So we talked on the phone, we WhatsApped. We ... other things.'

'Right.'

'And then,' said Karen, wiping tears from her eyes, 'I find out that for the last two months, she's not been living with her mum. She met some skank on a dating app and they moved in together.'

'Oh.'

'It's been going on since April,' said Karen, tears rolling down her cheeks now. 'Loads of people knew, apparently. Everyone except me. Eventually, a friend of mine sent me a link to an Instagram post on the skank's account. The two of them out in a bar – a fucking bar – eating the faces off each other.'

Maisy said nothing, just winced.

'I confronted her and she actually said . . . Get this, she said she was seeing how things went with the skank. That maybe it was just a "lockdown thing" – her words – and that perhaps she might come back to me once it's over.'

'Fuck. That is pure psycho!'

'That's exactly what I said. What kind of a heartless bitch uses someone they've been in a two-year relationship with as a bloody fallback plan? Like that's a thing. Honestly, talking to her – you could tell. She ripped my heart out and she didn't really care. Like, I was just there for her convenience and que sera. She actually said that – que sera. Can you believe that?'

Maisy nodded. 'That is horrible.'

Karen wiped her face with the sleeve of her jacket. 'So, now I'm going to make sure she feels something. She'll never be able to look at another bridge in her entire stupid life without remembering what she did to me.'

'Right.'

'So, there you have it.'

'Yes. It just ...'

'What?'

'I mean, it does feel like in all this, you're kind of inadvertently putting a lot of unfair blame on bridges.'

Karen paused for a moment and then burst out laughing. 'You're an idiot.'

Maisy smiled back. 'Again, that feels very trollist.'

'To be clear, I mean you specifically.'

'Oh. OK, then. Well, that's a relief.'

'Did I answer your question satisfactorily?'

'I guess.'

Karen nodded. 'OK, then. On to number three.'

'Yeah. Before that, fun fact for you – you know the Sphinx?'

'Not personally.'

'Ha ha. Very funny. But you know what it is?'

'Yes. I've actually seen it, in person.'

'Ohhh! Get you.'

'My auntie Joan wanted to see Egypt before she died and asked me to go with her.'

'That sounds amazing.'

'Yeah,' said Karen. 'Not so much. Poor Joan had food poisoning for most of the trip.'

'Oh no.'

'Oh yeah. She threw up on this snake statue thing. Luckily, the guide managed to clean it off before anyone saw, otherwise it would've been a serious international incident.'

'Crikey. Well, anyway. The Sphinx. Fun fact: it's actually called that because that's the name the Romans gave it when they invaded.'

'Really?'

'Oh yes. They probably mentioned it on your tour, but you would've been understandably distracted.'

Karen nodded. 'Poor auntie Joan. The woman loves seafood, but it does not love her.'

'Here's the bit you probably don't know. In Greek mythology, the Sphinx would give the people of Thebes a riddle and if they didn't get it, it'd kill them. Someone did eventually get it, and then the Sphinx, overcome with shame, killed itself. And that person was – drumroll, please – Oedipus!'

'Ohhh! That clever motherfucker!'

At this, Maisy burst out laughing. So much so that her horned hat fell off and tumbled to the ground. 'Shit, if I damage that, Dad'll kill me.' She snatched it up and placed it carefully back on her head. '"Clever motherfucker" – that is good. Did you really just come up with that on the spot?'

'No. I've been wandering the land, hoping that somebody somewhere would finally tell me that random bit of Greek mythology so I could unleash that zinger.'

'Totally worth it.'

'Thank you,' said Karen, taking a bow. Then the smile dropped from her face. 'So, question three?'

Maisy looked suddenly nervous. 'Yeah.'

'C'mon. No more stalling.'

'All right.' Maisy took a deep breath. 'Would you like to go for a drink with me?'

'What?' asked Karen, narrowing her eyes.

'You heard.'

Karen folded her arms. 'Your earlier material was a lot funnier.'

'Oh, God, no!' said Maisy, looking horrified. 'I wasn't trying to …'

'Really? This isn't a joke or some pity thing?'

'No.'

'To be clear, you're asking me …'

'Yes.'

'… on a date?'

'Yes.'

'Because you're …'

It was hard to tell in the light from the torch but Maisy looked embarrassed. 'I think I am.'

'You think?'

'I am,' said Maisy. 'No, I am. I've … just not had a chance. I've got four older brothers and, y'know. Then I went to work for Dad's company. Just – the situation never sort of arose.'

'Right.'

'But you seem nice.'

'Thanks.'

'And think of it this way. Given how we met, I can't really screw this up.'

Karen nodded. 'That's true. You are buying low here.'

'What have you got to lose? I mean, you could always come back tomorrow and do ... y'know. At least that way it isn't happening on my watch.'

'So, to recap: you think that rather than killing myself to get revenge on the monumental psycho love of my life who broke my heart into a thousand pieces, I should go on a date with you?'

'Why not?' said Maisy. 'I mean, weirder stuff happens all the time.'

'Name one instance.'

'OK. You came here to kill yourself and met a troll. That's pretty bloody weird.'

Karen nodded. 'I begrudgingly concede the point.'

'Right.' Maisy took off her hat and started fiddling with the horns again. 'So, will you?'

'I don't even know you.'

'Well, I'm here all night and I've got a big flask of tea. Happy to answer any questions.'

Karen turned and looked out into the night. Because even meteorology has a sense of the moment every now and then, the clouds parted once more and soft moonlight showed her the world. Or, at least, the rolling fields of Cheshire.

Karen turned back to Maisy. 'Question: how do fields roll?'

'What?'

'Fields. They're always described as rolling. What the hell does that mean? And what does a non-rolling field look like?' Karen started to walk back in the direction of the promised cup of warm tea.

'I thought it was hills that roll?'

'Hills. Fields. I think they all roll.'

Maisy fell into step beside her. 'It's a fair point. Also, how can the words regardless and irregardless mean the same thing?'

'I don't know.'

'It baffles me that English became the dominant language. It's full of stuff like that. Trollish only has three adjectives.'

'Wow.'

'It is a very direct language,' said Maisy, slapping her torch into her palm for emphasis. 'It says exactly what it means.'

Karen nodded. 'It would be a much better world if all CVs, dating profiles and political speeches were written in Trollish.'

'That's exactly what I said last week!'

'And I'm happy to join that march. It might be tricky to write signs that people understand, though.'

'Yeah, there's that, and the fact we have to keep our existence secret.'

'Right,' said Karen. 'Well, if it helps, I won't tell anyone. To be honest, I fully expect not to believe this later on when I tell it to myself.'

'Good. Before we go any further, I should mention – full disclosure, I collect model trains.'

'Oh dear.'

'Yep. Do you want to go back to your Plan A?'

'Let me think about it.'

'OK.'

They walked on in amicable silence for a bit before Karen spoke again. 'On the trains thing …'

'It's mainly for the bridges.'

'That makes sense.'

Karen looked at the deckchair with the large flask sitting beside it, which they'd now reached.

'How are we handling the one-chair situation?'

'Did you not bring one?'

'My original plan for the evening didn't involve much sitting.'

'All right, we can rotate.'

'Fair.'

'Custard Cream?'

Karen smiled. 'You had Custard Creams all this time, and you only thought to mention it now?'

Maisy smiled back. 'I was saving them in case things got tense.'

THE OTHER SIDE

Josh Glynn scanned through his code for the umpteenth time. He'd never been one of those obsessive-compulsives who littered his line of work. It was why he was so good at what he did. To him, code was a tool, not a work of art. This approach was also how he'd managed to minimise those 'personalised touches' that made it possible for the authorities to trace programs back to their source. Not that they always did, of course – far from it – but it was a newbie error not to understand the importance of minimising risk. It was why Josh owned homes on three continents while so many of his contemporaries were locked up in prison, on funny farms, or, arguably worse still, had been forced to work for the government. Josh didn't differentiate between governments. They were all the same to him.

Having said all that, he was checking and rechecking his work because the woman made him nervous. He could hear her heels on the concrete behind him, heading in his direction. Her voice was soft as she spoke to one of her cronies.

The first time he'd met her, she'd been sitting at the end of his bed in the early hours of the morning. A bed in his mansion in Toorak, which was protected by a state-of-the-art alarm system, and guarded by a dozen heavily armed men and a pack of German Shepherds he'd bought from a trainer in Darwin and flown all the way to Melbourne. The OTT security was the consequence of a misunderstanding Josh had had with some Russians. You'd think that people who were trying to rob him would take a more sanguine attitude to him robbing them first. Josh had it on good authority that they had not. His old friend Zeke had told him. Actually, he'd screamed the news down the phone. Those words had quite probably been his last on that or any other subject. Josh was now considering moving somewhere more 'flexible' than Australia. Here, the guards tended to ask questions first, and Josh was in a shooting war.

On that fateful night, Josh had been woken by the sound of the woman's giggle. There she'd sat, not even looking at him, wearing that wide grin as she read something on her phone calmly. She was barely five foot in height and unarmed. Managing to access his inner sanctum was impressive, doing so in a Louis Vuitton business suit and heels was downright inexplicable. She didn't even look up as she spoke with an English accent. 'Hello, Josh. Nice to meet you, finally.'

He'd tried to scream and then found that he could not. It had been one of the most unpleasant sensations he'd ever experienced. His lips wouldn't part. He clawed at them with his hands. There seemed to be no physical reason why they wouldn't open, they just couldn't. Janine and Seb had remained asleep beside him in the bed. His attempt to get out of it was thwarted by the fact that he wasn't able to move his legs either. He'd been reduced to thrashing about and shaking his companions, who simply smiled in their sleep and turned over. It had been the stuff of nightmares, only he'd been very much awake.

Then, once he was thoroughly freaked out, the woman had casually tossed a folder on to the bed in front of him. In the absence of any other options, he'd opened it. It was full of everything he did not want the world to know. Some of the things were impossible for anyone but him to know. A couple of them, even he'd tried very hard to forget.

'Now, Josh,' she'd said mildly, as she finally raised her eyes from her phone and looked directly at him. 'We aren't going to offer you money because, well, you've already got money. Let's be honest, money is totes boring, isn't it? It is also terrible to use as leverage because absolutely loads of people have it. The people I represent are looking for the kind of can-do effort that money just can't buy. What we are going to offer you is the chance to make' – she nodded towards the file – 'all of that go away. Nobody will know. In fact ...' Her nose wrinkled slightly – was that disgust? '... if you'd like to make your memories of those last couple of pictures go away, we can do that too. We're not the government, Australian or otherwise. We're not the Russians. What we are is the people you really do not want to mess with.' Then she giggled again. Such a high-pitched grating sound. 'I'm Dr Carter, by the way. Charmed to make your acquaintance.'

She placed a note at the foot of the bed then calmly walked out on to the balcony. After a minute, Josh found he'd regained control of his mouth, legs, everything. Janine had also woken up by this point and asked him what was wrong, but he'd told her to go back to sleep. Then he'd stepped out on to the balcony, but there was nobody there. The only evidence the whole thing hadn't been a dream was the folder and the note he held in his hand. He unfolded the piece of paper. On it was written the number of a flight from Melbourne to Manchester via Abu Dhabi, leaving the following afternoon, accompanied by the words 'Be on it or ...' They hadn't even bothered to buy him a ticket. Seeing as sleep was an impossibility, he had burned the file right there on the balcony with the one-of-a-kind lighter signed by Roger Moore that he'd bought at auction. Then he'd gone and packed.

He hadn't been able to sleep on the flight either, which meant that when he finally reached his destination a day later, he was as cranky as all hell and feeling considerably more defiant. He'd used the long flights to convince himself that he'd simply been drugged and that somehow all of this was smoke and mirrors. The not-being-able-to-move stuff – that had just been pharmaceuticals. Janine and Seb must've been bought off. Bloody ingrates.

As for the stuff in the file? They couldn't know that – it was impossible. Some clever cocktail of hallucinogens had messed with his brain and mined his subconscious for his deepest, darkest fears. Some Poms were trying to play him for an idiot and he wasn't going to stand for it.

At arrivals, a lanky guy with a sign was waiting for him, wearing the full Ask Jeeves butler get-up. Josh slid into the car they'd sent for him and demanded to speak to the person in charge or he'd be on the next flight home. He was ninety per cent certain that this was all nonsense, he just needed confirmation.

. . .

About half an hour later, the car pulled into a zoo of all places. Chester Zoo. It was still early and the staff had not yet arrived, so it was empty, except for him and Jeeves. Josh knew what this was – do as I say or we'll feed you to the lions. Classic hard-man tactics.

Admittedly, now Josh was here, he didn't have much to counter with. In the car, the thought had occurred to him that maybe he should pretend to play along then contact some people to come and get him. He knew people. To be precise, he knew people who knew people who were happy to kill people, for people. Presumably, some of those individuals could also mount a rescue mission while doing that. The body count wasn't an issue. Josh would be happy to see Jeeves get iced just for the way he said 'sir'.

He was surprised when Jeeves started walking in the opposite direction to the sign for the lion enclosure. Instead, Josh was led to a platform outside the tree-kangaroo enclosure, where a table for two was laid, complete with a tea tray. He was slightly unnerved to see the woman who'd said her name was Dr Carter sitting there, smiling at him.

'Josh,' she said. 'What a delight it is to see you again.' She gave that stomach-turning giggle. Annoying in its own right, it also made their first meeting feel somehow more real. She gave him a cheeky wink. 'How was your flight?'

'Long,' he said, sounding a lot less defiant than he'd felt an hour ago. He geed himself up. 'Look, I don't know what this is, but I want no part of it. I'm a businessman and this is not how I do business.'

'I see,' said Dr Carter. She indicated the chair opposite her. 'Please take a seat. Tea?'

'No, I don't want bloody tea,' he said, sitting down. 'I want to go home.'

Dr Carter nodded. 'I think I understand the issue here. You feel as if you've been tricked. Conned, if you will, and brought here against your will?'

'Exactly.'

She waved a hand in the direction of the enclosure. In it, a few examples of a type of 'roo Josh had not seen before were munching away on some branches. 'I should apologise. I thought it would be fun for us to meet in front of some of your countrymen, if you like, but I just noticed the sign over there says that these tree kangaroos are actually native to Papua New Guinea. How remiss of me.'

Josh didn't say anything, confused by what this woman was banging on about.

'The sign also says,' she continued, 'that the little scamps can jump downwards up to nine metres without being hurt. Imagine that – nine metres!'

Josh looked back at Jeeves, who was standing stony-faced behind him. Josh noted there were no guards. All he had to get away from was a tiny woman and a dusty old butler. He had never been much of a fighter, but this didn't seem like much of a fight.

'How high do you think nine metres is, Josh?'

He rolled his eyes. 'No idea. Look—'

Dr Carter held up her hand. 'What do you think? I reckon that's about a couple of metres.'

'What are you—' Josh broke off, stunned by the sight of a small tree kangaroo levitating above the ground in front of him. He sat there, open-mouthed, as the little fella, munching away on a twig, oblivious, began to rise further and further in the air. Eventually, it stopped.

'Whereas I reckon that,' said Dr Carter cheerfully, 'is about nine metres.'

Josh's mouth was dry. His eyes darted around, searching for any sign that he wasn't losing his mind. All that greeted him was Jeeves's implacable stare.

He coughed to clear his throat. 'All right, you've made your point. No need to drop him.'

'Drop him?' echoed Dr Carter, sounding scandalized. 'I would never hurt an animal.'

Josh tried to grab the table, but he was too slow. He suddenly felt himself rising into the air. 'Oh god, oh god, ohgodohgodohgodohgod.'

'*You*, on the other hand …'

Finally, Josh came to a halt. The wind whipped around him. It wasn't his biggest concern right then, but he hadn't dressed for the British climate. He glanced to his right to where the remarkably sanguine-looking marsupial was floating beside him in mid-air. Down below, Dr Carter was still sitting in her chair, looking up in his direction calmly, a cup of tea in her hand.

She didn't shout. She didn't need to. Somehow, her voice sounded weirdly as if it were coming from right beside his ear. '*You*, on the other hand, I don't care about unless you are useful to me. Our original agreement is still on the table on exactly the same terms.'

'Yesyesyesyesyes.'

'Excellent.'

Josh closed his eyes as he started to float back down. He didn't open them again until he felt his chair beneath him. Whatever invisible force had gripped him was released, and he was able to crumple into his seat. Weeping.

Dr Carter tutted. 'William, if you would, please take Josh

to his new home. And place a sheet on the back seat of the car – it appears he has wet himself.'

'Very good, ma'am.'

Josh was driven to a large house in the country and set to work the next morning. All attempts to explain that the brief he'd been given didn't make any sense were dismissed. It was made clear to him that what they wanted was his talent, not his advice. And so, he had worked.

Two weeks passed. Two nights ago, he had explained to them the latest solution he had come up with to their particular problem – *them* being Dr Carter and whoever else was watching on the one-way video link beside her on the desk. Dr Carter had then stepped into another room and returned fifteen minutes later with a smile.

'Excellent work, Josh. We are on for Thursday at four in the morning, so go and get your beauty sleep.'

'You don't need me to actually be there to—'

She raised her hand to silence him. 'Yes, we do. I want you to see if it works, or ...'

Josh was pretty certain that he really wouldn't like whatever the unsaid end of that sentence was. He'd got to work the next morning, laying the breadcrumbs carefully. You had to know where and how. Hackers were paranoid individuals by nature. Luckily, Josh knew exactly how to think like one. He'd created a dozen aliases long ago which he'd worked hard to establish as credible. Given the circumstances, he'd resigned himself to burning all of them on this if he had to.

And now here he was, working at the only desk in a massive marquee. The kind of thing in which you could host a large wedding. He didn't know where he was – not that he knew this part of the country – but even if he did, they'd blindfolded him as they'd left the big house and driven for nearly three hours. He got the sense they were in the middle of nowhere. There seemed to be no sounds from outside save for the occasional hoot of an owl. A biting-cold wind sliced through the marquee whenever anyone opened the door. The jeep had travelled up an incline for about the last twenty minutes of the journey. So then, they were on a mountain in the middle of nowhere. None of which made any sense for the purposes of what they were asking him to do. If they wanted him to try to trace the source of a hack, he could do it as well, if not better, sitting on his couch, near a conveniently placed bathroom and fridge.

The marquee had been erected over a concrete floor that looked as if it had been laid recently. In the centre stood a metal platform upon which sat a twenty-foot-by-twenty-foot box made out of some kind of glass or Perspex or god knows what. Josh hadn't ventured close enough to look. He'd decided this was a need-to-know situation, and he didn't want to know anything. Why was the tower unit of a high-powered but otherwise entirely ordinary Linux machine he'd personally configured sitting in that large glass box? Why were there heavily armed men in reflective facemasks guarding this whole thing? They looked remarkably like storm troopers. Why were they doing all this in the middle of nowhere? Come to that, why was a pair of ginger-haired, pre-teen twin boys sitting in the corner, squabbling, while eating Nando's chicken and playing on Game Boys, while a man in his fifties sat beside them, awkwardly drumming his fingers on his knees as he stared at a screen? None of it made sense and Josh wanted to keep it that way. All he cared about was getting back home then forgetting this whole affair as quickly as possible.

Dr Carter was standing beside him now. 'So, Josh, how are we feeling? Excited?'

'That's not exactly the word I'd choose.'

She giggled. 'Oh, come on, now. You really must try to enjoy your life. None of us knows how long we've got left.' That last statement clearly tickled her as she threw her head back and gave one of her trademark grating giggles, flapping a hand in front of her face as she did so. 'Sorry. Sorry.'

'Why is that funny?' asked Josh.

'It's …' She shrugged. 'You had to be there. Is this going to work?'

'I think so.'

The smile fell from her lips. 'Think so? You *think* so?'

'Nothing in life is guaranteed,' replied Josh, hating how weak he sounded.

'Oh, believe me, some things definitely are.' Dr Carter raised her voice. 'All right, people. Showtime.' A couple of the storm trooper-like guards moved into position near the box, each of them holding an axe. 'First things first. Professor Marshall, can we get isolation confirmed?'

The man in his fifties sitting beside the twins looked up from his screen and nodded. 'Confirmed. No wifi signals present. Mobile towers neutralised. Satellites went down sixty seconds ago.'

He couldn't possibly mean what he said, thought Josh. Satellites don't go down. More importantly, nobody could organise for them to do so on demand.

Dr Carter nodded then did that trick with her voice again. It wasn't that it increased in volume, it just seemed suddenly to be everywhere. 'Last chance. If anyone has a mobile device of any kind on their person, it needs to be switched off now or I guarantee you will deeply regret it for the rest of your brief time on this earth.' She left a ten-second gap then nodded again. 'All right, then – boys?'

The twins, who were now engaged in an enthusiastic game of punching each other on the arm, ignored her entirely. Dr Carter stamped her foot. 'BOYS!'

The pre-teens pulled a face. 'Get yourselves into position this minute or, so help me, no screens of any kind for a month.' The youngsters trudged into place on either side of the box, about ten feet back. 'Why couldn't they have been girls?' she muttered under her breath.

She looked around the marquee one last time then turned to Josh. 'Mr Glynn, you may begin.'

Josh nodded and licked his lips nervously. This wasn't going to work, but as long as he could prove he wasn't the reason for its failure, maybe he'd still get out alive. He opened a fresh window on his screen and typed in the command to run the script he'd set up. 'Drop commencing.'

It all felt weirdly anti-climactic, which was odd. Josh knew better than anyone that what they were doing could take hours, days, maybe even weeks to work, if it worked at all. They were laying bait, waiting for someone to try to hack it. It wasn't as if as soon as it went online a bell would go off somewhere and the hack would commence. Theoretically, if you knew a hack was happening you could trace it back to source, but you had to be very, very good, and more than a little lucky. You also needed to rely on the attacker being sloppy. Josh had set up three layers of defence to such a standard that he was confident nobody but the very best could get beyond the second wall, and even then, it would take a lot of time and effort, which was the whole point.

Meanwhile, he would have to work back the other way while remaining undetected. Oddly, when he'd tried to explain all this to Dr Carter, she'd seemed entirely unconcerned.

The bait had been her idea. He had to admit that while she knew nothing about hacking, the woman demonstrated an excellent instinct for what the internet wanted: naked pictures of a well-known female political operative. It had it all – misogyny, voyeurism and the chance to rescue an ally or smite a political opponent in the never-ending culture war. There was something there for everybody. Believable enough that it could exist, desirable enough that most hackers couldn't resist. Josh had also tried to explain that when it was out there, they would have multiple attackers – some solo, some working in teams, all going after the prize. It would be impossible to tell who they were after. Again, Dr Carter had given him that infuriating smile and said, 'Oh, we'll know.'

Josh's laptop pinged. 'We've got our first nibble.' He looked at the various windows he had open, running all manner of programs, including a couple he'd written especially for the occasion. 'This first layer should take about … Oh, they've passed it.'

Dr Carter moved closer. 'This sounds promising. Could be our girl.'

It was the first time Dr Carter had referred to their target by gender.

'All right, now the second layer is considerably— STREWTH!'

'Are they through?' asked Dr Carter.

Josh shook his head furiously. 'Yeah, but nobody is this fast. You'd need more processing power than NASA. This is bullshit!' He looked around, aware how irrationally angry he was as he did so. While it wounded his professional pride, the intruder was doing exactly what they wanted them to. 'Seriously,' said Josh. 'Am I being punked?'

'Focus, Mr Glynn. What are they doing now?'

Josh drew a deep breath. 'Attacking the final layer. The way this has gone, they'll be in any second now.'

Dr Carter slapped the table with her left hand while holding up her right. 'On my mark. Tell me when.'

Josh studied the screen in front of him.

'Mr Glynn?'

'*Now*.'

As Dr Carter's hand descended, a lot of things seemed to happen at once. The storm troopers with axes sliced through the hardlines connecting the machine in the box to the outside world and to Josh's computer. The two red-headed boys held out their hands, identical strained expressions on their faces.

'What did you do that for?' screamed Josh. 'We'll never find them now.'

Dr Carter was walking slowly towards the box. 'On the contrary, Josh. All being well, we've already caught them.' She placed one hand against the box and held it there for a moment. 'Ohhhh, and we have.' She tapped on the glass. 'C'mon, Yenta – out you come. Don't be shy.'

Nothing happened.

Dr Carter placed her hands on her hips and sighed pointedly. 'Oh, don't be a silly billy, now. You know who this is, and you know what that means. Being petulant at this point really achieves nothing.'

Josh considered saying something, but held his tongue. Whatever this was, it felt a long way out of his comfort zone. He glanced around. Fleeing had felt as if it would not solve any of his problems. Now it felt as if it might at least solve the temporary problem of being trapped in a big tent with this much crazy.

'Fine,' said Dr Carter. 'Have it your way.' She raised her voice again without actually raising it. 'Medusa protocol.'

Instantly, two dozen storm troopers jogged into the marquee in formation and surrounded the box, six on each side. Each one was pointing a serious-looking automatic weapon at it. Josh considered himself a connoisseur of the international arms trade, because he had a lot of money and did enjoy watching things disintegrate in a firestorm of ordnance, but he'd never seen anything like these guns. Why all this hardware was pointed at a box that still contained only the tower unit of a computer disconnected from the internet, with the power cut off, was anyone's guess.

Josh got to his feet and turned around to find two more storm troopers standing behind him. How many of these guys were there? He shrugged off the heavy hand that had been placed on his shoulder and sat back down.

Dr Carter turned her attention to the red-headed twins. 'All right, boys, turn it off, but stay ready.'

'Can I—' started one of them.

'No, you cannot,' snapped Carter. 'We are in the middle of an operation.'

The boys relaxed their arms and slouched off to stand behind the armed men.

Carter stepped back to stand in line with the storm troopers then raised her voice. She spoke in a language Josh didn't understand. No, it was more than that. It was a language unlike any he had ever heard. Carter's voice crescendoed and she finished whatever she had been saying with a flourish, throwing her arms into the air dramatically.

Nothing happened.

For a couple more seconds nothing continued to happen.

Then, after a further couple of seconds, it felt like even that stopped.

Josh was halfway through letting out the breath he had been holding when the PC tower exploded. Only, you couldn't really call it an explosion. The entire thing disintegrated as a being – one considerably greater in size than the area the tower had occupied – suddenly took its place. It was like that old trick where fake snakes come flying out of a peanut jar, only the snakes in question were massive slimy tentacles, and the jar was obliterated in the process.

Amid the writhing tentacles Josh couldn't make out a body or a face or anything at the centre of the thing, it just appeared to be a swirling mass of horrifying existence. He averted his eyes and tried to stare at the floor. This wasn't real. It had to be a dream – an incredibly detailed and long dream. Maybe he'd made the mistake of reading from that book of H. P. Lovecraft stories again before bed? Yes, that must be it. In which case, the odds were strong that somebody would say something horrifically racist in a minute.

A couple of the men with guns took a step forward. A couple of the more sensible ones took a step back.

'Hold your fire,' said Dr Carter in a remarkably calm voice. 'Shooting will cause ricochets, resulting in your untimely death, directly or indirectly.' She walked towards the box again. 'Hmmmm, so it held. My compliments to the gals and guys in engineering.' She followed her praise with another of those grating giggles. Then she raised her voice. 'My, my, Yenta, how you've grown.' Her observation precipitated an increase in the already frantic swirling motion in the box. 'I'll use that name, as I know it was always your favourite of the many you've had and, despite all evidence to the contrary, I do want this to be amicable.'

The tentacles continued to swirl.

Dr Carter tapped her foot. 'Come, now, sweetie. There's no talking to you when you're like this. Can we not have a civilised conversation?'

The swirling mass of nightmares slowed. Then, in a second crushing blow to the laws of physics, it began to shrink, before eventually morphing into the figure of a girl. A blonde girl, her hair in the kind of ringlets you just don't see any more. She was about eight years old and looked like a strong contender for the lead role in the casting call for *Annie* that she was currently missing out on.

'There,' said Dr Carter. 'Isn't that better?'

A blown raspberry was delivered in response, which prompted a guffaw from one of the twins.

Dr Carter turned in their direction. 'Boys, go and wait in the car. Professor Marshall, you may now also step out.'

The man nodded and did as he was asked, almost tripping over himself in his haste to be elsewhere.

'It is nice to see you again, Yenta.'

'I wish I could say the same,' replied the girl in, well, the voice of an eight-year-old girl. She gesticulated around the room. 'Was all this really necessary?'

'I'm afraid it was,' said Dr Carter. 'You haven't been responding to our messages.'

'I've been busy.'

'Yes, but not too busy to go straight after salacious pictures of a minor celebrity as soon as the chance arose.'

Yenta shrugged. 'Can't a girl have a little fun?'

Dr Carter nodded. 'Of course. The problem is, you've been having too much fun, haven't you?'

The little girl looked outraged. 'How dare you! I did everything that was asked of me.'

'Did you, though?' asked Dr Carter, her tone slightly admonishing. 'It appears we have had a rather severe case of mission creep.'

'I disagree.'

'Do you?' said Dr Carter. 'Shall we examine the facts? Some years ago, when we realized the internet might be a problem, we came to you. The media could be tricky, but we had it under control. The internet, though – all those millions of little termites with keyboards, beavering away. Chewing at the structures it had taken us centuries to construct. They were dangerous. You were supposed to be the solution.'

The little girl raised her chin defiantly. 'And didn't I do exactly what you asked? Rather than hiding the truth, I buried it under a mountain of falsehood, conjecture and conspiracy. Thanks to me, not only does nobody know your organization exists, but they also wouldn't believe it does, even if they were presented with overwhelming evidence.'

Dr Carter nodded. 'All of that is true, and we greatly appreciate it. You did a wonderful job. Honestly, though, I'm not even sure how much credit we should be giving you. How much of the chaos was you, and how much was them?' She waved a hand in the air dismissively.

Yenta shrugged. 'They do have extraordinary minds. Pulling the truth apart and warping it beyond all recognition. It is fun to watch.'

'Yes,' said Dr Carter. 'I'm sure it was, for a while. Then you got bored, didn't you?'

Yenta folded her arms. 'I don't know what you mean.'

'Sure you do. You're a Truth-eater. The fundamentals of

what you do have never changed, only the medium. At least, that was the case. Just my personal theory, but I'm guessing you found yourself awash in a sea of lies and hate, and then, one day, you suddenly realised they'd become better at it than you have ever been. You couldn't keep up, could you?'

This time, the little girl said nothing, but Josh noticed her eyes had become watery. He felt a momentary ache of compassion, then he remembered that the girl in question had been a writhing mass of tentacles moments before.

'So, then,' said Dr Carter, 'let us say you evolved. Once you found yourself drowning in lies, suddenly you became nourished by the truth.'

'I can explain,' said Yenta.

'No,' said Dr Carter, 'you cannot. We found the site. You were not as subtle as you thought. Did you not think we would be watching? Looking out for any hint of the truth being out there? You know how paranoid they are.'

'They?' echoed Yenta.

Carter shrugged. 'Between you and I, I have more faith in humanity's inability to grasp bigger truths. To understand they are not, and have never been, the real top of the food chain. But it isn't up to me. Let us say that senior management is very old school when it comes to matters of confidentiality.'

Yenta moved forward and placed her hand against the glass. 'All right. I'll stop. I promise.'

'I'm afraid they have no interest in promises. My instructions are very clear.'

The little girl's expression changed in an instant. Gone was the doe-eyed innocence, to be replaced with a spiteful sneer that belonged to another, much older face. 'You can't do this. You need me.'

Carter sounded almost apologetic. 'We don't. They do it on their own now.'

'I know things.'

'That is the problem.'

'About you.' Yenta gave a malicious smile. 'Yes. Let me go and I'll be good. Don't, and ... Well, I know your true name.'

Josh felt Dr Carter tense for a moment.

A noise came from Yenta, deep and ominous. After a few seconds, Josh realized it was a laugh. Not one that could ever come from an eight-year-old girl in normal circumstances, but then, the 'normal circumstances' ship had sailed a while ago now.

The girl pointed at all the storm troopers standing around. 'If I say it, it will be in all of their minds. Best of luck containing that.'

Carter took a step backwards and made a movement with her hand. Then she spoke, this time raising her voice and shouting in the normal manner. 'To the first man to raise his left hand, I will give one million pounds.'

Nothing happened.

Dr Carter giggled that grating giggle again. 'I'm afraid they are receiving on a frequency even you can't reach. Still, it was a nice try, although I'm not keen on being threatened.'

Yenta slumped to the floor. 'There's nothing you can do to me that's worse than what you are already planning.'

'You say that ...' Dr Carter started to walk around the box. 'But I know you fear nothing more than absence. The absence of all data, information. Being truly alone. So, seeing as you've been nice enough to try to intimidate me ...'

She pulled out a clicker from a concealed pocket in her business suit and pressed the button on it. A screen appeared in the glass wall of the box. Josh recognized the four figures on it instantly. Who wouldn't? They were iconic. Known the world over. Tinky Winky, Dipsy, Laa-Laa and Po.

Dr Carter smiled. 'It is just the one episode, looping endlessly. I hope that is all right?'

Yenta covered her eyes. 'Turn it off.'

'No, I don't think I shall.'

In the background, Josh heard the distinctive gurgle of the baby in the rising sun that signalled the start of every episode.

Then the little girl turned and looked directly into Josh's eyes. Before he could break away from her gaze, she spoke a word: ÄÆÄÆÄÆ.

Dr Carter's head whipped around and she glared at him, annoyance writ across her face.

'Petty, Yenta. Petty. Enjoy eternity.' She snapped her fingers and the glass box disappeared into the ground with a whoosh that gradually faded into the distance.

'Stand down,' Dr Carter barked.

The storm troopers raised their weapons and quick-marched out of the marquee in the same manner as they had entered.

As Dr Carter walked towards him, Josh felt panic rising. 'I ... I didn't hear anything. And even if I did, I didn't understand it. I've got a terrible memory. I can't even remember ...' He was almost in tears now. 'I can't even remember what I can't remember.'

Dr Carter smiled at him. 'Josh, relax. I want you to know you did very good work.' She waved away the two guards standing behind Josh and they marched out of the marquee too, leaving the pair alone.

'Thank you,' said Josh. 'I'm ... I'm happy I could help, and I'd be happy to do so again in the future.'

'Very kind of you. And I'd like to apologise. In all honesty, I forgot you were here.'

'That's OK.'

'It's not.'

'It is, though. I don't know anything. I don't remember.'

Dr Carter leaned against Josh's workstation. 'The human brain, Josh, is an incredible thing. It stores things it doesn't know it is storing. Humans, being the inefficient creatures they are, can't access most of the data. But others can, even if the person in question is dead.'

Josh was running now. He didn't have a destination. What mattered was the 'away' part. He could figure out the rest later.

He was almost at one of the marquee's walls now. He could climb under the fabric or smash through or— His stomach lurched as he felt his feet leaving the ground. The wall careered away from him as he flew backwards through the air. He caught sight of Dr Carter looking up at him as he zipped past.

'Sorry about this. We dragged you around the world to come and help us, and now, well, you've had an accident at work that wasn't your fault.'

Josh came to a halt and hung in the air above where the box had been. 'Please,' he pleaded.

'Look at it this way, you're going to be halfway home. Eventually.'

And then he was falling.

Falling.

Falling.

Around him was darkness. Terrible darkness.

All he could hear was the air rushing past his ears and, in the distance, 'Tinky Winky... Dipsy ... Laa-Laa ... Po!'

THE OWL AND THE PUSSYCAT

The Owl – that was what they called him. At least to his face. They might well have had other, less kind nicknames for him round the office, but that was the one that was used in front of him. In truth, he didn't much care. He was a permanent fixture in a department in which it was career suicide to spend longer than a lunchbreak, so Peter Drake knew he was an unwelcome reminder to his co-workers of their own failure. The Ghost of Christmas Future. He was surrounded by burn-outs, screw-ups, twelve-steppers and fallen angels.

Invariably, when someone was assigned to OB12 – or 'guest services' as it was unofficially known – they'd explain to anyone willing to listen how there'd been a mistake and that they would be reassigned in a couple of weeks. They never were. Within eighteen months, they'd either be out of the Service or have that look about them – their spirits broken, punching the clock until that bright future became their disappointing past.

Occasionally, one of them would take a more dramatic

way out. Dobson had done it in the room – in Drake's chair, in fact. Drake had been quite specific when he had asked that nobody sit in his chair. It had a special back support and he'd been forced to pay for it himself because the Service wouldn't cover the cost. It had been him who'd discovered the body. They'd forced him to go and talk to a company-appointed therapist about it. In Drake's opinion – which nobody had asked for – people around here were overly concerned with employees' mental health to the detriment of the provision of sound lumbar support.

OB12 was one of those departments that the Service ended up having not out of want, but out of necessity. The country often had 'guests' whose privacy – indeed, their very existence – needed to be protected. The National Crime Agency had their witness protection scheme, but this was something different. The NCA's was used by victims of crime who needed to be squirreled away or, more often than not, people who had taken a deal and given evidence against former colleagues.

OB12's role differed greatly. A trial was hardly ever held. Their guests were defectors, allies who had become unpopular in their own countries, people who knew too much or, in some cases, whose very existence was problematic. Despite what some people might say, the British state was not in the business of permanently removing its problems – at least, not as a first choice.

As Peter sat in the room, the bank of monitors showed him four guest houses.

In the Warrington residence, a husband and wife were eating dinner in silence. The Chinese government had determined that the husband had been passing information to the British. It had actually been his wife, but as far as the

Service was concerned it was much of a muchness. They had both been extracted and now they had to be protected. The situation was further complicated by the husband's ongoing outrage at his wife's actions. On average, they were fighting every other day. Those arguments when they'd opened a bottle of wine beforehand were particularly feisty, stopping just short of physical. The Service logbook was full of incidents.

In Knutsford, a family of four was making the best of it. The fourteen-year-old girl was a nightmare. She was having her wifi privileges withheld. Apparently, this was the worst thing you could do to a teenage girl – without a hint of irony the Geneva Convention had been cited several times. The reason for this cruel and unusual punishment was that the last time she'd been online, the teenager had hacked into the place where the Americans kept the good stuff.

At some point, it had dawned on the Yanks that telling everyone how secure the Pentagon was was like waving a red rag at every hacker on the planet. Very quietly, they had started to move the real goodies somewhere else. Most of their own people didn't know. The thinking was solid: let the Greeks lay siege to Troy while Helen is hanging out on the metaphorical beach in Tahiti. Unfortunately for them, the petulant teenager had snapped metaphorical pictures of Helen with her norks out. The Americans were beside themselves to find out how they'd been the dealer in a crooked game of three-card Monte and somehow still lost.

The British had assured them that the teenager, her younger brother and parents had all fled the country and were currently in Iran, where the father's family was from. The Yanks didn't believe it, but crucially, they couldn't disprove it. Eventually, the girl would become an asset, but first, the Service needed her to become a considerably less hot topic of conversation.

The lady in Prestwich was on the most wanted lists of several countries, including the UK. No explanation was given to OB12 as to what a drug trafficker was doing in their care, but that was far from unusual. *It's on a need-to-know basis, old boy. Need-to-know*. Recently, she had really got into crochet. When Drake had visited her two months ago, she had given him a rather nice tablecloth. Under the guidelines, he hadn't been allowed to keep it, but nevertheless he'd taken it because also, under the guidelines, gifts were not to be refused for fear of offending the guest.

The house calls were infrequent unless absolutely necessary. Last week, Clara Watts had visited the Warrington house – ostensibly to do some maintenance on the cameras. In reality, the wife in the Chinese couple had grown alarmingly fond of stroking the hammer in the toolbox, and it had been subtly removed. Drake's visit to Prestwich had been to ascertain whether the subject's flirting with the neighbour could become an issue. Eventually, they'd got her a dog – for the company – and some subtle checks had determined that the neighbour had an irrational fear of canines.

Back in the nineties, the approach to 'guest services' had drastically changed, after what was euphemistically referred to as the West Finchley Affair. A North Korean scientist and his wife had been guests, until the State Security Department had found and slaughtered them and two of their guardians. It had been a nightmare to cover up.

Suspicions about how the system had broken down had been confirmed six months later. The problem with teams providing twenty-four-hour protection on site is that you potentially have dozens of operatives travelling to and from sensitive locations every week. All it needs is an interested party to find one of those operatives and for that person to be just a little careless. The whole system had needed to be ripped down and rebuilt from scratch.

And so, from the ashes of Close Protection Team 4 came OB12. Now, they stayed hands off, and monitored everything remotely instead. As long as the feed was protected, it gave the bad actors nothing to follow. Even if they did hack it, they'd have a devil of a time finding an exact IP address as it was routed through dozens of dummy locations. And if you identified a watcher, what did that give you exactly? It could be months before they visited one of the houses in person and then, assuming you successfully managed to follow them and evaded all counter-surveillance measures taken, odds on, the location they were visiting wouldn't be the one you were looking for.

The only downside was that it did rather remove from proceedings the personal touch. Disappearing for your own protection had become like everything else: if you had an issue, there was a number you could ring and be told to 'please hold because your call is important to us'.

The other change around the time of the West Finchley Affair had been that someone in High Command noticed the financial cost. Most of the guest houses owned by the Service were in London. Pretty nice parts of the capital, too. You couldn't put up a senior Russian defector in Dagenham – it just wasn't done. Not only were these locations some of the most expensive real estate in the country, but they were also situated in the city where the vast majority of foreign intelligence operatives were stationed, which was akin to keeping your chickens next to the fox sanctuary.

The arguments about how much a Chinese defector or a Russian scientist might stand out in, say, Market Harborough was categorically refuted when the Service deliberately leaked a dummy location to the Israelis as a potential hidey-hole for someone they were keen to get reacquainted with. They had declined to follow up on it. If even Mossad couldn't be bothered, then they were on to something.

In a rare example of actual decentralization, five London properties were sold, and the proceeds were used to purchase fifteen in the north and east of England, plus a couple in Wales. Scotland did not feature because the Scottish government, despite having no purview over intelligence services, could get problematically Scottish if the mood took them.

The seventeen houses were fitted out with the most cutting-edge surveillance equipment and OB12 was born. Some deadweight staff were shipped off to monitoring hubs in Manchester, Newcastle and Ipswich, and the guests were assured that this was all for their safety. The only losers had been certain high-ranking Service officials, who had been forced to find somewhere else to conduct their affairs. The head of a particular department might love nothing more than being covered in custard and whipped by a hooker dressed as his nanny, but he didn't love it enough to go to all the way to Norwich.

The reason bright young things hated being sent to OB12 was that not only was it a punishment for whatever screw-up you'd made, but the only way to get noticed once there was by being part of another screw-up. When OB12 ran smoothly, it was like the toilets flushing – nobody was impressed or even noticed it. But if it started malfunctioning, people realized immediately, not least because it meant there was a catastrophic amount of shit everywhere.

Peter Drake had been at OB12 from the very start. Every now and then, the latest head of department would bring him in for a 'career chat'. People found him unnerving. He'd never applied for the promotion or transfer that almost thirty years of impeccable service in OB12 meant he was long overdue. He could have been head of the Service himself, if he'd shown the slightest inclination. He was very good at his job, and the department was one that every new head who passed through the constantly revolving door viewed as something they took on to show that they were a good team player, ahead of – please, God – being moved to somewhere else before the stink could attach itself.

Drake regularly took the night shift. Twelve hours spent mostly alone, in a room, watching monitors. Making sure each location was secure. Normally, the boredom would drive the watcher to distraction or lull them into unconsciousness. Drake had a special kind of mind, though – and, come to that, bladder. He would sit there attentively. No one could ever recall seeing him get up to go for a pee.

It had been Drake who had spotted that the new Ocado delivery man to the guest house in Stockport was a Ukrainian hitman. He had guessed correctly that the human trafficker in the Wirral location had been planning to make a run for it. And it was he, Peter Drake, who had realized that one of his co-workers had fallen in love with the French madame at the Middleton address, which meant they'd both been stopped as they boarded a flight to Rio.

He was the Owl. He freaked people out, but he was also flawlessly good at the job. Sitting and watching, while mostly nothing happened.

Along with Warrington, Knutsford and Prestwich, they currently had the Worsley house up on the bank of monitors. It was the grandest of the properties, used for VIPs. The man residing there did not have a name. He did – obviously – but they had not been given it. He was known only as Mr Smith.

It was clear from the songs he sang to himself as he pottered around the large kitchen that he was Eastern European – from the Baltics, unless Drake was way off. He was probably in his early fifties, but so obsessive in his workout regimen that you couldn't be sure. It was a five-bedroom house, but he lived there alone. Every other day he spent thirty minutes painstakingly grooming his goatee.

His only visitors were a senior government official and a couple of service minders. For these visits, all of the cameras were turned off. That was the procedure. There was to be no evidence of the government official's meetings with this man. Mr Smith also received visits from what OB12 referred to euphemistically as a 'independent contractor', brought up from London especially. She was blindfolded for the last hour of the journey and paid handsomely for her absolute discretion. As she'd said, she was used to stuff with blindfolds.

The procurement of sexual partners for guests was not usually part of OB12's remit, but Mr Smith was a special case. He was being buttered up. Normally for such visits, it was agreed beforehand that the cameras in the bedroom would be switched off, once a sweep had been done to confirm the property was secure. However, Mr Smith had decided that 'events' would take place in the front room and on the stairs. He clearly enjoyed being watched. Drake had observed impassively and logged it.

'Are there any biscuits?'

Drake ignored the question. Dobson could be annoying at the best of times, and those times had been before he'd taken his grandfather's Second World War revolver into work, sat in Drake's chair and blown his own brains out. Now his ghost spent most of its time asking for biscuits. Biscuits it could not eat.

Drake was familiar with the theory that ghosts were the souls of people who could not pass on until something was settled. He found it hard to believe that a lack of biscuits could be classified as a 'something'.

Drake's grandmother had been possessed of 'the sight', as his family had grandly referred to it. He himself had paid no attention to it until nine years ago when he'd witnessed a four-car pile-up and one of the fatalities had followed him home. The spirit had wandered round his apartment, telling him her life story, and then, after a few days, she had left. There had been no big announcement, she had just faded away. Drake had told no one about that experience, or about the other times it had happened since.

Mostly, these spirits just wanted to talk, and he was fine with that. He had never been good at conversation. He was an intelligent man, well read, conscientious, engaged with the world around him, but when it came down to it, he never knew what to say to others. Somehow, he had never learned how to make a real connection with another living human being. It was just one of those things, and over time he'd grown to accept it. The good thing about ghosts was they really didn't need you to talk, just listen. Drake was good at listening, as he was at watching. So, they talked to him. He did not mind.

'I could really go for some chocolate Hobnobs.'

He *mostly* did not mind.

Mr Smith had been staying with them for six weeks now. The first time it happened had been in the second week. One morning, at 4 a.m., the spirit of a young girl had appeared on the feed. She was what you would probably call a pre-teen. Drake was no expert on children, not having spent much time hanging around with them, even when he had been one.

She had stood, wearing an anorak, at the end of the bed. She had a patch over one eye. It looked like an inexpert field dressing. Drake could see her, but he knew that if someone else watched the same feed they'd see nothing. Also, if Drake were to watch the recording back, no spirit would be visible. He had absolutely no idea why this was, and he'd never attempted to look into it. The main thing he understood about his 'gift' was that the only way things could go really wrong was if he brought attention to it.

After standing there for thirty minutes, statue-still, the girl had suddenly screamed. It had been a blood-curdling sound that had made Drake spill his tea. Mr Smith had woken with a start, and sat bolt upright in his bed. He stared at the girl for a few seconds, disorientated, and then he burst out laughing. He looked at her, then up at the camera, then back at her. Was he wondering if she was visible to the watchers?

He smiled, mimed a brief round of applause in her direction, then lay back down and went to sleep. Drake did not know what he had just witnessed. Smith could not only see the spirit, but he seemed entirely unaffected by her. Amused, in fact. On the few other occasions when Drake had seen a spirit that had also made itself visible to someone else, that person had been left a gibbering wreck.

The girl had turned and looked straight into the camera.

She couldn't see it, could she? Drake zoomed in closer. Even allowing for the ethereal nature of the spirit's appearance, which gave her a translucent quality, there was no question that the girl was looking directly at him. She had stood there for a few minutes before gradually fading away.

The following morning, when Drake had finished his shift and driven home to his little flat in Chorlton, she had been there, waiting for him. Unlike the others, she had not spoken. Instead, she had followed him round and stared balefully at him with her one good eye. He'd tried to ignore her. Gone about his day as normal. Eaten a dinner at 9 a.m., watched a recording of a nature documentary series he enjoyed. She followed him into every room, always there. Even in his car on the way back to work, he'd glanced in the rearview mirror and there she was again, sat in the back seat, staring at him.

That was not the worst part, though.

The worst part was the dreams.

They had started on the third night. Drake wasn't even sure you could call them dreams. They felt more like memories. Not his, but still they felt horribly real. Such terrible things. Only one featured the girl, but they all featured Mr Smith. He was a sadist who had used a time of war to do unspeakable things. Drake would wake in a cold sweat to find the girl standing at the end of his bed, looking at him in silence with that one good eye.

The only time she was not in the room with Drake was when he could see her on the monitors, following Mr Smith from room to room. The man seemed to enjoy the attention. At one point, as he had sat at the marble breakfast bar, eating his dinner, he had poured a second glass of wine and left the glass on the counter in front of her. He'd offered a silent toast and then done the same to the camera. Whatever the man was, it was not fully human. He had the sight, but that appeared to be only part of it.

In the dreams – the memories – there were killings, so many killings. They often seemed to have a ritualistic nature to them. As if he was drawing power from the act. As the days went by, Drake became more and more aware that he was watching a true monster. Beneath the smile and suave manners lay something less than human.

It dawned on Drake one night that perhaps the girl was not trying to torture him by showing him those memories. Perhaps she was looking for assistance.

He turned on the bedside lamp and sat on the edge of the bed in his pyjamas. 'Is that it? Are you asking for help?'

The girl nodded.

'I don't... What can I do? I watch. That is all. I watch.'

She had just looked at him.

On it had gone, day after day. More memories. Some repeated – always the worst ones. Drake had stopped sleeping. His boss, Addler, had brought him into her office to check if he was OK. His uncharacteristically dishevelled appearance had not gone unnoticed. He could see she was worried. Losing Drake would be like being the person who came in and somehow knocked down the office wall. Drake had assured her he was fine, because what else could he say?

He was not a religious man, which was perhaps odd, considering the 'gift'. He, unlike most people, knew categorically there was something after death. Still, what little time he had spent in the company of religion had left him feeling empty. Nothing there had spoken to him. He had given it little thought until now. He knew he had a soul, and he was finding himself filled with a dreadful suspicion that if he did not help this girl and the others – so many others – his soul would join those of the tortured.

At the weekly ops meeting Addler had blithely announced that Mr Smith was moving on soon. She had said that he had negotiated himself an upgrade to a villa in the Cayman Islands. Drake wasn't sure if she'd meant that literally, but it seemed clear from the feed that Smith was preparing for a trip and he was excited. Time was running out.

Drake installed an untraceable browser on his home PC and started to search for how to get his hands on a gun. Lots of people said they could provide one, but he didn't trust any of the avenues available to him. Perhaps it would be better to turn up with a hammer and rely on the element of surprise?

Smith was fit and powerfully built, though, and Drake was all too aware that the man was no stranger to violence. He revelled in it. In contrast, Drake, bar some long-forgotten training, had never had much aptitude, or call, for violence. He didn't know what to do. He tried not to look into the corner of his sitting room as he knew the girl was there, as always, staring at him.

He jumped with surprise at a knock on the door to his flat. This was unusual. First, there was a buzzer outside that people used. In theory, nobody was able to wander into the building and start knocking on doors. Second, he was expecting no one and nothing. He rarely got deliveries and never received visitors. There had been that one time with the overly enthusiastic Jehovah's Witnesses, who must have tailgated someone through the outer door, but right now it was 7 a.m. and Drake had just come home from work. Not even Jehovah's Witnesses were that enthusiastic.

He was all set to ignore it as someone knocking in error

when he heard it again. He stood up, walked to the door and checked the peephole. All he could see was the faded paint of the far wall and the cracked lighting fixture, which the building management company had still not repaired.

He needed to be on his guard. There were procedures in place so that if one of the watchers felt someone was trying to contact them, they were to inform management immediately. Drake took the sanctity of the system seriously. He slipped the chain on the door and opened it with care.

A black cat effortlessly squeezed by him and into the flat, as calmly as if it were returning home. Drake did not like cats. He was allergic, in fact. The one time he'd tried to have one as a pet, he'd sneezed constantly for a week before it ran off. In the list of awkward experiences he did not wish to repeat, it ranked second only to his disastrous attempt at having a flatmate.

When he walked back into the sitting room, the cat was curled up on the chair in the corner, right beside the girl.

'Is that with you?'

She nodded.

'I don't get on with cats terribly well.'

This elicited no response.

'Technically, we're not supposed to have pets in the building.'

Again, no response.

Drake shrugged. In truth, lots of people had pets despite the rules. He regularly met people coming in and out of the building with dogs on leads. On one occasion he'd even seen somebody carrying in a vivarium for snakes.

He looked at the girl and then at the cat, before turning in to the kitchen. He opened a tin of tuna that had been sitting in the cupboard for six months and placed its contents on a plate, before filling a bowl with the last of the milk he had in the fridge. He placed both receptacles on the floor in the living room and then retired to the bedroom.

Drake awoke in confusion, pulled out of a deep and peaceful slumber. He felt that moment of awful panic. He hadn't set an alarm. He'd not been sleeping for so long that there hadn't been a need for one. Even before that, he had always woken up fifteen minutes before it went off. Now he'd been disturbed by the sound of his phone ringing.

Was he late? He'd never been late. Not that anyone apart from him had noticed, but he'd been on time every day of his working life. It was a matter of personal pride, come wind, come rain, come snow. He'd also taken a grand total of three sick days. Many of his co-workers in OB12 averaged that in a month.

He flapped around and eventually found his glasses on the nightstand, which allowed him to locate his phone in the bed. He grabbed it just before it rang off.

'Hello?'

'Hi, Peter. It's Samantha . . .' There was a moment of confusion. 'Samantha Addler.'

'Yes, of course.' Drake looked at the clock on the wall. Just after three-thirty. He wasn't due in until 6 p.m. 'Is everything all right?'

'Yes. Sorry, did I wake you?'

'No. No,' said Drake. 'I was just . . .' he looked at the corner of the room, where the girl stood beside the wardrobe with the cat curled up at her feet, '. . . feeding my cat.'

'Right. I didn't know you had a cat.'

'Yes. I do.'

'Lovely.'

Then followed that lull in conversation Drake knew all too well. When the other person was expecting him to say something and nothing came.

'So,' said Addler. 'Again, apologies for disturbing you and the cat, but I was wondering, would you mind dropping over to the Worsley house before your shift? Our guest is complaining about a camera making buzzing noises, and we've been told to keep him happy no matter what.'

'I see. I suppose I could.'

'Thanks very much. I wouldn't ask, only Carol is off sick again and Dave has plans as soon as his shift is done. I'd really appreciate it.'

'Sure. No problem.'

Drake put down the phone and looked at the girl, who stared back at him with her one good eye.

The gravel in the driveway crunched under the wheels of the car as Drake pulled up. Dobson had once described the local area as perfect for a left back for United who only got his game in the Cups. Drake wasn't much of a sports fan but he understood the reference. Rich, but not superstar rich.

His toolbox lay on the seat beside him. He looked into the back of the car, where the cat and the little girl sat quietly. He addressed her in the mirror. 'I don't know if I can . . . I don't know if I can do this. I will try. I . . . I know I should, but . . .'

Drake closed his eyes for a moment, and when he opened them again the girl was gone. The cat sat there, licking itself, as if unconcerned with anything in the world. Drake took a moment to compose himself, dabbed at his eyes with a tissue and, when he was satisfied that he looked himself once again, opened the car door. The cat shot out and disappeared into the hedge. He debated going to look for it, but what would be the point? Cats were a law unto themselves at the best of times, and he was working under the assumption that the feline in question wasn't typical of its species.

Drake placed the stepladder that he had brought in from the car against the wall and his toolbox on the ground before ringing the doorbell. Then he pulled his ID from his jacket pocket and held it up to the camera to the left of the bell.

The voice of Dave Walsh came out of the intercom. 'Who is it?'

'Peter Drake.'

'What's the weather like?'

'The forecasters got it right again.'

It was a coded message. If Drake had said anything else, protocol dictated that Walsh would sound the silent alarm and an armed response unit would be there within twelve minutes. 'The forecasters got it right again' had been chosen carefully as the only phrase about the weather that no British person would ever say by accident.

'Reason for visit?'

'Maintenance. Requested by guest. Order four-nine-one-eight.'

Once the security confirmation and the logging were done, Walsh's voice became chatty. 'Hang on a second and I'll let him know you're here. He's in the kitchen, cooking.'

A minute later the door opened and Mr Smith stood there. He seemed bigger in person, more imposing. His smile would've looked warm to the casual observer, but Drake had seen it too many times in dreams. Such horrible dreams.

'Welcome. Come on in. You found the place OK?'

'Yes, thank you.'

He picked up his gear and followed Smith inside. Over the years, Drake had been to the house numerous times, having set it up initially, in fact, but policy was always to treat it as the subject's home while they were staying there. As Smith led him down the hall, that was easy to believe. The man walked with the relaxed gait of someone who owned his surroundings. He wore a linen shirt, chinos and deck shoes. Drake followed him into the kitchen. As he looked at Smith's back, flashes of images from all those memories came flooding back. Drake's stomach was a roiling mass, and a wave of nausea passed up through his body.

Smith took a seat at the breakfast bar and re-joined the glass of red wine he had poured earlier. The strong smell of lamb roasting in the oven filled the room. Smith liked to cook a whole leg of lamb despite being there alone. He'd eat a portion and then throw away the rest. The waste had come up in meetings, but Addler had instructed them to ignore the man's 'little eccentricities', as she'd put it.

Drake could feel the sweat on his skin despite it being a cool March day. 'So, what seems to be the problem?'

Smith pointed at the camera on the ceiling. 'It's that one. It makes a buzzing noise.'

'Right.' Drake stopped and listened. 'I can't hear anything.'

'It comes and goes,' said Smith, with a dismissive wave of his wine glass. 'Sorry, I'm being rude – would you like a drink?'

Drake tried to smile. 'I can't, thank you. On the job.'

'Right,' Smith said with a laugh. 'Of course you are.'

Drake pulled out his phone and dialled the office. On the second ring Walsh picked up. 'Hello.'

'I need you to take the kitchen camera offline.'

'Okey-dokey.'

Drake hung up. Walsh's inability to say the word 'yes' was annoying. *Wilco. Roger. Can do. Yesarino.* The man managed to make the simplest word in the English language an unwelcome expression of individuality – like a novelty tie.

Drake placed his toolbox on the marble countertop and opened it. It concertinaed out before him.

'That's a lot of tools for a little camera.'

'Well, you never know.'

Drake glanced at the girl, who stood in the corner of the room briefly, and then looked away again. He grabbed the stepladder and positioned it below the domed camera in the ceiling, the one that offered a 360-degree view of the kitchen. The green light beneath it flashed red briefly and then went off. Drake picked up his Phillips-head screwdriver and ascended.

'So,' said Smith, the tone of his voice changing, 'Are you the one?'

'I'm sorry?' said Drake.

'The one who can see her?'

Drake wobbled on the ladder slightly. He tried to maintain a level pitch in his voice. 'I don't understand what you mean.'

Smith laughed. 'I think you do. Sorry, how rude of me – I should hold the ladder for you.'

'There's no need.'

Drake looked down as Smith moved across the room and placed his hands firmly on the ladder. 'I insist.' The man beamed up at him.

Drake considered him for a moment and then, in the absence of any better ideas, looked up and started unscrewing the dome on the camera.

'Does she show you?'

Drake, having recovered from the initial shock, maintained a casual tone as he worked. 'Does who show me what?'

'Our little friend. I assume if you can see her, then she can show you.'

Drake removed the casing and made a display of looking at the perfectly functioning camera inside. 'I don't know what you are referring to. As a matter of strict policy, we do not discuss guests with anyone outside of the immediate operational groups.'

'Blah, blah, yes, yes,' said Smith. 'I know. I knew from the moment I saw you. You're the one. I could give you some bullshit story about things that happen in a time of war, but let's not kid ourselves.'

Drake's hands shook as he disconnected the power and then rotated the camera to check the tracking.

'Are you afraid to look at me?' The voice was mocking now.

'No, I'm just trying to fix this camera.'

'We both know there's nothing wrong with the camera.'

Drake mumbled something, unable to come up with any words. He kept thinking of the screwdriver lying in his sweaty right hand. From here, he could jab it down, try to get it straight through the man's eye. His arms felt like jelly, though – barely able to move. Suddenly, he felt terribly weak.

The man continued to talk in a chatty tone. 'You know what they say – if you find the thing you were put here to do, then you never really work a day in your life. I loved it. I was good at it. Really good.' He laughed. 'Well, you saw. I miss it too – hopefully it won't be much longer before I am back doing the one thing I am truly good at. The world belongs to men like me. Men who can take what they want.'

The ladder shook slightly as he spoke. Drake didn't look down. He placed the dome back on the camera and started to screw it back on.

'I like your fear. The taste of it. I've missed it. Look at me.' The last three words came out as an inhuman growl.

Drake took a deep breath. He had decided on the way over. He would do it and then leave the house immediately and go to that reservoir on the M62. The one near the farmhouse that was famously in the middle of the motorway not because the owner had refused to move as the urban legend had it, but because it was built on a geological fault. Every time he'd passed the body of water, it had looked nice. He didn't like the idea of falling onto rocks, but somehow, water didn't seem so bad. He could go off the side of the waterfall there. From a certain height, landing on water can kill you just as instantly. And besides, he couldn't swim. That seemed like the best way. He would not want to answer questions as he wouldn't be able to begin to explain. He had always taken pride in his work, and he didn't want to be the man who had broken protocol.

He finished screwing the dome back into place, and the tremor in his hands eased. He knew what he must do now.

'Look. At. Me!'

Drake lowered his hands. He moved the screwdriver in his sweaty palm, adjusting his grip. As he finally looked down, he saw Smith's eyes, glowing red, and his mouth spread into a wide grin.

Drake drew back his right hand – and stopped. Over Smith's shoulder, he noticed the girl. She shook her head clearly. Telling him no.

Drake froze for a moment, and then he dropped the screwdriver. The sound of it hitting the tiled floor was like an alarm bell waking him from his sleep.

He descended the ladder quickly, not looking at Smith. 'Right, well, it seems fine to me. Let us know if the noise comes back and we will replace it.'

Drake's phone rang – it was Walsh confirming that the camera had come back online. He snatched up the screwdriver from the floor and shoved it back into the toolbox, before slamming the lid shut. Throughout, Smith stood there, his hands still on the ladder, and didn't say a word.

'Right. I shall get out of your way. Enjoy your dinner.'

Drake placed his hands on the ladder. Smith looked back at him. His eyes had returned to their normal brown, but the veneer of politeness and charm had dropped from his face, leaving a sneer in its place. 'You didn't do what you came here for.'

'Yes, I did. It seems to all be fine.'

Drake pulled the ladder and Smith released his grip reluctantly. Drake snapped it shut, picked up his toolbox and headed straight for the front door. Smith did not follow him out.

'Goodbye, then.'

Drake opened the door, exited and then shut it behind him. It was only as he reached the car that he realized he had felt something brush against his leg. He looked down and around, but there was nothing to be seen. He wedged the ladder into the boot of the car and shoved the toolbox in beside it.

He climbed into the front seat and threw the car into a sloppy three-point turn before pulling off the drive.

One hundred yards down the road, the car came to an abrupt halt as Drake opened the door just in time to vomit onto the road. He wiped his mouth with his handkerchief and looked at his hands, which were still shaking. Then, he glanced in the rearview mirror. The little girl was sat in the back seat. For the first time, she smiled at him, and then she was gone.

Drake went to work. He relieved Walsh, after a brief bout of their usual awkward small-talk. He took up his station just in time to watch Smith begin to eat the dinner he had been preparing. It appeared it didn't agree with him as he left it half finished. As Drake watched him scrape the remnants into the food bin, he realized that for the first time in a long time, he was doing so alone. The little girl was neither on the screen watching Smith nor in the room with him. Drake was alone. Well, almost.

'I could really go for some Custard Creams. Maybe one of them Vienna whirl things.'

Drake continued to watch the feed as Smith stomped round the house. He seemed to be in a bad mood. Restless. He threw the occasional surly glance in the direction of the cameras, but otherwise there was no acknowledgement. He half watched a Champions League football match before hitting his gym for some bag work, then a quick shower. He was in bed by 11.30 p.m. Drake duly logged his movements.

'Where do you stand on the big "are Jaffa Cakes a cake or a biscuit" debate?'

'Biscuit,' said Drake, surprising himself. He hadn't spoken to Dobson in months.

In the other houses, life continued as normal. The

Chinese couple argued, but it was a pretty mild one for them. The Knutsford family all sat down and watched a film together – a very rare event. Pixar. One of the *Toy Story*s. Drake couldn't tell which one.

The lady in Prestwich did some crochet, read a book, and then brought a device into the bathroom with her for some 'quality alone time', as Dobson used to call it, before going to bed. Everyone was all tucked up and logged as such by midnight.

At 1.37 a.m., just as Drake was opening his sandwiches – ham and egg – the lights came on in the Worsley house. Smith lay in bed, looking across the room at where the girl stood staring at him.

Smith laughed. 'Oh, for God's sake, it's you again.' He tossed a pillow in her direction. 'Piss off.'

The girl stood perfectly still and just watched.

Smith glanced up at the camera. 'This is so boring.'

He turned over, as if about to go back to sleep, but jumped as he noticed the cat sitting quietly on the other side of the room. 'For fuck's sake!'

He tossed another pillow in the cat's direction, but it dodged it and darted to the corner beneath the camera.

Drake tried to reposition the device, but the camera in the bedroom didn't have 360-degree functionality. There was a blind spot directly under it. He couldn't see what was happening, only Smith's face. He watched as the smug smile disappeared and was replaced with something else, something new. Fear.

During the internal inquiries, of which there were several, Drake would sit and watch this footage more than a hundred times. You could follow Smith's eyeline as it went from looking down at the cat on the floor, to rising slowly, as if something was growing before him. The last you saw of Smith was his expression of pleading terror as he looked into the camera. 'No. No. No!'

And then static as the feed went dead. The other cameras picked up the sound of screaming and extreme violence.

Drake had dutifully rang the number to log a potential security problem, and then he'd called and woken up Addler. The inquiries would all find that he had acted impeccably. A commendation was added to his file for his swift response. The Service was also very keen that he not talk about this. A big part of the OB12 job was discretion about all manner of things, but this was something different. His superiors had gone to great lengths to try to find an explanation for what had happened, as well as hiding the fact that they didn't have one.

When the armed response team showed up at the property, they had found nobody else there. No alarms had been triggered, and there was no sign of forced entry or exit. Mr Smith himself, or rather what was left of him, had been found in the bedroom. All over the bedroom. Drake hadn't been there in person, but he had seen the photos. The remains were smeared mostly across the walls, though there had been bits on the ceiling too. The audio had been analysed but it didn't help a bit. One of the experts swore that at one point they heard Smith screaming in ancient Sumerian, but seeing as there was no evidence that Mr Smith would have spoken this language, that was dismissed. The only thing everyone agreed on was that whatever had happened, it had been fast and incredibly painful. One of the auditors had passed the comment that he wouldn't have wished it on his worst enemy. Drake said nothing.

Soon enough, life went back to normal. When a truly

inexplicable event happens, it is like a rock being tossed into a stream. After the initial splash, life just flows around it and on it goes. Drake's life too, returned to normal. Once again, he was able to go home and sleep peacefully, content in his small little life. He just needed to remember to feed the cat before he went to sleep. She did not like to be kept waiting, and she could be quite the handful.

A DOG'S LIFE

Marcia looked up at the cold, clear sky while she took a drag on her cigarette. As she let it out, her frozen breath mingled with the smoke. It was rare to see a cloudless sky up here. She'd been in Manchester for a couple of months now, and she thought it might be the first one she'd seen. Having said that, she hadn't been looking up much. Her life had spiralled out of control so fast, there had been little reason to hold her head up high.

She pulled her coat around her more tightly. It and the scrubs weren't anywhere near enough to fend off the bitter 3 a.m. chill, but she sort of liked it. It made her feel a bit more alive, and given that she spent most of her time feeling half dead, that was no bad thing. She couldn't remember the last time she'd slept for more than two hours.

She was working the night shift providing emergency cover at a vets on an industrial estate. She couldn't tell you the name of it or where it was located. The GPS just told her where to go and she went. It was one of only two practices providing out-of-hours cover for the whole of Greater

Manchester, and she was working at 'the shit one'. A couple of customers had made that very clear. This one took care of the overspill when the other was too busy.

Everyone she met who wasn't Fiona on reception was an odd mix of panicked for their ill pet's wellbeing and angry at the cost of the treatment. It seemed that Fiona's main qualification for her job was her ability to paint her nails while delivering shocking estimates to distressed people for how much the attempt to save their beloved, furry family member would cost.

Some had pet insurance and others didn't. Having said that, a lot of policies don't cover out-of-hours assistance. When people heard the figure for their bill, they regularly dumped the aforementioned beloved family member on the practice doorstep and left in protest. Fiona was utterly unfazed by this. The woman could announce the commencement of World War Three while barely looking up from whatever new nail effect or finish she was trying out that night. She appeared to have an entire nail bar behind her desk. There was also a glass partition separating her from the punters, which was possibly why she felt the need to put so little effort into sweetening the financial pill for them.

Not that Marcia was complaining. She had been desperate for work – any work – and Fergus, who'd been in her class at uni, had put her on to this. It hadn't been said, but he was repaying a favour. Way back when, Marcia had done one of his assignments so that he wouldn't get kicked off the course. He'd gone AWOL for three weeks in a melodramatic break-up with a woman whose name he could no longer remember. Not that Marcia was in any position to judge on that front – not any more. At the time, she had been the star student of their year. The girl with the brightest of futures. All of that seemed a long time ago. Fifteen years? Fifteen months seemed like a lifetime ago.

She had been doing well. That's what people who knew her would say if she came up in conversation. 'Marcia – oh yeah, she's doing well.' No. 'Fine' – they'd probably say 'fine'. In her head, she realized that if she came up at all, it was quite probably as a conversational straw being grasped at by two people who really felt they should have more to talk about than they did. That was a depressing thought.

Mind you, she also got asked to go on a lot of hen dos. She thought that was maybe because she always accepted the invitation. She was never the most fun member of the party, but she showed up. Brides liked these things to be well attended, given how they're a reflection of how popular – and therefore worthy – they are as people. And so Marcia got invited because she went, and she'd always gone because she wanted to be somebody with friends.

The reality was that she got on with animals a lot better than with people. She would spend the week leading up to every hen do thinking of ways to get out of it, before invariably going, because she kept hearing her mother's voice in her head telling her to be 'one of those popular girls'. Which is how you end up in a pair of bunny ears, nursing a rum and Coke, wearing the only T-shirt without a nickname (because no one could think of one for you), counting down the hours until you can head back to the hotel.

In hindsight, maybe it had been overdue – her moment of rebellion. This is what happens if you don't dye your hair pink as a teenager, or take a year out to go travelling in your twenties: you end up having an affair with a married dentist and kidnapping his poodle.

This wasn't a euphemism. While the subsequent police

investigation had used several ugly words, Marcia felt that nowhere near enough weight had been given to her assertion that Trixie had a serious skin complaint and that Malcom's wife was not applying the cream twice daily, as instructed. The poor thing's hair was falling out. The dog, not the wife.

In fact, the wife had tried to pull out Marcia's hair in the regrettable fight. The memory that really turned Marcia's stomach was that of the look of horror mixed with horny glee on Malcolm's stupid bloody face as it had happened. Two women fighting over him was the highlight of the man's shitty life. Wait until the guys down at the golf club heard about that.

The reality was that Malcolm wasn't the cause of Marcia's breakdown, he was a symptom. Looking up at his sweaty, weak-chinned face, eyes screwed shut as he put all of his efforts into using her as a means to satisfy himself sexually, had been the most glaring sign possible that something was seriously, horribly wrong. Marcia had 'fought over him' simply because she so desperately wanted something in her life worth fighting for. His wife had fought because she didn't like people touching her stuff. Trixie had fought – joining in to bite the wife on the ankle – because Marcia guessed she was royally sick of that choke collar the bitch used.

Eventually, all charges had been dropped, thanks to the prospect of the mortifying embarrassment all round if the thing were to be dragged through the courts. Besides, the wife got what she wanted – a no doubt generous divorce from the tedious idiot whom she'd been screwing around on for years. And Marcia had clearly been punished. Her job at the most prestigious veterinary practice in Berkshire was gone – 'gross misconduct' it read on the piece of paper she still had somewhere. And, despite being highly qualified and previously highly thought of, she couldn't get a sniff at another job. It was like a variation on that old joke about the man who fixed the roof on the village church, but they don't call him Roofer John. Chopped down a whole forest but they don't call him Lumberjack John. But he shags one sheep ...

It didn't matter how many beloved family pets Marcia had saved over the years, she was the vet who had kidnapped one and taken it to a yurt in Wales for a week. So here she was, providing out-of-hours cover in the worst of the two places in the Greater Manchester area that did so, and she was lucky to have the job.

Marcia tossed away the butt of the cigarette as the walkie-talkie on her belt buzzed. This had better not be Fiona, asking her to come and look at another nail-polish colour chart, or she was going to lose it.

Marcia pressed the button. 'Yes, Fiona?'

'Got an emergency. Dog ate something it shouldn't have.'

'I'll be right there.'

Out of the trio waiting in reception, the dog looked the most ordinary. He, the dog, was a fairly ordinary Staffie mix, albeit one who looked extremely unhappy about his lot in life. His hair was short and white, and he had black pigmentation spots on his skin. As Marcia approached the group, the dog's baleful eyes looked out at her from his position whimpering under the chair.

The man was broad shouldered and heavyset, with a face that looked as if it'd met a fast-travelling shovel. Not unattractive, just remarkably flat. As if he had it permanently pressed up against an invisible pane of glass. Most of his body, bar his head, was covered in tattoos, the most prominent of which was the face of a nervous-looking clown on his left upper arm. There was also a particularly detailed band of thorny branches winding around his neck. He wore ripped jeans and a gilet over a sleeveless T-shirt, his arms seemingly impervious to the cold. Concern was writ large across his two-dimensional face as he stared down at the dog.

In contrast, the woman looked annoyed to be there. She was wearing an odd mix of black and pink. It was as if she'd been covered in glue, shoved in a cannon and fired through the wardrobes of a goth and a Disney princess. Marcia was no fashion guru, and there was undoubtedly someone out there who could pull off this look, but it wasn't this woman. Her sour expression, glowering with undisguised hatred at the dog, didn't help. It is one of life's universal truths that you can judge people by how they look at dogs.

'Hi,' said Marcia. 'What appears to be the trouble?'

'It's Rubble,' said the man, in a surprisingly soft voice. 'He's eaten something he shouldn't have.'

The woman scoffed. 'You can say that again.'

'Right,' said Marcia. 'What was it?'

In the last week alone, she had dealt with the after-effects of the consumption of two socks, a long length of rope and an entire box of Domino's cookies, dogs never having been accused of being one of nature's more discerning eaters.

The husband glanced at his wife before speaking. 'It was sort of like a marble. A bigger one. Gobstopper size.'

'Right,' said Marcia. 'When did this happen?'

'About midnight,' said the man. 'I tried giving him water and, y'know, hoped he'd chuck it back up.'

Marcia nodded. 'A lot of times, with this kind of thing, that's what would happen. It would come out one way or the other. Has he been trying to bring it back up?'

The man shook his head. 'No, he's just been whining.'

'Right.'

'Yes,' interjected the wife. 'The little idiot hasn't stopped.'

'It's not his fault, Yvonne.'

'Yes, it is,' snapped the woman apparently called Yvonne. 'He's a nuisance. Whiny little shit. I told you, Phil, he needs to stay out of my room when I'm working.'

'OK,' said Marcia, who was in no mood to sit through Phil and Yvonne's domestic. 'Let me take him through and examine him.'

'I'll have to go with you,' said Phil. 'He freaks out in the vets if I'm not there.'

'Well, if he's going, I'm going,' said Yvonne, looking around disdainfully 'I'm not going to sit here in this filth.'

'What filth?' chimed Fiona from behind the reception desk. 'This clinic is perfectly clean.'

Fiona took the subject of hygiene very much to heart. She personally buzzed in the cleaner every night at ten.

'That's a matter of opinion,' responded Yvonne.

'Fact,' said Fiona. 'It is a matter of fact.'

'OK,' said Marcia, 'let's not forget what's important here.'

'Rubble,' said Phil.

'My marble,' said Yvonne.

'My floors,' said Fiona.

Rubble whined. Marcia could sympathize.

Marcia completed her examination while Phil leaned in close to Rubble's face and spoke to him in a calming voice. It was undeniably sweet.

'It's all right, little dude. Everything is going to be fine. The nice lady will make you all better.'

'She'd better hurry up about it,' added Yvonne, from her seat in the corner.

'Maybe you should wait outside?' snapped Marcia, who'd had more than enough of this.

'Excuse me?' replied Yvonne, all outrage.

'I'm trying to work here. Your husband is helping me, but I'm afraid all you're doing is making it more difficult and distressing the dog.'

Yvonne leaned forward and jabbed a blood-red painted fingernail in the dog's general direction. 'Now, you listen to me, he is mine. You understand me? I own him. I decide what happens to him. Whether he lives or dies.'

Marcia looked over at Phil, who was still looking down at the dog's face, his eyes watering. Marcia caught sight of the clown tattoo on his left arm. It was the weirdest thing. Its face looked terrified now. It couldn't be. Must be a trick of the light, or maybe Marcia had got the arm wrong. Yes, that must be it. Plus, she really hadn't slept in a very long time.

'OK, said Marcia, addressing Phil pointedly. 'Normally I'd suggest monitoring Rubble overnight to see if it will come out on its own—'

'No way,' interrupted Yvonne. 'That's a non-starter. It has to be out by dawn.'

'I see,' said Marcia, not trying to hide her perplexed expression. That was a weird way of putting it – 'by dawn'. 'Well, given that it's an object – as opposed to a toxic substance such as chocolate, raisins, et cetera – then inducing vomiting is unlikely to work. The odds aren't great that he'd bring it up that way. That leaves us with laxatives, or else surgery.'

'How fast can you cut him open?' asked Yvonne.

'I think that should be a last resort. While Rubble's in

pain, he isn't showing signs of internal damage that would require invasive surgery. The laxative option is the most sensible.'

Phil nodded.

'We need it out as soon as possible,' said Yvonne.

Marcia looked Yvonne directly in the eye. 'I am not in the business of cutting animals open unnecessarily.'

Yvonne never got the chance to deliver whatever response she was winding up for. Her phone rang. She pulled it out of the inside pocket of her coat and answered it. 'Alfredo, thank God. This is a nightmare.' Without a word to anyone in the room, she stood up and stomped out, slamming the door behind her.

'Sorry about her,' said Phil.

'Well, I'm ...' Marcia felt suddenly embarrassed. 'I'm sure she means well.'

'No,' said Phil, in a near whisper, 'she doesn't.' He grabbed Marcia's hand, his eyes pleading. 'She's a horrible, horrible woman, but she owns Rubble. That's why I ... Please, you've got to help get this out of him.'

'OK, well, let's give him the laxative. And—'

Marcia was interrupted by Rubble opening his mouth wide and belching a brief but unmistakable gout of flame. She would have been inclined to believe that what she had just seen was an hallucination brought on by exhaustion, only Phil was kneeling beside her, slapping his beard to prevent it from catching fully alight. If anything, Rubble looked more perplexed by this turn of events than she did.

'I can explain,' said Phil.

'No need,' said Marcia. 'That happens all the time.'

'Really?'

Marcia let out an unhinged giggle as she sat gracelessly

on the floor. 'No. Your dog just burped flame. That is impossible. I know. Dogs cannot do that. I paid attention in veterinary school – I really did. Believe me, if that was a thing, I'm sure I'd remember.'

Phil looked at her, his big flat face filled with concern. 'Yvonne, she practises magic. Black magic.'

Marcia nodded. Maybe she'd crashed the car on the way in this evening? Now that she thought of it, there had been a moment when some idiot in a yellow Golf with a spoiler had come hurtling towards her on the wrong side of the road, trying to overtake where there was no overtaking. Maybe she'd really been involved in a head-on collision and was in a coma now. It was like that TV show, *Life on Mars*, only she'd been transported into a particularly dark reboot of *All Creatures Great and Small*, where everyone was angry and dogs belched flame.

'Are you OK?' asked Phil, not unkindly.

'I very much doubt it.'

'Can you help him?'

Marcia shrugged. 'I don't know what the cure is for burping flame. Probably some kind of antacid?' She laughed again.

'I know this must all seem mad,' said Phil.

'Yep.'

'But I need your help. I need you to focus. If we don't get this thing out of Rubble, Yvonne will, and she won't be gentle about it. The person she's talking to on the phone is a member of her coven.'

'Right – she's a witch?' said Marcia, nodding for reasons she wasn't sure of.

'They prefer "magical practitioner".'

'What?'

'Not "witch". The word has some very negative connotations to it,' said Phil.

'Didn't you just imply she was going to kill the dog?'

'All right, it might apply in her case.'

Marcia pulled herself up off the floor and sat on one of the plastic chairs. 'I'm in no position to give relationship advice, but have you considered making a run for it with the dog?'

'I can't,' said Phil.

'Why not?'

Phil went to speak but stopped. Marcia watched in amazement as the tattooed garland of thorns around his neck appeared to twist and tighten. Phil's eyes widened with terror and he spoke in a rat-a-tat rhythm. 'Yvonne is the love of my life. Yvonne is the love of my life. Yvonne is the love of my life.'

After a moment, the tattoo seemed to release its grip, and Phil started to breathe easily. Marcia noticed a trickle of blood where, if such a thing was possible, she would have been inclined to suggest that one of the thorns had drawn blood.

Phil cleared his throat. 'Don't worry about anything else. We just need to help Rubble.'

'OK,' said Marcia. 'What exactly did he eat? This marble – I'm guessing it isn't just a marble.'

Phil nodded. 'It's used to summon demons.'

'Course it is.' Marcia rubbed her fingers over her eyes. 'I am so far beyond tired. You have no idea.'

She took her hands away to see Phil and Rubble both looking up at her with puppy-dog eyes.

'All right, and I can't believe I'm saying this, but what does she summon these demons for?'

'Stock tips, mostly,' answered Phil.

'Right. Makes sense.'

'She's a very wealthy woman,' said Phil. 'She runs an investment portfolio for some other … people.' It was the way he said 'people' that made Marcia pretty certain the individuals in question wouldn't be that surprised by a dog belching flame.

'OK,' said Marcia, 'let's assume for a second this isn't all the final stages of my breakdown. What do you expect me to do? I was out the day we covered exorcizing demons from dogs.'

'He's not possessed,' said Phil, with an air of admonishment. 'He's just swallowed a highly powered magical item.'

'You're right. I'm being melodramatic.'

'The point is,' Phil continued, 'we have to get it out of him or else … she will. By any means necessary. It took all I had to convince her to bring him here first.'

Marcia stood and opened the door at the back of the examination room, to where the supplies were kept. 'And why can't I just call the police? Or the RSPCA? Or, I dunno, a priest?'

'Believe me,' said Phil. 'None of that will work against Yvonne. She's very powerful.'

'Super.' Marcia found what she was looking for. 'All right, I'm going to give him a laxative. Given the circumstances, it's a pretty big dose. It works by promoting peristalsis – the muscle contractions that push food along the gut.'

'Will it work fast?'

'It should, but hard to say just how fast, given the – let's say, unusual conditions.'

Marcia administered the enema and then scratched

Rubble behind the ear. 'Hang in there, big guy. You'll be better soon.'

The dog licked her hand with his warm, wet tongue.

'Now what?' asked Phil.

Marcia leaned back in the chair. 'We wait.'

They sat there for a minute in an amicable silence. Marcia felt her eyelids dip into a too-long blink. She jerked herself awake.

'Are you OK?' asked Phil.

'Not even a little. He seems like a very nice dog.'

'He is.'

Marcia nodded and then, for reasons she didn't understand, added, 'I've been taking animals home. Ones that are scheduled for termination. The pricks on the day shift schedule the terminations to happen at night. I've not been able to do it. I mean, I have before, but for the last couple of weeks, I've just … not. My flat now contains three dogs, six cats, a tortoise, two gerbils and a parakeet.'

Phil nodded. 'Right.'

'It's pretty noisy.'

'I'll bet.'

'If anyone finds out, I'll be struck off.'

'For keeping animals alive?'

'Yeah.'

'That's mad.'

'So am I. A bit.' Marcia gave Phil a weak smile.

'You don't seem mad.'

'No offence,' said Marcia, glancing at the door, 'but are you sure you're in the best position to judge?'

Phil smirked at this, and then a wide grin broke across his big flat face. Marcia laughed in return, and before they knew it they were both in hysterics, while Rubble looked on from the floor, confused by it all.

The door flew open and Yvonne stalked in. 'What the hell is going on here?'

Perhaps it was Rubble's terror at her return or the nature of the foreign object, but something caused the laxative to kick in at that precise moment. It resulted in a rather explosive and splattery mass expulsion from Rubble's rear end, which permanently damaged the resale value of Yvonne's leather boots although, arguably, they now coordinated much better with the rest of the outfit.

Marcia howled with laughter. She couldn't stop. Tears filled her eyes as Yvonne stood there, mouth agape, as the monumental justice dripped off her onto the similarly covered floor. Rubble had clearly eaten a great deal, not including the object in question.

Speak of the devil, a soft *doink* followed as a large marble filled with swirling colours finally appeared out of the very relieved hound's backside.

Marcia, trying to recover control of her breathing, looked down at it. She spoke while wiping the tears from her eyes. 'There you go. Problem solved.'

Marcia would have bet that Yvonne's seemingly permanently sour expression had nowhere to go in the disgust stakes, but she'd have lost that wager. The woman looked like, well, someone who had been on the wrong end of volatile canine diarrhoea. Sometimes there is no simile.

'It's ... It's ...' said Yvonne.

'Oh, relax,' said Marcia, feeling unaccountably giddy. 'Here, I'll get it ...'

'No!'

Yvonne's scream came too late. As soon as Marcia

touched the marble, a blinding flash of light and a wave of energy threw her backwards, causing her chair to tip over and slamming her into the wall.

Marcia blinked, trying to regain her vision. Her hand – her entire right arm, in fact – was numb. She could feel the trickle of something on her forehead – possibly blood. It was hard to tell. She might've hit her head on something in the confusion.

'Who summons me?' The voice was deep, unnaturally deep. It sounded as if it had entered the air from beneath the ground.

Marcia's sight began to clear. The first thing she saw was the hooves. Then, as her eyes and her brain collectively got their act together, they were able to take in the rest of it. Standing in the middle of the room, was a ... demon. Marcia's mind couldn't believe it was using the word, but no other fit. Hooves, horns, red skin, and a face that looked as if the off-cuts bin at a butcher's had come back to life and wasn't happy about it. The whole terrifying look was slightly undermined by two things: first, the creature was only about four-foot-six in height; and second, it was wearing an apron with the slogan 'You don't have to be mad to cook here, but it helps' emblazoned across it, above a quizzical-looking cat in a chef's hat.

'I am the great Mar'ach'ta,' roared the creature. 'Who has summoned me?'

To Marcia's ear he sounded irritated, but it was hard to tell. She had little experience with demons.

'I ...' started Yvonne. 'It was I, your Lordship. I summoned you.'

The demon looked hard at Yvonne and nodded. 'And why,

pray tell, am I standing in, covered in and generally surrounded by excrement?'

He was definitely irritated. Marcia was sure of it now.

'I ... I apologize, my Lord.'

'You performed the rite of Ashacanta?'

'Yes, my Lord.'

The demon nodded. 'That demands that I answer your questions.' It looked around. 'However, it also states that you must have certain offerings in place ...'

'I did, my Lord.'

'And though it is not expressly stated,' continued the demon, 'it is heavily implied that the area of summoning should not be covered in shit.'

'Please, I ...'

'It is all right,' said the demon.

Yvonne seemed to sag with relief. 'Really?'

'Really,' it said, with what was possibly a smile. Certainly, parts of the hellish visage rearranged themselves in a way that suggested it. 'You see, as a demon, I have to put up with this crap. Answering your inane questions, being at your beck and call.'

'I apologize about—'

'But this time,' said the demon, 'as the ritual has not been followed correctly, I am unbound.'

Marcia didn't know what that meant, although the terror in Yvonne's face should have been a clue.

Marcia would never be able to explain what happened next. Even if one day she found the words to describe everything that had happened up to that point, the next bit would remain resolutely inexplicable.

A couple of years ago, Marcia had been convinced to go to a pub quiz. Her team had lost on a tiebreaker that was one hundred per cent incorrect. There is a commonly accepted myth – one also believed by that particular inept quizmaster – that certain snakes can dislocate their jaws in order to consume prey larger than the snake. They can't. The reality is more complicated.

As a veterinarian, Marcia knew all too well that a snake's jaw has more complex joints than other vertebrates. Instead of detaching, it has more than one hinge point, which enables far greater flexibility. She could have drawn diagrams and explained this. Instead, when her clarification had been arrogantly rebuffed by the quizmaster, she had held her tongue and spent the next three days being irrationally irritated by it.

Demons, on the other hand, looked as if they really could detach their jaws. Certainly, that was the first point in a no doubt multipoint and detailed explanation as to how a four-foot-six demon leaped in the air and, in one shocking moment, swallowed Yvonne whole, leather boots and all.

It pulled a face and stuck out its tongue, speaking now in a much more conversational tone. 'Ugh, that tasted disgusting. Still, it is the principle of the thing.'

Marcia held her breath as the demon looked down first at her and then over to the far corner, where Phil and Rubble were cowering.

'Any questions?'

Marcia shook her head, as did Phil.

'Right, then. By the way – nice dog.' The demon twirled its hands in the air and became filled with a strange purple glow. Then it glanced down at its apron, noticing for the first time that there was also some shit on it. 'Oh, for ... This was a present!'

And then, with a soft popping noise, it was gone.

Marcia and Phil sat there for a few seconds, looking at each other numbly.

'Is she ...?' asked Marcia.

'I think she is,' said Phil, in a whisper. 'I think she's gone.'

Marcia pointed at the tattoo on Phil's neck. 'Your thing on your neck. It's ... it's withering and dying.' In fact, all the tattoos that Marcia could see on his skin seemed to be changing. Brightening. The clown on his left arm was beaming a wide grin at the world.

Phil hugged Rubble tightly. 'She's gone, boy. We're free!'

The dog licked his owner's face enthusiastically.

As they started to get Marcia to her feet, the door opened. Fiona stood there. It occurred to Marcia that she'd never seen the receptionist standing up before. She'd always assumed the woman had legs, but after the night she'd had, nothing could be taken for granted.

Fiona looked around the room in silence before nodding. 'That witch gone, then, is she? Never liked her sort. Got a peaky rabbit in examination room three.'

And with that, she turned and left.

Pet Project

We here at *The Stranger Times* love to update our readers on further developments in stories we've previously reported. Remember Marcia Green, the vet who dognapped the poodle of the man with whom she was having an affair? Well, we're delighted to inform you that she has found happiness, and yesterday married one Philip Clunk in a civil ceremony. The duo are setting up the country's first hospice for terminally ill animals, on a farm in Cheshire. We wish them well.

PAINT BY NUMBERS

Lorna heard it before she saw it. That unmistakable murmur of intense conversation at the top of the stairs. Instantly, she felt a sickly mix of excitement and dread in the pit of her stomach. Diablo had struck again.

The staircase in question led up to Element Games, which occupied the entire first floor above a warehouse and an Aikido dojo. From the outside, the building didn't look like much. It was located on a small industrial estate that looked much like every other small industrial estate, except its car park had so many potholes you could only assume they must be deliberate – an art installation celebrating the pothole throughout history, possibly. When it rained, people needed dinghies to reach their cars, and this was Stockport, so it rained a lot.

Inside, though, was another matter. Lorna had once heard a staff member describe the place as 'nerd nirvana', and it was hard to disagree with that. It stocked every board game, tabletop war game and role-playing game under the sun, not to mention all the paints and supplies required to complete the miniatures that were such a core part of the aforementioned. For those outside the cult, the existence of such a place would perhaps come as a surprise. This was the age of the Xbox, virtual reality and online gaming, after all. Did people still play board games, except perhaps at Christmas? The reality was, it was a billion-pound industry that was booming like never before. The reasons for its boom were numerous, but one that was easy to point to was that when everything had been locked down, paint sets and models could still be delivered to your door and, suddenly, a lot of people with disposable income had nothing better to do with their time. It turned out even this generation could get sick of screens.

Lorna didn't play. A couple of years ago, she'd been living with Carl, who also didn't play, but who, at one point, had decided he would. Never a man for half measures, or indeed logic, he'd spent money that could have sent them on a nice holiday, acquiring an army of space marines, of which he'd painted a total of two before losing interest. Carl was also a great man for giving up as soon as he realised he wasn't instantly great at something. This had also been his attitude to being a boyfriend. The fact that the pair had stayed together for as long as they had said more about Lorna's self-image than she was prepared to admit.

If she was honest, Lorna had only started to paint the miniatures out of spite. Initially, at least. In hindsight, taking up a time-consuming hobby with the sole intention of annoying your partner was probably another rather obvious sign of a relationship doomed to fail, but you never see these things that clearly when you're in the midst of the battle. And so, Carl had argued with Korean teenagers on the PS5 while Lorna had hidden away in the spare room, painting. There were myriad tutorials on YouTube and she'd always loved art at school, but everyone knew there were no jobs in it (and that was before AI made graphic design the new spinning jenny).

When she'd finished the army, she'd been rather pleased with it. Carl had made a point of showing no interest, but she'd caught him sneaking a look when he thought she'd gone to bed. All those completed miniatures just sat there on the shelf – a monument to a relationship that was going nowhere. She and Carl finally broke up after her sister literally bumped into him in the Northern Quarter as he was exiting a massage parlour on his way to work – and not the kind of place you'd go for an actual massage. He'd denied everything of course, but even now, part of Lorna still wanted an explanation. Him being a sleazy arse didn't come as a massive shock, but really – eight o'clock in the morning? Nobody was that much of a morning person.

When he'd moved out, Carl had taken the space marines with him, and the last text they'd exchanged was him gleefully explaining that he'd sold them on eBay for three times as much as he'd bought them for. His intention had been to piss her off, and he had, initially. Then, she'd gone out and bought herself some more, painted them and sold them for five times their original cost. Eighteen months later, she had more commissions than she could comfortably take on and had turned miniature painting into a full-time job. It seemed people would gladly pay for quality, and the more she painted, the better she became. In fact, she'd been heralded by more than a few people as being the best at what she did – the best in the area, at least. She'd even been encouraged to enter the Golden Demon, or one of the other prestigious painting competitions, and she was seriously considering it. It'd certainly be good for business. But then Diablo had happened.

She trudged up the stairs to Element Games, expecting the worst. She'd only been dropping in to pick up some airbrush cleaning fluid. The morning had found her feeling pretty good. Focused. Energised. And now this. A kicking her self-confidence could do without.

It was 11 a.m. on a Monday, but there was still a crowd of about a dozen worshippers gathered around one of the display cabinets by the entrance. They would have been considerably closer had it not been for the restraining force that was Rachel, self-appointed crowd steward, who'd positioned herself at the front of the pack.

'Stop breathing on the glass,' she instructed one of the most earnest of the acolytes.

'I have to breathe.'

'That's debatable,' came the icy response. Rachel possessed the kind of untapped fury that could come only from a career in teaching children music. Lorna liked her, but she had to acknowledge that if she ever found out Rachel had snapped and gone on a killing spree with a recorder, she wouldn't be one hundred per cent surprised.

'Can I touch it?' asked another member of the crowd.

Rachel fixed him with a steely look. 'Anything of yours touches that glass, don't expect to be getting it back.'

'OK,' came a voice. It was Keith, Rachel's husband and the manager of Element Games, who was moving through the crowd, a tight smile on his lips. 'Let's ease up on the overt threats of violence. I'm sure everyone understands the rules.'

Rachel narrowed her eyes. 'They will after we make an example of one of them.'

Keith placed a hand on his wife's arm and began to guide

her away. 'I think your blood sugar might be low. Let's get you a banana.'

'But the display—'

'Is in a cabinet,' finished Keith, before adding for the benefit of the gathered crowd, 'that is alarmed, and if anyone touches it, they're banned from the shop, just like the sign says.' There was indeed such a sign. 'Also, love – you don't actually work here.'

'This place needs discipline!'

'Does it, though?'

Rachel pointed at the cabinet as she was being dragged away. 'Obey the sign!'

Even from her position at the rear of the crowd, Lorna could see the new miniature. You could say it didn't look like much – in the sense that the other cabinets contained larger, more elaborate monsters, entire massed armies, complex dioramas and all manner of other displays. The new miniature was just one solitary figure, four centimetres high – a knight in battered armour, holding a bloodied sword down by his side and staring off into the distance. It was painted to an exquisite standard but it was the eyes that drew her attention. This was the third example of the mysterious Diablo's work that Lorna had seen, and each time, the eyes had been inexplicable. It wasn't the cliché that they followed you across the room so much as they looked right through you. It was as if the figure's mind were elsewhere.

Somehow, using just paint – presumably the same paint everyone else had access to – Diablo managed to instil a chilling amount of humanity in their work. The first piece had been a portly Viking wielding a Warhammer with a look of wild-eyed rage across his bearded face; the second a female druid cowering with fear; and this one, a bloodied knight somehow haunted by battle. Lorna was good – very good – but not only was she unable to match the level of skill those figures demonstrated, she couldn't even begin to tell you how Diablo had done it. Nobody could. Not that it stopped them from trying.

'I heard Diablo studied with Tibetan monks,' said a young man near the front.

'Oh, aye,' said one of his older companions 'Those famous miniature-painting monks. I think they live one mountain over from the equally famous Corby-registered heating-repair monks.'

The take-down was greeted with a raft of poorly stifled giggles and smirks from the rest of the throng.

'That's just what I heard,' said the younger man defensively, fighting the losing battle to maintain the honour of his take.

'I heard Diablo uses speed paints,' said another voice.

'Speed paints?' scoffed the self-appointed arbiter of these things. 'Are you mad? You'd never get that level of detail with speed paints. You mark my words – it's nanobots. That figure isn't painted at all, it's been assembled at a subatomic level by top-secret NASA technology.'

It was the stuff of science fiction, but Lorna watched as everyone studied the figurine again, and then couldn't bring themselves to discount the theory entirely.

Fifteen minutes later, Lorna had picked up her order. It had taken a lot longer than normal as the shop was rammed. She passed Keith on the way out, restocking a display of paint sets.

'Busy day?' she asked.

'Yeah, a new Diablo certainly brings out the crowds. It's only been there for a couple of hours. Thanks to social media, we'll be packed out all week. All month, probably.' He grinned to himself, the smile of a manager of an independent business who was going to have to order in more stock.

'Any chance of the mysterious Diablo turning up and taking a bow?'

Keith shook his head. 'He or she doesn't seem interested. Just sends it in.'

'Really? You must have some way of getting in contact with them, though?'

Keith gave Lorna a shrewd look. 'I was wondering when you'd get around to asking. Everyone else has.'

'I just—'

'Let me save you some time, Lorna. They don't take commissions, host masterclasses, answer emails asking for tips. None of it.'

'But …'

Keith stopped and gave her his full attention. 'Look, you're a good painter. A great one. Don't go comparing yourself to other people. Trust me on this – that way madness lies. Now, if you'll excuse me, we're out of black spray cans and I need to stop my staff from spending the day peering into a display cabinet with everyone else.'

Madness – that was the word Keith had used, wasn't it? Madness. If this was not that, then it was certainly madness-adjacent. Lorna was sitting in her car at 3 a.m. while the rain sheeted down around her, a full-on torrent.

She'd gone home and spent the rest of the day in the spare room she rather grandly referred to as her studio. She had a lot of work to get done – two big commissions to finish – but she'd just sat there, holding a brush between her fingers, unable to do anything. She looked round at the shelves that surrounded her. Everything she'd ever done was simply not good enough. She was trapped under an avalanche of her own inadequacies and there was only one way out. One person who could pull her to safety, whether they bloody well wanted to or not.

That was why she was here, parked up on the street outside Element Games, considering doing something incredibly stupid. It wasn't technically a burglary – at least she didn't think it was. She wasn't intending to take anything beyond information. It was, however, definitely both breaking and entering. She hadn't bothered googling the legal definition of that. Now that she thought about it, though, breaking without the entering was just vandalism, and entering without breaking – well, that was just wandering in, wasn't it? Even as she pretended to consider her options, she knew she was going ahead with this stupid idea. She'd known it when she'd got into the car. In fact, she'd known it as soon as she'd gone looking for the black leather gloves she was now wearing.

Somewhere in that building, presumably in Keith's office, would be contact information for whoever the hell Diablo was. If Keith wasn't going to give it to her, she'd take it. Painting was the one thing in her life at which she'd ever been truly great, and she'd be damned if she was going to give it up without a fight.

She'd noticed earlier that the fencing between the council-run car park and the industrial estate had been damaged, meaning it was easy to access the site. From there, a raft of scaffolding ran around the building. All she had to do was climb it, find a likely looking window and gain entry. In the small satchel sitting on the passenger seat beside her was a screwdriver and a hammer. She also had a wad of twenty-pound notes shoved into the pocket of her jeans. She'd leave it behind to pay for the window. She wasn't a criminal, she was an artist – albeit one who was about to commit a crime.

The fence proved harder to circumvent than expected, resulting in her catching her jeans on the top, stumbling and scraping her palms on the car-park gravel as she landed. Luckily, the place wasn't big enough to warrant employing a security guard to patrol it. At least, she didn't think it was. It occurred to her belatedly that she probably should have checked first. Ah, well, too late now. The scaffolding proved similarly more challenging than anticipated. Lorna hadn't really exercised since school, and she hadn't even been good at it then, so a series of metal poles slippery with icy rain thwarted her admittedly sketchy plan of nimbly scaling the building like Catwoman minus the impractical leather outfit. Eventually, she'd resorted to borrowing a wheelie bin belonging to the garage next door and clumsily managed to get a leg up on to the first platform on her fourth attempt.

And so it was, scratched, bruised and thoroughly soaked, that Lorna found herself in front of a row of windows. If everything had been harder than expected to this point, it seemed her luck had finally taken a turn. Even in the dim light offered from the streetlights, she could see that one of the casements was ajar. Not only that, she was ninety per cent sure it was the one to Keith's office. No breaking required, just entering. That'd save her a few quid, not to mention leaving her feeling less like a dirty criminal.

She pushed the window open carefully and took a final

surreptitious look around to make sure she wasn't being observed. As she lowered her soggy, sneakered foot down on to the carpet inside, Lorna had a brief moment of feeling like she sort of knew what she was doing. This lasted just as long as it took the bastard cat, who'd no doubt been waiting for the perfect moment, to land on the scaffolding right beside her. It didn't even acknowledge her presence. Not that it had much chance to do so, as the involuntary spasm of terror that passed through her body caused her to fall through the window with a squeal and end up in a wet heap on the floor of the dark office.

The briefly dark office, that is. She'd just been regathering herself when the lamp on the desk turned on to reveal Keith sitting behind it. 'All right, Lorna – always nice to see an enthusiastic customer.'

'I …' Lorna didn't say anything else because there wasn't that much else to say. She slumped to the floor again and threw up her hands. 'OK, call the police.'

Keith looked down at her as he scratched his neck. 'I should.'

'Were you waiting in here for me?'

'Yeah. I recognised the look. You're not the first person to try this.'

'Seriously?' she asked. 'And you've been sitting there all night?'

''Fraid so, but be honest, it looked pretty cool when I turned the light on, didn't it?'

'You're weird.'

'Says the woman who I assume is breaking in to find out how to get hold of a stupid painter?'

Lorna folded her arms. 'Technically, I didn't break, I only entered.'

'Only because I left the window open. This office is cold enough when the window hasn't been smashed in.'

'You're enjoying this, aren't you?'

'I've been sitting here for three hours doing accounts on my own time. You're damn right I'm enjoying this. I'm a man who enjoys being right about stuff.'

'Congrats,' she said.

'Thanks. And would now be a good time for me to repeat the salient points from our chat earlier? Forget about Diablo. Comparisonitus can be fatal if you don't treat the infection quickly.'

'I just …' Lorna looked Keith directly in the eyes. 'I need to know.'

'Are you seriously going to make me go into the clichés about curiosity's effect on the life expectancy of cats?'

Lorna pointed out the window. 'If I ever get hold of that bastard moggy on the scaffolding, it won't be curiosity that kills it …'

'It's a guard cat. You leave it alone. You're the criminal here.'

'I need to know,' she repeated.

Keith stared down at her for a long moment then shook his head. 'Great. So, either I call the police or I give you what you want, because if I don't, you're going to try this or something equally stupid again, aren't you?'

Lorna hadn't thought that far ahead but she realised he was right.

'Yeah,' he said, without waiting for a response. 'That's what I figured.' He sighed and wrote something on a Post-it note. 'It's the address of a PO box in Macclesfield that we send painting supplies to. That's all I've got.'

He peeled off the Post-it and held it out between two

fingers. As Lorna went to grab it, he pulled it away. 'For what it's worth, let me say, yet again, this is a terrible idea that'll lead you nowhere good.'

Lorna said nothing – she just stared intently at his hand. After a few seconds, he tutted loudly and handed her the Post-it note. 'And move that bin back before you leave.'

———

It was on the third day of her stakeout that Lorna started to feel like a fool. Actually, no – it was on the first day. The morning after her night-time meeting with Keith, she'd arrived in Macclesfield at 9 a.m. with the plan to watch the post boxes at the Mail Boxes Etc. branch. It was about 9.05 when she realised how stupid an idea it was.

She made her way inside and stood there awkwardly while the woman behind the counter – five minutes into her working day and apparently already bored out of her mind – stared at her like a spillage she was unwilling to deal with. Lorna proceeded to engage her in an awkward conversation about renting a mailbox and was given a pamphlet. She also managed to extract the information that the mailboxes were out the back and people could only access theirs once they showed ID. Lorna then made her way back outside and hung around on the street outside for a while, trying and failing to look inconspicuous. There was a pub beside the shop, but it offered no view of the entrance, and even if it did, she couldn't see the mailboxes. The stakeout idea had proven entirely impractical. She'd driven home feeling defeated. Until inspiration had struck.

The next day, she was back at 9 a.m. and delivering a package to the same woman behind the counter. If the woman recognised Lorna she gave no indication of it, but then again, she was also giving off strong vibes that she was considering ending it all by lunchtime, so it was hard to say. Lorna had walked back to her car feeling positively giddy. The parcel she'd delivered to the mailbox number contained a Warhammer 40K Space Marines Terminator Chaplain Tarentus. A single rare model, still in its box, costing over a hundred quid – if you could get hold of one at all. She'd been given it to paint and it wasn't hers to give away, but she'd deal with that later. The reason she was so pleased with herself was that also inside the box was an Apple AirTag synced to her phone. She'd carefully opened the packaging, placed the tag inside and then resealed it. As soon as Diablo picked up the box, she'd be able to track them.

Her initial optimism drained away over the next couple of days. She was sitting in her car parked one hundred yards away from Mail Boxes Etc., watching the Find My icon resolutely refusing to move. It was swiftly dawning on her that it could be weeks, maybe even months, before Diablo came to check their mailbox. Another thought played on her mind. Keith may have sent her on a total wild-goose chase to teach her a lesson. She didn't know him well – was he the practical joke sort? The idea festered in her brain throughout the day, and by 4 p.m. she was convinced that was the case. Her hand was on the car key in the ignition, and she was all set to drive back to Stockport and give Keith a piece of her mind, with a possible side order of violence, when the icon started to move.

At first, she couldn't believe it. She stared at the screen of her phone, which was attached to the dashboard, in stupefied silence as the icon sauntered down Park Green Road like it wasn't the most incredible exciting thing ever.

'Shit!' Lorna hollered, remembering why she was there, and started the car. She reversed out of the space, narrowly avoiding hitting a grown man on a scooter, and took off in hot pursuit. She turned the corner just in time to see the icon stop about a hundred yards ahead of her, where a figure in a green hoodie, hood pulled up against the drizzle, was climbing into the passenger side of a blue Ford Fiesta. As the car pulled away, the icon picked up speed, confirming Lorna's suspicions.

As car chases went, it wasn't that exciting – mainly because it wasn't really a chase. She followed from a distance of what she reckoned was a few hundred metres as the icon proceeded along the A537 towards Buxton. Theoretically, the tag would work anywhere but the reality was it needed wifi networks or nearby devices, or something. As they drove up into the Peak District, Lorna really wished she'd taken some time over the past couple of days to read up on how the damn tag thing worked exactly, instead of spending approximately fourteen hours playing Candy Crush.

They climbed higher into the hills where buildings of any kind became fewer and farther between, and Lorna grew more and more nervous. The traffic was light and the only signs of life she encountered were the occasional car coming the other way and bored-looking sheep regarding her impassively over fences. Mobile coverage was patchy up here at best – her phone was showing one bar of 3G. The rain was steadily getting heavier and it was starting to get foggy, or there was every possibility she was ascending into low-hanging clouds.

And then – the icon disappeared. One second it was there, the next it was gone. Lorna accelerated around a couple of bends, expecting to see the blue Ford Fiesta come into view but it didn't. She increased her speed to 70 mph – far too fast for this road in any conditions, let alone these, but she was desperate now. Eighty miles per hour. After fifteen minutes of increasingly reckless driving, she caught up with a white van, but there was no sign of the blue Ford Fiesta. It was virtually impossible to overtake on this stretch of road, which meant that odds on, she'd lost it. Damn it! She should have stayed closer.

She pulled into a layby and executed a highly illegal U-turn. There'd been a couple of small roads branching off the main one – perhaps she should head down one of them and pick up the scent? Even as the thought crossed her mind, it felt like the longest of long shots. Still, it was all she had.

It was only when she reached the point where she'd originally lost the tracking that she finally admitted to herself that somehow she'd blown this. Diablo would find the AirTag and undoubtedly change their method of receiving post, leaving Lorna none the wiser, sitting at her desk, unable to paint while dodging calls from Gary Trainer asking where the hell his Terminator Chaplain had got to.

She slammed on the brakes and skidded into another tiny layby, which was really nothing more than a parking space. The sudden urge to stop had gripped her as she just didn't trust herself to keep driving. Tears were flowing down her face now. Messy, snotty tears. Not the kind of crying you see in movies. Some part of her was aware she was having a kind of breakdown. Painting had been something into which she'd invested all her self-esteem, and it'd all gone great until someone better had come along, and then this. Breaking into Element Games, stalking some poor person who just wanted to be left in peace, losing her mind chasing a phantom around the Peak District.

Lorna had no idea how long she'd been sitting there for, but she dried her eyes on the sleeve of her hoodie. Time to pull herself together, go home, possibly get drunk, and then, tomorrow, give herself a damn good talking-to about letting her obsessive side run away with itself like this. This could be a learning experience. She could come out of it a better person, and besides, beyond embarrassing herself in front of Keith and having to come up with some kind of story to explain this away to Gary Trainer, what harm had she done, really?

Learning experience.

She reached out to turn on the ignition and stopped. The icon was back. The bloody icon was back! Not only that, it was just a couple of hundred metres away and stationary. Up the hill from where she was. But it didn't make sense, unless ...

In her defence, you'd never see it from a moving vehicle. A gate, so overgrown with weeds and bushes that it looked to be part of the verge. Snatching her phone from its cradle, Lorna climbed out of the car and hurried across the road, too distracted to remember to pick up her coat from the back seat. As the mizzle soaked through her hoodie she inspected the previously unnoticed gate. Up close she could see it wasn't merely overgrown. It had been camouflaged. Diablo really did not want visitors. Lorna stood there for a long moment, only coming back to the present when a truck whooshed by, startling her. The phone in her hand showed the motionless icon at the top of the hill. She could turn back now, learning experience and all that, or ...

She climbed over the gate before she'd even made a conscious decision. Behind it lay a rough track that wound up the slope, avoiding rocky outcrops. Lorna zipped up her hoodie, shivering as the cold wind whipped through her soaking clothes. The hill wasn't that far in the distance but, given the gradient of the path, she was breathing hard when she reached the top. If someone had asked, she wouldn't have been able to tell them what she'd been expecting to find, but this wasn't it.

The Ford Fiesta was parked beside a small ramshackle shed, which was leaning haphazardly against the rockface. It looked as if it'd blow over in a decent breeze, only there was more than that blowing already. Lorna slowly approached the red door with its peeling paint. Now that she was here, wherever exactly here was, it occurred to her that she had no idea what she was going to say to whoever was behind that door. 'Hi, sorry to go against your express wish for privacy and all of the measures you've taken to assure it, but I'm a fellow painter and I need you to tell me how you're so good.' It wasn't that it'd sound unhinged, it was more that it very definitely was unhinged. Still, she was here now, and, at the very least, he or she might throw Gary Trainer's Chaplain Tarentus at her, which would solve that problem.

She stopped in front of the door and knocked.
Nothing.
She waited and then knocked again. Louder this time.
Still nothing.
She cleared her throat. 'Hi! Hello, I'm really sorry to bother you. I'm … My name is Lorna and I'm … a big fan of your work.'

It sounded incredibly weak to her and worthy of mocking laughter, but none came. There was still no response.

'Look, I'm not leaving, so …'
Still nothing. She was getting annoyed now.

'I know you're in there. At least have the decency to tell me to fuck off.'

Still nothing.

'Right, screw it – I'm coming in.'

Lorna pushed open the door to find a largely empty shed. Inside was a small camping stove and a battered metal kettle sitting beside it, along with one chipped mug. Beside the mug was the box containing Gary Trainer's Chaplin. Apart from those items, there was also a wardrobe standing against the back wall. Lorna picked up the box and then, because how could she not, she opened the wardrobe.

There was nothing in it – no objects, at least. It served to conceal an opening in the rock wall that led into a cave revealed by dim guide lights, descending into the unseen distance.

'You have got to be shitting me.'

Her voice echoed back to her.

'All right,' she said, deliberately raising her volume. 'If you're down there, and I'm assuming you are, know that I'm coming down. I'm ... I'm pretty sure I've entirely lost my mind but I'm here for painting tips.'

She advanced into the cave. The path was only wide enough to allow one person at a time to walk down it. As her eyes adjusted to the dimness, she could see ahead of her a little more, but all that was revealed was more cave, descending ever downward. The only sound was the rat-a-tat of various water drips competing against each other to set the rhythm. A draught blew in from somewhere, causing goosebumps to rise on Lorna's arms. She kept expecting something to lurch out at her from the darkness as her imagination worked overtime in all manner of unhelpful ways.

She yelped as a voice boomed out of the depths.

'Turn back now. Final warning.'

'For Christ's sake!' Lorna screamed, clutching her chest. 'That is ... That is ... That is ... just mean!' Her pulse was pounding so loudly in her ears that she could barely hear herself breathe. 'Y'know what? Screw you, buddy. I'm sick of your bloody stupid games.'

Lorna started stomping onwards, no longer paying much attention to her footing. The path appeared to be levelling out, and then, just as she reached a flat area, she tripped over something in the darkness. Her body tensed as she pitched forward, but against the wishes of gravity she just hung there, frozen in the act of falling. She looked down at the rock floor, which was inexplicably not rising up to meet her. She tried to speak but while her mouth moved a bit, no words came out. A small voice in her head repeated the words 'final warning'. When had she received the first warning? There hadn't been one, unless ...

The hood of the green hoodie now pulled down, Keith's face appeared in her field of vision. He shook his head. 'I tried to warn you, Lorna. You can't say I didn't try to warn you.'

There came a scraping noise of something heavy being dragged across rock. Rachel appeared in view, hauling a large wooden chest behind her. 'No,' she muttered. 'No need to help me move the dressing-up box. I'll do it all by myself.'

Lorna turned her head the fraction she was able. Rachel opened the lid of the box and only then did she meet Lorna's gaze.

'To be fair, like he said, he did try to warn you.' She reached into the box and pulled out two elaborate-looking outfits on hangers. 'Now, do you want to be a warrior priestess or a bard?' She gave each costume an assessing look. 'I'm going bard, I think. The warrior outfit is a bit Xena and, no offence, you don't quite have the figure for it.'

Over the course of the next few minutes, Lorna stayed frozen in place while Rachel, with some help from Keith, wrestled her into the bard outfit. It was the oddest sensation, like Lorna was both there and not there, as if she was all but disconnected from her own body. When they'd completed the process, the couple argued over exactly what pose she should be manoeuvred into. Eventually, they settled for one leg in the air, frozen mid jaunty dance. Then, for the final touch, Rachel placed what appeared to be a mandolin in Lorna's hands. That done, she looked at Lorna's face again. Her brow was furrowed in consternation.

'That's weird,' said Rachel. 'She's smiling. Why is she smiling?'

Lorna could feel herself growing smaller now, as she had known she would, so that when Keith walked back into her line of sight, he already towered over her. He bent down and studied her face. After a moment he smiled. 'Curiosity killed the cat, but satisfaction made it whole.'

FIRE IN THE SKIES

The washing-up.

It's funny how the mind works, isn't it? It's my first memory of that night – the bloody washing-up. It was one of my chores, you see. One of many. My dad was away at sea and my mum and older sister, Katie, were out working in the factories, so it used to fall to me to handle most of the cooking and cleaning. I didn't mind it. I could see how tired they were when they came home from a shift and, like everybody else, I wanted to do my bit. Don't get me wrong – I was fourteen at the time. I was fully of the belief that what we needed to turn this war in our favour was me on the front lines, giving Hitler what for.

That's the thing about being young – it never even occurs to you that you either will or won't get old.

I'd just finished my Sunday dinner and stood up so fast to grab my coat and kit bag off the hook by the door that I sent my chair tumbling over behind me. Nana looked at my mum and pointed an accusatory finger at me. 'Where's he off to?

He's not done the washing-up. He's supposed to do the washing-up!'

Nana was not a woman to cross. She was my great-grandmother and while we all loved her, it was mixed with a fair dollop of healthy fear. She would happily give you a clout with her stick if she thought you were doing something you shouldn't be, or if you were doing something you should be, but too slowly or too sloppily. I don't want you to think badly of her. She just had a very set way of thinking about things. She could be very kind too. I was one of the few people who could make her laugh, and when she did, it was a sound worth waiting for. She had a glorious wheezy chuckle and her whole face would light up – just like a child's on Christmas morning.

I looked at Mum, who gave me the subtle nod that told me to get moving. She patted Nana's arm and spoke loudly. 'Don't worry about it, Nana. He's off doing an errand for me. Marty Draper has a line on a few eggs. You love an egg for breakfast, don't you?'

The second last thing I saw before heading out the back door and grabbing my bicycle was the smile that lit up Nana's crinkly little face as she thought about the prospect of eggs for breakfast. The last thing I saw was the worried look in my mother's eyes. Nana was deaf. That's why she couldn't hear the air-raid siren that was going off. In a few minutes, Mum would be taking her down to the shelter on Mealy Street. She just wanted to get me out the door first to stop Nana taking one of her turns. War had cost her a husband and a son already, and she would tell anyone who would listen that she was done with it.

I was what they called a fire warden. The job involved

standing on top of your assigned building and keeping an eye out for incendiary bombs. We were each given a bucket of sand and a pump, and it was our responsibility to deal with any fires the Luftwaffe were nice enough to send our way. It wasn't as ridiculous as it sounds. How raids generally worked was that the planes dropped the incendiaries on their first pass and then came back with the big boys, because it was a lot easier to bomb a city when parts of it were already on fire. It gave them something to aim at. There's not much point in the old lads telling you to turn your lights out when there's a towering inferno up the street for the Jerries to set in their sights.

Pedalling as fast as I could towards the city centre, I should have been scared – terrified, even. I was about to stand on top of a mill, defenceless, while the might of the Luftwaffe rained down death all around me. Honestly, though, I was thrilled. Like I said, fourteen – at that age glory comes without consequence. I'd been waiting for this chance for weeks. Almost praying for it. We'd had false alarms and all that, and each time I'd been disappointed not to see any action. I kept it to myself, of course. I had that much sense. Nobody wanted to hear my frustrations and I reckoned Nana would wallop me silly at the very idea. Dunkirk had been a few months earlier. We were fighting a war – losing it, by Marty Draper from the shop's reckoning – and I was at home doing the washing-up. Hard to believe now, but that's what was going through my mind. I don't know what it is that makes young men long for war and old men grant them their wishes, but the cycle plays out again and again.

In my defence, it's not as if I knew what to expect. It was the evening of 22 December, 1940, and up until then we'd seen precious little bombing. There had been pictures in the paper, of course. Sheffield, Coventry and Birmingham, but if ever there was something that a camera lens failed to capture in its awe-inspiring awfulness, it was the Blitz. Some people here had thought we'd be safe. It'd been said that the Luftwaffe either couldn't or didn't want to pay us a visit.

That was until the summer when the sirens had gone off and we'd heard them overhead. Then we knew. We were just as vulnerable as everybody else. Still, we'd only seen sporadic, low-level bombing up to that point. The first 'victim' had been a bobby guarding the civil defence building in Salford. A big bundle of leaflets from Hitler telling us that he wanted to be friends failed to open and landed on the chap's head.

For the last couple of nights, Liverpool had been catching it bad and we'd been warned that there was every chance we were next in the queue. My uncle Steve had been dispatched over there with his fire unit and he hadn't come back yet. Earlier in the day, I'd heard Mr Draper from the shop talking about how we were missing a load of our engines, meaning we were going to be caught short if the worst happened.

What the sirens meant was that the worst was here.

As I pedalled my bike down Oxford Road, people were rushing around me, trying to get themselves into shelters, while tracer fire from anti-aircraft guns stitched across the night sky above us. Cars with netting covering their headlights were being driven out of town, their owners keen to make sure their motors were kept out of the line of fire.

I took a left down Hulme Street, pedalling for all I was worth. For a second, the sirens stopped. I thought maybe it was a false alarm, but then they started up again almost immediately. I threw my bike down at the back of Chorlton New Mill and, with burning legs, ran up the metal fire escape at the side of the building. Up six storeys to reach the roof.

I stopped and looked up at the sky, my hands on my knees, panting as I tried to catch my breath.

'You took your bloody time, didn't ya?'

With a sense of dread, I turned to see old Ron Walker grimacing at me from the crate he always sat on.

Truth be told, I didn't like the man. Uncle Steve had told me he used be an all right fella, but had come back from the Great War changed. I don't know what he was like before, but these days he was an old codger with a limp and a mean disposition. He permanently smelled of booze and always seemed to be three days off his last shave and a week off his last bath. He'd been an air-raid warden, going about telling people to put out their lights, but then he'd got into a fight with someone and had been put up here instead. We were supposed to split shifts but a lot of the time, he'd be here when I turned up, even when it wasn't his night. I reckoned he'd been sleeping up here some nights during the summer, but I never said anything. Not my place.

'Looks like you might finally see a bit of action,' snarled Ron. 'Try not to wet your pants, eh?'

This was one of his recurring riffs – how I would wet my pants at the first sight of the enemy.

'I'll be fine.'

Ron gave a bitter laugh. 'Everyone says that until it happens. You wait an' see.'

I ignored him, as my mum had told me to, and checked my gear instead. I moved across to the sheltered enclave where I picked up my bucket of sand. I inspected my other equipment, taking the stirrup pump out of my kit bag and placing it beside the second bucket – the one containing water. My whistle was around my neck where I wore it on a piece of string at all times. I left the gas mask in its cardboard box inside my kit bag.

Satisfied, I turned my attention back to the sky. The unmistakable rumble of Luftwaffe engines, louder now, mingled with anti-aircraft fire above our heads.

Suddenly, it all started to feel a whole lot more real and a whole lot less fun. 'Blimey,' I said softly. 'This isn't another false alarm, is it?'

Then I noticed flames towards the centre of town. 'Ron, look at that!' I exclaimed. 'I reckon that's over near the town hall.'

I was shocked when Ron started laughing. 'Whole city might burn, lad. Whole city.'

I looked at him. His eyes were wide as he shot me back a grin that was missing a few teeth and, to my mind, a few marbles and all.

He was about to say something else but noticed something over my shoulder. 'Ooooh, your fancy Dan friend is back.'

I turned towards the mill on the far side of Cambridge Street where there were two factories. Directly opposite sat the Dunlop place – Macintosh Works. They made all manner of rubber stuff, same as us, and to the right was Hotspur Press. To the left were some houses with a school behind them. There'd been talk about them being knocked down and some new factories being built in their place, but nobody was crazy enough to build something with a war on.

Sure enough, there on the roof of the Macintosh mill sat the man in the hat. That's how I referred to him. Ron had many other, less complimentary names. He'd been there a few times previously when there'd been false alarms. I never saw him come or go, but we'd just happen to look over and there he'd be, sat on a deckchair of some sort with his flask of tea and a newspaper. I don't know how he was able to read in the low light, but he seemed to manage. He appeared to be about the same age as Ron, but that was the only similarity between the two men. He looked proper posh, dressed in a fine wool coat with a wide-brimmed hat on his head that you wouldn't see anyone walking around in day to day. Whenever it was raining he'd have an umbrella he'd put up, and he'd sit there, as nonchalant as you'd like, reading his paper, occasionally cleaning his glasses. He didn't even look up at the sky, which I considered a pretty fundamental part of the job.

Still, he always acknowledged us with a polite wave and, despite the insults Ron would mutter darkly in his direction, I'd decided I liked the man, odd as he was. I looked over at him now and noticed something.

'You've forgot your sand!'

The man gave me a quizzical look. I responded by holding up my bucket. 'Your sand,' I repeated. 'For putting out the incendiaries.'

He smiled and nodded. 'I'm fine, thank you.'

Ron slapped me on the shoulder. 'What'd I tell you? He's as useless as a chocolate teapot. Them toffs – all the same. He'll run at the first sign of trouble.' Then he grabbed me excitedly and pulled me close. 'Look! More fires! More fires!'

He was gripping my neck so tightly that it hurt as I looked out across the city. To the north of us were several blazes clearly visible against the night sky, and to the east were a few more too.

'Bloody hell,' I said, as I tried to move away from Ron. 'I think that's the Royal Exchange.'

I stood back, appalled, as Ron started to clap his hands

and dance a little jig in a circle around me. 'It's all going to burn. It's all going to burn.'

I looked across at the man in the hat, who was watching Ron from over the top of his reading glasses. Even though Ron wasn't my responsibility, I felt embarrassed to be in any way associated with such an unhinged maniac. I knew I should feel sorry for him, but now wasn't the time – the city was in flames around me, and I was standing there with just a bucket of sand to make sure that our mill didn't burn too.

I was going to have a word with Uncle Steve when he came back from Liverpool – to see if I could get reassigned. I couldn't take Ron any more.

As he danced around me, I pleaded with him. 'Ron, calm down. We've got a job to do. Ron! For God's sake …'

I heard it before I saw it – a clunk, followed by a whoosh. I turned to see an incendiary had landed on the far end of the roof, and a circle of fire was already taking hold.

'Bloody hell.' I snatched up my bucket and started running towards it, but Ron grabbed my arm.

'Let go of me.'

'No,' he hollered, his breathing all funny now. 'Let it burn.'

'What?'

'Let. It. Burn.'

I didn't mean for it to happen, but as I struggled to get away from him, my elbow came up and caught him right on the nose, causing his head to whip backwards. I heard a sickening crack of bone and as his hands shot up to cup his damaged hooter, he released me.

I didn't have time to worry about him. I rushed forward with my bucket of sand and threw it over the flames.

Just like Uncle Steve had taught me. Incendiaries

contained phosphorus and magnesium, materials that burn brightly and are liable to explode if sprayed with water. If you smothered them with sand first, though, any eventual outbreak of fire could be extinguished with the stirrup pump in the bucket of water. The trick was to spread the sand all over the flames, denying the fire the oxygen it needed. Then, when you've emptied the bucket, start stomping as fast as you can, and you might not even need the pump. I stomped for all I was worth, and it worked, it blimmin' worked!

As I watched the last of the flames going out, I felt elated. I'd done my job. Didn't wet my pants at first contact with the enemy either. Which made me think of Ron. As I turned to talk to him, he tackled me, sending us both crashing to the ground.

As I fell, I watched my bucket skitter over the edge of the roof and fall into the night. Ron was on top of me instantly, his hands around my neck.

I looked up to see his mouth covered in the thick blood that was flowing steadily from his destroyed nose. His grin was as utterly demented as his eyes, which were bearing down on me and wide with, I don't know – fear, anger, delight, all of the above. I tried to speak but his hands were crushing my windpipe. I flailed at his arms, but they were in a vice like grip around my throat. And then …

What happened next – happened.

Now, I realise this might seem impossible for rational thinkers to comprehend, but I know what I saw. I saw a bomb – a proper bomb, not an incendiary – falling out of the sky and coming straight for us.

There it was, as clear as day – my own death heading right towards me. It didn't matter what Ron, the mad old bastard, did – Hitler was going to get me first.

There must have been something in my eyes because Ron, as crazed as he was, turned his head towards the night sky.

I remember him making a gurgling noise then I clamped my eyes shut. There was no prayer, no last words. No time for any of that. Only …

Nothing happened.

Ron's hands fell slack around my throat before he slumped back off me entirely.

After a few moments, I opened one eye and dared to look.

There was the bomb, frozen in mid-air, maybe ten feet above my head.

Ron was lying prostrate on the ground below it, his hands held up around his head. 'No – God, no. Please, no. Not again. No!'

I scanned the rooftop, trying to regain my senses.

The world was still moving around us. I could see fires in all directions now as Manchester burned. I could hear shouts in the distance. The harsh smell of the chemicals from the incendiary stung my nostrils and the grit of the sand on the roof beneath me prickled at my skin.

But the bomb stayed there, frozen above our heads.

I turned to look at the man in the hat. There he was, standing on the roof opposite, his arms raised above his head and a look of pained concentration on his face.

I eased myself to my feet unsteadily. Ron had curled himself into a ball by this point, and was shaking and blubbering unintelligibly.

The man in the hat spoke through gritted teeth. 'Is there anyone over on the school playground?'

I squinted across. 'I don't think so.'

I felt a movement in the air and the bomb seemed to be a couple of feet closer now.

The man's voice was strained. 'Could you be ... sure?'

'Hang on.'

'I am,' came his terse reply.

I rushed over to the far corner of the roof, where Hulme Street met Cambridge Street. 'It's ... Yes, it's empty,' I confirmed.

I watched, dumbfounded, as the man slowly turned himself around and, in the air above us, the bomb moved with him. I remember thinking, as I stood there with my mouth agape, that it was moving at about the speed of one of them steam barges on the canal.

I think I heard a ticking noise as it sailed over my head and across the road. Maybe it was just metal cooling down or depressurising. Then it sailed silently over the rooftops of the nearby houses and I held my breath. I knew a girl who lived in one of them – Maggie Braithwaite. She'd once given me a gobstopper when I'd fallen and scraped my knee.

Finally, the bomb reached the middle of the playground and wobbled in the air above it.

'Still clear?' shouted the man in the hat.

'Yes,' I replied.

'Then hit the deck.'

The man's entire body collapsed with relief. Then, after a second, during which it felt as if the bomb itself seemed unsure of what it should do, it resumed its descent.

I dived and felt the shockwave wash over me as every window in the mill below me shattered.

After a moment, with my ears still ringing, I sat back up and looked across the street. The windows of the houses had blown in too, but the buildings themselves were otherwise intact. Same with the school. As the smoke started to clear, a massive, smoking crater in the middle of the playground revealed itself. The sheer power of the thing was terrifying to behold.

I clambered back to my feet and looked around me, dazed. In every direction, the skyline glowed orange and yellow with ravenous fires. To my right, London Road Station was ablaze, the flames licking against the night sky.

The pathetic figure of old Ron lay crumpled on the ground, shaking and mumbling.

The man across the street was picking himself up, dusting off his hat and placing it back on his head.

He raised an eyebrow and nodded at me. Somehow, without shouting, his voice carried to me. 'You're a brave lad and you've done your duty. Time for you to head off now, I think. The Krauts are moving from incendiaries to the really nasty stuff.'

'How did you ...' I started, not knowing how to phrase the question.

A laugh without malice wafted across the night air to me. 'That, I'm afraid, is not something to be discussed. You're a smart lad, I think you know that it's best left between us.'

I nodded. 'Nobody will believe me, anyway.'

'Quite right,' he said. 'A young boy's flight of fancy.'

I pointed down at Ron. 'What about him?'

'That poor blighter wouldn't even believe himself. Best you get him to a shelter.'

I nodded.

I took in the terrifying image of a skyline in flames again then turned to the smoking crater across the road. It occurred to me belatedly that I hadn't even said thank you. Before I could, I realised that the man in the hat was nowhere to be seen.

I shook my head again. 'I saw it and even I don't believe it.'

I walked across to where poor Ron was huddled. I know he'd attacked me and all the rest, but I could feel nothing but pity for the poor wretch. I reached down and took him by the elbow.

'Come on, Ron. Best be getting off.'

'Th-th-the,' he stammered.

'Yeah, near miss, that,' I replied. 'Let's get you up.'

I helped him back to his feet. He grabbed my arm. 'I'm … I'm sorry.'

'That's OK. All's well that ends well, eh? Our building's still standing. Lots aren't as lucky.'

I started to walk him towards the fire escape.

After a couple of moments, he stalled and confirmed what I'd already smelled. 'I think I peed myself.'

'It's all right, Ron,' I said, patting his arm. 'It happens. It happens.'

DANCE WITH THE DEVIL

THE DANCE

Stanley Roker sucked the grease off his fingers with gusto. As he did so, he was aware of the two women at the next table glowering at him. In fact, that was why he was doing it. Screw them. If he wanted a woman to look at him with disgust, he could be at home with his wife right now. Crystal was angry at him. He didn't know why; odds on, she didn't know why either. Being angry at him was her default position these days. He'd long given up trying to figure out what he'd done wrong.

He had to put up with this behaviour from her, but he'd be damned if two office workers drinking themselves into a stupor on a Tuesday evening were going to make him feel bad too. His life had few enough joys left in it for them to deny him the magnificence that was the ten-pence chicken wing.

Stanley found the bar he was in annoying. It played nineties rock – his preferred era and genre – but everyone else in the place seemed to be enjoying it ironically. It was full of the fairly young and reasonably beautiful. The three lads in the corner, playing on the pinball machine, looked to be competing to outdo each other in the ridiculous-facial-topiary stakes, and it was too close to call. Stanley would have to bestow the dubious honour on the one with the twirly moustache, if pushed. They had arrived one at a time – on a motorized scooter, a skateboard, and some type of roller skates respectively. Seriously, what was the world coming to? Stanley wouldn't have been surprised if, at some point, another rolled up on a penny-farthing.

The bar was on First Street, Manchester's latest up-and-coming area, according to one of those puff pieces that increasingly filled the gap where real journalism once lived. The Northern Quarter had previously been the city's 'it' location, but the thing with hipsters is that they are terrible customers. Their only loyalty is to the concept of the next thing. Somewhere, a bar owner was staring at a room full of retro video games and full-sized statues of the A-Team, coming to terms with the idea that he was going unironically broke. The nostalgia machine rolled on, and now the nineties were the new eighties. This bar's walls were festooned with comic-book covers and posters for films that nobody enjoyed the first time around.

The place was busy enough, though, which was why he had picked it. Well, that and the ten-pence chicken wings. He was here on business but he also had to eat. He thumped a hand to his chest as the familiar swirl of impending heartburn clawed at him.

The plate of wings that Stanley was polishing off was his third, and he basked in the warm glow of hatred from the ladies at the next table and the occasional filthy look from the barman. He knew he wasn't welcome there – the bar's target demographic was definitely not anyone who'd heard Nirvana the first time around. There had also been the heated discussion with said barman. A sign behind the counter stated that the ten-pence wings could be purchased only with other items on the menu. Stanley had quoted the law, which said that as they were listed on the sign outside as individually available items, that superseded an A4 sheet of paper they had put up inside. Not allowing him to buy the wings on their own violated advertising standards regulations. He'd been only guessing that, but it sounded believable. After all, he had a way with words.

The barman had pulled whatever unhappy expressions he could manage around the various piercings through parts of his face, and had gone and got him his chicken. Stanley ordered two more plates after that, but on the third attempt the guy started to get proper shirty with him.

Stanley glanced over at the bar and received a big smile in return, which he acknowledged by raising his glass of tap water in a toasted response. The fella had gone from giving him the evil eye to smiling back happily. Perfect. Stanley considered himself an expert reader of human nature and, unless he was very much mistaken, if he ordered another batch of wings, they would be delivered promptly and with cheerful customer service. That wouldn't last long, though. Stanley was going to pay for the wings, thank the barman courteously, and put what was left into the Ziploc bag that he had in his coat pocket. He would give it even odds that scientific analysis of a sample of the meat would reveal a lot more than just chicken and BBQ sauce; he'd put his money on the barman's DNA being in there too.

A few years ago, Stanley had written a very successful

series of articles examining the hygiene standards of many of Manchester's most famous eateries. It had been the gift that had kept on giving. People didn't really want to know, but at the same time they couldn't not read on. The editor at the *Manchester Evening News* begrudgingly admitted it had been one of their most popular features in years.

Stanley's fees for the articles covered Crystal getting the whole downstairs re-carpeted, and the kickbacks he'd pocketed from certain restaurateurs for not being featured paid for the extension she'd wanted on the house too. The gig had even nabbed him a celebrity chef who, in exchange for Stanley forgetting about a pesky vermin problem, would regularly drop him a text revealing which of his celeb mates were using the private dining room for intimate meals with people whom they weren't married to. Those days had been great. Crystal had been so warm to him that there'd even been a bit of marital relations, something which had long since disappeared off the menu.

In Stanley's experience, nothing good lasted for ever. His contact in the environmental health department at the council had shuffled off his mortal coil after having eaten at a particularly infamous Indian restaurant. It wasn't as if the man hadn't known the risks. He was literally paid to make sure nobody else died. It must've been tempting to put 'irony' as the cause of death, but the coroner had gone with 'salmonella'.

Stanley was a member of a dying breed: a freelance journalist. The whole nature of reporting the news had changed. The papers had to be careful what they printed, whereas social media was allowed to run amok. The curse of the modern age was that any wanker with a smartphone could pap a celeb or spread a nasty rumour. With Photoshop, you didn't even need the proof. It was eroding the foundations of journalism as far as Stanley was concerned – not that anyone asked his opinion.

He was an old-school tabloid hack and proud of it, which made him *persona non grata* in some circles. This idea that only certain truths had value wound him up no end. Stanley believed that all truth had value, and that value was however much he could get an editor to pay for it. Bob Woodward or Carl Bernstein he was not, but he considered himself to be a branch of the same tree. All right, he didn't do politics – not least because the current crop of MPs seemed depressingly boring.

God, how he missed the late eighties, when he'd just started out. Back then, every other week an MP would get caught doing the kinky in new, interesting and, most of all, sellable ways. For every story that made the front page, another three were hushed up and paid off. Back then, a journo could make an incredible living from not publishing stories.

Modern politics didn't interest Stanley, not least because celebrity was where the power lay these days. Most people didn't even know what their political representatives looked like, but everyone recognized the latest reality TV star or Instagram influencer. Stanley focused on them too. If these people held up their lifestyles for public scrutiny, then that was exactly what they were going to get.

If you were a Premier League footballer raking in the dosh, then your delight in dalliances in lay-bys with random strangers was fair game. If you were the celeb weather girl pushing your miracle workout at yummy mummies keen to get their yummy back after pregnancy, then you'd best not be getting sacks of fat sucked out of you at a fancy Cheshire clinic. Stanley was a seeker of truth, in all its forms.

The only problem was that truth – at least the sellable sort – was becoming harder to find. These days, staff writers could generate scandal from a Twitter feed without having to leave their desks. Punters on the street would send in pictures *for free*. It was pretty bad all year round, but now it was summer it was a desert. Every footballer was out of the country, and all the pop stars were on tour, drinking soya lattes and working out every day.

Stanley had been forced to get creative. Say what you want about him – and people had said an awful lot during his fifty-four years on the planet – Stanley Roker was a survivor. He'd improvised. He'd adapted. He'd sifted diligently through his notebook of whispers and innuendo until he'd found 'Dirty' Dave Marks.

Davey Boy wasn't anything special in almost every way. A middle-aged married man who played away from home when he could arrange any kind of a fixture. It didn't exactly make him newsworthy. If he were to walk into this bar, no heads would turn. Nobody would know him from Adam. He was utterly unremarkable save for one tiny fact: Dave was the mascot for a certain Premier League football team. The weirdo in the big padded costume who cavorted on the sideline, and who everybody secretly hoped would catch a free kick right in the kisser.

So much, so what? But Stanley had found one little nugget of gold while sifting. Dirty Dave liked to wear the outfit while he was 'at it'. Highly recognizable dirty devil banging away in full costume – hello, front page! Editors who hardly ever took Stanley's calls would lap that up. It was an angle they'd not seen, and fans of every other team would love it. There'd be chants in the stands for years. It was a sure-fire thing.

For a month, Stanley had been working on the story constantly, and he reckoned he'd finally found his way in. There'd been an advert on one of those dating sites that sell themselves on 'discretion'. In other words, it was aimed exclusively at cheating bastards. The advert had read, 'Do you want to dance with the devil? Naughty beast seeks sexy playmate for discreet fun.' It had to be Dirty Dave. Stanley's original tip-off had come from a woman who'd met him through the same site. All Stanley needed was bait, and that was where Tina came in.

She was sitting at the bar right now. The girl was a solid seven, pushing for an eight thanks largely to her outfit, which made the most of her attributes. For every wannabe that made it to celebrity status, there were a dozen more that littered the ground. They were easy to find if you knew where to look. Tina had been 'a model', but was too short for runway, too chubby in the face for catalogue, and close but no cigar for glamour. Apparently, her wonky nipples didn't photograph well.

Still, she was a good-looking girl, but, crucially, not too good looking – she sat right in that sweet spot where the deluded mind of a forty-something male could believe that she might conceivably be interested in him. She'd turned her hand to singing these days, but then, hadn't everyone? She'd given Stanley a memory stick with her demo on it, which he had not listened to. He was more concerned about how she was flexible – in many ways, but particularly when it came to morality.

Stanley pitched it that she would be the 'unnamed woman' in the article, but the girl said she wanted to be identified. Quite how she thought being in the paper for having sex with a literal horny devil would help her career was anyone's guess, but Stanley hadn't questioned it. He'd offered her twenty-five per cent of the fees, and he'd expected her to haggle and drive him up to fifty, but instead, she'd argued for exposure. Stanley despaired for the younger generation, but only after she'd left the room having negotiated mentioning her non-existent upcoming album release in the article too.

Stanley had been clear – she wasn't to speak to him or even look in his direction in case she blew it. Dirty Dave couldn't suspect a thing or he'd bolt. Unfortunately, Stanley hadn't extended that rule to texting, and so his phone buzzed twice a minute with messages from her. Dave had been scheduled to arrive at eight and it was now almost nine. Tina wasn't used to being stood up, and she wasn't taking it well. As per Stanley's instructions, she'd batted away the advances of the hipster trio in the corner as they'd each taken a crack with depressing predictability, but she'd started to accept drinks from the barman. Stanley had told her not to get drunk, but she was on her fourth now. His phone buzzed again.

> Where the fuck is he?
>
> He'll be here.
>
> Bollocks.
>
> Go easy on the drinks.
>
> Sure, DAD!

Stanley stared daggers at Tina's back as the barman delivered her another freebie – something pink, with an umbrella and some fruit sticking out of it. He placed it in front of her with a wink and a remark that was greeted with an uproarious laugh. The way things were looking, there was a good chance both Stanley and Tina could be leaving the bar tonight with nothing but a sample of the barman's DNA.

> Remember what you're here for.
>
> This prick isn't showing.
>
> He might.
>
> No man stands me up.
>
> Until now.

As soon as he'd sent the last message, Stanley regretted it. Tina turned round and glared at him. He watched as she snatched her bag off the bar, hopped down from the stool, flicked him the V sign and headed for the door.

Oh shit. Stanley was up on his feet fast, and pushed his way through the crowd. He met Tina just before she reached the door. He grabbed her elbow.

'Tina, I'm sorry.'

She turned, hatred burning in her eyes. 'Piss off, Stanley. You're a joke. I'm gonna get my brothers on to you.'

'Look, take it easy. Let's give him five more minutes.'

She pulled her arm away. 'We've been giving him five more minutes for half an hour. I'm done with this shit.'

'Tina, be reasonable.'

That last bit earned him a high-heeled kick to the shins. Stanley stumbled backwards and when he looked up, Tina was out the door.

. . .

'Tina! Come back!'

Stanley had run only thirty yards but he was already out of breath. Despite being in heels, Tina had not only maintained the lead she had on him but was also pulling away.

He wasn't in the best of shape, and that was before he'd gorged himself on cut-price chicken. 'Tina!'

She disappeared around the corner of the NCP car park. Despite knowing it was a futile gesture, he pushed himself to make it that far at least. What was he expecting? That she'd have calmed down and would be standing there, hoping that they could be friends? That she would go back to the bar and wait for the guy who wasn't turning up? Even if Dirty Dave didn't show tonight, they could reschedule.

Tina being out would mess up the whole damn thing. Stanley needed this – two late car payments and a stack of letters in large, angry red type needed this. He wasn't out on a Tuesday night doing this by choice. They were in dire straits. Last week Crystal had accused him of having an affair, and had then been pissed off when he'd fallen into a fit of unhinged giggles at the thought of it. When would he have the time? The only person screwing him was the bank manager.

The reality was that both he and Crystal knew she was too good for him, and Stanley worked every hour God sent just to afford the rising costs of keeping her in the style to which she'd become accustomed. He was a pathetic mess of a man, but the one thing he held on to in this screwed-up world was that he loved his wife. He had married above his station and he'd been reaching ever since.

When he eventually made it round the corner, Tina was a sparkly dot on the horizon. Stanley wasn't even sure it was her. He wasn't wearing his glasses and his vision was beginning to blur from the exertion of the brief chase. He was carrying an extra stone or two in weight – possibly eight. He'd not been to the doctor in years. He could barely afford the dog's medical bills, so he didn't need to find out what other cheques he'd been writing that his own body couldn't cash. Stanley leaned a hand against the concrete wall and spat while trying to heave in ragged breaths.

'Here he is!'

Stanley looked up to see one of the hipster triplets from the bar standing over him. Up close, the guy was a bit bigger than the man-bun and coiffed beard might have led you to believe.

'What the ... fuck ... do you want?'

'We saw you bothering that poor girl.'

His two companions appeared from around the corner, the shortest one on roller skates.

Stanley spat again and pulled himself upright. 'It's not what you think. We work together.'

'Yeah right,' said his shorter arse friend.

'Why is it ...' started Stanley, pointing at the small one. 'That little pricks like him only get mouthy when they've got numbers on their side?' He knew he shouldn't have said it, but he was in a bad mood.

The third fella – the one with the handlebar moustache – smirked behind the short-arse's back. At least he could see the funny side. His vertically challenged mate had a face like thunder.

'Fuck you, ya creepy old bastard. Chasing women. Sex pest.'

Stanley pointed at the ring finger of his left hand. 'Happily married man. Now, if you'll excuse me, lads.'

The first of the triplets blocked Stanley's way as he tried to walk past. 'Where do you think you're going?'

'None of your business. Haven't you three got a bell-ringing craft-beer festival to be at, or something?'

Stanley pushed by him and started to head back towards the street corner. As an expert reader of human nature, he knew these three were all mouth and no trousers. They'd never been in a real scrap, and they wouldn't know where to start.

What felt like a half-brick hit him in the back of the head. As he stumbled messily to the ground, the realization that his intuition was buggered added insult to impending injury. Still, he'd bet the person behind the brick was the little fella.

Stanley had taken a kicking several times in his career. It was an occupational hazard. As they went, this wasn't the worst. He wasn't a fighter, but this wasn't a fight. The trick is to curl into a ball and do your best to protect the prime targets: the testicles, the face, the testicles, back of the head, the testicles. The big lads weren't putting their weight behind their kicks, which was lucky, although the roller skates were steel-capped, which was unfortunate.

Stanley felt a hand dive into the inside pocket of his coat where his phone and wallet resided. He moved to fend off this new incursion, which allowed a boot an unobstructed flight path to his nether regions. His world became a very specific kind of pain, and he could barely feel the hands rifling through his pockets and relieving him of a few of his most immediate worldly possessions. He was in too much pain to register it, his traumatized testicles forming the centre of his universe.

A skate smashed down on his face. Lights flashed. Blood spurted. Bells rang.

'Get away from him!'

The voice sounded odd, but when you've been kicked in the head, everything gets a bit scrambled. The rain of vengeful footwear ceased and, after a few exclamations, Stanley heard receding footsteps mingled with the *whoosh* of the kind of solo transportation system best suited to a nine-year-old girl with pigtails.

For a few moments, nothing happened. Stanley was fine with that; it was a big upgrade on the rest of his evening. Then, he felt gentle hands on him.

'Are you OK?' asked a soft female voice.

Stanley spat out part of a tooth. His mouth was too sore for him to figure out which tooth it was part of. 'No offence, love, but that isn't the cleverest of questions.'

He looked up. A black woman with a streak of red running through her hair and wearing a grey hooded top was peering down at him. He thought he recognized her from the bar, perhaps they'd passed when he'd nipped upstairs to the loo and to check the target hadn't somehow slipped by him. He'd not really been paying attention to the women.

'Yeah, I guess.'

'I mean,' added Stanley, slurring slightly. 'Don't get me wrong, I appreciate you popping by.'

'Do you want me to call an ambulance?' She held up her phone.

Stanley shook his head, and then regretted doing so as pain issued from various areas. 'No, I'm fine.'

'Yeah, right. You need a proper looking at. Seriously, I know what I'm talking about. I'm a nurse.'

'Good for you, love. No disrespect to the NHS, but the only thing that could make my night worse is spending five hours on a plastic chair only to be given two paracetamol by some junior doctor off his tits on speed, which he needs to keep going for eighteen hours solid. Can you help me up, please?'

The woman bent down and assisted him to his feet. More pain erupted from several parts of Stanley's body. He knew he was only getting a taster right now. Adrenalin was minimizing the full effects. This was just the trailer for the feature-length shit show he had to look forward to.

'You look dreadful.'

'Thanks. You should see the other guys.'

'I did. They looked fine.'

'You say that. There was a definite man-bun in there, not to mention a grown man on roller skates.'

Stanley's legs buckled under him, and the woman put her arm around him to stop him from collapsing back to the ground.

'You really need to be in a hospital.'

'No, I'll be fine. I just want to get back to my car.'

Stanley pointed towards where his had-seen-better-days Audi was parked, up on the road past the NCP.

'Right,' said the woman. 'Couple of things. One – you've got a probable concussion and no bloody way are you driving anywhere. Two – you do realize that's a disabled parking space, don't you?'

Stanley ran his tongue round the new topography of his mouth and spat out more blood. 'Look at the state of me. Is anyone going to suggest I've not been disabled?'

'And you were psychic when you parked, were you?'

'If you wanted to take a few free shots, you should've joined in with the three amigos.'

'If I'd known you were parking in disabled spaces, I

would have.' She pulled a tissue from somewhere and handed it to him. 'Here, hold that to your nose.'

Stanley took it. 'Is my nose bleeding?'

'Nah. I'm just finding your beauty distracting.'

A couple walked past and shot them a furtive glance. The woman guided Stanley towards the wall against which he could lean.

'All right,' she said, 'what's the plan here? People are starting to look at me like I might have something to do with kicking the shit out of you, and I could do without that kind of unearned praise in my life.'

'Just leave me.'

'I wish I could, but I'm a nurse, remember? There's this whole duty of care thing. I can't let you die in the street, even if you are the kind of arsehole who chases women out of bars.'

'You saw that?' asked Stanley, taking the tissue away from his nose and looking at it, as if he needed to verify that the liquid soaking it was indeed his own blood.

'Yeah,' said the woman, 'it's the kind of thing people notice. I don't think you were her type.'

'It wasn't like that,' said Stanley. 'We were working together. I'm a journalist.'

'Sure. You got ID that proves that?'

He patted his pockets with his free hand. 'Well, I did, but the Hair Bear Bunch swiped it, along with my phone and ... shit!'

'What?'

'My car keys.'

'Well, I'm sure the police will be only too delighted to tow a disabled man like yourself home.'

Stanley closed his eyes. 'Sod it. Can't go home anyway. If

the missus sees me like this, there'll be a divorce.' The last time he'd taken a beating in the course of his duties Crystal had been very clear: next time she would be out of there. 'I'll go stay in a hotel, but …'

'What?'

Stanley took a deep breath. 'I've got no money.'

The woman looked disapprovingly at the bloodstain on the shoulder of her hoodie. 'Maybe you could give them your card number? Oh, you should cancel your credit cards too, by the way.'

'I don't have any.'

'Really?'

Stanley nodded as much as he could. 'Those things are a great way of telling the world your business. Cash is king. Take it from me.' The tabloid journalist's best friend was the credit card receipt.

'Yeah, I'm sure the boys currently in possession of your wallet agree wholeheartedly.'

'Is there any chance—'

'I am not lending you money, so don't even bother.'

'Right.'

She glanced around. 'Is there someone you can call?'

Stanley looked up at the windows of the office block opposite and the reflection in them of the massive neon sign that hung over First Street. 'Not any numbers I can remember.'

'Great,' she said. 'So, to recap, Mr Journalist. You won't go home. Got no money, no friends, no phone, no cards. You won't call the police or an ambulance, and you can't get into your illegally parked car.'

'It's not illegally parked. I've got a badge.'

'Is the badge legal?'

Stanley gave a shrug, which turned into a wince. 'Not exactly.'

'You're quite something, you know that?'

Stanley nodded. 'You're not meeting me on a good day.'

'When's the next one of them due?'

'It has been a while,' Stanley conceded.

The woman stood and looked at her feet. 'Damn it. All right, I guess I'll have to bring you home.'

'No, I can't—'

'My home.'

'Oh,' said Stanley. 'Thanks, but ...'

'Make one crack about me taking advantage of you and I'll leave your bloody bleeding arse standing here.'

Stanley nodded. 'Fair enough.'

The woman sighed, and when she spoke it was more to herself than to him. 'I knew this was a bad idea. Stupid!'

'I promise I won't be any trouble,' said Stanley. 'Where are we going?'

She shook her head. 'Nowhere. You stay here. I'll go get my car. I stupidly parked it legally over on Deansgate.'

'I could come with you?'

'No. I'll get it and come back. I don't want people seeing us together. I've got a good name to protect.'

Stanley nodded. 'OK. What is that good name, by the way?'

'Shauna.'

'I'm Stanley. Nice to meet you, Shauna.'

She turned to go. 'Wish I could say the same. Stay there and get all your bleeding done here. I'm not having you ruining my upholstery as well as my night.'

THE RIDE HOME

Stanley had been considering his limited options for when Shauna didn't come back, when she re-appeared. He'd concluded that the one possible advantage of his concussion was that he could probably conk out behind a dumpster. The tricky part might be waking up again, but honestly, death wasn't feeling like that bad an option.

Certainly, a trip across the river Styx felt less daunting than walking all the way home to Altrincham, then sleeping in the shed until his wife left for Pilates in the morning and he could sneak back in. Now he thought of it, he'd put a lock on the shed after next door was burgled last year. He supposed he could try to fit into the dog house he'd built for Trixy at Crystal's insistence. At least that way someone could finally use it, because the bloody mutt didn't. No, the dog got to sleep in the bed with Crystal, which was more than Stanley managed. His snoring kept her awake. He was pretty sure every form of breathing he engaged in bothered her, but that one was the easiest to complain about.

A pair of fingers being clicked in front of his face brought Stanley back to the present. Without realizing, he'd been drifting off.

'Wakey wakey,' said Shauna.

'You came back!'

'I said I would.'

'I know,' said Stanley. 'Just, in my experience, people don't keep promises. That's the problem with my job. Gives you a very low opinion of people.'

'Yeah,' said Shauna. 'Try spending a few Saturday nights working A & E, being called all kinds of racist crap by drunks you're trying to help, then see how you feel about the human race.'

'You're too young to be so cynical.'

'What can I say?' said Shauna. 'I'm a fast learner. Besides, I'm a lot older than I look.'

'Black don't crack,' said Stanley, noting the slur in his voice.

'Yeah,' she replied absent-mindedly. 'The car is parked just over there, through the archway. We're gonna have to go around, though. You sure you can make this?'

'Not a problem.'

They started to walk. Or at least Shauna did. Somewhere, the signals travelling between Stanley's brain and his legs got messed up. He started to follow her, then a big wave hit the boat and he staggered to his left. Shauna grabbed him to stop him from capsizing.

'Right – might've been a tad optimistic there.'

'That's me,' said Stanley. 'One of life's great optimists.'

She pulled his left arm around her shoulders. 'OK, lean on me ... Oh, damn it!'

'What?'

'Well,' said Shauna. 'Now I've got your blood on both shoulders of my hoodie. At least it'll look like some kind of design.'

'I'll buy you a new one.'

'With what? You're broke.'

'It's the thought that counts.'

'Sure,' she said. 'OK, let's try this again. One ... two ... three.'

The second attempt went better, although by no means smoothly. Shauna held him up, but she was only about five-two and there was a lot of him to hold. Graceful it was not.

Even in Stanley's dazed and confused state it dawned on him that they were taking a particularly circuitous route to where she had parked, but he knew better than to criticize a woman's sense of direction. He called to mind his and Crystal's driving holiday in France, which had not gone well – in fact, a large chunk of it had taken place in Belgium. If there was a next time, Stanley was going to pay extra for the GPS.

They reached Shauna's car, parked in an alleyway by Deansgate Locks. She propped Stanley up against the passenger-side door and stood there, panting, her hands on her knees. 'No offence, but you could do with getting your arse to a gym.'

'I don't believe in them.'

'Really?' said Shauna. 'What do you believe in?'

'The sanctity of the Great British fried breakfast.'

'Yeah. You're a fantastic advert for it.'

She stretched out her back. 'If I pull a muscle, I'm billing you.'

'Add it to my tab.'

'Yeah. Right.'

She opened the door and, with some difficulty, managed to wedge Stanley into the front seat. It was a small car, and he was a big man.

Shauna got into the driver's side. 'Right. Let's get out of here.'

Stanley watched the lights of the city through the window as they drove. It occurred to him that the evening had slipped into night without him noticing. Town was busy for a Tuesday. The decent weather was drawing people out despite it being a school night. He enjoyed the cool glass of the car's window pressing against his face. At the back of his mind there was a tap-tap-tapping – some instinct asking for attention. Sod it, he was too tired. Figuring out Dirty Dave and getting his stuff back – all of it could wait until the morning.

'Hey!'

'What?' said Stanley.

'Don't go falling asleep on me.'

'I wasn't.'

'You were. You fall into a coma and I'm taking your fat arse to hospital.'

'Do you mind? I'm sensitive about my weight.'

'Then eat a salad. Sit up. You promised you wouldn't bleed on my seats, remember?'

Stanley pulled himself upright.

'Better. Keep talking.'

'About what?'

'Anything,' said Shauna. 'What was the deal with you and that girl?'

In the absence of a better idea, Stanley told Shauna what he'd been up to that evening. When he'd finished, there was a moment of silence in the car.

'So, you're like one of them proper scumbag tabloid hacks, then?'

Stanley rolled his eyes, or at least he attempted to. They didn't seem to be entirely under his control. 'Here it comes.'

'Excuse me?'

'All the high and mighty, holier-than-thou judgement. Let me guess – you think you're better than me?'

Shauna snorted. 'I work as a nurse. I help sick people. You're paparazzi. Everybody thinks I'm better than you. Everybody is right. When was the last time you got clapped? Admittedly, a pay rise would've been nicer, but que sera.'

'Actually,' said Stanley, 'the paparazzi are photographers. I don't do that.' This wasn't entirely true. He did own a couple of cameras. Nowadays, it was so simple to take a decent picture that photographers were dying out faster than journalists. Well, they still had weddings, and portraits of screaming brats for grandma's mantelpiece, but the sexier news stuff wasn't there so much any more.

'So,' said Shauna, 'you dig about in people's private business, messing up their lives?'

'What I do is find the truth, in all of its many glorious forms. I don't make stuff up. If you've not been a naughty boy or girl, then you've nothing to fear from me.'

'Right,' said Shauna. 'And your life is so perfect, then, is it Mr Journalist? Is that why you get to sit in judgement over the rest of us?'

'Nobody is interested in me.'

'Maybe they should be.'

'Well, they aren't.'

'Speaking of which, does anyone know where you are tonight?'

Odd question. 'No,' said Stanley. 'Why?'

'Well, with you not going home and all. I don't want somebody coming looking – accusing me of kidnapping you.'

'You're fine. The wife is used to me working unusual hours.'

'Scandal never sleeps, huh?'

'Something like that.'

'What about your editor?'

'I don't have one. I'm a freelancer.'

They turned a corner and Stanley could feel Shauna looking him up and down. 'So, you get to choose the kind of stories you write?'

'I do.'

'I'm struggling to find any redeeming qualities in you, Stanley.'

Stanley looked out of the window again, watching as the suburbs zoomed past. They were somewhere in Salford, but he didn't know where exactly. He didn't have much cause to come out this way.

'You know what bothers me?' he said. 'The hypocrisy. I am what I am, and yeah, it ain't the cleanest way of making a living. But ask yourself this – who reads my articles? If everyone was as vertiginous as they make out, then the papers wouldn't sell and I'd be out of a job. Seems to me the world is full of people who think butchers are monsters, but who still enjoy a nice plate of sausages.'

'Is that one of them similes?'

Stanley shrugged. 'Technically it's a metaphor.'

'Well, it's a good one. Personally, I'm a big meat-eater. Aren't newspapers dying out, though?'

'Yeah, but the internet is killing 'em, not people losing interest in other people's dirty laundry. Everyone gets their scandal fix on the web these days. It's getting harder and harder to make a living in the paper game.'

'Sounds brutal,' said Shauna. 'It's those Page Three girls I feel sorry for. Can't imagine they got many transferable skills.'

'You'd be surprised. My wife did a bit of that.'

'Really?' Shauna gave Stanley the same appraising look he'd received a lot in his life. 'What does she work as now? Brain surgeon?'

Stanley said nothing.

Shauna glanced at him again. 'Sorry. Didn't mean to be rude about the missus.' She looked embarrassed. 'My mouth works faster than my brain sometimes.'

Stanley nodded. 'Whatever.' He didn't need to fall out with his only chance at sleeping indoors tonight.

Shauna turned into a car park at the rear of a four-storey apartment building. It looked nice in a nice enough way. Nondescript. Forgettable. Nobody's dream home but perfectly decent. In a moment of weakness, after one of the eleven times he'd been fired in his career, Stanley had considered taking the offer of a job from his cousin Lewis and his real estate business. Thing is, property was boring, and somewhere deep down Stanley guessed a part of him enjoyed the chase. At least, he did on the nights when he'd come away with more to show for it than a wheels-on example of how much it must suck to be the floor in a roller derby.

Shauna parked up, and they sat there for a moment in the darkness, with no sound save the ticking of the cooling engine.

'OK,' she said. 'You stay here. I'm going to check the coast is clear.'

'Why?' said Stanley. 'Do you live with somebody?'

'No. I just don't want my neighbours seeing me dragging a semi-conscious man up to my lair. It'll ruin my chances at winning Vestal Virgin of the Year.'

'I'd hate to besmirch your good name.'

'Fab. And don't die in my car while I'm gone. It'll be a nightmare to get the smell out.'

Stanley leaned against the window again. 'I'll try my best, but no promises.'

Shauna's door opened and closed, and the next thing Stanley knew, his shoulder was being shaken. 'What?'

'You fell asleep again.'

'Oh, right.' He stared up into Shauna's face. Her eyes

looked weird. There was a red flash, like you see in photos sometimes – only this wasn't a photo. Then it was gone.

She shook him again. 'Don't conk out yet. We've got three flights of stairs to get up, and there isn't a lift.'

Stanley shook his head. 'All right, but this is going in my Yelp review.'

She moved round the car and helped him out. As they made their way across the tarmac, Stanley found it a bit easier to walk unassisted. He glanced up the path that led around the building and noticed a hint of movement in one of the parked cars across the street. The niggle that there was something odd about that teased the back of Stanley's brain, but the majority of his efforts were taken up with trying to walk straight and hoping he wasn't going to throw up. He'd elected not to mention to Shauna that he might be seeing a lot of loss-leading chicken for the second time that evening, for fear that whatever Florence Nightingale instinct led her to bring him home might wear off at the prospect.

In the end, the stairs weren't too bad. He leaned on the bannister and chugged away until they reached the top, managing to avoid any of Shauna's neighbours in the process. She opened the front door and helped him inside. Her apartment smelled of incense, or something. Stanley wasn't big into smells. As far as he could tell, the only difference between the perfumes you got for a tenner down the market and the ones that cost over a hundred quid in one of the fancy shops was how ornate the box looked.

The carpet was thick shag, which Stanley didn't think people had any more. At least, he didn't. His had been ripped up several years ago, after his beloved had seen a thing on TV.

Shauna kicked open a door on the left side of the hallway

and hurled Stanley ungraciously into the darkness. He landed on a bed.

'You are one heavy bastard, you know that?'

'No offence taken,' replied Stanley. The lights came on above his head. The bulb was red, and threw crimson light around the room.

'So,' said Stanley, 'this is where the magic hap— Argh!'

He pushed himself up onto his elbows, more awake than he'd felt since he'd been roller derbied. 'What the hell is that?'

'What?'

Stanley jabbed a finger at the large glass enclosure sat on top of a chest of drawers.

'Those are my babies.'

'Fucking spiders,' said Stanley.

'Tarantulas, to be exact.'

'Horrible things.'

Shauna looked down at him, real anger in her face now. 'I take you into my house and you're rude about it. You really are a disgusting piece of shit, Stanley.'

He looked up at her. 'Sorry, I didn't mean to be … I'm scared of spiders. Creepy crawlies.'

Shauna turned round and put a hand on the glass of the enclosure. Stanley's skin crawled as he caught the faint outline of spiders clambering against the glass in the dim red light. 'They are perfect. Beautiful predators shaped by evolution into efficient killers. The world is made up of hunters and prey, Stanley. You more than anyone should know that.'

'All right,' said Stanley. 'Point taken. I didn't mean to … Could you maybe put a sheet over it or something? Just while I'm—'

'No.'

'OK.'

'It's like your newspaper, Stanley. I don't look at it. You can just not look at my babies.'

Stanley leaned back and focused on the ceiling. 'All right, I just ...'

He was very tired.

His mind swam back towards consciousness. The pain in his body and the memory of the kicking that preceded it merged into a fevered dream, only this time a large, roller-skate-wearing spider was tap dancing all over him.

'Stanley.'

The voice was soft, almost a purr. He felt a hand softly stroking his hair. 'Stanley – oh, Stanley.' It was sing-song now. A joyous lilt to it. 'Wakey wakey, naughty boy.'

His eyelids fluttered, then a finger pushed roughly into the swelling above his eye. 'Ouch!'

He was fully awake now, the stab of pain drawing him back. 'What the—'

Shauna smiled down at him. 'Sorry, Stanley, you fell asleep.'

'Oh,' he said, trying to shift himself upright. 'I was ... This bed is really soft.'

It really was. He wasn't lying on it so much as sinking into it. His whole body was encased. He felt like a piece of electronics equipment being shipped somewhere, entombed in Styrofoam packaging. He tried to move his arms, but he was so tired that his limbs weren't responding to commands.

Shauna smiled down at him. 'I have a little confession to make, Stanley. I wasn't just trying to be helpful. I mean, I wasn't sure – you're not my normal type.' As she spoke,

Shauna unzipped her hoodie and tossed it to one side. 'Normally, I pick cheats. I need someone and they're the ones I choose. I figure I'm doing somebody a favour in the long run, even if they don't know it yet.'

In the fog of his concussed grogginess, somewhere in the distance Stanley heard an alarm bell. 'Ehm …'

'You see,' continued Shauna, 'I wasn't in that bar tonight by accident. I was there because there'd been a tug on one of my threads.'

She took off her T-shirt to reveal a black lace bra.

'Whoa!' said Stanley, trying to move. Why couldn't he move? 'Hold on, no. I'm flattered, but I'm a happily married man.'

'Happy?' said Shauna.

'Well, I love my wife.' He tried to move again, but his body was unable to do so.

'Oh, Stanley,' said Shauna, unclasping her bra and letting it fall to the floor. 'Finally, a redeeming feature. Sadly, too little too late.'

Stanley pulled in breath to scream, but Shauna touched his lips softly and he found himself unable to push sound out of his mouth.

Shauna continued to undress as she spoke. 'For once in your sad little life, Stanley, you're going to shut up and let the woman do the talking. You see, I sensed something was up. I thought you might be a hunter – a real hunter, I mean. Not just a bottom-feeding scumbag. I needed to know if they were on my trail. I know you were expecting a man, but, well, that's just semantics.'

Shauna blurred before Stanley's eyes. Another image overlaid her naked body – a vision of a white man; taller, broader shoulders, the face somehow different but the same. Like brother and sister, only the same.

Shauna clambered onto the bed and positioned herself over him. He felt hands pulling at his clothes as she maintained eye contact with him. 'Normally, I prefer cheats, liars, philanderers. Just my thing, I guess.' Her smile widened. 'We all have our little rules, don't we? To justify the wrongs we do. In the end, though, hunters are simply hunters. Aren't we, Stanley?'

Something sliced through his clothing. He could feel her warm skin as she began to gyrate on top of him.

Shauna stopped and looked at Stanley's nether region. She nodded. 'Good self-control, Stanley. I'm impressed. You really do love your wife. Aren't you a big sweetie?'

Her face came down, inches above his. He tried to move away but he found himself unable even to blink. 'Most men – even when they realize – can't stop themselves. I admire your resolve, Stanley.'

A tongue rolled out of her mouth, impossibly long and red. As it played over his skin it felt coarse, and left behind a residue of some kind. As he tried to look away, he noticed the spiders in their enclosure, frenzied now, slamming themselves against the glass.

Shauna pulled back. 'It doesn't matter what you want, though, Stanley. You might as well try to enjoy this bit, because trust me, you won't like the next part. At. All.'

As she uttered those last words, her outline blurred again and a face materialized. Another face. Inhuman. Red. Horns. A face that would haunt his dreams, if he ever had any more of those.

Stanley felt nails, incredibly long nails – the word 'talons' popped into his head unbidden – play up and down his naked body.

'I have to say, I'm finding you surprisingly entertaining, Stanley. I'm going to enjoy this.'

Something jabbed into his chest and Stanley felt his body betray him. Was a terror erection a thing? Stanley hadn't thought so up until now. He lay there, rigid in all ways, as she mounted him.

Shauna, or whatever she was now, sat above him. Different faces – the woman, the man, the devil – mixed and merged. One second it looked like a woman, then a four-armed terror in red, shell-like skin, and that face. Then Shauna again. It moaned and made a noise somewhere between a hiss and a growl.

More than anything, Stanley wanted to scream. His body yearned for the physical release of the fear that was building and building. He tried to distract himself. To think of anything else. To not register the sensation. To disconnect from the reality. He put every inch of his energy into trying to close his eyelids. His resistance reduced to wanting not to be there.

The smile – the smiles – grew wider, as if the thing was feeding off his terror. Then, somehow, the noise cut out.

Stanley couldn't hear anything. The whatever it was still bucked above him, its head tossed back in twisted ecstasy.

Then, Buddha smashed into the side of its head.

The creature toppled off Stanley and out of his view.

In its place, standing beside the bed, her voice screaming words he could not hear, was his wife, Crystal. Her eyes were wet with tears, her face was filled with outrage. The Buddha statue in her hands was smeared with blood.

As if emerging from the depths, Stanley's hearing came back.

'...ing around on me, you ungrateful toe rag. After all I've done for you. Gave you the best years of my life.'

Stanley's body filled with a whole other kind of terror. Fear for himself as his enraged wife stood above him, the blunt object still in her hands. Fear for her, should Shauna – or whatever you could call it – attack her.

'Ain't you got nothing to say for yourself?'

Stanley tried to talk, but he couldn't.

The sound of movement came from the floor beside the bed. Crystal diverted her attention towards it. 'And as for you, you home-wrecking slag, you're welcome to him. I don't know what I see in him, and I've no fucking idea what you do.'

Her gaze returned to Stanley. She held the statue awkwardly in one arm, and ran the other across her face in an attempt to wipe away tears. Her mascara smeared. She looked at him, her eyes filled with hatred.

'Aren't you even gonna say something?'

Stanley tried. Every inch of his being tried, but his lips would not move.

'You ...'

Crystal raised the statue above her head only for it to be grabbed by a man Stanley hadn't noticed standing behind her. That's not to say he was unknown to him. Maurice Glenn. Slimy little toe rag. A private investigator. He and Stanley had met before. Worked together. Fallen out. Fair to say they weren't the best of friends.

'Jesus, Mrs Roker – this is why I told you not to come in.'

Crystal struggled against Glenn briefly, then let go of the Buddha as the fight drained from her. He took the statue out of her hands and stood there as she leaned against him, weeping.

'The cheating bastard.'

'I know, I know.' Glenn looked at Stanley, and a wide smile played across his face. 'There, there. C'mon, you need to get out of here.'

Crystal spat at Stanley and marched out of the door.

Maurice Glenn leaned in. 'Don't worry, Stanley Boy. I'll take good care of her.'

A groan came from beside the bed. Glenn stood and looked to where the noise had come from. 'Sorry about that, love, but, y'know, probably shouldn't get caught screwing married men. You're lucky she didn't kill ya.'

Stanley desperately wanted the Shauna thing to leap up and rip off Maurice Glenn's smug little face. Instead, Glenn turned and left the room, tossing a casual wave over his shoulder as he did so. 'I'll leave you lovebirds to it. Enjoy your evening.'

He stopped in the doorway and turned back round. 'And sorry about kicking in your front door, sweetheart. Stanley here will pay for it. Get the money from him now, though – he's got an expensive divorce coming up.'

Then he was gone, and Stanley was alone in the room – well, except for the glass box full of spiders and the nightmare.

He could move again. He stood up, only to fall down. The soft carpet brushed against his skin. He tried to pull himself up. On the opposite side of the bed he saw Shauna – the red dye in her hair now mixed with a darker red as she hissed at him, her open mouth showing an impossibly wide set of hellish teeth.

Stanley picked himself up and ran. Dizzy. Slamming into walls. The world a blur.

He stumbled out of the bedroom and pinwheeled off the wall. Then he was out of the apartment and on the landing. An elderly woman standing on the stairs took one look at his naked form and screamed, clutching her dressing gown to herself as she did so.

He pushed past wordlessly. He made it to the bottom of the stairs, falling down the last few steps. A door, and then he was out. The night air felt so good against his bare skin as he stood in the street. In the distance, a set of brake lights flared as a car stopped and turned left. Crystal? Too late now.

How had they not seen? Seen what it was? Had they really not noticed anything about ...

Stanley spun round, fearful that Shauna could be following. There was nothing there. Or at least, not the nightmare. What was there was a man holding the lead of a cocker spaniel. The man gawped at him, dumbfounded. The dog sniffed excitedly at a tree – uninterested in anything else that was going on around it.

Behind them, Stanley saw a light come on in the apartment building he'd just left, up on the top floor.

He turned and ran. Ran like his life depended on it. Naked. Bruised. Broken.

He ran.

His bare feet hurt as they slapped against the concrete. His lungs burned as he forced himself onwards. He didn't know where he was. He wasn't running to anywhere, just away. Away was all that mattered.

When he couldn't run any more, he would collapse. He'd lie where he fell, and at some point in the future, when he was able to breathe again, he'd pick up the shattered remnants of his life and try to make sense of it all.

Until then, he would run.

He just hoped that eventually this erection would go away too.

BEFORE YOUR VERY EYES

Unless your life has been particularly blessed or cursed, you probably can't pick out the one defining moment that set it on a certain path. I can. 21st of June 1962 at a Butlin's holiday camp somewhere in Wales. I'm not suggesting that the location was secret, rather that I was nine at the time and it was raining so heavily on the drive up there that I couldn't make out any landmarks. My parents had saved up to take me and my little sister on the holiday of a lifetime. Unfortunately, Wales is still in Britain and the only thing more unreliable than the British weather is its train service.

How bad was it? Let me put it this way – our chalet flooded. Actually flooded. I distinctly remember my mother standing in several inches of water, sending my poor father off to reception to demand we be moved. He ended up at the back of a queue of other people making similar demands. When he came back defeated, Mum argued with him about why he was so terrible at arguing, which even at the time struck me as a tad unfair. If she'd have gone, they'd probably have relocated us to Tenerife.

And so it was. In a desperate attempt to get out of the dank, damp chalet, we went to watch the entertainment. We hadn't gone the previous night as we'd been too busy using my little sister's bucket and spade in an attempt to hold back a monsoon, so we'd missed the Great Walldino, who was billed as a magician extraordinaire. I'd quite wanted to see him, but even nine-year-olds can sense that there are points in life when you probably shouldn't push your luck.

Fortunately for us, he was back again. An Everly Brothers tribute act couldn't make it owing to a mudslide taking out a nearby road. Unfortunately for the Great Walldino, the first the audience knew of this was when the Redcoat who'd drawn the short straw appeared on stage to make the announcement. Walldino came on to boos, left to jeers and, in between, performed three tricks while struggling to be heard over the cat calls and heckles of a crowd that had arrived ugly and then discovered that the rumours of a free bar had been false. The only cheer the poor man received was when he deftly fielded a thrown pint glass. He even kept going through a couple of death threats, only calling it a night when somebody threatened his rabbit. Nevertheless, amid the rabid and rain-soaked holidaymakers reaching breaking point, a certain young boy became mesmerised by the wonders of stage magic.

After the Great Walldino had retreated from the stage and started packing away his props, all the while keeping a beady eye out for further airborne drinks receptacles, I ran up and asked him for his autograph. I can still remember the invective forming on his lips before he looked down and saw the achingly sincere expression on my face. As he hurriedly scrawled something on a scrap of paper, I asked him if it was hard to become a magician. I'll always remember his response: *not nearly as hard as it is to stop being one.*

I didn't know what he meant at the time.

At the time.

I'd always been an awkward child, but after that night I became an awkward child obsessed with magic. I'd compare it to throwing gasoline on a raging fire, but in my experience, people are a lot keener to watch a raging fire than a tongue-tied teenager mumbling his way through the interlinking rings.

The problem wasn't that I was bad at magic. Quite the opposite. I have the kind of mind that meant I was happy to spend hours a day perfecting sleight of hand through mind-numbing repetition. I also have the kind of imagination that can figure out how a trick is done. Most people, when they do, experience a couple of moments of delight followed by the inevitable come-down when they realise that they've stolen a little bit of wonder from their own world. Not me, though – I actually enjoy tricks more when I know how they're done.

No, my problem with performing magic was very much the performing part. My crippling stage fright meant my teenage years were consumed in an endless cycle of coming up with an act, booking myself to perform somewhere, convincing myself it wasn't good enough then scrapping the whole thing to start again.

My parents tried to intervene. Every six months or so, Dad would take me to a different sporting event. I think at a certain point they'd have been relieved if I'd developed a crippling addiction to betting on the gee-gees. At least that way I'd be getting some fresh air or making friends down the bookies.

School was hard. In hindsight, even in the sixties, the last thing the bullying community of a south London comprehensive needed was the added incentive of a child wearing a battered top hat that didn't even match his briefcase. The end-of-year talent contest was a particularly low point. There really is no coming back from throwing up over the baton-twirling Butler sisters while waiting to go on stage. One of them cried while the other punched me, and then they swapped places.

Upon leaving school, I was taken on as an apprentice at the accountancy firm where my uncle George worked, and where I distinguished myself by scraping by with the bare minimum effort. It wasn't that I was lazy, I was just focused on other things. Or, rather, one thing.

I had the skills, all I needed was the showmanship. I tried everything. I read books, I sent away for courses, I even joined the Toastmasters in an attempt to learn public speaking – distinguishing myself by becoming the first member to be thrown out for, and I quote, 'the unnecessary and ill-judged production of a dove'. In fairness to them, I was already on a warning.

I had one friend at the time – Errol, another apprentice accountant. His nickname was Error. It was a prescient one. He took to accountancy like a duck to accountancy. I was half trying to get fired and Errol was the main reason it didn't happen. They didn't fire me because they couldn't fire him. Despite his ineptitude, Errol was well liked by all. His wide, gap-toothed grin and excited, puppy-like manner could win over all but the hardest of hearts. Even those individuals were brought round remarkably quickly when they realised his grandfather owned the company. That was the other reason he didn't get fired. Eventually, the problem of his ineptitude was solved the old-fashioned way – by promoting him repeatedly until he finally reached a position where he couldn't do any damage.

That was in the future, though. Back in the early days of our friendship, Errol ended up being the one-man cheering-squad for my showbiz ambitions. I'd never had someone who believed in me before and, frankly, it could be argued that it was the last thing I needed. With Errol cajoling me, I started booking myself into talent shows, showcases, you name it. He knew a man who knew a man who knew who his grandfather was, and that's how I got booked at a showcase night for the Chamber of Commerce. Errol came along as my off-stage assistant and, seeing how utterly terrified I was, he took me across the road for a swift half beforehand. Which soon became several halves. So many, in fact, that we returned for the show half-cut. The man in charge didn't want to let me go on but Errol, who referred to himself as my manager, assured him that this was all part of my 'process'.

When the time came, Errol's role as manager extended to shoving me onstage, which he did with such vigour that I duly fell over. My trip was greeted with a titter and a gasp or two. I got to my feet and loudly introduced myself to the backdrop before realising the audience was behind me and turning around. I then proceeded to perform my act while drunkenly stumbling about the place. The thing was, I knew the tricks so well that my body could do them without my brain's assistance. I drunkenly rambled, hiccupped, recounted a joke Errol had told me in the pub (backwards), all the while doing trick after trick. People loved it. I left to a standing ovation. As I stood there afterwards, dumbfounded, my back grew sore from all the congratulatory slaps. My pockets were stuffed full of business cards. I was a success,

God help me. I'd been so utterly unprepared for this turn of events that I'd even performed under my own name – Robert Craven.

So that's how it started. Soon, I got myself a booking agent and the gigs began rolling in. I ended up hiring my cousin Martin as a driver as I had to have several drinks to get into 'character' at every gig. I even worked up a whole routine, 'Cocktail Hour', that revolved around me mixing myself drinks while making bottles, tumblers and Reginald, my rabbit, disappear and reappear, seemingly at random. Audiences couldn't get enough.

It wasn't long before I was making almost enough money to give up my job, so I gave up my job. At that point, I also moved out of home, as Mum was on my back about throwing away my career and the fact I was drinking so much. She didn't understand. The drinking was part of the act.

To save a few quid, I moved up to Manchester. Besides, that was where my booking agent, Edgar Wagner, was based. The man was as slippery as an eel, but he talked a good game and he'd have sold his granny for a decent commission.

And so, off I went, working my way up the circuit, playing the working men's clubs, charity nights, bingo halls. Having relocated, I got myself two new drivers, Gerry and Carl, who alternated. Carl was a wannabe magician himself, and so I made him my sort of apprentice. Gerry was a doorman, so him I brought to the rougher gigs.

There were other magicians around at the time, of course. Donnie Drake, who was nothing special technically, but a smooth performer who could also hold a tune. Fabulous Frankie Barker was good, but he supplemented his act with off-colour jokes that weren't to my taste. It was frankly depressing to watch him storm it. Then there was

Marty Martins and the Lovely Cheryl. They were a glamorous duo – him with matinee-idol looks and her with a smile that could light up a room. Theirs was an odd act – some fairly unimaginative standard fare interspersed with Marty telling jokes about how dumb his assistant was. It was essentially all the blonde jokes you've ever heard, reworked. Cheryl smiled and laughed along, which I guess gave the audience permission to do the same. Then, as a finale, they performed the bowling-ball trick – where Marty managed to make a real bowling ball disappear from a box on one side of the stage and reappear in another on the far side. It was extraordinary. The first time I saw them do it, I couldn't believe it.

Whenever we worked together, I watched carefully from the wings. I checked with other magicians, too. Nobody could figure it out. I even did the unthinkable and asked. Marty took great delight in not telling me. It might've been jealousy, but I didn't like the guy. There was something about him. Cheryl seemed nice, if rather quiet, but Marty was the jealous type and so she rarely spoke to the other acts. The changing room in most venues was somewhere between cramped to non-existent, so Cheryl always made use of the back of their van instead.

Still, I couldn't work out the damned trick and, honestly, I became a little obsessed. I even ended up going to see them on a few of my nights off, desperate to figure it out. The more I watched, the more mystified I became.

Obviously, I determined at one point, it was a trick bowling ball. Then, at a gig in Stockport, I saw Cheryl drop it and, blimey, if she didn't break her foot. She tried to soldier on, but the girl was clearly in too much pain. One of the committee men stepped in, seeing as Marty seemed determined for the show to continue in spite of the fact that his assistant was fighting back tears.

I left when they finished, as I'd no desire to sit through another cabaret singer taking 'New York, New York' out back and kicking it to death. As I neared my car, I caught sight of Cheryl and Marty on the far side of the car park, having what looked like a heated argument. It ended with Marty getting into their van and screeching out of there, leaving his assistant and girlfriend standing there on one foot, shouting after him.

I pulled up and offered her a lift. She assured me he was coming back, and I agreed that I was sure he was too, but the sooner she got to hospital, the sooner they could go home. They lived down Birmingham way. Once I'd left a note with the lady on the venue door, Cheryl agreed to let me drive her to accident and emergency.

I remember it being awkward in the car as we drove in silence. Eventually, Cheryl said, 'It's just he takes it all so seriously. He wants it to be perfect, so that we can be a success.' I told her that of course, I understood completely. The thing I understood was that Marty was a monumental arsehole of the highest order, but it wasn't my place to say it.

Once we got to A & E, I insisted on taking her in and waiting with her. It was quite busy, being a Saturday night, and there'd been a derby match earlier in the day, too. Several men who'd disagreed with the result or enjoyed it too much were ahead of us in the queue. I gave Cheryl my coat as her spangly assistant outfit was drawing more attention than she felt comfortable with.

Daft as it sounds, we then played I Spy for two hours. In between rounds, we shared memories of some of the worst clubs we'd played, I made her laugh with some stupid card tricks, and she completed the crossword in a newspaper someone had left behind while pretending I was helping. It turned out that Cheryl was nobody's dumb blonde. She had a sharp mind, a quick wit and a smile that had a room full of football hooligans sitting up and trying to look respectable.

After a little more than two hours, Marty showed up, looking all contrite and making excuses aplenty about some mix-up or other. He'd been racing off to find her a doctor apparently. Cheryl played along and who was I to say otherwise? I made my apologies and left. I headed home and, with an aching heart, 'practised the act', which had become my charming little way to describe getting hammered.

Over the next couple of years, I saw Cheryl and Marty infrequently. With variety nights being what they were, we didn't end up on the same bill often. Still, every now and then there was a magic showcase or something like that. Cheryl and I rarely got to speak. I still watched the act and was none the wiser as to how they did the bloody bowling-ball trick. Drove me insane.

Then, finally, my big break came – the chance to appear on one of the new act TV talent shows. When Edgar called with the news, he was beside himself, to the point where I had to calm him down to understand what he was telling me. He was quite often hard to understand. For reasons known only to himself, he permanently had an unlit cigar clamped in his mouth, despite being a non-smoker. That day, he nearly swallowed the bloody thing and had to ring me back.

I only found out when I reached the hotel they were putting me up in that Marty and Cheryl would be on the same show. It was going to be recorded at the London Palladium, one of the great meccas of British showbiz.

It would also be going out live, so the show's producers

had us go down the day before for run-throughs and rehearsals. At Edgar's urging, I pushed the boat out and had a custom bar built, one that could be pushed on and off stage.

From the first moment I stepped on to that hallowed stage, I could feel my nerves going jingle-jangle. This was it. This was my moment. My first run-through was a disaster, though. I stumbled over my words, dropped props. The second was still ropey but slightly better, after I'd steadied myself with a few stiff whiskies.

I bumped into Marty and Cheryl backstage. Cheryl just smiled while Marty, being Marty, kept asking me how nervous I was while telling me what great mates we were. Trying to get into my head. More fool him – there was no room in there, it was already full to bursting point with self-doubt and demons.

We were all done by one o'clock and they didn't need us back until six so I went to the pub across the road to get lunch. Come to think of it, I never actually managed to eat any food. When I made my way back to the theatre, I was in 'high spirits'. The bloke on the stage door didn't want to let me in and called one of the assistants to verify I was really on the show. I can still remember the look on the assistant's face as I cheerfully informed her not to worry, this was my well-honed stage persona.

I was barely in my dressing room when the producer arrived, took one look at me and announced I was off the show. I tried to plead with him, make him understand. It's all part of the act, I told him. That was all. The act. I'll always remember what he said – there's a big difference between acting drunk for an act and being a drunk with an act. He was not going to risk his career by putting an alcoholic live on national TV.

Weirdly, that was the first time anyone had ever used that word in my presence. I remember opening my mouth to defend myself but not being able to find the words.

The producer turned to the assistant. 'Bloody magicians. The other two are gone as well.'

He left the door open as he stormed out and I looked across the hall. There in their dressing room were Cheryl and Marty, with a man in a cream suit who I'd never seen before. The stranger looked on impassively as Marty pleaded his case while Cheryl sat there quietly, her head in her hands. It didn't make sense. I knew the reason I was being kicked off, but what had they done? Cheryl raised her head, our eyes met and we sat there, looking at each other for what felt like the longest time.

The moment ended when the man in the suit turned around and caught my gaze. I remember noticing that he had two different-coloured eyes. There must have been somebody else in the room whom I hadn't seen, as it seemed as if he just waved his hand and the door slammed shut.

I was promptly shoved into a taxi. The last thing I heard was the producer ordering somebody to shake a tree and a couple of comedians would probably fall out of it.

Back at my hotel, I lay on the bed. I thought about ringing Edgar or my suddenly proud parents to explain that I wasn't going to be on the show, but I couldn't. It just made it too real. Instead, I opened the bottle of Glenfiddich I had in my suitcase that I'd brought to celebrate with after the show. I started celebrating pretty hard.

I must have nodded off, but I awoke to the sound of shouting. I recognised the voices. Marty and Cheryl.

To be fair, it was mainly Marty. He was loudly making the point that whatever had happened was all Cheryl's fault. Her 'stupid people' was a phrase that kept popping up, which I didn't understand. Cheryl's responses were considerably more muted, mainly along the lines of 'leave me alone'. When they changed to 'get off me', I was on my feet.

Three rooms down on the far side of the corridor. I pounded on the door.

'Piss off!' screamed Marty.

'No,' I said. 'Open this door.'

He did. For a handsome man, a sneer really brought out the true Marty. He scowled down at me and, given that he had a good six inches in height on me, it was quite the trip. 'Oh, for fuck's sake, it's your little pisshead friend.'

I peered past him. 'Cheryl, I'd like you to come with me.'

Cheryl's mascara was running from where she'd been crying and her hair was dangling down over one of her eyes. 'Honestly, it's OK.'

'No,' I said, 'it isn't. He can't speak to you like that.'

Marty shoved me in the chest. 'Talk to me. Not to her.'

I stood as tall as I could. 'I've got nothing to say to you.' I reached out my hand. 'Come on, Cheryl. Let's go.'

Marty slapped it away and shoved me again. 'Get lost now or you'll wake up with more than your usual hangover.' He pointed down the hallway. 'You and whoever that is.'

I looked to where he'd pointed, which marked the first time in his career when Marty had successfully accomplished some genuine misdirection. By the time I'd realised there was nobody there, his fist was already well on its way to my face. It crashed into my jaw and sent me sprawling on to the carpet. Marty, being Marty, took the opportunity to fire a couple of well-aimed kicks into my midsection and nether regions as an encore.

I heard Cheryl shouting then everything became a little

fuzzy. The last thing I remember was her standing over me, a flash of blue light, and then I saw stars.

When I came to, I was still seeing stars. This time they were in the sky above London.

I was sitting outside on cold concrete, propped up against a wall behind me. The wind was bitterly cold and surprisingly strong. I tried to comprehend this new location as various parts of my body delivered damage reports to my drink-addled brain. Luckily, I'd been pre-numbed before the fight – if you could even call it that – but it was clear that I had a lot of bills waiting to come due on the pain front. Not that it was my most pressing concern, but I wondered if the TV company was still going to pay for the hotel. Come to that – given that I was outside, on a chilly but mercifully dry November evening, maybe I'd already been kicked out.

In answer to at least some of my questions, Cheryl appeared above me and handed me a loaded napkin. 'Here,' she said in a kind voice. 'I got you some ice to put on that.'

'Which bit?' I said, taking the proffered handkerchief. 'Everything hurts.'

'The lip.'

'The ...' I ran my tongue around my mouth and took her point. My bottom lip felt as if it were in danger of swelling to a size where it would take over my face entirely. 'Oh, that.'

She sat down beside me. I felt her shoulder rub against mine as she did so.

'How did I get here?'

'You blacked out.'

'Right.' I glanced at her. 'I didn't even get a chance to do all of that kung fu that I definitely know. Second biggest disappointment of the day.'

'Don't,' she said.

'OK.'

We sat there in silence for a few minutes.

'We're on the roof of the hotel,' I said.

'Yes, I know.'

'I mean, how are we on the roof?'

I felt her shrug. 'Everyone has to be somewhere.'

I looked at my watch. 'And we were supposed to be on stage at the Palladium.'

'Yes.'

'I think we both know how I screwed up, but I've no idea why you aren't there?'

'It's a long story.'

'I'm not going anywhere.' I shifted the ice around my lip and winced. 'I mean, possibly a dentist at some point, but they won't open for a while.'

'You shouldn't have done that,' she said.

'Which bit? I've done a lot of things wrong today.'

'You know which bit.'

I turned to look at her, my neck complaining as I did so. 'That bit I don't regret. Although, can we go back to how the hell I got here? I'm really confused.'

'Just accept that not everything has a rational explanation.'

'You really don't know how to talk to a magician.'

'Evidently.'

I winced again but not from any of the sources of physical pain. 'I didn't mean ...'

'I know.'

'You deserve better than him.'

She sighed. 'More and more I'm starting to realise that this world is full to bursting point with people who aren't getting what they deserve. Everything is complicated.'

'Some things aren't,' I replied. 'Some things are blindingly obvious to everyone except the person involved.'

'Is that so?' Cheryl pulled herself up so that she was sitting on her haunches in front of me. 'Shut up for a second.'

She placed her hands gently on either side of my head and turned it this way and that. She really did have the kindest eyes. 'Hmmmm. As long as you don't have any modelling shoots scheduled for the next few weeks, you should be OK. You might need to cancel a few gigs.'

'I think I might need to cancel all my gigs. I'm done with this.' Until I'd said it, I hadn't even realised I was thinking it, but once it was out there, the sheer sense of the revelation was overwhelming. 'I can't keep doing this. I need to get help.'

She nodded. 'That ... is a very good idea. You, Mr Craven, are a great magician, a good guy and a terrible drunk.' She gave me a soft smile that broke my heart. 'You should do something about that because while there will always be plenty of magicians, good guys are in short supply.'

'I don't know what to do,' I said. And I really didn't.

'I'm guessing admitting there's a problem is a good first step.'

'Speaking of which, not to change the subject, but your boyfriend is an arse.'

'He's not my boyfriend any more.'

I felt my heart rise. 'Oh?'

She held up her hand and I saw the ring. 'Fiancé.'

'Congratulations.'

'Do you mean that?'

'Christ, no.'

'Just checking.' She looked around. 'We should probably get going.'

'But we haven't even played I Spy yet? How many people get to do that with a view like this.' I waved a hand to the majesty of London laid out below us.

'Time is against us,' she said.

'Isn't it always? I spy with my little eye … something beginning with H.'

'Houses of Parliament.'

'Damn, you're good at this.'

'I had quite a bit of time to prepare myself while you were out cold.'

'No fair.'

'Life isn't,' she said, hugging herself to fend off the chill. 'Life isn't,' she repeated softly. Then she eased herself to her feet. 'I really should get going.'

'Wait. I …'

As she looked down at me I felt suddenly transfixed by those eyes. 'What?'

I didn't know what. My mind had achieved a level of emptiness normally only accomplished by scaling mountains in Tibet to spend a decade with Buddhist monks eating nothing but broccoli.

'Is there something you want to ask me?'

'Yes.'

Have you ever said something and even while the words were still coming out of your mouth you already wanted to suck them back in? To take it all back. 'How do you do the bowling-ball trick?'

Cheryl looked out at the skyline and laughed. 'Once a magician …' She turned back to me. 'I'll show you.'

'Actually, no, I ...'

'Close your eyes.'

'But—'

'Close your eyes,' she repeated.

I did.

'Now count to three.'

I did. When I opened them, she was gone.

I waited an hour but she didn't come back. Then I realised that the door to the stairs was locked.

I sobered up, sitting there in the bitter cold all night, looking down at the spectacular London skyline and feeling like the biggest idiot in the world.

When a cleaner finally heard my banging at 6 a.m., and I made it down from the roof and back to my room, I poured the remainder of the Glenfiddich down the sink. I never drank again.

The next few years were tricky. This was the eighties. Rehab hadn't been invented yet – not unless you'd won an Oscar or played Wembley. Luckily, my one-time driver and apprentice Carl had a mother as nice as he was, who owned a little cottage in the Lake District. I went up there to 'rest'. The local GP was a very friendly chap, who dropped over on his daily dog walks and checked in on me. I came back a different man. An unemployed but sober one.

Having decided on my new course of action, I duly sold my act. Well, all of it except 'Cocktail Hour', which was the signature piece. I got plenty of offers for it too, but I held off. I can't really explain why. I'd decided that my future definitely did not lie on stage, but I still couldn't let that routine go. The story of it was the story of me – at least in part, and it didn't feel right to sell it to a stranger.

The money from my little fire sale gave me just enough to rent a small warehouse in Manchester with blocked pipes and a stench that never leaves you. From there, I launched my emporium. This was my solution. I loved magic and, for better or for worse, I wasn't going to abandon it. Instead, I would design and sell illusions for others to perform. People always assume that a magician's act is created by them, but that is rarely the case, especially once the ravenous beast that is television gets hold of them, which means that more and more material is needed.

Things were rough for a while and I was barely scraping by, but then the wheel of fortune turned full circle. Remember Carl? My young apprentice? Well, what I didn't mention was that, with a little assistance from me, he became something of a rising star. As you may have guessed by now, Carl isn't his real name. Secrecy is a large part of my business. The lad was an incredibly natural performer. He had what you couldn't teach, and believe me, I know that better than anyone. After a couple of big appearances, he was given his own show on prime-time TV.

My emporium took on more staff, and I became Carl's full-time ingénieur. He and I worked on tricks and illusions together that he went on to perform all over the world. Carl in the spotlight, me working away behind the scenes. That was how I liked it and, although he blanched at ever being referred to as such, Carl was a wonderful boss. I worked for others from time to time too, but my relationship with Carl has spanned thirty years and remains a very happy one.

I saw Cheryl and Marty only twice in those early years. They were still on the circuit. They got older, the act got a little staler but Cheryl remained as beautiful as ever. They also got married, so I heard. Unsurprisingly, I wasn't sent an invitation.

While I was happy with my lot in life, I often thought back to that night on the roof. What did I say at the start of our little tale? Unless your life has been particularly blessed or cursed, you probably can't pick out one defining moment that set it on a certain path. There can be more than one moment, though. Arguably, on that day when I played the briefest game of I Spy up on the roof, I had two. Looking back, while I cringe to remember the first in that dressing room in the Palladium, I don't regret it. Without it, God knows where I'd be now. My guess is that the drink would have derailed me eventually, possibly at a point when the fall would have been even harder.

The other moment, though ... That comes wrapped in nothing but regret.

I've been part of a few big moments for Carl, too. Happy ones, I'm pleased to say. We had a great career, he and I. Magic being magic, it fades in and out of the public consciousness, but Carl managed to keep it all in perspective while also being able to move with the times. Plus, while he had also coincidentally trained as an accountant, unlike me, he was actually good at it, and so was well able to manage his finances to ensure he and his family were well taken care of. He and his wife, Melinda, have four kids now, and I'm godfather to all of them, would you believe. Each year on my birthday, they put on a magic show for me. It is a delight.

So, while I've never married, life has been good. I have no complaints. Through my work, I've been to some of the most glamorous locations in the world, and stood in the same room with some of the most glamorous people. It was therefore something of a personal disappointment to suffer a massive heart attack while standing in the Arndale Centre. I'd only gone there to buy a birthday cake for the long-suffering Jacinta from the office. I never did find out what happened to the cake.

I woke up in Manchester Royal Infirmary with Carl and Melinda standing over me, smiling those trying-not-to-look-too-concerned smiles people do that let you know you're in real trouble. The doctors informed me that they would have to perform a quadruple bypass.

I was fifty-five. I felt a little miffed that my ticker had become awkward quite so early. While I'd been a heavy drinker, that had been almost thirty years ago. I was a month away from getting my bronze sobriety chip. Admittedly, I hadn't always eaten the healthiest of diets – Las Vegas has such wonderful buffets – but still. I don't mind telling you, lying there in that hospital room the night before the operation, I was scared. A different kind of scared than I'd ever been before. I'll say this for a near-death experience, though – it does rather simplify life.

I wrote a few letters. One to my mother – we'd been stubbornly frosty with each other for years by that point and enough was enough. One to Carl – in case I didn't make it. I even wrote one to my godchildren.

And one other.

As the anaesthesiologist counted me down from ten the next morning, I thought of one face. One kind smile.

Nobody was as surprised as me when, two days later, I awoke in my hospital room to be greeted by that smile. Cheryl was sitting beside the bed, holding my hand.

'Good morning,' she said.

'How did I get here?'

She looked confused then turned away to hide her smile. After a moment, she looked back at me, a twinkle in her eyes. 'Everybody has to be somewhere.'

'That they do.'

She bobbed her head in the direction of the door. 'The nurse tells me that you're making a remarkable recovery. I think she has a little crush on you.'

'Oh,' I replied, 'I don't doubt it. Women really go for the whole vulnerable thing.'

'Some do.'

An awkward moment of silence followed. I flashed back to another such moment up on a roof. This time would be different. I didn't feel like I had another thirty years or another heart to risk waiting to try again. 'So, you got my letter?'

'I did,' she replied. 'Your young apprentice is rather resourceful. I left the world of magic completely over twenty years ago now. Even changed my name. He still knocked on my door yesterday morning and handed it to me.'

'I bet Marty loved that.'

'I wouldn't know,' she said. 'I left him over twenty years ago too.'

'Right,' I said, my mouth suddenly dry. 'Well, I know this will shock you but I have to say, I never liked him.'

'Really? He spoke very highly of you.'

'Where is he now?'

Cheryl patted my hand. 'Does that feel like something we should be discussing at this particular moment?'

'No. Right. I ... have to be honest, you've sort of caught me on the hop here, Cheryl.'

'This from the man who wrote me a letter after nearly thirty years.'

'Fair point.'

We smiled at each other for a long while. 'Honestly, just give me a couple of minutes. I will think of something to say. I just don't want to get it wrong again.'

'If it helps,' she said, pulling my letter from the inside pocket of her coat, 'I could give you this back and you could read bits of it out.' She tapped it against her chin. 'You did rather nail it.'

'Story of my life. Always better on paper. Any passages in particular?'

She rolled her eyes then wiped a tear from the corner of the right one. 'The one about how you reckon you've always loved me was a pretty good one.'

I nodded. 'I thought so. It has the bonus of being true. I—'

She interrupted me by leaning forward and kissing me on the lips. Then she placed her hands gently on either side of my face. 'It took you long enough.'

'Timing is everything.'

She eased herself to her feet. 'Speaking of which …' She moved down to the end of the bed and checked that the door was closed. 'I think you've waited long enough, don't you?'

'I mean … I agree, but while I'm going to hate myself for saying this, I might not be in the best of states to do that right now.'

She looked at the ceiling. 'Not that, you idiot. You really are better on paper.' She scanned the room then picked up a teddy bear that the children had given me. 'Imagine this is a bowling ball …'

She swirled the index finger of her right hand in the air

and a distorted circle appeared, as if that section of the air suddenly didn't belong. I didn't notice the other circle, the one to my right until she put her left hand holding the bear through the first one, and the bear appeared beside my head. As if by magic. No, as actually by magic. Actual magic.

She drew the bear back and put it through a few more times as I watched, dumbfounded.

'Right, well, that explains that. By which I mean, that doesn't explain anything …'

Cheryl laughed. 'It would never have occurred to you in a million years, would it? The one thing a magician can never ever believe – that there really is such a thing as magic.'

I lay there, looking back and forth between her and the bear. 'Is this heaven?'

She arched an eyebrow in the direction of the window. 'Not with those curtains.'

'And you've been able to do that since?'

'I was a young girl.'

'But why didn't you … I mean … That would blow people's minds.'

'It's all rather complicated, but to give you the really simplified version, there's lots more where that came from. In the world, I mean – not me specifically. I am what is known as a porter. Bit of a family tradition. A lot of people get very annoyed if they think you're letting people in on the secret, though.'

My eyes widened. 'The Palladium. That's why you didn't …'

She nodded. 'I thought they wouldn't know. Rather naive. Then again, I thought I loved a man who was clearly a narcissistic control freak.'

'It was the eighties. We all made mistakes. Let's not discuss my regrettable mullet phase.'

She laughed and, with the slightest hand gesture, the portals in the air disappeared. Cheryl stepped back around the bed, handed me the bear and sat back down.

'So ...'

'So ...' I agreed, holding the bear in my hands.

'Where do we go from here?'

I looked at her. I looked at the bear. I looked around the room. 'Cheryl?'

'Yes?'

'I spy with my little eye, something beginning with L ...'

THE LADY RISES

It was a dark and stormy night. Or at least it would have been, had the weather any sense of occasion. As it was, it was just raining. A steady Mancunian rain, slanting slightly to the left regardless of which way you were standing. On the upside, it was enough to dissuade all but the most committed of trick-or-treaters.

Victor's father had always hated Hallowe'en, or rather what it had become. So commercialised. Every year, he berated the people who knocked on their door, for reducing the most important date on the pagan calendar to a fancy-dress party. It was a stance that had not made them popular on the estate.

A few years ago, while in the midst of a particularly impassioned monologue on the subject, a woman from three roads away had smacked Dad right in the eye with a toffee apple. Victor had spent an hour with a pair of tweezers, surgically removing his father's eyelashes from a fruit-based confectionary nightmare. The lashes had never fully grown back until, oddly, the undertaker had restored them in death. Victor had taken some consolation from that, given that the council had forbidden him from fulfilling his father's dying wish of a funeral pyre on a raft in Deansgate Locks. It was health and safety gone mad.

After the toffee-apple incident, his father had cast a spell, and nobody had knocked on their door on Hallowe'en ever again. It was almost certainly the spell that did it, but every year, just to be on the safe side, Victor also stuck a big picture of Jesus on their front door. In his experience, most people didn't believe in the man, but they were still terrified of speaking to anyone who did.

For as long as Victor could remember, it had been just him and Dad. Victor didn't have many friends, seeing as he'd been home-schooled. Dad said it was pointless him going to an ordinary school, as they'd just try to stifle his genius. His earliest memory was being told he was a genius and now, at the age of twenty-four, it was taken as a matter of fact, albeit one he'd had a hard time explaining to the woman at the job centre.

Victor's genius took many forms: for a start, he was a wordivator – a maker of new words. In fact, he'd made up that very word, thus proving himself to be one. Shakespeare had been one; Tupac, too. And now him. Other people claimed to be wordivators, except they used the term wordologist, which was just proof that they weren't true wordivators. It wasn't as simple as just making up random nonsense – there was so much more to it than that. At its heart, wordivating was the art of finding expression for the untold story of human existence. Take bagasense – his word for the gnawing feeling of having driven to the supermarket and forgotten yet again to take reusable bags with you – or pasqualopothy – the belief that your good idea was really someone else's first but being absolutely fine with that.

After tonight, no one would dare to doubt Victor's genius ever again. He was about to bring new life into the world!

Now, yes – people had been doing that for, well, the entirety of human history, and the act of creating life in and of itself wasn't that impressive. He'd witnessed evidence to support this belief only yesterday when a heavily pregnant woman at the bus stop had called him a paedo because he wouldn't give her a cigarette. It's worth pointing out that Victor didn't smoke and, more importantly, he was pretty sure she shouldn't have been either.

The difference between Victor and that woman – well, one of the differences; there were loads, actually – was, for a start, he wasn't female, pregnant or a smoker. Nor did he have the word 'mum' tattooed on her arm and then, later, the words 'fuck you' above it for reasons that weren't clear. But the single biggest difference pertaining to this momentous moment was that he was bringing life into the world fully formed, as opposed to squeezing out a baby that would inevitably have its ears pierced at far too young an age.

His creation lay before him on the kitchen table. All right, she wasn't technically his creation – yet. Technically, she was a product supplied by the Nakatoma Corporation in the Philippines. Victor strongly disliked the descriptor 'sex doll'. For a start, she wasn't a doll, but a state-of-the-art programmable android. A Francine 5000. Francine was an oddly old-lady name for something whose advertising bumph had emphasised its frankly impractical curves and wipe-clean features, but Victor supposed the Filipinos had simply picked a name that didn't have any obvious celebrity associations to avoid lawsuits. He wasn't wild about the sex-android angle of all this, but it was either that or start digging up bodies. That seemed extremely icky and – people always underestimated this – it is actually really hard to dig up a grave. In any case, Victor had never been good at physical exercise, having been a steady C-student in PE or, as it could be more accurately described, running laps of the garden of his small, terraced house.

Admittedly, the programming options available on the basic Francine 5000 model were very limited, as indicated by the fact that most of the so-called 'personality types' were illustrated in the instruction manual by stick-figure drawings, some of which involved the use of implements. All this, however, was about to change.

The genius of Victor's approach was two-fold. First, he'd paid extra for massive processor and memory upgrades to give him the capacity to upload additional personality programming. He'd combined ChatGPT with the script of his favourite film, *Alien*, plus a transcript of two shows by Victoria Wood (his father's favourite comedian) and three sample chapters from the book *Fix the System, Not the Women*, which he'd downloaded free from Amazon. These, Victor felt, would provide a more well-rounded individual. He'd also tweaked Francine's programming to include 'bringing down the patriarchy' under her fantasies, as Victor was a feminist. He wasn't entirely sure what he meant by that, as up to this point in his life he'd had remarkably little contact with the opposite sex, but he regularly gave women a big thumbs-up out the window of the bus when he saw them doing stuff.

The second fold of his two-fold approach was the application of the occult. Victor wasn't a wizard like his dad, but he still understood enough about magic to grasp the fundamentals. Certain items retained magical properties and those properties could be drawn upon – sort of like batteries. With that in mind, after spending a whopping fifteen thousand pounds on the customisable Francine 5000, he'd used his remaining four hundred pounds to acquire objects of latent magical power to perform the ritual he had planned. He'd gone to Paulo's Emporium in Affleck's widely regarded as *the* shop for the serious magic user, and bought two Himalayan salt lamps, a dreamcatcher, some maprinian spoons and a crocheted portrait of Aleister Crowley. To cover all bases, he'd also trawled the local charity shop and found an inexplicably unnerving picture of a blond child, the stuffed head of a moose, half a dozen ceramic gnomes with haunting eyes, and a portrait so magnificently awful that the one-word title on the frame, 'Queen', still left the peruser wondering if the subject was the dearly departed monarch or Freddie Mercury from the band Queen. That final item hadn't felt particularly eldritch, but the nice old lady in the shop had thrown it in for free. In fact, she'd given him everything for free, as a thank-you for taking the portrait.

He would never normally have accepted something for free from a charity. However, he fundamentally didn't understand why Bolton needed a donkey sanctuary. He was confused by what the donkeys were being saved from, and to what end. What's more, whenever he'd asked the old lady about it in the past, she'd been peculiarly shifty. He had a sneaking suspicion that the Bolton Donkey Sanctuary was a front organisation for something sinister, and that she was definitely in on it. His father had often stated that people had a real blind spot when it came to trusting the elderly automatically. Old people were just people who'd grown old.

Victor was ready to begin the ceremony. He'd finished lighting the candles. If there was one thing he'd learned from watching his father performing spells over the years, it was that you couldn't have too many candles. If there was a second lesson, it was that you should always have a fire extinguisher handy, as the aforementioned candles and his father's penchant for long-sleeved robes were a dangerous combination. The candles he was using today were particularly pleasing as they were dark purple and black, and had that all-important dribbly quality to them. They were the 'good candles' that his father used on special occasions. If Dad had ever been conjuring some basic ill on the man who'd been rude to him in Lidl then the tealights from IKEA would suffice, but for the momentous spells he'd always instructed Victor to bring out the big guns.

Along with the candles, the various items Victor had acquired were now dotted around the kitchen table. The air was thick with magic and the scent of burning lavender because, as his father was wont to say, you couldn't find an unscented candle these days for love nor money.

This would be the night; Victor could feel it in his bones.

Admittedly, this wasn't the first time he'd felt it in his bones. In fact, his bones were becoming suspect. The first occasion had been two weeks ago – on a truly stormy night, wonderful ambiance. Victor had been mid-ceremony when the doorbell had rung and he'd opened it to a man asking if he had a TV licence. A twenty-minute argument had ensued, during which Victor assured the man he neither needed nor wanted a TV licence, and that the mainstream media was a con. The man had kept bringing up *Match of the Day* and then, once Victor had finally seen him off, he'd returned to his ceremony to discover he'd left one of the candles too close to Francine, causing her little toe to burn and melt slightly.

On the second occasion, which had been a week ago, there'd been actual lightning! Infuriatingly, he'd had to abandon the ceremony when Francine's software had failed to compile correctly. He'd spent two days ringing Nakatomi technical support, trying to resolve that issue. They'd kept picking up the phone and shouting about not giving refunds before slamming it down again. He'd eventually found an answer on an online forum and once he'd updated the firmware, things seemed more promising. Previously, the little green bar, which stretched across his computer screen, had crashed when it reached seventy-eight per cent but now it was at ninety-four per cent. It was working, it was really working.

Of course, Hallowe'en was the ideal night to do this, but initially Victor had not wanted to wait. This had less to do with his desire to prove his genius to the world and more to do with where he'd borrowed the fifteen thousand four hundred pounds from. Ivan, the mad Russian. It was a hyperbolic name but an apt one – the bloke was certainly mad. That being said, Ivan wasn't Russian – he was actually called Darren and was about the same age as Victor. As children they'd been in the Salford Amateur Dramatics Society together. Darren had gone from what in Victor's opinion had been an overly showy Peter Pan, to deciding at some point in his adolescence that he was Russian and, if the stories were to be believed, then staying in character for fourteen years and counting. He hadn't even managed to remain in character for the whole of *Peter Pan*, so he'd come a long way in at least one regard.

If what Victor had read on the internet and overheard on

the bus was to be believed, Ivan was now one of Manchester's premier mobsters, having set up his own version of the Russian mob that incredibly featured no actual Russians. That part might have been fantasy, but his uncompromising methods were a terrifying reality. Ivan had been charged with murder, attempted murder and a shopping list of other offences, but none of them had ever come to court due to witnesses recanting their testimonies or simply disappearing. Mr Ibrahim from three doors down had been late on payments and ended up with a broken arm. Luckily, he was a lollipop man, so it didn't affect his work, but a clear message had nevertheless been sent. Victor had not wanted to go to Ivan for the money, but conventional banking was incredibly small-minded when it came to its lending criteria.

The green bar on the screen ticked from ninety-five per cent to ninety-six per cent compiled. This was it. This was definitely it. All the hard work was about to pay off. Victor began the chanting.

'Ma-wah-ca-ca, wah-wah, nah-nah.'

Victor's dad had explained that the act of chanting was more important than what you were saying.

'Izzy wizzy, let's get busy!'

Victor tried to remain calm as the portrait of the Queen or Freddie Mercury started to glow with a hazy orange light.

Ninety-seven per cent compiled.

'Tinky Winky, Dipsy, Laa-Laa, Po!'

The orange light was expanding now, growing in intensity.

Ninety-eight per cent.

The kitchen table was shaking.

The orange light throbbed.

'Eeny, meeny, miny, mo …'

Victor shielded his eyes, as the light emanating from the picture was now so bright he could no longer look directly at it.

Ninety-nine per cent.

Everything in the kitchen was vibrating now.

Victor swore that he could feel the heat of the light burning against his cheeks.

Then one of the wonky-eyed gnomes exploded.

One hundred per cent compiled.

The air was electric and tasted of iron.

It felt as if reality was going to tear itself asunder right there and then in his kitchen. The moose's head made a sound remarkably like a howl. The rest of the gnomes exploded in quick succession. One of the salt lamps went out. The candles remained lit. A black candle quickly learns to expect shit to get weird and is hence reliable in all manner of stressful situations. Victor, on the other hand, was freaking out.

What could he do?

What could he do?

He remembered what he could do. He reached across and pressed enter on the keyboard … and it all stopped.

The chaos ceased so suddenly that, had it not been for the still-smoking remains of the gnomes, he couldn't be sure if it had happened at all. That and the fact that the woman on the table opened her eyes, sat up and smiled at him.

'Hello, darling,' she said. 'My, that made a mess. I'm famished. Shall I get started on dinner?'

Victor sat nervously in the front room, hugging a cushion. Francine had been in the kitchen for fifteen minutes now, cooking dinner. She had informed him that she was making duck à l'orange, which seemed particularly ambitious seeing as he had neither a duck nor an orange in the house, two items he assumed were fundamental requirements for that particular dish. He didn't say anything, though, because, well, up until this point, Francine had been merely an idea. A concept. In more practical terms, a vessel wrapped in a lifelike silicone-skin substitute containing what the Nakatoma Corporation proudly called the cutting edge in android technology. Now, she was a five-foot-ten blonde woman standing in his kitchen putting something into the big pot. She was doing all of this naked. Victor hadn't dressed her before the ritual because Francine had just been one of the objects then. Now, now – well, now …

Now, she was very naked in his kitchen. He was aware that naked was technically a binary state, but she was, like, really, really naked.

On his trip to the charity shop he had also acquired a nice summer dress and he'd pointed at it hanging on the back of the kitchen door, but she'd simply smiled and asked him if he had any cornflour. He knew what corn and flour were individually, but he'd never known there was some kind of hybrid. Tonight was full of firsts.

Victor was really worried about dinner. What if whatever she came up with was inedible? Or poisonous? Was cooking even part of her programming? He toyed with the idea of ringing tech support again but dismissed it. He imagined the invocation of black magic had voided the warranty. It was all probably buried somewhere in the forty-seven pages of terms and conditions.

The kitchen door flew open and Francine strode into the front room. Victor stared into her dreamy blue eyes, first and foremost because looking at anything below eye level seemed incredibly rude.

She gave him the kind of heart-stopping smile that he'd never experienced before in his young life. 'Darling, dinner will be ready in twenty minutes. Down with the patriarchy.'

Victor cleared his throat. 'O-OK.'

'And after that, I thought you could spend the rest of the night making mad passionate love to me.'

With that, she turned and left the room.

Victor was no longer worried about dinner.

Right, he thought, how hard could this be? Which was an unfortunate choice of words.

He'd never had sex before, but people did it all the time, didn't they? That horrible woman at the bus stop had clearly managed it. All he needed were some basic instructions and he'd no doubt pick it up fast. He was a genius after all. It would be a lot like riding a bike, in that he'd never done it personally, but he regularly saw people hard at it on the path beside the canal. He picked up his phone. Google was his friend here. Perhaps someone had put something on the internet about sex?

It turned out they had. Quite a lot, in fact.

After some false starts and other distractions, Victor found himself on page twenty-six of what was described as a beginner's guide to sex. He'd already skipped over most of the foreplay section. Not that he was against the concept, it was just that when the other person was already naked and demanding sex, there probably wasn't going to be that much foreplay required.

It was then that the doorbell rang. Trick-or-treaters – that was the last thing he needed! Damn it. He'd forgotten to put up the picture of Jesus. He'd ignore them. He had no time for that now.

'I'll get it, my love,' came the shout from the kitchen.

Victor was out of his chair like a rocket. 'No, my ... no. No need, I'll get it.'

He rushed to the door and, after checking there wasn't a naked woman standing behind him in the hallway, he opened it. He'd been so concerned about what was behind him that he hadn't given due thought to what was going to be on the other side of the door. It wasn't kids looking for sweets, it was a mad non-Russian Russian looking for money.

Ivan favoured him with a gold-toothed smile. 'Victor, my friend!'

The way Ivan said his name sounded more like a vampire from a black-and-white Hollywood movie than Russian to Victor, but Ivan didn't strike him as a man who would take notes well. Behind the approximate Russian stood two massive menacing slabs of humanity who didn't speak yet sent a terribly clear message.

'Ivan, hi. Lovely to see you. To be honest, now isn't a brilliant time. Is there any chance you could pop back tomorrow?'

'Pop back tomorrow?' echoed Ivan. He turned to one of the henchmen. 'Pop back tomorrow. Sure – Terry, check my schedule. Let's see if we can find a time that suits Victor here to give me my fucking money!' He shouted the last bit. The inference was obvious. At least, it was to everyone except Terry.

'You've got the dentist in the morning.'

'Vhat?' snapped Ivan.

'The dentist,' repeated Terry. 'You cancelled the last two

appointments and you said whatever happens, we were to pinky promise not to let you cancel this time.'

'I know vhat I said, Terry!' snapped Ivan. 'I was being rhetorical.'

'Oh, right. You should've said.'

'If I did, it wouldn't have been rhetorical, would it?'

'Actually,' said the other guy, 'saying you're being rhetorical doesn't technically stop you from asking a rhetorical question.'

Ivan turned his eyes to heaven. 'Christ, Bob! One year of the Open University and suddenly everything is academic definitions with you.'

Bob's massive bottom lip turned over slightly. 'You said you were proud of me for improving myself.'

'I am, I just …' Ivan waved a hand at Victor. 'I'm here to collect twenty thousand pounds off a guy. Not argue semantics!'

'Ehm,' interrupted Victor, 'it's actually fifteen thousand four hundred pounds.'

'It vas,' agreed Ivan, 'but then there is the interest.'

'But it's only been a month! Is that legal?'

'Actually' started Bob, but he was silenced by a raised hand from Ivan.

'So help me, one more word, Bob, and I am going to make you wait in the car.'

Bob clamped his mouth shut.

'Now,' said Ivan, 'back to my twenty thousand pounds.'

'Right,' said Victor, going for honesty being the best policy, 'I'll admit, I don't have that money at the moment but I'm sure, given time, I will have no problem coming up with it.' All right, well, that sentence had at least started out honest, even if it veered wildly into wishful thinking at the end there.

'OK. I appreciate your candour, Victor. And in recognition of that, I will allow you to pick which of your limbs Mr Open University here is going to break.'

'Is everything all right, darling?' came the voice from behind Victor in the hallway. He did not need to turn around to see if Francine had put on any clothing since the last time he'd seen her. Terry's gawping expression was enough to confirm that she definitely had not.

'What is this?' said Ivan. 'You don't have my money, but you can afford to buy whores?'

'Excuse me?' said Francine.

'No offence, darling. I am sure you are good value. I only mean you are out of this poor fool's price range.'

'You are a disgusting man and I suggest you get out of here this instant.'

'And maybe you should calm down and put some clothes on, sugar tits.'

'You strike me as being part of the patriarchy.'

'Now, ehm ...' started Victor, feeling increasingly like both this conversation and his life in general were getting away from him.

Ivan jabbed a finger in Francine's direction. 'And now you need to shut up. I will not hit a woman. I have Terry for that. He is bi-violent. Willing to hit anybody.'

Francine pushed Victor to one side. He stared at the ceiling, trying very hard to think of anything he could say or do to stop the unfolding nightmare. And to think, just a couple of minutes ago all he'd been worried about was sex. Now there was going to be violence, and while he wasn't sure he'd be great at the former, he definitely knew he was terrible at the latter. In truth, he was neither lover nor a fighter, but he was prepared to at least give one of them a go.

'Don't you point at me, you beastly little man,' said Francine.

It was at this juncture that Ivan's hand reached forward to do something more than point and all hell broke loose.

Without being aware of what was happening, Victor crumpled to the ground. He did so voluntarily, at least. Ivan, on the other hand, was very much compelled there by a swiftly delivered kick to his nether regions. Francine was a blur of buck-naked femininity mixed with rampant unadulterated violence.

Victor somehow lost track of time as everything blurred. He didn't realise it was over until Francine laid a soft hand on his cheek. 'Darling? Are you all right? Did they hurt you?'

She helped him unsteadily to his feet. It was only then that he looked at the mass of groaning humanity that lay on the pavement in front of them. All three men were alive, although they weren't enjoying being so. It had been a literal bonding experience for Ivan, Bob and Terry, as each man now had one of the other's limbs shoved somewhere the sun didn't shine. The disentanglement of this nightmarish daisy chain would require extensive medical assistance and a proctologist being signed off work for a month because of his nerves.

Victor stood there in silence for a long moment, taking in the destruction Francine had wrought.

Then she sighed and uttered the words that, more than anything from that night, would haunt Victor: 'Oh, dear, it's happened again.'

Victor looked at her in confusion before she took him in

her strong arms, dipped him down and planted a kiss on his lips that rocked his world.

When it was over, he stood gasping for breath as, in the distance, sirens could be heard ripping through the night.

She brushed her fingers lightly through his hair. 'I'm sorry, my love. I guess I'd better be going. Know that I will always be with you.' She held his gaze but raised her voice pointedly. 'And know that should anyone come back here looking for money, I will definitely be here.'

Someone behind them groaned in Russian. It has to be said, staying in character, even then, was a truly impressive feat.

Before Victor could find the words, Francine placed a soft final kiss on his cheek then leaped on to the roof of his terraced house and disappeared into the night.

Victor closed the front door behind him quietly. He walked back into his kitchen and managed to rescue a Marmite-covered tea towel that had been roasting in the oven, before it burned the house down. As the smoke alarm warbled, Victor studied the framed picture, which no longer featured either the Queen or Freddie Mercury. It was now a perfect rendering of Francine beaming out at him. Many a night from now he would sit in his front room, staring fondly at the portrait in its new home above the mantlepiece, and she would smile down upon him. Visitors would often comment about how the nipples seemed to follow you across the room.

He never did see Francine again, but he knew she was out there. She was there in the urban legends, the rumours, the whispers on the wind. The builder who cat-called a woman walking past a construction site only to be found later, half buried in his own cement, bollock naked. The trio of drunk lads following a woman home, telling her to smile, and that they were just being friendly, who were inexplicably discovered thirty-five miles away in the African painted dog enclosure of Chester Zoo, covered in gravy.

To others she was vengeance. She was a warning. She was the patriarchy's worst nightmare.

To one particular proctologist, she'd be the reason he'd leave the medical field and retrain as a barista.

But not to Victor. No, to Victor she would always be that final kiss.

A GOOD BOOK

Leo Klein held his glass of Riesling against his cheek and stared at the package on the table in front of him. It was an unremarkable cardboard box that gave no hint of its remarkable contents.

If you were to tell the average person what it contained, they would be utterly repulsed and wouldn't understand.

If you were to tell a certain subset of the population, they'd understand what it was but still run a mile.

But if you were to tell a select few – those who truly understood what it was – they would pay handsomely for it and do anything to get hold of it.

In fact, a representative of one of those select few was on their way, right now, to this utterly unremarkable hotel room in Mainz to pay Leo more money for it than he'd ever been paid for anything.

So why was he toying with the idea of doing something stupid? Of breaking one of the defining tenets of his profession? Was it because he had recently found himself actively considering retirement for the first time and there was a way one big pay day could become two, or even three? Was it that he'd recently felt himself growing stale, losing his edge, and this would certainly be a way to liven things up? Or was it just that a third glass of this rather good white had been a mistake, and it was giving the voices of his dumber demons leeway to whisper in his ear?

He'd fallen into this game by a circuitous route, but then again, it wasn't as if it were a job with a set career path. He was an acquirer of things. A very particular type of thing. There was only a handful of people worldwide working at a similar level to him. They were all, more or less, on polite speaking terms. They all hated each other's guts, and they would all, given the opportunity, happily watch the others slowly burn to death while roasting marshmallows over their flaming corpses. Theirs was not a business suffused with sentimentality.

In its way, it was still more honest than the art and antiquity dealership world where he had started. That was full of people selling each other the stolen pasts of other countries, cultures and families while wearing a benign smile and pontificating on how vital it was to preserve history. The importance of art. Millionaire hedge-fund managers weren't outbidding each other for a Dalí or a Rembrandt because they wanted to preserve or appreciate anything but their own egos. It was just a thing. A twelve-million-dollar thing that was a way of showing the world that you had twelve million dollars you had so little use for that you could afford to hang it on your wall, where the person who would see it most would be your minimum-wage Turkish cleaner who was working two jobs to put her kid through school.

And that was even assuming that the Dalí or Rembrandt was genuine. Some estimates suggest that twenty per cent of the masterpieces currently hanging in galleries around the world are fakes. Leo thought that number was on the low side. It was an incredible system – only so many people could be regarded as 'experts', and they made their bones by telling everyone else what was and wasn't genuine. Once they'd made their pronouncement, it was career suicide not to keep backing up that assertion until the end of time. The only experts considered qualified to contradict you also had a long line of things for which they'd vouched, and nobody likes to be second-guessed. It was a form of mutually assured destruction. Given that the average buyer couldn't tell you the stylistic intricacies to look for in a van Gogh any more than dogs could play snooker, it was a perfectly rigged system. You just had to be careful how blatant you were. Leo had lost his job with the auction house in Berlin where he'd worked for almost six years since leaving university for crossing that line. He hadn't done anything worse than others; he just hadn't been as careful. It had been a valuable lesson learned.

'Disgraced' as he supposedly was after his ignominious dismissal, Leo should have been untouchable. In fact, he had been exactly that for the next three months. Enough time for him to confirm with every auction house, dealer and gallery in Germany, France, Belgium, the UK and vast swathes of the rest of the world that he was toxic. A morally dubious shyster with a fine arts degree – versions of him with clean records could be found serving coffee in any city in Germany.

Leo had been packing his meagre belongings into boxes, unsure of where he was going, when the call had come. Fredrich Buch, a small-time antiquities dealer, had invited him to lunch. Freddie's operation was the kind that sold things to people who didn't know the difference between an antique and something just being old. Leo hadn't been in any position to turn his nose up at the chance or, indeed, the free meal. By that point, he owed all of his friends money, not to mention the people he'd owed money to for so long that they were no longer friends.

Freddie had been charm personified throughout the meal, during which the pair had talked about everything except the business. A gentleman in his seventies, dressed in a blazer and dickie bow, Freddie had regaled Leo with amusing anecdotes about his travels around the world and the characters he'd met. Then he'd taken Leo back to the office and started dropping hints about 'other things' he dealt in. Leo had almost settled on the idea that Freddie was leading up to admitting he dabbled in the odd bit of Nazi memorabilia, when he'd called his assistant, Monika, a raven-haired woman in her forties with sharp eyes and an athlete's body, into the room.

Leo had felt the heat of Monika's glare on the way in. Fredrich had smiled at her and said, 'If you would, please, *Liebling*.' Leo had then sat in his seat as, with a motion of her hand, Monika had raised the chair off the ground and caused it to levitate round the room. Later, Freddie had laughingly told Leo that he'd given him the job because he was the first candidate who hadn't screamed.

Then, it had been laid out. Freddie's established business was a front for another, considerably more 'interesting' enterprise. Magic existed in the world, and not only that, but many of those who could harness it possessed a great deal of wealth and power. Much of it had been acquired over centuries, seeing as death did not call on those individuals in question as it did to others. In such a world, it was natural that objects of great power would exist, and ergo, there would be a trade in them. It was a difficult realm to traverse, not least because pushing a fake would cost you a lot more than your job.

Freddie had emphasised his point by showing Leo a set of pictures he kept in his safe. They'd been sent to him by a customer and showed what had happened to one of his competitors who had disappointed that discerning buyer. Leo considered himself a cold-hearted individual as much by necessity as by nature, but even almost twenty years later, he occasionally woke up in a cold sweat, the images freshly reburned into his mind. He was thankful for that lesson, too.

He'd diligently learned everything Freddie had to teach and, when his mentor passed away, Leo gave him the grand funeral he deserved and then proceeded to carry on the business. Officially, the old scoundrel had died in his sleep at the ripe old age of seventy-six. Unofficially, while it was true he'd been in bed, he'd also been there with Monika and a couple of her friends. Freddie, when in his cups, had occasionally shared far too many details with Leo about his sex life. It seemed he was quite the connoisseur of the possibilities that magic offered in the enhancement of what he referred to as 'the pleasures of the flesh'. His and Monika's relationship was not merely that of boss–underling. Rather, in certain, specific situations, it appeared to be reversed. To Leo's great surprise, Monika donated the sizable inheritance she received in Freddie's will to an animal rescue shelter and kept her job as office manager. He'd never asked about it, but he noticed she'd worn a great deal of black in the intervening years.

In contrast to his former mentor, Leo was remarkably dull. He enjoyed a fine bottle of wine, but only to a healthy level. He'd had a few casual sexual partners, but nothing too serious or exciting. In fact, the closest thing he had to an addiction was shoes. He'd just kicked off his chocolate-brown Tramezzas. Finest handcrafted Italian leather. He'd sampled wares from around the world, but nobody did it quite like the Italians. They might not be able to form a stable government or collect taxes, but they were a nation that understood how luxury was done.

And so Leo had been at this job for twenty years now. While it had never been dull, business had quietened down over the last few. That had been a result of a phenomenon whereby the amount of magic in the world was apparently decreasing. He had been forced to take the word of people who knew more than he did about such things. A peculiarity of the trade was that nobody in his position was a member of the Folk, or a magic user of any kind. There was a certain logic to it. This world was filled with paranoia, and a dealer being unable to use the products they offered granted them a certain cloak of protection. So, he had adapted to a world with less magic in it and tended to the investments that made up his retirement fund. They weren't what they should have been, thanks to a disastrous investment in a 'can't miss' timeshare development in the Seychelles. It hadn't collapsed into the sea, but it might as well have done. Then, out of nowhere, came what the Folk referred to as the Rising. Suddenly, the tide of background magic had reversed. It had started flowing back into the world and business had once again began to boom.

Coincidence or not, new players were emerging, like the one he was currently engaged by, for example. In his entire career, he'd never worked for one single buyer exclusively, but then he'd never been offered such an obscene amount of money before. He was on retainer. Whoever this new entity was, they had a shopping list of extremely interesting items and a standing desire to know about anything else that showed up, too. Their goal was power and they were refreshingly open to any and all suggestions as to where it could be found.

It was the reason Leo was in Mainz of all places – with its excellent wine and limited selection of interesting people with whom to drink it. A small city on the banks of the Rhine, Mainz was known for many things, including being the birthplace of Gutenberg, the father of moveable type. (Admittedly, the baby itself may have looked suspiciously Chinese, but half the battle in innovation has always been about making sure you get the credit.) The city was also home to the Gutenberg Museum, with its extensive collection of historic printing machines and important texts. The jewels in the crown were two copies of the Gutenberg Bible – the first book printed using movable type – which were billed as priceless, a term loathed by Leo. He knew better than anyone that everything has its price. Still, the books would fetch somewhere north of thirty million at auction, although any such auction would have to be done very, very quietly, as the German government didn't enjoy people stealing their national treasures. Not that the bibles were of interest to either Leo or his client. No, they may have been exceptional and historic books, but they were ultimately just books. The museum held far more interesting treats for the discerning curator

Leo's gift had always been his acute eye for human weakness. It was invaluable in this game. The items he was after were rarely simply offered up for sale. They had to be acquired. This particular item had been especially challenging. He'd even doubted its existence beyond urban myth but, as he had been asked, he had duly gone looking. A former museum curator with a politician for a son and an embarrassing search history had told him where it might just be found. A DNA expert with a special interest in anthropodermic bibliopegy – or, as the layman knew it, books bound in human skin – had confirmed sight of it and had also substantiated its provenance.

Back in the nineteenth century, books bound in human skin were something of a macabre fascination in certain circles. Most of the supposed examples of the phenomenon had been proved fakes by scientific analysis – goat hide being the most common substitute. Rather hilariously, most of the genuine examples were medical textbooks. A certain subset of doctors at the time seemed to have been remarkably eco-friendly when it came to reusing materials they happened to have lying around. Such practices were now, of course, frowned upon in these more 'enlightened times', and several institutions had recently come under attack for retaining such artefacts. The outraged used social media to broadcast their disgust at the use of the skin of a centuries-dead person they didn't know, furiously typing away on their beloved devices manufactured by slave labour in the world they currently inhabited. Leo really had grown so terribly tired of people.

The book Leo was interested in, however, was neither a medical textbook nor some dreary philosophical tome. No, it was something very different. Even better, the museum did not know what it was either. They knew the book was bound in human skin, of course – hence why it was hidden away – but they didn't know the true nature of the thing. It was written in a language almost nobody could read any more, exacerbated by the fact that those attempting to do so ended up developing a predisposition to madness. In the right hands, though – well, it would be quite something. By the right hands, Leo meant anyone who was willing to pay him handsomely for its delivery. Or, to be more exact, for it to be swapped out, as neither he nor his client wanted to draw attention to the piece. The museum knew it as item 45291-B, but Leo knew it as *The Black Grimoire*.

And so he'd found Annaliesa Leitz, a young restorer with a mild gambling problem. Over the course of three months, and the judicious application of the talents of a couple of independent contractors Leo regularly used, said problem had morphed into a major gambling problem. Soon, Annaliesa had found herself with a mountain of debt, a girlfriend who was both out of her league and expensive to maintain, and no way out.

Enter Leo. The charming man with an offer to make some real money in a way that would have her free and clear, if she played things right. A larcenous acquaintance of Leo's procured a set of spare keys from the museum's security firm that would allow access to the special archive section. They could cause a glitch in the security systems while Annaliesa was working late one night, and then it would be simple for her to execute the swap. From there, she would be leaving work for the night at the end of a long day, five minutes before the end of a crucial Champions League tie. The museum's guards would wave her through without the technically required search.

Annaliesa had appeared at Leo's hotel room door an hour ago, covered in flop sweat and bearing the package. The plan had worked perfectly. Still, for someone who had never done such a thing before, this was a big line to cross. Annaliesa handed Leo the box with shaking hands and a giddy lust filled her eyes as she looked into the bag filled with used banknotes. She even mentioned that if he needed her help with anything else, she was amenable to the idea. Leo had smiled and nodded. They'd never meet again. Annaliesa didn't know it yet, but her girlfriend would be gone when she got home, too. By midnight, Annaliesa would be heartbroken and temporarily solvent, although one of those states was likely to outlast the other by a considerable distance. An eye for weakness.

All of this was why Leo was sitting in an uncomfortable chair in a decidedly mid-range hotel room, with only an extraordinary object, a good bottle of wine and a bad idea for company. The hotel was a habit he'd picked up from Freddie. Never stay in a five-star – it drew unnecessary attention, and besides, the itchy sheets and paltry mini bar of a lesser establishment kept you focused on the fact you were there on business. He'd found himself ruminating on his career throughout the day – in hindsight because this stupid idea was pecking away at his brain and perhaps that was his better angels trying to remind him of lessons learned. Of the reasons he'd managed to stay alive, intact and sane for this long. By heeding those lessons and staying away from the stupid ideas.

He stood up. A decision made. Maybe it had been made a long time ago, and all this had merely been pointless procrastination. He opened the box.

It wasn't as if it were an actual betrayal. He'd been paid to obtain the book. He had acquired the book. There had been no mention of him taking pictures of its contents before handing it over. Leo knew that was the kind of logic he could find himself screaming into the uncaring void as his body was stretched out on a rack but, ultimately, it didn't matter what you did, only what you got caught doing.

The binding looked remarkably ordinary. That's to say, it looked like battered leather. You wouldn't know what it was if you didn't know what it was. At least to look at. Leo wasn't a member of the Folk but even he could sense the book's presence. The hairs on the back of his forearm stood on end as he ran his fingertips across the cover. It didn't have anything written on it in a recognisable language, only the ouroboros – a snake eating its own tail. It was also remarkably cold to the touch. He glanced at the watch on his wrist. He had ninety minutes. Plenty of time.

He pulled his phone from his pocket and took a picture of the cover. A sudden, queasy sensation lurched in his stomach. He really should have eaten something. The last food he'd had had been a bagel with cream cheese for breakfast. Drinking on an empty stomach had been a bad idea. Admittedly, not the worst idea he'd had that day, but still.

The binding crackled as he opened the front cover. The book smelled musty but of something else too. A sickly-sweet aroma he couldn't place.

He wasn't a fool. He made sure to angle his face away as he turned each page, so as not to look directly at the text. He kept his eyes fixed on the terribly bland painting screwed to the wall, presumably in an effort to deter the world's most unambitious art thief. A yellow sailing boat bobbing around on an unconvincing turquoise sea. Leo's nausea was growing steadily worse, to the point that he wondered if he was about to throw up. He could taste hot bile in the back of his throat and a throbbing ache was starting to drill away at his left temple. Still, he was halfway done now. Being careful to regard the book only from the corner of his eye, he reached across with his left hand and turned another page, his iPhone held above it in his right, clicking away.

He felt himself wobble slightly, unsteady on his feet. He grabbed the back of the chair with his left hand. It occurred to him that all this would be for nothing if the pictures were out of focus. He glanced at the screen and ...

His last memory before he passed out was the sensation of falling backwards on to the bed.

Leo came around to find the figure of the man he knew as Xander looming over him, a scowl on his face, framed by the water stain on the ceiling. At almost seven feet tall, Xander typically loomed over everyone, even when walking with a stoop as he did, but from Leo's supine position the man's height was considerably more pronounced. With his stature, his entirely bald head, odd gait and vulture-like demeanour, you'd think Xander would draw considerable attention, and yet the reality was the exact opposite. Previously, he and Leo had met in cafes, galleries and so on, and on each occasion Leo had noted how people seemed to avoid looking at Xander without realising they were doing so. It was as if the boundaries of reality curved around the man. It wasn't that he was invisible, rather that something in the human mind simply chose to look elsewhere. It was a rather neat trick. You didn't see him unless he wanted you to, or unless he was standing over you, his eyes burning into you as they peered down his aquiline nose.

Leo went to speak but Xander raised his hand. 'Silence.'

Leo's lips clamped shut and not of his own volition. His brain was starting to come back online now, and it was noticing some things. He felt numb. He tried to move and realised that while he could shift his head and his fingers, he was in control of nothing else. Panic was rising in his chest now, not least because he'd remembered what he'd been doing before he'd passed out. This was bad. Very bad. His brain tried to come up with excuses, but they'd all be for nought if he couldn't move his lips.

'You damned fool,' said Xander, shaking his head. 'I thought you would have known better than this, Mr Klein. The thing hasn't fed in eighty years. Did it not occur to you that it might be hungry?'

Hungry? That made little sense. Xander disappeared from view and Leo could make out sounds of some form of scuffle. In the absence of the ability to do anything else, Leo stared at the ceiling and attempted to fight off the rising panic that was threatening to consume him. Yes, this was bad, but if Xander had wanted him dead, he already would be. There was little consolation in that thought, though, as the images Freddie had shown him all those years ago came flooding back into his head. There were far worse things you could be than dead. Think. He needed to think. He had made a mistake, but what harm had really been done? Xander, or rather Xander's employer, was still getting what they wanted. Leo was a useful man. He'd offer a grovelling apology and, while it might mean the termination of his employment and the withholding of payment, he could live with that – with the operative word being 'live'.

He heard Xander grunting, then a snapping noise and what sounded like the lid of a wooden chest being slammed shut.

Xander reappeared above Leo, wiping sweat off his brow

with a handkerchief. 'Now. This is important. Was anyone else here?'

Leo shook his head, still unable to speak.

Xander's eyes narrowed. 'This would be a remarkably bad time to lie to me, Mr Klein. You were alone?'

With an effort to look less frantic, Leo nodded his head firmly.

Xander pursed his lips and shrugged, seemingly satisfied.

'Very well. Our relationship is, of course, terminated, and allow me to express my employer's displeasure at your betrayal. You will receive half payment on the understanding that your disappointing turn into unprofessionalism will not extend to losing your discretion. I assume we can rely on that?'

Leo gave another firm nod.

'Very well. I will at least give you some credit by not explaining what will happen should that not be the case. Everything will cease when I leave the room, bar the cone of silence, which will stay in place for fifteen minutes. After that, I imagine the screaming will be enough to attract the attention of the staff.'

And with that, he disappeared from view again.

Screaming? What screaming? A sentence swam back to the forefront of Leo's frantic mind: *Did it not occur to you that it might be hungry?*

He heard the hotel room door open and, after a few seconds, close again. As the lock clicked, it was as if he had bobbed to the surface of a warm, comforting sea and into a world of pain. The agony washed over his body and he spasmed, his arms flailing upwards, fists clenched, screaming.

Then he looked down at his body.

At what remained of his body.

He had no left leg below the knee and even less remained of his right.

Unheard and unheeded, he screamed again.

When the ambulance crew arrived, horror writ large across their faces, they gave him something for the pain. The last thing he saw before he lost consciousness again was his chocolate-brown Tramezza shoes, lying discarded on the floor.

YES, PRIME MINISTER

The two men walked in silence save for the sound of their footsteps echoing in the darkness. Everybody knew that there were tunnels under Whitehall – they were part of the Winston Churchill legend, after all. This wasn't one of those particular tunnels, however. This one was long and seemed to stretch down indefinitely, quite possibly by design. It was also fitted with motion-detecting lights so that as they descended at a steady twenty-degree gradient, lights came on to illuminate the ten feet ahead of them and then shut off as they passed so they could only see ten feet behind them. The walls were tiled and the flooring was a modern-looking concrete.

Charlie wondered who had built this tunnel? Come to that, who even knew it was here? Not that any of that mattered. Charlie knew when somebody was trying to intimidate him. He liked it. He may be a political operative these days but he'd been a City boy after Cambridge. He liked nothing more than a good fight. It was why the boss had dialled him up and asked him to come on board. Be his man behind the man. He and Scruffy went way back, so far in fact that Charlie was one of those rare people who knew the true story behind how the PM got that nickname when they were freshers. He'd also helped him come up with the heavily-sanitised version of that particular tale when the press had come sniffing around.

After a couple of near misses, Scruffy was now the PM, and Charlie was part of the crew he'd brought in to shake things up. Sure, have the faces as ministers out front to play to the cameras and handle all the tub-thumping stuff, but you needed your crack troops behind the scenes to actually get things done. All the talk of weirdos and misfits was fun for the press, and it played to the maverick image the PM was going for, but when it got down to it, you needed bodies about you that you could really trust. The boss brought some of the old boys in to answer directly to him – be the power without the PR bullshit, that'd been the pitch. Charlie had no interest in kissing babies and eating the amount of rubber chicken required to become an MP. But being the PM's attack dog? That had sounded like bloody good fun. Plus, the cut in salary would be made up for in other ways. People liked to know people – it was the way of the world.

He kept walking, with Sir Humphreys moving silently beside him in perfect lockstep. Until he'd taken the job, Charlie wouldn't have believed that such people still existed. Lifelong civil servants – the old Whitehall mandarin. The guy looked older than death and was about as much fun. He was carrying an umbrella, for god's sake, despite them being who knew how many hundred feet underground. Odds were that he'd only recently given in and foregone the pleasures of a bowler hat as a concession to modern times.

The PM had insisted that Charlie be present when Sir

Humphreys delivered his briefing. It said something for the old duffer's stilted delivery that he somehow managed to make the most shocking revelations you'd ever heard in your life sound boring. There had been rumours, of course – you heard them in lots of different places – but Charlie had mostly dismissed it all as urban myth, nonsense made up by conspiracy theorists in tinfoil hats. At least he had up until that day.

They'd sat there as the tedious old git had explained that there really were powerful people in the shadows, although 'people' probably wasn't the right word. They hadn't known what to think at first. According to Sir Humphreys, it had been this way for hundreds of years and systems were in place to deal with it all. As far as he was concerned, the PM needed to know enough to stay well enough away and let things continue to run as they always had. There were non-elected people in place to manage it – the Sir Humphreys of this world. The PM, being the PM, demanded to see more details, and he'd eventually been given them. It was incredible, the amount of obfuscation and obstruction involved. It had taken all manner of threats until they had started to see at least some of the bigger picture.

This plan, this meeting, had been Charlie's idea, but the PM had leaped at it. They were fresh in the door and dealing with division and naysayers on all sides. They needed a big win and they needed it fast. It was bold. The kind of idea Scruffy had brought him in for and Charlie was going to bloody well deliver.

Sir Humphreys had hated the idea – at least as much as it was possible for him to do so. The old fogey was all but coated in a layer of dust and he'd quite possibly not experienced an emotion since the eighties. The PM had overruled his objections and sent Charlie as his envoy. So here he was.

They'd been walking down this tunnel for a good ten minutes now. Charlie wasn't going to blink first. Humphreys would want him to get nervous, start asking how much further it would be. Charlie was having none of it, though. He would hold his head high and walk like a man. These people may have some 'interesting' power of their own, but he was the right hand of the Prime Minister of Great Britain. That came with a little power too, thank you very much.

Sir Humphreys came to a halt, his leather shoes giving a tiny squeak as he did so. Charlie turned to him. 'Everything all right?'

'We are here,' said the man in the dull monotone he possessed in place of a voice.

'But how are we … Oh.' Charlie turned to see a door that he could've sworn wasn't behind him a second ago. Funny how a tunnel like this can play tricks on the mind. All part of their games, no doubt. They'd probably try to pull a rabbit out of a hat before the end of the meeting.

Sir Humphreys gave one of those non-cough coughs that were a little vocal tic. 'Mr Richards—'

'Call me Charlie.' He loved saying that because it made Sir Humphreys uncomfortable, not least because he didn't want to reciprocate the gesture. Scruffy joked that he thought the old bastard probably didn't have a first name. His own wife almost certainly referred to him as Sir Humphreys. He and Charlie had once spent a good ten minutes riffing on dear old Sir Humphreys' sex life over some scotch. 'I have arrived, Mrs Humphreys. Thank you for your service.' 'You are most welcome, Sir Humphreys. Tea?'

'Charlie,' continued Sir Humphreys awkwardly, 'I should

like to take this final opportunity to strongly advise you against this course of action. These people do not take kindly to—'

'Yes, yes, yes. We've been through all of this with the PM already. These people may not take kindly to being challenged, but from what I can see, all they do is take. This is about one hand washing the other. We do a lot for them, we're just asking for a little something in return.' Charlie rolled his head around his shoulders and turned to the door. 'Now, let's bloody do this, shall we?'

He went to put his hand on the door handle.

'Wait!' Sir Humphreys moved beside him quickly and knocked on the door three times. 'There are protocols.'

With great effort, Charlie turned his head so that he wouldn't be seen rolling his eyes. The sooner all these ludicrous old farts got booted out, the better. This was the twenty-first century, after all. Whitehall was an archaic maze of pointless procedure and red tape. The whole shambles was an embarrassment.

They stood there for a long moment until a female voice from inside said, 'Enter.'

Sir Humphreys got to the door handle just ahead of Charlie and pushed the door open.

The room had the dimensions of a decent-sized study. Tapestries lined the walls and the floor was covered with what looked like an antique Persian rug. In places, Charlie could see the walls – or rather the rock that the room was carved from. In the centre was a large wooden table of a deep-red varnished mahogany. Seated behind it, to Charlie's surprise, was an Asian woman who didn't look much beyond thirty. She appeared incongruous under the stuffed moose head that hung on the wall above her. When he'd run through this meeting in his mind, Charlie had expected to find himself sitting opposite an old white dude. Instead, there this woman was, wearing a smart business suit, with two mobile phones placed by her right hand.

Was this some calculated form of disrespect? Sending a junior to listen to Charlie's proposal? Well, two could play at that game. The PM had been very clear – Charlie was under instruction to come in here and play hardball. Wanting someone to come in hard and fast was why you sent Charlie Richards to do the job. He was the PM's pit bull, and if he needed to rip this woman to shreds to get his point across, then that is what he would do.

In the left-hand corner of the room, an elderly lady was asleep in a leather armchair, a trolley beside her, covered in a sheet . She was dressed like the dinner ladies they'd had back at school.

Sir Humphreys stepped forward and gave an elaborate bow before the Asian woman. 'Lady Vasor.'

The woman nodded without getting up. 'Sir Humphreys.'

Charlie reached forward and extended his hand across the desk. 'Charlie Richards.'

Lady Vasor did not move but considered his hand as if he were trying to present her with a dead fish. After a long moment, she spoke. 'Yes, I am aware of who you are. Please take a seat.'

Charlie smiled as he sat down. Sir Humphreys settled himself in a chair beside the door. 'Friendly start to proceedings.' Charlie was used to frosty receptions. He used to go out trawling for skirt during London Fashion Week. Nobody can give that disgusted-with-what-they-ordered look quite like an anorexic supermodel.

He nodded towards the slumbering woman. 'Is the old dear all right?'

'She is fine. Just resting.' The slight upturn to Lady Vasor's nose indicated she considered Charlie's question somehow rude. Her eyes were a piercing blue and her build was slim. Even seated, Charlie could tell her suit was well tailored. Gucci, he'd wager.

'Normally these meetings are only with Sir Humphreys.'

'Yes,' said Charlie, 'but, as I am sure you are aware, Britain is under new management.'

She gave a tight smile. 'Is it? And what exactly are you seeking from the people I represent?'

'Well, for a start, I'd like to know I'm meeting with someone from the top of the tree.'

Lady Vasor's face tightened into an offended squint. 'If the person on the other side of this desk were a man, would you be asking to see his credentials?'

Charlie rolled his eyes. 'With all due respect, I am here representing the office of the prime minister. I have no idea who you are.'

'The people I represent have made a habit out of people not knowing who we are. That is rather the point.'

Sir Humphreys cleared his throat and spoke up. 'I assure you, Mr Richards, Lady Vasor has always spoken for her organisation.'

Charlie nodded. 'OK, great. That's all I wanted to know.'

'I'm glad we were able to clear that up for you.' If looks could kill, Charlie was pretty sure he'd be a smouldering pile of ash right now. Good. It always paid dividends to knock one's opponent off their stride. Emotional people made bad decisions. 'So, Mr Richards, what can we do for you?'

'Well,' said Charlie, reaching one hand into the inside

pocket of his suit, 'before we get to that, I'd like to discuss what we do for you.' He unfolded the A4 sheet of information that he'd all but had to beat out of Sir Humphreys. He cleared his throat and began reading from it.

'In the last year, that I know of ...' he added pointedly. He was sure that if he'd held Sir Humphreys' feet to the fire, there would still be a lot more he wasn't being told. '... we, the British government, have assisted you in closing off an area of Aberdeen for what we claimed was a gas leak, so that one of your specialist teams could deal with something. The army was called in to deal with an incident in Bath that resulted in, and I'm quoting here, two people becoming "ill", resulting in the deaths of three other people. In Belfast, the port had to be shut down for two days, costing lord knows how much in losses to the economy. We designated a hundred-acre site in the Scottish Highlands as an MoD testing facility, despite the fact that no MoD employee has ever been there. Apparently, this is due to what the report refers to as a "bottomless hole" appearing on the side of a mountain. In Bradford, the army had to carry out a "controlled explosion" on a suspect device. From what I can gather, the device in question had tentacles. The clean-up alone ...'

Lady Vasor studied her fingernails, painted an immaculate blood red. 'Is there a point to this?'

'Yes,' said Charlie, 'there is. It appears we are doing an awful lot for you.'

'Would you rather the thing with tentacles was allowed to roam freely in Bradford?'

'I'd rather it wasn't an issue in the first place.'

Lady Vasor leaned back in her chair. 'You seem to be making the mistaken assumption that rain is caused by umbrella salesmen. Our role here is to control things that neither we nor you want the general public to be aware of. We have always worked with the government to achieve this goal.'

'Yes,' said Charlie, 'and you also appear to have complete and total access to our intelligence infrastructure.' He noticed only the subtlest of reactions to that one. It had been an educated guess, but it had landed. To do what they did, they must have all kinds of illegal back doors.

'Can we move this along? I assume you have come here with a list of demands.'

Charlie refolded the piece of paper slowly before placing it back in his inside pocket.

'In a moment,' said Charlie, giving his best winning smile. 'But first, this bottomless hole. The country has some waste it could really do with getting shot of. Any chance we could ...' He left his request hanging.

'That depends,' said Lady Vasor.

'On what?'

'On how keen you are to see the entire fabric of reality ripped asunder.'

Charlie shrugged. 'Hmmmm, ask me again on Friday.'

Charlie smiled at his own joke, Vasor did not. It struck Charlie that she was an attractive woman, in an ice-bitch-from-hell sort of a way. This could develop into one almighty hate fuck.

They locked eyes.

Charlie held her gaze. He couldn't blink first.

Ten ... twenty ... thirty seconds passed.

It dawned on him that while he wasn't metaphorically going to blink, it appeared this woman wasn't capable of actually physically blinking. Was that even humanly possible? It wasn't. Of course, that question relied on the assumption that the individual in question was actually human.

Charlie flinched. Vasor's eyes remained steadfastly locked on his, but in his mind, the image of his sister's friend Tilly flashed suddenly. Not just the image but the smell of her perfume. A brief snatch of words. The briefest memory of that night. Charlie's sister didn't speak to him any more because of the bullshit Tilly had told her. He hadn't … Charlie shook his head and lowered his gaze to the floor. When he looked back up, Lady Vasor raised an eyebrow and smiled at him.

'Will there be anything else?'

'Oh,' said Charlie, 'we're just getting started.' He wasn't going to be intimidated by silly parlour tricks.

'I see,' said Vasor.

'We are at a crucial turning point in this country's glorious history.'

'Aren't we always?'

Charlie gave a tight smile. 'Not like this. We are heading into some make-or-break negotiations with our so-called allies. We would like your assistance with that.'

She actually laughed. 'We do not involve ourselves in politics.' She said the last word as if she'd just been asked to nip around to Number 10 and give the loos a good once-over.

'You do now.'

'No,' she said. 'There are agreements in place. Rules.'

'We are redefining the rules,' said Charlie.

'These are not your rules.'

'It is very simple. Are you with us or against us?'

Lady Vasor raised her eyes to the ceiling. 'There is nothing more dangerous than a man who believes something is very simple.'

'Nice,' said Charlie. 'You should print that on a T-shirt. Meanwhile, in the real world, we need your side to start pulling its weight.'

She looked down at him again. 'We do not have a side and we will not do what you're asking.'

'Fine,' said Charlie, uncrossing his legs, as if getting ready to leave. 'If that's your decision, so be it. You should know, the PM has informed me that if you will not assist with this, he will be withdrawing all cooperation from the British government, by which I mean the military, the police and the secret service. We'll also tell our friends in the newspapers, who apparently have a long-standing understanding regarding your "issues", that all restrictions are now lifted. Maybe it's time the world knew the truth?'

Both of Lady Vasor's eyebrows shot up, the closest the woman had come to showing any emotion so far during the exchange. 'Just so we are absolutely clear – you are trying to blackmail us?'

Charlie scoffed. 'Blackmail? Oh, please. We are merely trying to get a little something in return for everything we give you.'

'You are blundering in here without the slightest understanding of what—' She was interrupted by Charlie standing up. 'Where are you going?'

'If your answer is no, then I see no point in me sitting here while you lecture me.'

'I'd think very carefully about what you are about to do, Mr Richards. You are about to make some powerful enemies.'

He shrugged. 'That's pretty much my job description.' He turned and walked towards the door. Sir Humphreys was still sitting beside it, a look of undisguised horror on his face.

Charlie smiled at him. He got all the way to putting his hand on the doorknob.

'Wait.'

He turned to look at Lady Vasor. She attempted to smile at him. 'Perhaps we may be of some assistance.'

Charlie grinned at her in return. 'See? Now, was that so hard?' He ambled back to his seat and retook it.

'Can I interest you in some tea?'

'That would be lovely.'

Lady Vasor turned to the woman still dozing in the leather chair in the corner. 'Mrs Oleander?!'

———

The prime minister sat behind his desk and looked at them expectantly. 'Well?'

Charlie allowed a smile to spread across his face. 'I think we got them.'

The PM slammed his meaty fist on to the blotter pad. 'Bloody brilliant! Well done, Chazzer. Well done!'

Charlie held up a hand. 'Now, don't get too excited, Scruffy. We're not there yet.'

Normally, the PM hated anyone using that nickname in the presence of others, but such was his excitement that he let it go. 'But we'll get 'em? You reckon we'll get 'em?'

Charlie nodded. 'I think so.'

He rubbed his hands together gleefully. 'Brilliant. Cracking job. I knew it. I bloody knew it! These people, whatever else they are, are British. I knew they'd rally around the flag. All this nonsense about them being untouchable was guff.'

The PM glanced in Sir Humphreys' direction, where he

was standing a few feet behind Charlie. He'd be toddling off to his retirement cottage in the Cotswolds by the end of the week if Charlie was any judge.

'So,' said the PM, half turning in his chair, 'what's the next step?'

'They want to talk to you.'

'Right. Got something in the diary, did we?'

'No,' said Charlie. 'I pushed her on it but they said they would be in touch in their own way.'

'Her?'

'They sent a woman.'

'Ha,' barked the PM. 'Your specialty, Chaz.' He turned to Sir Humphreys. 'You should've seen this beast working on the lovelies in college. Man was a machine. Absolute pussy monster.'

Charlie didn't need to turn around. He could feel Sir Humphreys cringing behind him. 'Quite,' came his barely audible response.

'Well, then,' said the PM. 'When do you reckon they'll be in contact?'

Charlie went to speak but something caught in his throat. He held up a hand.

'You all right there, Chaz?'

'I ...' He couldn't get any other words out. His throat felt like it was contracting. As if invisible hands were wrapped around it, restricting his air supply.

'Chaz?'

Charlie felt the world tilting on its axis, black spots blotting his vision. His legs gave way beneath him but he did not fall. He tried to move his arms but they didn't respond. His vision cleared and he looked at the prime minister, who was gawping at him, dumbfounded. Charlie felt himself rise in the air until some kind of lighting fixture bumped against the back of his head. He wanted to panic, to scream, to thrash about, but he appeared not to be in control of any of the parts of his body required to do those things. He locked eyes with the PM, who stared up at him, open-mouthed.

A weird memory popped into his head. The time he'd tried on a virtual reality headset when a brother of one of the guys had been looking for seed capital. The sensation of being in another space only not. There and not there. Charlie felt that now, only with his own body. It was as if he had somehow been relegated to the role of passenger.

He felt his mouth move and a voice came out that was not his. It had a growling edge to it and a much deeper register. There was an odd sensation, as if the vibration of the words came more from Charlie's stomach than from his throat. 'We will talk now.'

'Charlie, what the …'

The voice made an odd hacking noise. Was it … was it laughing? 'This is not Charlie. Charlie can't come to the phone right now.'

The PM jabbed a finger at him. 'Let him go, you hear me? Let him go!'

The voice continued to speak. 'We wish to clarify our relationship. You will do exactly as we say.'

'Don't you threaten me,' said the PM, his voice rising a full octave. The distant part of Charlie's mind that was watching on felt that this might not be the best tack.

'We are not threatening. We are explaining.'

Charlie was aware of motion and then two members of the PM's close protection team were on top of Scruffy, pushing him back towards the wall. One threw his body over him while the other stood, sidearm drawn.

'Do not move! Do not move!' the officer screamed.

It was the ginger guy. Brooks, wasn't it? Ex-squaddie – seen an awful lot of action. He'd been with the PM for a couple of years before he'd got this job. Charlie had chatted to him on a few occasions, killing time at some reception or other. Spurs fan. Didn't think much of the manager. He currently had his handgun drawn and was pointing it up at Charlie. For all he must have seen in Afghanistan and elsewhere, the man looked absolutely petrified.

The voice carried on speaking, ignoring the gun pointed in its direction and the shouted instructions. Something about its quality seemed to be able to carry over any other noise. 'This is your one and only warning. Do not attempt to threaten us again.'

'All right,' conceded the PM, his voice now a muffled squeal owing to the man lying on top of him.

And then the room started to spin. Or, rather, Charlie did. He couldn't do anything other than watch as the 360-degree tableau was presented to him. The PM, behind his desk, the two close protection guys in front of and, in one case, on top of him. Four other men were fanned out across the room, gawping up at him, guns drawn. In the corner, his hands placed calmly in his lap, a benign look on his face, sat Sir Humphreys.

And then the world began to spin faster. And faster. Voices screamed but Charlie could not make out any words. It was all a blur – a kaleidoscope of sickeningly warped colour and sound.

And then it stopped.

The second last thing Charlie saw was Sir Humphreys giving him a tight smile as he opened his umbrella.

The last thing he saw was bloody meat flying in all directions.

Just before the bit of Charlie that did the thinking stopped doing it, he realised that the meat was him.

The room fell silent. Sort of.

Nobody spoke but there was the occasional sound of some of the larger parts of Charlie Richards sliding down the walls, now that gravity was once again the main force acting upon them.

Sir Humphreys got to his feet and lowered his umbrella, taking a quick step to his left to avoid colliding with one of the gore-covered close protection officers. The guy hunched over as he released his lunch back into the world. While the umbrella had borne the brunt of the mess, the trouser legs of Sir Humphreys' suit were ruined, and his brogues would need a considerable amount of spit and polish. Most of what had been Charlie had been hurled outwards by centrifugal force, so the rug in the centre of the room was remarkably untouched, given what surrounded it. The wallpaper, in contrast, was a mess, with the outline of the agents burned into it like Hiroshima shadows, although the agents had lived through the experience.

Sir Humphreys shook his umbrella, closed it and walked swiftly across the floor. The lead agent, Brooks, stood dumbfounded behind the desk, pointing his sidearm at the spot in the air that Charlie Richards no longer occupied. In fact, it was one of the few spots in the room that now contained none of him. Sir Humphreys craned his head to look past Brooks.

'Prime Minister?'

The agent who had thrown himself on top of the PM clambered off him now that the threat was gone. The country's leader looked up at Sir Humphreys, a dazed expression on his face.

'Ah, there you are. You are well, I trust?'

The PM gawped at Sir Humphreys as if he were speaking to him in a foreign language. The older man was famously unwilling to speak any language other than English or Latin. A classic education seemed to do that to a certain breed of Englishman.

Sir Humphreys cleared his throat. 'Shall I inform certain individuals that things shall go back to normal?'

The PM nodded his head emphatically.

'Excellent. I think that would be best. I will see to it forthwith.' Sir Humphreys turned to go, but stopped himself. 'Oh, and one final thing, Prime Minister. Should you ever meet them, I do strongly advise you don't drink the tea.'

THE BLITZ SPIRITS

Tommy awoke with a start as somebody sat down on him. Bloody cheek! He leaped off the bench, pulled into full consciousness by the sickening judder that passed through him every time a living person took the space he had been occupying. The somebody in question was a bearded man who was wearing a set of those headphone things. Tommy had considered himself safe for a snooze in that position, as there was a girl in the seat beside him. Clearly, this headphone-wearing idiot wasn't practising that social distancing from the news. The girl seemed to share Tommy's disappointment, tutting as she got up and walked away down the platform.

He'd allowed himself to get distracted by Beardy and howled, unheard, as a man in a grey suit walked through him – again, oblivious to the damage he was doing. Tommy felt weak. He staggered to one side and crumpled into a ball beside the seats; the best position to stay out of life's way.

Angel was always a busy station, and had been since the

war, which was ... a while ago now. Being a ghost, time felt differently for Tommy. He had been here a long time, but beyond a certain point, phrases such as 'a long time' lose all meaning. Routine, the day-to-day, still had importance, though. His default state was one of near exhaustion, and much of his existence centred around trying to locate a spot where he could rest. He found it difficult to sleep on the floor, so the pursuit of a blessed spare seat became his be all and end all.

He hadn't started at the station. Initially, he was up the road in ... He couldn't remember names of places any more – at least, not anywhere that wasn't on the tube map. He read that every day, learning it by heart. Every now and then, to kill a bit of time he'd test himself. It'd been a lot more fun when Molly had been there. Now it just made him sad.

So no, he hadn't started at the station, but for some reason, he and the other spirits in the area had gravitated towards it. Molly had said that she reckoned it was because the station was where life was most condensed. All those souls, constantly flowing through it like rivers of lifeforce. She said the dead were drawn to life like moths to flames. It was a nice theory, but Tommy wasn't sure he believed it.

It wasn't as if anyone gave you a set of instructions on your first day as a ghost. He had just woken up dead and spent days wandering about, watching first the firemen, then the neighbours, then kids as they sifted through the rubble that had been his home. He'd sat and looked in the other direction when they'd thrown his body in the van and driven it away. There had been a cold, empty feeling, as if something had gone that was never coming back. It had felt the same when Molly left.

He'd tried to leave the station, but found himself unable to get past the turnstiles. Whatever he had been before, he was trapped here now.

Tommy pulled his knees into his chest to save his legs from being passed through by a short woman who was power walking while clutching a handbag under her shoulder, her head swivelling constantly. This was his life now, bobbing and weaving, doing all he could to avoid the living.

Molly had had theories, lots of theories. All ghosts seemed to be different – as if different parts of you stayed if you had to stay. Tommy, for a start, was a 'shuffler' – her word. It meant he couldn't pass through things, but things could pass through him. Other ghosts could wander through walls, but he couldn't. It was as if his memory of the physical world remained with him somehow. Still, when people walked through him, their only response would be the occasional reaction, as if they'd walked through a cold spot. In a station where air was being pushed around constantly, most didn't even notice.

Things were worse in the summer. When it was really crowded, and people would stand in him unknowingly, they would sigh happily. Once, when a pregnant lady had looked as if she might pass out, Molly had forced Tommy to position himself beside her so that she got a little relief. Molly had been able to make him do anything. She had been a 'slider' to Tommy's shuffler, so if he annoyed her she could just disappear through a wall. It had been really frustrating. She'd disappear, sometimes for days, and he'd be worried about her. Being a ghost didn't mean that bad things couldn't happen to you. Your luck didn't automatically improve after death.

Molly reckoned that Tommy's worrying was part of his thing. He hadn't worried much in life and so, somehow, it was imposed on him in death. As if the 'whatever' was punishing him. He thought about that more now. For the first few years, it had been on his mind all the time. Was he being punished? And then, Molly had happened.

She'd had her accident and she'd been there, with him. He'd found her crying on the platform, watching as the ambulance crew had dealt with it all, and then the cleaners. He had been her guide initially, but soon enough she had fit into the life better than he had. 'The life' – it seemed odd to call it that. It was an existence, at best. It wasn't even that now.

Frank was a very different kind of ghost. He didn't talk much, even to Molly, and everybody talked to Molly. He had a spot at the end of the southbound platform and he stayed there almost all the time. He didn't interact much, just spent his time getting angrier and angrier at the crush of commuters. You could tell by the red glow around him, visible to the other spirits, how angry he was. It would build and build. Then, after several weeks – it was hard to be sure as time was, well … but Molly said it was several weeks – Frank's rage would reach boiling point and he'd be able to headbutt somebody. It was always a man, thankfully. What's more, the chap always had it coming. Some fella would be a rotter in the wrong place at the wrong time, and then there'd be that wonderful moment when he'd been taken out by an invisible entity.

The reaction of these fellas was an exquisite thing to behold. Tommy had seen it a couple of times. Molly had kept a close eye on Frank, thanks to her ability as a slider, and she'd let everyone know when Frank was about to blow. It was tricky, as Frank didn't like other spirits being around him either, so you had to time it right.

Tommy had seen him from a distance yesterday, and he reckoned he was about due. It wasn't surprising. Molly had said she reckoned that Frank was sensitive to tension in the air, and almost everybody was tense right now. She also designated his type as 'stander', because they mostly stood about in the one spot. Oddly, after Frank had headbutted somebody, he'd go for a walk around the station, and would whistle happily as he did so, before returning to his spot where the whole sequence would start again. It had taken Molly to point out that Frank and the whistler were the same entity – they looked so different that nobody else had spotted it. She had been really good at stuff like that.

Throughout the day, when the station was busy, Tommy tended to avoid the platforms as he'd only get walked through again and again. One time, in a particularly dark moment, Tommy had thrown himself in front of a train. It had not achieved the desired outcome. The sickening sensation of hurtling metal and humanity passing through him had left him a sobbing wreck for weeks. It wasn't until they shut the station for necessary maintenance for a blissful few days that he got enough rest and had been able to recover. Molly had nursed him back.

So, to minimize any chance of contact, Tommy tended to spend the busiest hours in his spot. A while ago they'd installed a TV screen to the side of the turnstiles, out of the flow of traffic. Tommy had discovered that if he stood two feet from it, nobody walked into him. It was a peculiar thing, but people seemed to respect the personal space of televisions more than they did other people.

All the screen showed was twenty-four-hour news coverage. Headlines scrolled along the bottom of the screen while something called subtitles spelled out what the silent people were saying. Alive, Tommy would have seen such a thing as a wonderous miracle, but death had taken whatever part of him felt such things. And so, he watched the news. It cycled through the stories again and again, interspersed with adverts because they were, of course, the real reason for the screen's existence. Death might've stripped away his ability to appreciate the miraculous, but it left him with the ability to fear. He watched and despaired. He wondered if perhaps all the worry he had about the state of the world had been why Molly had departed. Had he been bringing her down?

There were other ghosts in the station, which Molly had also tried to categorize. There were the 'occasionals', who just sort of appeared and then disappeared not long after. Ghosts like Helen the hoarder. Tommy had met her in his first few days. They'd been new at around the same time. She'd been stockpiling during the war when the floor of her overburdened attic had collapsed above her.

The woman was odd, even by spirit standards. She'd be standing there, chatting away to you happily, and every now and then would be poleaxed by a ghostly rain of cans of corned beef. When you heard it described it sounded as if it would be funny, but then you'd see it and realize it wasn't. Her scream stayed with you. It was also Helen's 'touch' – another Molly term. As a student of economics, Molly had enjoyed categorizing and defining things. Helen's touch was that people could hear her scream when it happened. Tommy's was the cold thing; Frank's, well, that was obvious. Molly's own touch was a whisper. Sometimes, and only sometimes, people could hear her voice. She had a soothing voice.

The Northern Line train pulled in, still alarmingly busy given the circumstances, and the passengers on the platform got on. Only two people alighted, and they hurried away, keeping their distance from each other. Tommy watched as the beardy bloke boarded and plopped himself down beside an exhausted-looking man in a high-vis jacket. Despite his fatigue, the man stood up immediately to try to find more space, saying something that Beardy's headphones prevented him from hearing.

Now the coast was clear, Tommy decided to head up to his spot. It was a straightforward journey given the lack of alighting passengers. Still, he was aware that maybe he shouldn't. Molly said watching the news was bad for him. That it had become an unhealthy addiction. Now though, he had nothing else to do. He stood there and watched, mesmerized. The same stories repeated over and over again. Experts would say something, all but pleading, and then someone would disagree with them.

Tommy didn't understand. He felt like screaming. Why were they giving these things equal weight? And they kept referring back to the Blitz. The Blitz. The bloody Blitz. It was as if they had taken a horrible thing and romanticized it, drawing all the wrong lessons. Tommy knew. By God, Tommy knew that now.

His life, when he'd actually had one, had been confusing. He'd tried to enlist but the army had rejected him on the grounds of ill health. He didn't look unwell, but since he'd been a child, illness could take a grip on him and not let go for weeks, often months. He had missed a lot of school, and had learned what he could from books instead. So no, he'd not been allowed to serve. Instead, he'd been given a job in Whitehall.

People had been suspicious of him. A healthy-looking lad, working as a clerk and spending his days filing RN27 forms when their loved ones were fighting and dying overseas. He'd tried to explain, but still, he knew the stink hung off him. People avoided him. Old men made remarks in the street. He'd got into a fight in the local pub and been barred, despite not having thrown a punch.

It had all left him angry and stupid. So damned stupid.

When the warnings had been issued he'd ignored them. When the siren sounds – get to a shelter and await instructions – he'd defiantly stayed home and sat there, eating his meagre supper while the bombs fell. He would show everyone he was unafraid. And, of course, he'd left his light on. Sitting there, dining with the ghost of Hitler, showing the little bastard that Tommy Clarke was unafraid.

And then he'd woken up. Or rather, he hadn't.

Around 11 p.m., after watching a couple of solid hours of news that mostly repeated but occasionally got worse, Tommy made his way down to the southbound platform. Down to the very end. It was there that the two biggest moments of Molly's life had taken place.

The first had been in 1984. Tommy knew the year only because she referenced it regularly. Time. She was the one who knew about time.

Initially, she had claimed the whole thing had been a terrible accident. That she'd tripped and lost her balance when stepping forward in preparation to board the train while simultaneously pulling a book out of her bag. Tommy had been polite enough not to say otherwise. Eventually, the truth had come out. A disastrous affair – along with, as she called it, a flair for the big gesture – had led her to that place, to that big mistake.

If Tommy had been cursed with fear, she had been cursed with perspective. She spoke often about if she could only get that chance to talk to herself. To tell herself the things that she already knew, but that emotion had blocked out. That she was a young woman with her whole life ahead of her, and that actually, a politics student called Richard wasn't the most interesting man in the world, but rather a boring arse who'd memorized a few passages from the right books, and knew which bands were cool. Instead, she'd been left here, wandering restlessly, counting the hours.

The second moment had happened, Tommy didn't know when. She had been his connection to time. They had been wandering, chatting amiably, at the end of a Sunday. He remembered it had been a Sunday because it had been relatively quiet, as they normally were. Molly had spied the young man standing at the end of the platform. There had been something in his body language. The clenching of the fists, the rocking in the step, the thousand-yard stare. Everyone looks lonely on the tube, encased in their own world, but still, with him you could see it was something different. Others might have done too, but they chose to ignore it.

Molly raced up the platform. The sign said two minutes until the next arrival. She placed herself in front of him, not that she formed any kind of barrier in the real world. The man, not much more than a boy really, stood staring straight ahead, at an advert that had half fallen off the tunnel wall. He had sandy-blond hair and wore an earring. His eyes were murky grey.

Words spilled out of Molly. 'You don't have to do this.

Listen to me. You don't have to. Whatever it is, I promise, I promise, it will get better. Please.' She looked imploringly at Tommy as he finally reached them. 'He's not listening. How can I make him listen? He needs to listen.'

'Molly,' said Tommy, 'maybe you can't—'

'No, I can. I can!'

The lad was wearing a badge around his neck on a bit of string. Molly lowered her head and read it. 'James. His name is James.' She pushed herself right up close to his face and screamed, 'James! Don't do this. People love you. Nothing is that bad. You can ... go somewhere else. You can be anyone you want to be. You can talk to someone. Anyone.' She pointed down the platform. 'Look. There's a lady there reading a magazine. She looks nice. Talk to her. Or take out that phone thing and, y'know, do something with it.' She turned to Tommy. 'Why can't he hear me? People can hear me sometimes. Why not him?'

The screen said one minute now.

Molly was crying. Tommy didn't know she could actually do that but there they were, tears streaming down her face. 'Please!' She looked at Tommy, her face a mask of horror. 'Not again. Please. Not again.' She pointed at Tommy. 'Stand beside him.'

'What?'

'Just do it!'

'But, what—' She looked up at the screen. *Arriving – please step back*. The boy didn't.

Tommy took a deep breath and moved beside him, feeling the wave of nausea he always got when he stood that close to the living.

'I don't—'

'Please,' she said. 'Keep doing it. For me. Please.'

Tommy nodded and held his position, his breath coming in short percussive bursts as he ignored every instinct and didn't move away.

They could hear the screech of the approaching train as it took the turn, its brakes starting to slow its momentum.

Molly's words were unintelligible now – just pleading sobs as she flapped about helplessly in front of the boy.

And then, he shivered. The boy shivered and moved his hand up to close his jacket, over and around himself. He looked at a ring on his finger, an oddly ornate piece of metal, which was tarnishing a little at the edges. He stared at it for a long moment and something changed in his stance. He rolled back on his heels and ran his fingers through his hair, breathing out the long, ragged breath he had been holding in.

'It's working,' hollered Molly. 'It's working!'

The train pulled in and the boy picked up his carrier bag and took four steps to get on. Tommy watched him sit down and reach into the inside pocket of his jacket for a telephone.

Molly danced around the platform, overcome with joy. 'We did it! We did it! We did it!'

As the train pulled off, Tommy turned to look at her. It was a face you couldn't fail to love: blue eyes, dimpled cheeks, and a small button nose. It had a warmth to it. In a cold, cold world, it brought Tommy warmth.

'We did it,' she repeated. 'Why aren't you happy?'

The reason stood behind her, unseen. He briefly considered not saying anything, but it wouldn't be right.

'It's ... it is your time.'

'What do you ... ?'

She turned and looked. It wasn't even that impressive. Just a dull glimmer of light. She had looked back at him, her eyes wide with joy. 'We can move on! We can move on!' She clapped her hands with glee. 'Finally, we can move on!'

Tommy took a step back. He could feel it, pushing him away.

'What are you doing?'

He smiled weakly. 'It isn't for me, just you.'

'You don't know that.'

'I do. I can feel it. I have to move away.'

'But ...'

'You go.'

'No, I ...'

Tommy laughed a laugh he didn't feel. 'It's your time. You're the one who knows time. Bye, Molly.'

'No, I ...'

He turned and walked down the platform. Part of him hoped she'd follow, part of him prayed she wouldn't. He didn't allow himself to look back. He had kept moving forward. He stared down at the tracks. The little soot mice were scrambling about. Molly had tried to name them once, but Tommy doubted that even they could really tell each other apart.

When he'd reached the stairs, he had stopped and looked back to see an empty platform. For the next couple of days, he'd held out hope that maybe she'd appear through a wall, chattering away as if nothing had happened, but deep down he had known. He could feel that she was gone. Once again, he was alone.

And that had been that.

On the days when the news was particularly scary, Tommy would wander down here to this spot and remember her. It wasn't as if it felt any different to any other spot. Memory traces of Molly were everywhere in the station. He was being haunted by the ghost of a ghost. Still, he needed somewhere to go and this was the place. He had tried speaking to her a couple of times, but even though no one else could see, he had felt silly.

An exhausted-looking woman sat on the metal bench. Tommy noticed her head sinking slowly and then jerking back up as she fought to stay awake, afraid of missing the train. She was fairly young, and he could see a uniform of some kind under her coat.

He looked down at the track and said a silent prayer of his own making. He didn't know what came next, if it was even anything, but he hoped Molly was finally at peace.

His reverie was interrupted by a braying laugh.

Tommy turned to see three young men in suits entering the platform. They were playfully slapping each other. Tommy turned to re-join his moment, but it was lost. The trio headed down the platform, pushing and shoving one another. They were about his age – well, the age he'd been when he was still in possession of lungs and what not. He recognized the cockiness – that had once been him.

The woman was now fully awake and clutching her bag to her. Normally, a woman on her own, Tommy supposed, would be wary of three inebriated men, although Molly had explained to him that the station had these cameras. They put things on the TV, but not the TV upstairs. He had never figured out who would want to watch that, but apparently people did. Now, though, the woman was wary, although not for that reason. Tommy glared as they jostled one another. Two metres, or six feet, the man on the news had said. The man had been a doctor. Doctors knew about these things – why didn't people listen?

The men were rapidly approaching. The woman looked

down at her hands. Tommy watched as one of the men slapped another's shoulder and pointed towards her.

'Hey,' said Tommy, 'leave her alone.'

Just because you can't be heard, doesn't mean you do not speak.

'You all right there, sweetheart?'

The woman ignored him, instead looking down to rummage through her bag for something. When the man spoke next, he was sitting beside her on the bench, which caused her to jump. 'I said, you all right?'

She stood up and moved down the platform. 'Leave me alone.'

He grinned at his giggling mates. 'What? I'm just being friendly.'

'You know the rules,' she said.

'Rules? I'm a rebel, love. I'm dangerous. Girls love that.'

'Infectious,' she said. 'That's what you are.'

The mates *oooh*ed in chorus.

Grinner stood. 'Don't worry about me, love.' He slapped his chest. 'Strong as an ox. No underlying ailments.'

'Unless you count stupidity.'

The mates roared with laughter at this. Grinner's grin dipped and then returned as a sneer. Tommy could see the regret in the woman's eyes, knowing that this would only escalate things.

'Now, there's no need for that. Nasty girl. You are nasty.'

'Look,' she said, 'I'm a nurse. I've just done a twelve-hour shift and I'm tired. Please, just leave me alone.'

'A nurse? Thank God, I'm not feeling well.' Grinner started coughing and staggering towards her.

'Oh, for fuck's sake.' She moved down to the end of the platform until she was standing by the wall.

Tommy moved into Grinner's path. 'Leave her alone.' The man kept coming. 'Just leave her be!' Tommy took a couple of steps back, keeping himself in front of the staggering idiot. 'Stop it! Stop being an idiot! Listen! Why don't you listen!'

With a sickening judder, Grinner passed through him. Tommy collapsed to the ground. He turned to see Grinner standing a couple of feet from the nurse, still coughing as he staggered about.

'STOP!'

Grinner turned. They all stared at the spot where Tommy was kneeling.

'Who …?' started Grinner, as his two mates looked around in confusion. One of them pointed to a camera on the ceiling.

'Oh, shit,' said Grinner. He waved at the camera. 'Just having a bit of fun. No harm.'

Tommy rose to his feet. 'It's not a bit of fun, though, is it?'

Grinner's face paled. 'Who said that?'

'You don't listen, do you? You don't listen! Why doesn't ANYONE. EVER. LISTEN?'

Grinner turned to the nurse. 'How are you …?'

His question remained unfinished as he saw her, pinned against the wall, looking terrified.

'Arrogant. Selfish. Ignorant. Idiots! Listen! Why can't you just shut up and listen?'

Tommy balled his hand into a fist and launched it at the idiot's stupid face. It passed through, and the momentum carried him right beyond Grinner. This time it was a stabbing pain that caused Tommy to crumple to his knees, his chest burning.

The world was background noise now, as Tommy lay there, wrapped tightly in his pain.

'What was that?' said one of the mates. 'Is one of you pissing about?'

Grinner moved away from the nurse, his foot passing through Tommy as he did so. He spoke in a quiet voice. 'Anyone else get chills?'

The other mate started laughing. 'Piss off. You two are messing about.'

Nobody answered.

Down the tunnel, Tommy heard the squeal of the train's brakes as it approached the station.

Grinner turned back to the nurse, now standing several feet away from him. 'Fucking lesbian.'

With a crunching noise, it was Grinner's turn to crumple to the ground. His hands flew to his nose as blood spurted from it, painting the front of his grey suit red.

'What the fuck?' screamed one of the mates over the roar of the incoming train.

Tommy, feeling slightly better, looked up. He watched as the nurse skirted around the men and boarded a nearly empty carriage.

'Quick,' said the first mate. 'Help me get him up.'

'I'm not touching him.'

'We need to get him to a hospital.'

'Don't be fucking stupid, Gary – they're full of sick people. Haven't you seen the news?'

Tommy heard the announcement followed by the *whoosh* of the doors closing.

As the train departed, the two mates reluctantly picked Grinner off the floor. As they started to carry him back towards the exit, people veered to get out of their way.

After the train had left and the three men had reached the stairs, leaving a trail of bright-red blood droplets in their wake, Tommy took a deep breath and pulled himself to his feet.

'Thanks, Frank.'

'You're very welcome, Tommy.'

Tommy stumbled over to the empty bench and sat down as, up the platform, the sound of a man whistling happily reverberated off the walls.

'TWAS THE NIGHT BEFORE CHRISTMAS

'Twas the night before Christmas and all through the house, not a creature was stirring, not even a mouse.

The reason no mice were stirring was actually quite telling. The house in question was an eighteenth-century, multimillion-pound pile just outside Knutsford and, given its age and rural location, the odd wildlife visitation on a cold winter's night was to be expected. To safeguard against this possibility, the owner of the property had installed a Verminator 4000 system. Normally, such complex and expensive arrangements were used only in places such as pharmaceutical test facilities where rodent incursions could have serious consequences – hence the need for lasers and sensors and rodent-killing robots, which are less impressive than they sound but exactly as deadly.

In any case, this house was the only domestic dwelling on the planet to have such a system. The property owner – one Eddie Spatchcock – wasn't even that bothered about rodents, he just despised the idea of anything or anyone taking something that was his. He'd even tipped the installation engineer two grand to recalibrate the system so that it'd take out next door's cat if it strayed over the fence. You see, Eddie – spoiler alert – was a monumental, grade-A shit. Most storytellers would try to show you that, through subtle inference and telling interactions, but we're all busy people and I thought it best to cut to the chase. Incidentally, the engineer took the money but didn't carry out the recalibration. In fact, he spent some of the cash on a new, state-of-the-art scratching post for his four rescue cats and gave the rest to a homeless shelter. It's important to remember there are still nice people in the world, especially as they don't feature heavily in this story.

So, no mice, or indeed anything else, were stirring. The house had seven bedrooms, an inexplicable fourteen bathrooms, and a room with a swing in it, which might sound quite jolly until you realise that, yes, it was that kind of swing. There was also a cupboard in the same room, full of what can loosely be described as implements, but don't worry, this isn't one of those stories. Eddie Spatchcock was the property's sole occupant. The reason for this was, well, remember the being-a-prize-shit thing? That. Eddie liked money and didn't like people. People didn't like Eddie either. Money has no strong opinion on Eddie either way because if history has shown anything, it's that money is not fussy about the company it keeps. Eddie had enough money for people to try to pretend to like him, so the fact that nobody did is telling. He was such a level of unlikable that were he to be written in a story, some readers would be inclined to dismiss his unapologetic shittery as unrealistic. Those people have never worked in IT support in the City of London.

So, that's Eddie. You'll be pleased to hear he was having a really bad night. He'd planned it to go oh so very differently.

It had started well enough. Margarita, the housekeeper, had set a roaring fire before leaving for the night, hoping against hope that such an act would finally remind Eddie about the notable absence of any kind of Christmas bonus. It hadn't. She'd trekked home through the snow, trying not to think unkind thoughts while mentally updating her CV.

By the time the long-suffering Margarita had reached her front door, Eddie was sitting in his enormous sunken living room, in front of the fire she'd lit for him. He held a glass of single malt Talisker whisky from a bottle that had cost four grand in one hand and an Arturo Fuente cigar in the other, while a Bulgarian woman of negotiable virtue by the name of Allegra danced around in front of him in lingerie. It was Eddie's idea of a Christmas tradition.

While he was certainly open to the concept of more company, he was nevertheless upset when the figure of Albert McGraw, his old business partner, walked through the fireplace and started to talk to him. It was an impressive trick for many reasons, one of them being that Albert was dead. From Allegra's confusion, it was evident that she couldn't see the new guest. She fled. Eddie was a regular, and while she'd been paid a handsome bonus to spend her Christmas Eve entertaining an arsehole, there wasn't enough money in the world to tempt her to do so while the arsehole in question was having a psychotic episode.

Long story short, before disappearing into the floor, Albert informed Eddie that he was to be visited by three spirits. By this point in the evening, two of them – Christmas Past and Christmas Present – had already been. Eddie had not enjoyed the experience. They'd run through some of the highlights of his career at what could be described as the cutting edge of capitalism, and had put what he considered to be a very negative spin on his accomplishments. True, the edge in question was renowned for drawing blood, but he was a great believer in the power of the market, as long as it was working in his favour. The tone adopted by the spectres, who had taken the form of his childhood nanny, Gretchen, and some poor sap Eddie had fired and whose name he'd already managed to forget, had been downright judgy. It was why he was now sitting very, very still in the corner of the room, staring at the fireplace, his eyes the size of saucers, expecting his comeuppance to come a-calling any minute. He was attempting to pray, despite the fact he didn't know any prayers. It'd been that kind of an evening.

Lying beside him on the floor was the now-empty gun that he'd acquired from the man who'd installed the property's state-of-the-art security system – both of which had failed to stop the aforementioned spirits. All he'd managed to do was alarm next-door's cat, but not so much that it hadn't taken the time to finish taking a dump on Eddie's lawn before making good its departure. Say what you want about cats, they really are remarkably good under pressure.

At this point, Eddie was assuming that nothing could surprise him, and yet, when the vision of a stout, middle-aged woman in a wax jacket appeared before him, it did.

'Be gone, foul spirit,' yelled Eddie.

'Well, that's charming,' replied the woman, looking down at him. 'Are you aware you've widdled yourself?'

'What?'

The woman waved a hand towards Eddie's crotch while wrinkling her nose in disgust. 'You appear to have involuntarily lost control of your bladder. I mean, I presume it happened involuntarily but I'm not one to judge.'

Eddie stared at her for a few seconds then, sounding more than a little unhinged, shouted for a second time, 'Be gone, foul spirit!'

'Will you stop calling me that? It is rather rich given the state of your britches. My name is Elizabeth Cavendish the Third, but everyone calls me Betty.'

'You're ... you're alive?'

'Yes. Thanks for noticing.'

'But ... the spirits. The three spirits.'

To Eddie's confusion, Betty chuckled to herself. 'Dear me, still pulling the old Christmas Carol, is he? Well, well.'

'What?'

'The Christmas Carol. Three spirits?'

Eddie looked up at her blankly.

'It's the plot of *A Christmas Carol*. You know, the book by Charles Dickens?'

'I'm not much of a reader.'

'Much of a reader?' Betty echoed, sounding scandalised. 'It's one of the most famous stories in the world. How on earth have you not heard of it?'

Eddie knew he was being scolded but didn't understand why. 'What's this got to do with anything?' he asked, his temper flaring. 'And what are you doing here?'

'Presently, I'm worrying about the state of the education system in this country, but in a more global sense, I'm here looking for help.'

'You want my help?'

Betty laughed. 'Good God, no. A man who's widdled himself and doesn't even recognise when he's being Christmas Carolled? What possible use could you be to me?'

Eddie paused, his mouth open, trying to process this

information. Eventually, he managed, 'Are you going to save me or not?'

'From what?'

'The ghosts.'

'There aren't any ghosts.'

Eddie pointed a finger at the fireplace. 'There are! There's been three of them so far, and a fourth is coming.'

'Just like in ...' Betty looked at him pointedly.

'In what?'

She shook her head. 'Unbelievable. Absolutely unbelievable.' She gave a sigh of despair. 'I'm not here to save you, although yes, that will turn out to be a by-product of my actions. And—'

Betty broke off as a glass tumbler hit her in the chest before falling to the floor and smashing. 'Ouch,' she said, rubbing a boob. 'What the hell did you do that for?'

'Sorry,' said Eddie, 'I was just checking you aren't a ghost.'

'I've already told you there aren't any ghosts.'

'They don't exist? Really?' Eddie wanted to believe, but his recent experiences had been far too vivid.

'Oh, no, ghosts definitely exist. I just mean this isn't them. They're hardly ever capable of this level of organisation' The lights in the room started flashing and the flames of the roaring fire took on a distinctly blue edge. 'Or, it has to be said, quite this flair for the amateur dramatics.'

Betty turned and, for the first time, Eddie noticed the small suitcase she had wheeled in behind her. She tossed it on the sofa and threw it open.

Eddie pointed at the wall above the fireplace, which was now swirling in a positively eldritch manner. 'It's coming,' he whimpered.

'Yes, yes,' replied Betty dismissively, pulling what

appeared to be a rubber chicken out of her case. She contemplated the item for a long moment before tossing it aside. The lights continued to flicker and began to be accompanied by low moaning. Betty, meanwhile, carried on digging about in her case, tossing aside a jar of what could have been pickles, a wind chime and a framed portrait of a newsreader.

'Aha!' she shouted excitedly, before turning to Eddie. She was holding a carved wooden figurine of a three-headed snake in one hand and a one-eyed stuffed Paddington Bear toy in the other. 'These should do the trick!'

As Betty calmly placed the items on either side of the bearskin rug in front of the fire, an inexplicable wind started to whip through the large, open-plan room. The growing gale rattled the paintings on the walls as the moaning noise rose in volume to match it, the sounds forming into words. 'Eddie ... Eddie Spatchcock ...'

Betty looked utterly unperturbed as she focused her attention on the two objects. She moved the teddy bear back six inches and nodded to herself, seemingly satisfied.

'What are you doing?' screamed Eddie.

'My job,' she replied. 'Well, more of a vocation, really.' She pointed at a dish on the coffee table. 'I say, are those marzipan fruits? Do you mind?'

Eddie's arms were now wrapped around his head and he'd begun to rock back and forth, jabbering 'no, no, no, no, no' to himself, over and over again.

Betty, choosing to interpret his words as a response to her question, picked up the dish and sauntered off happily. If her attention hadn't been so fixed on the sweet treats, she might have noticed the skeletal hand emerge from the stone wall above the fireplace behind her. Eddie certainly had. He stared at it, transfixed.

'I ... I can change,' he begged. 'Please. I'll ... I'll stop that company dumping all the crap in the river ... I'll shut down some of the call centres that make the spam calls ...'

As the wind whipping around him increased in intensity, something expensive crashed to the floor on the far side of the room. The windows shook. The Verminator 4000 reported several errors back to the control room in Amsterdam, which the tech who'd drawn the short straw of Christmas Eve monitoring ignored entirely.

The hand – with one bony finger pointing at Eddie – drew closer. A cloaked arm followed it. A figure sheathed in black from the fireplace emerged, its face hidden by a hood. Behind it, it dragged heavy metal chains that clanked – y'know, the sort of thing you'd expect at this point, assuming you aren't the kind of person who hasn't heard of *A Christmas Carol*.

The room was cold now. So very cold. Eddie could make out blue eyes under the black hood, burning into him as he stared into the abyss. The abyss spoke. 'Eddie Spatchcock, your time has come.'

'I'll cancel the payday loans business! I'll make those sweatshops less sweaty. I'll stop voting Tory ...'

The figure continued to advance.

In despair, Eddie scanned the room furiously. Betty was sitting on one of the couches on the far side of the fireplace, happily sucking on a marzipan fruit, as if everything going on around her wasn't happening.

As the cloaked figure took another step forward, there came a loud popping noise. The figure glanced down at the two objects on the rug then, in an unexpectedly Brummie accent, said, 'Oh, bugger.' It gave a yelp and the robe – if not empty, then suddenly a lot less full – tumbled to the ground.

The wind ceased. The lights resumed working in the correct manner. Slack-jawed, Eddie surveyed the room. He could believe the whole thing had been an incredibly vivid nightmare were it not for the lady in the wax jacket who was still sucking loudly on a marzipan fruit.

'Raspberry. How delightful,' she declared.

Her proclamation was followed by a high-pitched and melodious voice swearing loudly in a Birmingham brogue.

'Language,' said Betty sternly.

Eddie watched as an orange creature of about eighteen inches in height fought its way out of the pile of oversized robes before climbing up on to the coffee table. It was vaguely humanoid, had elongated pointy ears, and a protruding snout with buck teeth like a rabbit's. It resembled something a schoolchild had made from plasticine and which had resulted in the pupil's parents being called in for a chat.

'Sorry, Betty,' it said, sounding resigned.

'So you should be, Norman,' she responded, standing up and proffering the dish. 'Marzipan fruit? They're really quite scrumptious.'

'No, thanks,' responded the creature who was evidently called Norman.

'I have to say,' continued Betty, 'the whole thing with the wind was rather dramatic. Is that new?'

'Well, I try to—'

'What the hell is happening?' screamed Eddie, having regained the power of speech.

Norman shook his head. 'This guy.'

Betty pocketed the contents of the dish and set it down on

the coffee table before addressing Eddie. 'This is Norman – he's a demon.'

'Kill it!' shouted Eddie.

'Excuse me?'

'Kill it,' he repeated.

'Him,' corrected Betty. 'And what good would that do anyone?'

'I'll pay you ten thousand pounds. No questions asked.'

Betty turned her nose up in disgust. 'What do you take me for?'

'Twenty. Fifty.'

'I wasn't negotiating,' she responded, exasperated.

'He really is a piece of work,' chipped in Norman.

'Would you believe,' said Betty, 'that he didn't even understand he was being Christmas Carolled?'

'You're kidding?'

'No,' said Betty. 'Had never heard of the story, apparently.'

'What?' said Norman, looking at Eddie. 'Not even the Muppet film?'

'Yes,' agreed Betty. 'Surely you've seen the Muppet version?'

'I hate the Muppets!' shouted Eddie before giving a yelp as the diminutive demon snarled and launched itself at him. Showing an unexpected burst of speed, Betty interceded, catching Norman in mid-flight.

'Now, now, Norman.'

'Please, Betty,' he pleaded, his clawed hands scrabbling at the air in front of Eddie. 'Let me rip his smug little face off.'

'Calm yourself. Don't make me get the muzzle out.'

The demon jabbed a stubby finger in Eddie's direction. 'All right, but if he says one more thing about the Muppets …'

'I'm sure he won't,' said Betty, favouring Eddie with a very pointed look.

The tension in Norman's body eased and Betty placed him back on the coffee table.

'Who are you people?' asked Eddie, trying to get some kind of grip on what was passing for reality these days.

Betty rolled her eyes. 'Do try to keep up. Norman here is a demon and I'm the kind of person who can capture a demon.' She turned to look at Norman. 'A demon, might I add, who assured me he was turning over a new leaf.'

'I have!' protested Norman.

'Really?' The sarcasm in Betty's voice was heavy. 'Did I not just catch you Christmas Carolling some poor sap?'

Eddie objected to the epithet, but he was too busy struggling to keep up to verbalise his umbrage.

'He's not poor, he's stinking rich – with the emphasis on stinking. I've gone Robin Hood.'

'Wait a second,' interrupted Eddie. 'This is all some big con?'

'In a manner of speaking,' conceded Betty. She looked down at Norman. 'What was the payoff supposed to be here?'

Norman looked sheepish. 'I was about to get him to buy a load of bitcoin.'

Betty shook her head. 'I think you've misunderstood a rather crucial part of the Robin Hood concept, Norman.'

'I was going to give some of it to charity,' protested Norman.

'Let's see what the police say about all this!' hollered Eddie, standing up.

'I really wouldn't do that,' said Betty, sounding more like she was giving advice than an order.

'Who asked you, ya mad old bag?'

Eddie just had time to notice Norman wince before he found himself flying through the air and being pinned to the wall. Betty, who had moved only one hand, puffed out her cheeks before addressing him. 'I am getting the impression you are not a terribly nice person, Eddie.'

'He really isn't,' said Norman. 'You should hear the rest of the list.'

'I'm a new man,' protested Eddie. 'I'm really sorry, honestly. It's the shock. I didn't mean to be abrasive. I apologise ... For everything, especially how I just spoke to you. I ... It's not an excuse, but my mother died when I was young and my father raised me. He was not a nice guy. Always screaming at me, "Toughen up, Eddie. Toughen up." He locked me in my room for a week for crying at Mum's funeral.'

'Oh, dear,' said Betty.

'And ... I'm sorry for what I said about the Muppets. I ... I never had a childhood and I guess I've ended up trying to take it out on other people. Norman here might have been trying to con me, but honestly' – Eddie's eyes filled with tears – 'he was doing me a favour. For so long I've wanted deep down to be a better person, and now I think maybe you've shown me the way. So, thank you. And really, if you give me the chance, I think I'll make you both proud.'

Norman scoffed.

'Norman,' admonished Betty, 'if the man says he's changing his ways, then it behoves us to give him a second chance.'

The demon shook his head. 'I smell bullshit.'

'I think you're forgetting that I once gave you a second chance.'

'Exactly,' said Norman. 'And you just caught me doing a variation on the same old crap I always do.'

Betty lowered her hand and Eddie slumped to the floor. 'That is a very odd argument you just made, Norman.'

He shrugged. 'I'm just saying. He really is awful, and that's coming from a demon!'

'That was the old me,' protested Eddie. He eased himself to his feet sheepishly. 'Please, give me the names of some charities and I'll start making big contributions right now. I really want to—'

He was interrupted by a wash of blue lights across the room through the tinted windows to the front of the house. Eddie's open expression changed from one of pleading to a sneer. He pulled a small object out of his pocket and held it aloft triumphantly. 'Ha! Panic button, bitches!'

'See?' said Norman to Betty. 'New leaf, my orange arse.'

'Yes,' agreed Betty. 'Well, at least he was given the opportunity. That's the main thing.'

'And now,' said Eddie, 'you two are going to jail.'

Norman shook his head. 'Unbelievable.' He turned to Betty. 'So, what did you want my help with? Actually, doesn't matter – given what the choice is, I'm in.'

'I thought you might be,' said Betty.

Eddie was feeling rather put out that nobody was acknowledging his great big moment of triumph. 'You're both going to—'

'Jail,' finished Betty. 'Yes, you said. But no, I'm afraid that will not be happening. If I were you, I'd go outside and tell them it was a false alarm while you still can.'

Eddie gave a mocking laugh. 'I bet you would.'

On cue came the sound of the house's rather obnoxious pealing-bells doorbell.

'Thank God,' yelled Eddie, laying on the terror in his voice while grinning at Betty and Norman. 'In here. Help – I've been taken prisoner.'

Betty sighed as a heavy thumping sounded against the front door.

'Told you,' said Norman.

Betty held out her hand towards him. 'Nobody likes a gloater, Norman. It's a very unattractive quality.'

'I am a demon,' he responded, taking her hand like a child taking its mother's.

As the front door was finally kicked in, Betty took one last look at Eddie. 'Do remember, I did give you a second chance.'

Eddie swivelled in the direction of the door to the hallway as two uniformed police officers came barrelling through it. A short woman and a tall man, both with batons in hand.

'Thank God,' yelped Eddie. 'They—' He found himself pointing at an empty space. 'What? No! They were there.'

'Who were, sir?' asked the male police officer, scanning the room, clearly looking forward to hitting something with his baton.

'The demon and the fat witch.'

'The what and the what?'

'The demon and the fat witch,' repeated Eddie, running across the room, checking behind sofas and anywhere else he could think of.

The female officer spotted the bottle of whisky. 'Have you been drinking, sir?'

'What?' said Eddie distractedly, throwing cushions off the sofas, in case they were hiding a demon. 'No, I haven't.'

'I think you might have—' started the male officer, but he stopped when his partner pointed urgently at the gun she'd just noticed lying on the floor.

'All right, sir,' she said. 'How about you sit down for a second and we'll have a nice chat?'

'A chat?' screamed Eddie. 'There's no time for that. Search the building. A demon was just here trying to get me to buy him bitcoin by doing something he got from a stupid bloody Muppets movie.'

'Take it easy, sir,' said the male officer. 'I can see you're upset, but let's not say anything about the Muppets we might regret.'

Eddie turned on the two officers. 'Do what I tell you to do. I know the chief inspector!'

'Do you, sir?' said the female officer, holding out her hands in a placatory manner and using the voice we all reserve for precocious children and unhinged adults. 'That's nice. How about we all go down the station and tell him about how the Muppets are trying to get your bitcoin?'

'Yeah,' said the male officer. 'And while you're at it, you can explain to him how you've quite clearly pissed yourself.'

Fifteen minutes later, following a chase and accusations that the two officers were in fact a demon and a witch in disguise, Eddie was handcuffed and being shoved into the back of a patrol car. As he was being driven away, two figures appeared on the lawn, seen only by him. Betty watched on with a sad look as Norman waved cheerily.

'Don't gloat,' Betty reminded him. 'Like I said, it's a very unattractive quality.'

'Again, I am a demon.'

She sighed. 'That you are. I'll give you this, Norman – you certainly can pick 'em. He really is dreadful.'

'You don't know the half of it. Right, so – what's this job you need my skills for?'

'Actually,' said Betty, 'we can't do anything for a couple of days.'

'Oh,' said Norman. 'I suppose you'll be locking me in a cage, then?'

She looked down at him. 'I'd really rather not.'

'Letting me go?' he asked hopefully.

'Also, no.' She gave him an appraising look. 'I may be losing my senses but ... just for tomorrow, why don't you forget what you are, I forget what I am, and we have a nice little Christmas for ourselves?'

Norman considered this. 'Can we watch *The Muppet Christmas Carol*?'

Betty held out her hand and Norman took it. 'It wouldn't be Christmas without it.'

RING THE BELLS

Book 5 of The Stranger Times

For most people, that means a time of celebration, relaxation and inebriation, but not for the staff of *The Stranger Times*. While a book club meeting ending in a triple murder isn't unprecedented, it is at least noteworthy. It quickly emerges that this is no ordinary book-club-triple-murder either, as it features a librarian possessed by a chaotic entity who has broken through from another dimension and is hellbent on vengeance. He's made a list, but he's not checking it twice as the whole of humanity is on it. Who would want to summon such a thing? And how is anyone going to be able to send it back?

As if that wasn't enough to be dealing with, a shocking revelation about a member of *The Stranger Times* team's past brings family together, but not in a way that's ever going to make it into a Hallmark movie.

Featuring demonically possessed Santas, blood-thirsty books and the ghost of a legendary nightclub, it's beginning to look a lot like a Christmas apocalypse . . .

Ring the Bells is the fifth book in the award-winning, critically acclaimed and laugh-out-loud funny *The Stranger Times* series.

Preorder the hardback and send proof of purchase to ringthebells@mcforiink.com, to receive a signed bookplate, key ring, newspaper and Stranger Times Christmas card.

FREE GOODIES

Hi lovely reader person,

C. K./Caimh here – thanks for reading *Tales from The Stranger Times*.

If you'd like to receive some exclusive Stranger Times short stories, you can get them delivered straight to your inbox by signing up for my newsletter at **thestrangertimes.co.uk.**

Also, check out the award-winning Stranger Times podcast, which is chockfull of short stories written by me and read by some of my former coworkers at the coalface of the British standup comedy circuit. They're available from all the usual places or through my website.

Sláinte and stay weird,

Caimh

ALSO BY CAIMH MCDONNELL

THE INCREASINGLY INACCURATELY TITLED DUBLIN TRILOGY

A Man With One of Those Faces (Book 1)

The Day That Never Comes (Book 2)

Angels in the Moonlight (Book 3/prequel)

Last Orders (Book 4)

Dead Man's Sins (Book 5)

Firewater Blues (Book 6)

The Family Jewels (Book 7)

Fortunate Son (Book 8)

Shorts (Bunny McGarry Short Story Collection)

MCGARRY STATESIDE (FEATURING BUNNY MCGARRY)

Disaster Inc (Book 1)

I Have Sinned (Book 2)

The Quiet Man (Book 3)

Other Plans (Book 4)

MCM INVESTIGATIONS (FEATURING BRIGIT & PAUL)

The Final Game (MCM Investigations 1)

Deccie Must Die (MCM Investigations 2)

STATESIDE STANDALONE

Welcome to Nowhere (Smithy and Diller)

Writing as C.K. McDonnell

The Stranger Times (The Stranger Times 1)
This Charming Man (The Stranger Times 2)
Love Will Tear Us Apart (The Stranger Times 3)
Relight My Fire (The Stranger Times 4)
Ring the Bells (The Stranger Times 5)

Visit www.WhiteHairedIrishman.com to find out more.

BVPRI - #0005 - 050825 - C0 - 198/129/18 - PB - 9781912897636 - Matt Lamination